A PERFEC
PARTNER

Maureen Ma_____
with five sisters and a brother. She moved to
London, fell in love with an Italian and returned
home to Ireland to bring up her children.
Travelling again she spent time in Bel Air where
she worked as an assistant to a mortician. She
is also the author of *Maddy Goes to Hollywood*
and *Annie's New Life*. She now lives and writes
in rural Ireland. Her website address is
www.maureenmartella.com

MAUREEN MARTELLA

A PERFECT
PARTNERSHIP

arrow books

Published by Arrow Books in 2004

1 3 5 7 9 10 8 6 4 2

First published in the United Kingdom in 2004 by Arrow Books

Arrow Books
The Random House Group Limited
20 Vauxhall Bridge Road, London, SW1V 2SA

Random House Australia (Pty) Limited
20 Alfred Street, Milsons Point, Sydney,
New South Wales 2061, Australia

Random House New Zealand Limited
18 Poland Road, Glenfield,
Auckland 10, New Zealand

Random House (Pty) Limited
Endulini, 5a Jubilee Road, Parktown 2193, South Africa

The Random House Group Limited Reg. No. 954009
www.randomhouse.co.uk

A CIP catalogue record for this book
is available from the British Library

Papers used by Random House are natural, recyclable products made
from wood grown in sustainable forests. The manufacturing processes
conform to the environmental regulations of the country of origin

ISBN 0 09 946919 7

Typeset by Palimpsest Book Production Ltd, Polmont, Stirlingshire
Printed and bound in Great Britain by Cox & Wyman Ltd, Reading, Berkshire

For Roberto

1

I parked the Honda Civic in a narrow side street and strode around the corner to the agency, my heels tapping a furious tattoo on the frosty pavement. My black mood didn't prevent me throwing a proud glance at the nameplate by the door. 'McHugh Dunning Detective Agency', it said in bright gold script. I had passed it daily for three years now, yet the sight of it never failed to thrill me. Except this morning.

This morning it would have taken a lot more than seeing my name etched in gold to cheer me up. Even the chorus of appreciative whistles from the building site opposite hadn't managed that. And it was all Gerry's fault. Gerry Dunning, the love of my life. My business partner. My life partner. A man so in love with me he had jumped at the chance of a solo trip to Kerry on his birthday, leaving me to finish our over-due tax returns. To add insult to injury, he had driven off at the crack of dawn in our brand new Jeep Cherokee. The one I barely got a chance to sit in before he commandeered it for what he called 'a special case'.

Special my arse, I fumed as I pushed open the agency door. His *special case* was a run-of-the-mill missing person's job that any of the agency's three investigators could have handled without breaking sweat. But Gerry, the great egalitarian, had pulled rank, unilaterally deciding that what this case needed was his personal attention – as well as a four-wheel-drive.

I had braved a freezing wind to follow him out to the jeep. My only protection a bulky dressing gown and scuffed Bart Simpson slippers, I was determined to confront him about his obsession with missing women. Then he turned and smiled at me, and my well-prepared speech disintegrated.

'I . . . you know I hate doing tax returns,' I said, my teeth chattering like castanets.

'Aw, but you're so good at it, Annie.' He threw his overnight bag into the back seat. A tad too enthusiastically for my liking. 'And someone has to do it. Either that or we'll both end up in the nick.' He grinned cheerfully.

'At least you'd be among friends,' I snapped. Well he did spend a lot of time with lawbreakers. Although, to be fair, that was frequently a requirement of the job.

He didn't take offence. Just laughed. That's the trouble with Gerry, he's a hard man to row with. Mainly because he's a man of few words, but also because he's too damn attractive for his own good. And mine. Even at such an ungodly hour I found him indecently appetising. But then the first time I saw him, at my friend Fiona's very first engagement party, I thought George Clooney was making a personal appearance. And judging by the reaction of the other female party guests, I wasn't the only one. I *was* the only one put off by the sight of his wedding ring. Fiona dismissed my concerns, saying he was separated, about to be divorced. But the sight of that gold ring still firmly *in situ* had worried me. I was once burned by a man wearing a wedding ring. And besides, separated men had never been my cup of tea. But then very few of them looked like George Clooney.

'I'll get back as soon as I can, Annie. We'll celebrate my birthday at the weekend.' He planted a kiss on my freezing lips and slid his fit body behind the wheel. 'We'll go to that Cajun restaurant you're so fond of. I might even try the gumbo this time.'

Coming from Gerry this was a declaration of love. An unreformed steak and chips man, he had little time for trendy restaurants. Or any kind of socialising, if it came to that. The job was his life. Sometimes I thought it satisfied all his needs. Well, nearly all of them.

Fiona says he was born into the wrong century. 'Gerry belongs on a big white charger, jousting with the other knights of honour, rescuing damsels in distress,' she once sighed as he rushed away from yet another of her stylish dinner parties, this time to answer a call from a despairing father whose only child was joining the Moonies.

Fiona could be right. Gerry does take missing persons cases to heart. Especially when they involve the young and vulnerable. Today's missing girl was barely fourteen. Three weeks of intensive Garda investigation had come up with zero. Her distraught family had contacted the agency, begging Gerry for help. Nothing unusual there. Our number was frequently slipped into the hands of distraught parents by sympathetic Gardai. Gerry had served on the force for eight years, and still had lots of friends there. And enemies.

Watching him turn up the collar of his sheepskin jacket I began to soften. After all, he was sacrificing the comfort of a centrally heated office for a long, hard drive down to the frozen Kerry mountains. Albeit in the new Cherokee.

Ashamed of my selfishness, I blew him a kiss. He waved, slipped his favourite Van Morrison tape into the player, and drove off, his hands practically caressing the steering wheel.

The noise in the agency hit me like a blow. Twenty decibels plus of shrilling phones, dog howls and Ronan Keating warbling with background static, it was head-wrecking.

I switched off the transistor, told Fred the dog to shut up, and picked up the phone.

'McHugh Dunning Detective Agency.'

'Gerry Dunning, please,' a gruff voice demanded.

'I'm sorry, Mr Dunning is not available right now. Could I be of any assistance? I'm his part—'

From behind the reception desk came the familiar chimes of the William Tell Overture. Sandra's mobile. Our receptionist/general factotum has strict orders to keep her Nokia switched off during office hours. 'Kill it, Sandra,' I hissed.

My caller hung up.

Sandra's shiny red head shot out from behind the desk. She took the phone from my hand, held it gingerly to avoid smudging her wet nails (a trick honed to perfection by long practice) and hit the line button.

'Good morning, McHugh Dunning Detective Agency. May I help you?' She listened wide-eyed for a second. 'Oh, don't worry about that, Mrs Murtha, we'll have that information for you before the week is out. Mr Dunning is working on it even as we speak.

No problem, Mrs Murtha. A pleasure.' She hung up. 'Shite! Gerry hasn't even looked at that feckin' file yet. What the hell is he doing driving down to bleedin' Kerry on a busy day like this anyway?' She blew on her nails.

'Testing the Cherokee?' I gritted my teeth.

'The new jeep? Jesus!' Her eyes popped. 'I bet you're sorry you bought that damn yoke?'

I was. But I wasn't about to admit it to someone who left sticky bottles of Deep Plum nail varnish on our, almost new, mahogany reception desk. *And* used her Nokia during business hours. 'We need it for work.' I evil-eyed the bottle of varnish. 'The van would never have passed its NCT. What is Fred doing here?' I shook the pumping dog off my already distressed leather boot.

Sandra gave her thumbnail a tentative little dab. 'Mags was on her way to mass. The new priest won't let dogs in the church. I *said* she couldn't leave Fred here. But you know Mags. She said Gerry wouldn't mind.'

'Well I do! We're running a business here. Not a drop-in centre.'

Gerry had once saved old Mags from hypothermia. Or so she claimed. He did get her a place to live after finding her sleeping in the churchyard below Christchurch Cathedral. In hot pursuit of a couple of church vandals he had tripped over a bundle of damp rags and was shocked to hear it give a muffled protest, followed by a muted bark. That night he let Mags and her faithful dog sleep in his car, and eventually found her a permanent place to stay. Mags decided that this made her and Gerry soulmates, and consequently persisted in calling into the agency to pass on every whisper of gossip she picked up on the streets. Against everyone's advice Gerry encouraged this by slipping her money. I wouldn't mind if she even occasionally used soap and water. Or put manners on her dog. He tried to hump anything that moved, reminding me of an episode in my life that was best forgotten.

I shook him off my boot for the third time. I was wearing my new knee-hugging boots, and a *very* brief skirt, for a specific purpose. Gerry is a leg man, and I hadn't yet given up all hope of him making it back tonight. Which was also why I hadn't cancelled the romantic surprise dinner in the tiny French bistro where a Romanian violinist tiptoes to your table to play tunes nobody ever heard of. The perfect place for me to ask Gerry the question that had been on the tip of my tongue for weeks. The question that, given the right reply, could make me the happiest woman on earth.

'I want you to keep Mags out of here, Sandra. She upsets the clients. She can still have the newspapers. Just don't let her—'

The door opened and Mags's wizened little face appeared around it. 'Gerry here?' she asked, her skin blue tinged with cold.

I sighed in defeat. 'Come in, Mags. You can have one quick cup of coffee. Then you'll have to leave,' I added, feeling Sandra's eyes on me.

'I hope it's not that decaffeinated stuff.' Mags pursed her toothless mouth.

Sandra put a steaming cup in her hand. 'Drink that and go. You and that dirty little dog.' Sandra hates dogs. Even ones who don't try to ride your leg.

Mags drew herself up to her full height. Nearly

five foot. Although she thinks she's a lot bigger. 'I have important information for Gerry,' she boasted.

'You'll have to give it to him another time.' Her nails now safely dry, Sandra put the varnish bottle away and busied herself sorting the post.

'No. He'll want to hear this.'

'He's not here, Mags,' I said.

'I have something *important* to tell him,' she sulked.

'We all have something important to tell him, Mags. But he's not here. Now finish your coffee and go home.'

'I don't have a home.' Her lip was starting to quiver.

'You do so! Didn't Gerry get you a room?' Sandra tore a leaf off her desk calendar, exposing a brand new platitude for the day – *You only get out of life what you put into it.*

'I wanted a flat.' Mags tone was scathing.

'Jesus, who do you think we are? The feckin' council? Here's yesterday's papers. Now buzz off. Go on over to the Financial Centre. They have *The New York Times* over there,' she added encouragingly.

Mags is an obsessive newspaper collector. Nobody knows why. She can't possibly read all of them. And since she no longer sleeps rough, she can't be using them as bedding. But as Gerry is fond of reminding us, ours is not to reason why. We just hand them over. Glad to be rid of them, once Sandra had removed any cutting that might be relevant to any of our cases.

Mags was slandering the Financial Centre and everyone connected to it when Barney arrived. At twenty-six, Barney is our youngest investigator, but destined for great things according to Gerry, who is viewed as a bit of an oracle in the investigative business. Barney sometimes comes to work wearing jeans so threadbare they leave nothing to the imagination. And biker boots that were distressed long before fashion gurus invented the idea. His excuse for this ragbag look is that his girlfriend Hazel, an emerging actress/dancer/singer, used to take care of his clothes and she left him three months ago. Packed up lock, stock and barrel for the bright lights of London. 'Took the keys of the wardrobe, did she?' Gerry had asked dryly.

But when Barney pulled off his crash helmet you could see why he was so popular with the cappuccino set in the Café Naturalle down the road. He could easily pass for the lead singer in a popular boy band. If he could sing. Or even mime.

'Morning.' He tossed back his floppy fringe of wheat-coloured hair and threw the *Irish Times* on the desk, green eyes twinkling in his golden sun-god face.

'Like butter wouldn't melt,' Gerry once described him to a client who was looking for someone to police his teenage daughter's birthday party.

'Don't send me someone who looks like a gorilla in a suit,' Billy Webb of Webb's Wonder Motors had stipulated, possibly because he's an expert on such types. He was so pleased when Barney turned up he was only just short of offering him his daughter's hand in marriage, as well as a reliable second-hand Ford.

'What's that smell?' Barney sniffed the air now.

'Barney!' I warned, always aware that under those pretty-boy features there lurks a will of steel. Admittedly no drawback in the investigative field, except when he clashes with Gerry or spots Mags hanging around the agency.

'Oh, it's fresh coffee! Just the job.' He flashed me

a dazzling smile and snatched the cup from Sandra's hand. 'Thanks, Sandra. Nice boots, Annie. Fancy!' He looked me up and down. 'I need to talk to you about that shoplifting case. Can we go up to your office?'

We took our coffees to the lift, leaving Sandra to deal with Mags. And the still hopeful Fred. The doors were closing behind us when there was a blood-curdling screech. 'Get off me, you randy little shite!'

Fred had found another victim.

Barney and I exchanged glances. 'The start of another day in paradise, huh?' He hit the button for the third floor.

The lift shuddered its way upwards. I pretended not to notice until there was no ignoring the waves of coffee splashing on to the sleeve of my new white blouse.

Barney rescued the styrofoam cup from my dripping hand. 'You'll have to get this lift sorted, Annie.'

I dabbed at the widening stain on my cuff. '*I* will?'

He took this to be a promise, and moved on. 'We're getting nowhere with that shoplifting case. The security cameras came up with zilch. The store detectives are flummoxed. Those thieves are like bloody magicians. The jewellery seems to disappear into thin air. We know it's being lifted. We think we know who's doing it. But we don't know how. Or where they put it.'

I raised an inquiring eyebrow.

'Nah. We did the body search. That nearly dropped us in it. If we try that again without hard evidence, *we* could end up in the dock.'

The lift gave a final shudder before halting on the third floor. Less than three years in service and

9

already it was the office joke. The doors refused to open until Barney punched them with his free hand.

My office phone was jigging on my desk. I hoped it was good news. It wouldn't take much to push me over the edge today.

'It's the Garda, Annie,' Sandra said from reception. 'They're looking for Gerry. It sounds serious. Do you want to talk to them?'

Christ. I hadn't even tasted the coffee yet.

'Put them through.' I directed Barney to a chair. He crossed to the window instead, looking out over the waking city.

'Sergeant Tom O'Neill here.' The voice on the phone was grim. 'I used to work with Gerry.'

Terrific. This was all I needed. Another garda looking to do a bit of moonlighting. Earn a little extra dosh by working undercover on his day off. Strictly off the books, of course.

I was already formulating a polite refusal, had the 'things are a bit tight right now' speech on the tip of my tongue, when he said, 'I have some news on that missing girl in Kerry.'

I guessed by his tone that it wasn't good. 'Is it *very* bad?' My stomach churned.

'It's not good.'

I held my breath.

'We've had an anonymous call. Caller thinks the girl might be a runaway. With good reason. Her older brother could be the real problem there. The caller hinted at abuse. We have a new address for the girl, but it's a long way from Kerry. We've already called in social services, so I thought I'd best give Gerry a shout. Save him driving all the way down there on a wild goose chase. The roads are somethin' terrible this morning. These March frosts can be a killer. We've had two fatalities already. Tell Gerry to sit tight. Not to budge till we have further information.'

Gerry had left Dublin at six. Intent on beating the traffic.

Barney was now pacing impatiently, his blonde fringe falling into his eyes with every step. He checked his watch, waving his other hand to draw my attention. 'Sorry to interrupt, Annie, but the store owners are meeting this morning and I'm supposed to be there. Like now.' He pointed to the time. 'One of them was dead set against bringing us in, from the start. Too costly, he reckoned. Now the case is dragging on, they're all getting their knickers in a twist. I need to know if I can offer them a deal. A special rate?' He didn't look happy.

'Are you still there, miss?' The voice on the phone didn't sound happy either. 'Will you tell Gerry I'll fill him in later? I'll leave you my number.'

I was scrabbling for a pen when Declan, our senior detective, came in, his face grim as a tombstone. He was on the dry again, which never made for a happy detective.

'Annie, Gerry's been on to me. Says he's been trying to get through all morning and would you *please* switch on your mobile. He says some of the figures for our tax returns can't be right.' His frown turned his already hawkish features even more forbidding. 'You're to redo the lot. And I'm to remind you that Friday is our deadline. Oh, and he said will you meet Mr Simon Boucher for him. It's too late to cancel, and you know how important that meeting is. Sandra has the details. He said you're to be extra careful. Treat Boucher with kid gloves, because he's a touchy bastard at the best of times. And we need that contract. I'm off to Dundalk.' He was gone.

'The number here is 014 89 . . .' the voice on the line was saying.

The clock on the wall said nine-twenty.

'Did you get that?' the Garda sergeant asked. 'It's azero awone afour . . .'

I hung up.

'What do I tell them at the meeting, Annie?' Barney stood over me.

'Tell them whatever you bloody well like! Sorry, Barney. I . . . I have a blinding headache. Look, you deal with it. Revise the hourly costing if you have to. I have *implicit* faith in your judgement.' I hurried out, leaving him staring after me.

I hit the lift running. Sandra kept the equivalent of a well-stocked pharmacy behind the reception desk, and I was in desperate need of something to ease my head. One of these days I was going to have my headaches checked out. One day when the sun was shining, and I got to actually taste my coffee before it got cold, and the lift worked properly, and I finally got to drive the Cherokee.

The lift gave a massive shudder before coming to a halt. Twelve inches above its target. I hit the emergency button. Nothing.

'Sandra?' I called through four inches of stainless steel. 'The lift is stuck again.'

'Give it a kick,' she bellowed.

'Ring the engineer,' I yelled back.

I could hear Fred barking, then Mags's high-pitched squeak: 'Is Gerry in there with you?'

'Fuck off, Mags!' I exploded.

There was a long silence. Then the sound of

Barney's calm voice. 'Make a fist, Annie. Hit the right door midway along. Level with the button. Hit it hard.'

I did exactly what he said. Nothing happened. For a second. Then the light blinked, and went out, and I was standing in complete darkness. Panic threatening to choke me, I kicked and punched both doors viciously. I was poised for another go when the light suddenly came on again, the lift gave a shudder, dropped and the doors shot open, catapulting me into reception. 'You mechanical bollocks!' I yelled, before catching sight of Barney's frantic hand signals.

The reason for the signals was standing next to Sandra. A tall, distinguished-looking man with immaculate grey hair and an air of deep gravitas. Mr Simon Boucher, managing director of one of the largest international financial institutions to have sub offices in Ireland, had arrived early for his appointment with Gerry.

I wiped my sweaty palm on my skirt and rearranged my face into a welcoming smile.

'Good morning, Mr Boucher.' I held out my hand.

His sharp eyes zeroed in on my stained cuff, his patrician nose twitching in distaste. Then we were shaking hands and he began to relax. We were even making eye contact when Fred made his move. He launched himself enthusiastically at Mr Boucher's beautifully tailored leg and began pumping.

Afterwards I kept thinking that maybe if Barney hadn't tried to boot Fred so indelicately off Mr Boucher's leg. Or if Mags hadn't leaped to her pet's defence and hit Mr Boucher with the *Financial Times* by mistake. Or if all our phones lines hadn't started flashing at once, making Fred howl like a demented banshee. But they did.

Agonisingly aware of the importance of the Boucher security contract, I kept my smile rictus-firm. 'Shall we go up to my office, Mr Boucher?' I indicated the lift.

He glared at me, his lightly tanned face turning brick red. 'Where . . . is . . . Mr . . . Dunning?' The tone was icy.

'Er . . . he was called away. An emergency,' I lied. 'I'm his partner, Annie McHugh. I run the agency when he's not here.' From the corner of my eye I could see Barney trying to push Mags out the door. She wasn't having any of it. 'I have *important* infor-mation for Gerry,' she shouted. 'Gerry relies on me for information, you ignorant bugger.'

'My office, Mr Boucher?' I widened my smile.

He turned on his heel.

I hurried after him, my heart rattling. If he walked out there would be hell to pay. This had been a bad year for us, and things were not looking up. There was plenty of investigative work on offer, but the competition was growing. The PI business was chang-ing, being overrun by Techno Techs, Gerry said. And our overheads were spiralling out of control. The IT consultancy which had been happily renting our two middle floors had crashed without warning, leaving us with two vacant floors and no other tenant in sight. A long-term security contract like the one Boucher had to offer would make a world of difference to us. I daren't let it slip through my fingers.

'Would you like to make another appointment, Mr Boucher? We're a little . . . under pressure this morn-ing. You know how it is. Busy, busy, busy! The price one pays for success! The roar of the Celtic Tiger and all that.'

He gave me a withering look.

'You have our card?' I persisted. 'You can ring us any time, day or night. We're always here. Always ready to facilitate our clients. Ready to provide you with a reliable, and superior, service.'

He was gone.

Watching him drive away I knew there was only one route left open to me. But you can't throw yourself down a lift shaft when you're on the ground floor. I had to be satisfied with banging my head against the wall.

'Don't worry, Annie, he'll be back.' Sandra put a consoling hand on my shoulder.

'Mr Boucher?' I turned hopefully.

'No!' She shook her head. 'Gerry.'

2

'Annie!' Fiona threw open her door to give me a close hug. Well, as close as she could given that she was preceded by the biggest pregnancy bump in living memory.

'You brought food?' She sniffed my canvas bag like a bloodhound. 'Fish balls in batter? Oh, Annie, you're a lifesaver.'

'Pino at work?' I glanced around her elegant living room. Pino is Fiona's husband. Her second. As gregarious as her first husband was timid, Pino is tempestuous and passionate and great fun, but inclined to be a food snob. But then, as the owner/manager of two of the most fashionable restaurants in Dublin, he's practically obliged to be. Fortunately Fiona isn't, because for close on seven months now she's had an insatiable craving for fish balls.

The glitterati of Dublin are rumoured to use blackmail, some say death threats, to get the highly coveted tables at Pino's restaurants. And not just to see and be seen. Or even because he has signed a major TV contract to allow filming of his monthly gourmet dinner nights. But because the food in both places is to die for. However, from the moment the two red lines appeared on her home pregnancy test, Fiona's taste buds went berserk.

She opened the brown paper bag with glee – 'I'll

give these a quick blast in the microwave' – and disappeared into the kitchen.

'You haven't eaten yet?' It was gone nine.

'Er . . . actually I have,' she called back from her palatial kitchen. 'We had Ribollita, Vitello Tonnato and brandy crêpes for dessert,' she shouted as she clattered around her spacious cooking area, which has more knobs than *Burke's Peerage*. 'But I've been *dreaming* about fish balls.' She came back, patting her bump. 'Besides, I'm eating for two, remember?'

How could I forget? With six weeks still to go, she already looked as if she had swallowed the Hindenburg. If it weren't for the scan confirming a single baby I'd have advised her to order multiples of everything. Her pregnancy had changed her beyond recognition. Practically overnight she had gone from being an edgy, fashion-conscious size ten to a spaced-out, yet blissfully happy, customer of rent-a-tent.

'So how goes it at the cutting edge of crime?' She wedged herself into a fireside chair. 'What's the word on the mean streets?' she teased.

'How should I know? I'm stuck in a bloody office all day.' I threw myself on to her cream linen sofa. 'Same old routine. Balancing the books. Filling in tax returns. Fouling up interviews.' I winced, recalling Simon Boucher's hasty exit.

'Oooh, do I detect trouble in paradise?' Her newly podgy cheeks dimpled.

'What *is* all this paradise crap?' I snapped. 'Barney said the same thing today.'

'Don't tell me you've forgotten?' She looked surprised. 'When you and Gerry opened the new offices you christened it paradise. Remember?'

'Oh, that was aeons ago.' I was in no mood for rose-tinted nostalgia. My viewpoint wasn't clouded by marital bliss. I didn't live in a haze of maternal expectancy and lemon-scented Pledge. 'I've had a *brutal* day.' Ever the masochist, I put my feet up on the immaculate sofa and waited for her to chastise me.

She didn't. The pre-pregnancy Fiona would have given me a slap on the head. This one stroked her bump lovingly. 'You're only miffed because Gerry's not around for his birthday,' she giggled.

'Am not!'

'Then why are you so crabby?'

'I'm not crabby, just fed up. I'm tired of being a dogsbody. Tired of buttering up pompous gits who only want to talk to Gerry. Pacifying old grannies who think their flea-ridden mutts have been kidnapped by Al-Qaeda.'

'But you love working in the agency.'

'Who told you that?' I snapped. Then realised it was probably me. But that was ages ago, back in the days when I considered it exciting, even borderline erotic, to be working with three attractive detectives. Well, two. Even Declan's mother wouldn't consider him attractive. But I had thought it a privilege to be typing out their badly written reports, helping with muddled expense sheets, discussing serial killers and axe murders as we drank gallons of black coffee laced with strong Bourbon deep into the recesses of the night. Oh no, cancel that last bit. That was in a movie I saw.

Fiona's baby-pink forehead crinkled sweetly. 'But didn't you say . . . ?'

'The *detectives* enjoy working in the agency,' I

sighed impatiently. 'And why wouldn't they? They get to do all the exciting things.'

'Like?'

'Like . . . like investigating,' I said.

She smiled. 'Would that be because they're professional investigators?'

'So? They're not FBI men. Hardly Crime Busters Inc.' I said nastily.

'Maybe not, but Gerry's a top detective. A highly regarded ex-cop.' She was always quick to defend Gerry. Mainly because they have been friends for years. Not close friends like me and her. But still. Fiona and I go back as far as junior school. We used to be known as the terrible two. Constantly in trouble with dark moustached nuns for climbing the wall of the convent orchard while the boys gathered round below hoping for an apple, or at least a glimpse of our navy school knickers. The bonds of friendship don't come stronger than that. Plus, I was the one who consoled her when her first marriage fell apart. Convinced her that there *was* life after divorce. In fact, I was the one who suggested we try a brand new Italian restaurant, whose proprietor turned out to be Pino Molino.

'And Declan . . .' she was saying, 'Declan is . . .'

'Permanently liverish? A failed law student!' I relished the words. 'Last time he failed his exams miserably.'

'Only because he went on the rip,' she frowned.

'And why did he do that? Because my nasty half-sister Francesca dumped him? Francesca dumps everyone. It's a fact of life. If all her ex's took to the drink, the country would run dry.'

'What's eating you, Annie?' She became concerned.

'Nothing!' I lied. 'I'm . . . deliriously happy.'

She didn't believe me. She was only pregnant, not witless. She knew there was something major stuck in my craw. The clue was possibly our lack of laughter. Our conversations, whether long or short, were always peppered with laughter. Even during the darkest days of her first marriage break-up, we could get a giggle out of something. Usually at the expense of her husband's infatuation with the muscular Russian engineer he met in Cuba. A woman. Although Fiona frequently questioned her gender.

She made a determined effort now to cheer me up. 'You've obviously had a bad day, Annie. But we all have *them*. Gerry will be home tomorrow and everything will be perfect again. You'll be on the blower to me, telling me how you love your job. How exciting it is to be working in a busy detective agency.'

'Huh.'

'I know it's hard when he's away. But he has to go where the work takes him, and the unsocial hours are all part of the job. You knew that when you met him. It's a bit late to start complaining now.'

'I'm not complaining about his job,' I said truthfully.

She wasn't listening. Too busy reminding me how lucky I was. How fortunate to have someone like Gerry and the chance to do three expense account sheets. Well, she didn't actually say that, but she meant it. As if I should be grateful to be the agency's bookkeeper because I get to shag a cool detective every night. Well, sometimes twice a night. But she didn't know that. Anyway, that wasn't my area of complaint. I wasn't being short-changed there.

She poured fresh orange juice into two lead

crystal glasses. It tasted fresh and cool. But I could have murdered a real drink.

'. . . I mean, everyone assumes it's a fun job, being a PI,' she topped up my glass. 'But where's the fun in hanging around doorways with a five-pound Nikon strapped to your wrist? Working night surveillance in midwinter? Having to pry into people's lives to get evidence strong enough to convince some bolshie judge? Do you ever think about that?'

'All the time. That's why I want to do it.'

'What?' Surprise had her dribbling orange juice down her front.

'That's what I've been trying to tell you.' I handed her a napkin. 'I want to be an investigator. It's been my dream for quite some time now.'

Only her huge bulk kept her from falling out of her chair.

'Why not?' I answered her shocked look. 'It beats being the agency dogsbody. Or sitting in front of a computer screen all day.' I raised my chin defiantly. 'I could handle an investigation. I know how it's done. I haven't been watching the detectives for three years without learning a thing or two.'

'Are you serious?'

'Sure!' I insisted. 'Don't you think I could do it?'

'Well . . .'

'All it takes is common sense. And patience. I have plenty of that, haven't I?'

'Oh, I don't know, Annie.' She seemed doubtful. 'I mean, I know you have common sense, but being an investigator? That's pretty specialised work.'

'Rubbish! I could do it.'

There! I had finally managed to say it. Out loud. Not to the right person, of course, but it was a start.

Next time I *would* say it directly to Gerry. Straight out. No more pussyfooting around. No more teasing suggestions or broad hints. None of that had worked anyway. He was convinced that I was happy to sit in the office all day poring over messy accounts, correcting badly written reports, while the detectives were out there leading exciting lives. Driving Jeep Cherokees.

'The thing is, Fiona, I thought life with Gerry would be different. That if I bought into the agency we'd be like . . .'

'Holmes and Watson?' She laughed. 'Starsky and Hutch?'

'Not exactly,' I smiled. 'I did think we'd be like . . . *equal* partners.'

'You *are* equal partners! He just happens to handle the investigative end of things while you . . .'

'Do all the boring stuff? Exactly!'

The microwave pinged. 'Stay there.' I patted her swollen hand. 'I'll get the fish balls.' I legged it to the kitchen.

She called after me, 'If you're so confident you can handle a case, why don't you just take one on? What's stopping you?'

'Three macho detectives?' I laughed mirthlessly.

There was a slight pause, then she said something that had me almost dropping the fish balls. 'Correct me if I'm wrong, but don't *you* allocate cases when Gerry's not there?'

'I couldn't take a case behind his back,' I flustered, but even as I said it an idea took root in my head. The Murtha case was just sitting there. Practically ignored. Left to one side while more urgent cases were dealt with. *And* it was pretty straightforward.

All it needed was a bit of close surveillance. A couple of nights should do it. That and a good camera with a telescopic lens. We were falling over cameras in the agency, almost all of them with telescopic lenses. I could handle a camera. It wasn't like I'd have to learn how to handle . . . an Uzi? I chuckled to myself.

'You OK, Annie?'

'Perfect.' Working on autopilot I put a napkin on a tray, collected silverware from a drawer, lined up a little glass cruet set. Lead crystal, of course.

All Mrs Murtha wanted was evidence of her husband's adultery. She couldn't care less who got it. The Murthas had been married for twenty-five years. Happily, she claimed. Now their children were grown he had taken to travelling up to Dublin every third Tuesday, staying overnight, sometimes on into Thursday. Business, he told her. She didn't believe him. Something about the recent change in his behaviour aroused her suspicions. Maybe the fact that he seemed so relaxed on his return. Or maybe it was the black lace 36D bra she'd found stuffed into the side pocket of his travel case. Either way, she wanted him followed.

I took the tray in to Fiona, putting it on what was left of her lap. 'Give these fish balls time to cool. They're dangerously hot.'

I prowled around the big living room, too wired to sit, my head bursting with ideas. The Murtha case was perfect for a beginner. Simplicity itself. Practically a training course for a rookie detective. You couldn't go wrong.

Fiona munched away blissfully, relishing each calorie-laden mouthful of the batter-coated fish balls, while I honed my plan to take on the Murtha case.

She'd been right about one thing. I *was* a full partner in McHugh Dunning. Didn't have to report to anyone. I was as much the boss as Gerry. But going behind his back to take a case. Was that sneaky? A bit underhand? Then again, some people just drove down to Kerry without as much as a by-your-leave. In the new Cherokee!

Fiona cleared her plate. Opened a box of Maltesers. 'I'll make coffee in a sec.'

'I'll do it,' I volunteered.

'Oh, would you? I'm too comfortable to get up. There's a strawberry cheesecake in the fridge. Bring it in, I'll cut it. Pino made it specially for me.'

A strawberry cheesecake? Was the man mental? I only brought her fish balls because she had a serious craving for them. And fish is fish. Packed to the gills with protein, even when it's covered in three inches of batter. But a cheesecake? At four hundred calories a slice? *The Murtha case was just sitting there.* Maybe Pino liked her plump. Maybe it was an Italian thing. *I could probably solve the Murtha case in two days. What could go wrong?* Maybe Pino equated luscious food with love. *It wasn't a complex case.* Pino himself wasn't exactly skeletal.

'How is Pino?' I called back to her.

'Not good. His mum had another bad turn. If they are ministrokes like her doctor suspects, he'll have to fly over to spend time with her. But he can't go until our head chef gets back from Naples.'

'But that won't be for another three weeks?' I puzzled.

'Eeeem?'

'Three weeks.' I shouted. 'What if you went into early labour?'

'Oh, you'll just have to step in then, won't you?' she said calmly.

The coffee spoon slipped from my hand and hit the floor. In a moment of madness I had said that in the unlikely event of Pino being unavailable for the gig, I would be her birthing partner. But I had meant it as a joke! Knew it would make people laugh. And it did. A party joke born out of three vodka Martinis, four glasses of champagne and the way Gerry was holding me as we danced to a romantic Italian song that I can never remember the name of.

'Pino wouldn't miss the birth,' I said, my voice a high squeak.

'Might habb to.' She munched happily. 'For his mother's sake. We all have to make sacrifices. In the name of love,' she thrilled, sounding like an off-key U2.

'So you'd . . . drop your plan for a home birth then?' I waited.

'No way! That's all arranged.'

This time a little china coffee cup went south. Hitting the shining floor tiles with a loud crash. I watched helplessly as it shattered into a trillion pieces on the imported Italian marble. Stood staring as the last little piece rattled endlessly before coming to a standstill.

'What are you doing in there, Annie? Wrecking my kitchen?'

'Sorry . . . just . . . a little accident.'

I don't even like babies. And the thought of childbirth is enough to bring me out in a rash.

Fiona sipped her special decaf and ate her way through a wedge of cheesecake as I sat on the arm of her chair, picking unenthusiastically at my slice, priming myself to tell her that I couldn't be anyone's birthing partner. 'Fiona, about your plans for the birth, I . . .'

'Have I told you about fatty acids?'

'Fatty acids?' I was still swamped in terror at the thought of having to witness a home birth.

'There was a brilliant programme last night on Sky. Called *Positive Pregnancy*. It said long-chain polyunsaturated acids are megaplentiful in oily fish, and that clinical tests have proven that eating enough of them during pregnancy will absolutely benefit your unborn child. In fact LCP's can positively guarantee a *brainier* baby. Isn't that exciting? Given my recent craving?'

Fiona should never have given up work. It left her with far too much time on her hands. There was more to come. 'Did you know that it's clinically proven that infants who absorb high levels of LCPs *in utero* not only learn faster, their overall health is superior!'

'To what?' I asked numbly. All I know about babies *in utero* is that women suffer excruciating pain in getting them out.

'To babies who *don't* get enough fatty acids, dumbo.' She nudged me playfully in the ribs.

I took a mouthful of cheesecake. She was so happy I didn't have the heart to tell her I'd rather be stabbed in the head with an ice pick than hear another word about babies. Or childbirth.

She looked up at me, her face glowing. 'I'm planning on eating the placenta.'

The room began to spin, its pale ivory walls closing in threateningly.

'Maeve says it's packed with nutrients.'

Maeve is her midwife. She's from Donegal and a fierce proponent of home births. When Fiona talks about her she becomes almost reverential. Calls her a true earth mother. I'd call her a mad bitch, but not to her face. She weighs at least twenty stone and has hands like cement shovels. And surely any woman who encourages another to eat her placenta should be committed? I was trying to think of a sensitive way to put this when the phone rang.

'Hi, darling.' Fiona stuck the receiver under her third chin. 'It's Pino,' she gestured.

I wondered if he was in on the plan to eat the placenta. Surely not. I once heard him forbidding her to even touch the steak tartare.

'I'm fine, darling,' she chuckled. 'Annie's here. We're discussing my birthing plans.'

I dropped a kiss on her forehead and headed for the door. 'I have to go. Tell Pino I said hello.'

'He says, back at ya.' She smiled at me. Then, 'I've just told Annie that she may have to be my birthing partner after all. No! She's fine with that. She is! Aren't you Annie? Annie?'

I sank slowly into the steaming hot bath. Bliss. I've never understood why anyone would choose to shower when there's a hot sudsy bath available. And enough scented candles to light a cathedral. I lay back and closed my eyes, letting the heat soak into my weary bones. I was nearly asleep when the door opened. The candles flickered wildly.

'Don't move,' a deep male voice said.

My whole body began to tremble. In the flickering light it was difficult to make out his features. Only his tall outline in the light of the open doorway.

He pulled off his gloves and dropped to his knees by the bath. My breath quickened. He put his hands on my throat, turned my head and kissed me, almost savagely, his mouth moving against mine as if he were famished. It wasn't exactly painful, but his rough stubble scratched my skin. To my shame I became aroused. My whole groin becoming engorged. Swollen with desire. As if he knew what was happening under the soap bubbles he trailed his mouth lower and lower until he was licking my wet nipples, which were now standing to attention like pink thimbles. Someone groaned softly. Me.

Grabbing his damp hair I said, 'You bastard, Gerry. You said you wouldn't make it home tonight.'

He sat back on his heels, his mouth glistening wet, his eyes hot. He gave me a slow teasing smile. 'Thought I'd surprise you.'

I feigned coolness. This *was* the man who'd left me to do his bloody tax returns. Who kept me stuck in a boring office when all I wanted was to do some investigative work.

'I have only one thing to say to you, Gerry Dunning.' I tilted my head back, letting my hair trail into the soapy water.

'What, baby?' he asked, his eyes devouring my jutting breasts.

'Happy Birthday!' I reached for his zipper.

3

Despite the mildness of the bright spring day, the atmosphere in the agency was several degrees below zero. So frosty I wouldn't have been surprised to see icicles form on the ceiling above Gerry's head. He had just learned that Simon Boucher had walked out on us. He called the whole staff to account. Lined us up like privates on parade. Well, not Declan because he was sleeping off a hard night's surveillance. Plus he hadn't been there when Mr Boucher got the hump.

'What the hell happened? How could you let him walk away? You all knew how badly we needed that contract.' A familiar little tic sprang to life in his tightly clenched jaw.

Barney, Sandra and I kept our eyes on the floor. All three of us tongue-tied with guilt.

'I asked what the hell happened?' The sharp tone made Sandra jump.

'Mags was here,' she said. 'You know what she's like.'

He shot her an icy look. 'So Mags lost us the contract?'

'She didn't help,' I found my voice. 'And you're the one who encourages her to come here,' I accused. 'You always . . .'

A lightening dart from the blue eyes silenced me.

Hard to believe those same eyes had gazed at me with such tenderness only a few hours earlier.

'I wasn't here yesterday,' he growled.

'Maybe that was the problem?' I said recklessly.

'What?' he practically spat.

'Don't shout at Annie! It wasn't her fault,' Barney defended me.

Gerry didn't appreciate this. I knew because the tic began working overtime as his colour rose angrily. 'She doesn't need you to speak for her. She has a mouth of her own.'

Yeah, and you made full use of it last night, you bastard. Wait until the next time you come home horny. It'll be a cold day in hell before you get to share a bubble bath with me again.

'I'm not placing the blame on any one person.' His controlled anger was even more scary. 'I think *all* of you messed up equally! I'm very disappointed in you, Annie.' He sounded it. 'You've always kept things running smoothly. But you're all going to have to take some responsibility for what happened. Every one of you knew how important the Boucher contract was. What it would have meant, financially, to this agency.'

Feet shuffled guiltily. Somewhere down the corridor a phone started ringing. Sandra half turned, as if she thought she should answer it. One look from Gerry was enough to make her drop that idea.

'What we need to do now is try to repair the damage. But we can't do that until I have the full facts. I need to know exactly what happened. Exactly *what* was said to Simon Boucher that made him walk out.'

He had every right to question us, of course. We

had messed up. But he had to take *his* share of the blame as well. 'Well, the main fact is that *you* weren't here,' I reminded him again. 'Mr Boucher didn't want to deal with anyone else.'

'Was that your impression, Barney?' His eyes narrowed.

'Yeah,' Barney nodded. 'OK, it probably didn't help that Mags and her dog were stinking the place out. But . . .'

'And that stupid lift went on the blink again,' Sandra cut in. 'Annie wouldn't have been cursing and yelling if the lift worked properly.' She gave me a supportive grin.

Gerry sat up ramrod straight. Always a bad sign. 'You were cursing and yelling, Annie? In front of Simon Boucher?' He looked at me in disbelief.

'No!' Barney said quickly. 'She was cursing in the lift! He couldn't have heard her.'

'Sandra did.' Gerry's body language became increasingly hostile.

'No! I . . . I didn't! I . . . just guessed.' Sandra lies as poorly as she does everything else. But she's never disloyal. Well not intentionally. 'We all curse and yell when the lift doesn't work. Don't we?' she appealed to Barney, her eyes huge.

He nodded. 'Only natural. When things don't work properly.'

'So you think if the lift had worked and I'd been here to keep my appointment, everything would have gone smoothly? We'd have that contract now?' Gerry waited.

'Er . . . yes.'

'Yeah.'

'Sure.' We all agreed.

'So apart from the troublesome lift, yesterday's fiasco is all *my* fault?' It was impossible to read his expression. He has this knack of closing off when he doesn't want you to know what he's thinking. It's partly what makes him such a good detective. But not the easiest person in the world to communicate with.

The three of us studied the floor again.

Gerry stood up. 'OK then. Well, thanks everybody. I'll see what I can do to repair the damage.'

'You can't! It'll take a qualified engineer to fix that stupid lift,' Sandra insisted. 'Only this morning it started chugging again, and you could hear it all the way up to . . .'

Barney practically dragged her out the door.

Outside in the corridor we held a miniconference. 'Whew!' Barney pretended to wipe sweat from his brow. 'But it wasn't as bad as I expected,' he cheered up. 'I thought he'd flay us alive.'

'I thought he'd fire us,' Sandra giggled. 'Well, not you, Annie,' her eyes widened. 'He can't fire you. You're a partner.'

Too angry to speak, I chewed my lip and tried to think of a way to regain my dignity. Gerry had gone too far this time. Lining me up with the rest of the staff like some kind of kind of ditsy office temp. Telling me off in front of them? *I'm very disappointed in you, Annie*! How dare he? I worked my socks off in this place. Plus I was a full partner here. My name was on the door. In gold paint. I was entitled to respect. Even if I had called the lift a bollocks.

'You all right, Annie?' Barney bent his long frame to peer into my face.

'Sure. Thanks for your support in there. Really

appreciate it.' I meant it. Barney was always there for me. Always loyal.

But Gerry was supposed to be in love with me. At one deeply emotional moment he had even proposed. I'd been the one who'd put *that* on the long finger. And OK I knew, and fully appreciated, his problem with public displays of affection. I didn't expect, or want, him to throw me across his desk and declare undying love for me in full view of the staff. But was showing respect for me too much to ask?

Barney put his arm around me. 'You know, when you bought into the agency I thought it would change everything. I was afraid it would be you and Gerry on one team, and the rest of us on the other. It hasn't turned out like that at all.' He sounded chuffed.

'Barney's right.' Sandra linked my arm. 'You're one of us, Annie. We're nearly like the three musketeers. Well, four if you count Declan!' she giggled. 'When things go wrong Gerry always gives out shite to you as well, doesn't he?'

He certainly does, I fumed silently. And he thinks he can get away with it? Making love to me one minute and treating me like an office junior the next? He'd been whistling happily in the shower this morning. I hope he enjoyed it, I told myself. Because he's going to be showering for a very long time. Cold showers.

I'm very disappointed in you, Annie. I'd show him disappointed.

'Sandra, can you get the Murtha file and bring it to my office?'

If she wondered at this sudden request, she didn't

say. Something in my tone may have warned her not to. She had the file on my desk in minutes.

I checked the calendar before ringing the small family hotel where Liam Murtha stayed when he came to Dublin. It took an age before someone answered.

'Beechmount Hotel,' a high childish voice said.

'Mr Liam Murtha, please?'

'Mr Murtha isn't here yet,' the childish voice said. 'He doesn't come until about nine. Off the train.'

'Nine o'clock tonight, you mean?' I kept my voice soft. Child-friendly.

'Yeah. Nine o'clock tonight.' He sounded about ten, or even a precocious eight, the type of child who spends too much time around adults. Listening to their conversations.

'And does he usually stay in for the night, then? Or go out . . . maybe to see a film . . . or something?' I prompted gently.

'He might go to a film. Or something. Mam says he *never* comes back until the next day. Would you like to leave a message?' Again he spoke in mini-adult tones.

'No thank you.' I ended the call with a song in my heart. How easy was this going to be? Taking candy from a baby was the expression that sprang to mind. Getting evidence against this dope would be a doddle. He books into his regular hotel as a cover then scarpers off to spend the night with his lover, without even attempting to cover his tracks? What a total wuss. And Fiona thought investigative work was difficult? I could do it with my eyes closed.

I found it hard to concentrate for the rest of the day. But I persisted, redoing our tax figures to Gerry's specifications, then typing out some of Barney's reports that appeared to be written in some kind of ancient hieroglyphics. Declan's were ultraneat as always, but almost as monosyllabic as his conversation. I worded a few tough letters to people who were always quick to employ us to collect any sums owing to them, but who were stricken with mysterious bouts of amnesia when they received our bills. Apart from the call to Mr Murtha's hotel, the most exciting thing I got to do was answer an inquiry about a missing dog.

'Mrs Green wants to know if there is any word on her Yorkie?' Sandra rang through.

'Oh God.' I slumped. 'Tell her I've checked with Interpol. Ditto Scotland Yard. And Mossad promised to get back to me before sundown. The second I have any news I'll report back to her.'

'OK so,' she chuckled.

Mrs Green is an elderly widow, and only slightly gaga. With more money than sense, her main passion in life is her pampered little one-eyed Yorkie. Twice a year he goes walkabout. Despite all the evidence, Mrs Green refuses to accept that he only goes missing when their neighbourhood bitches are on heat. She orders us to set up a worldwide search for him, persisting in the belief that her Flopsy is the target of international dognappers. When Flopsy comes home (of his own volition and with his one eye hanging out of his head) she sends us a cheque for four hundred Euros. I readdress it to the DSPCA.

Hardly surprising that I couldn't wait to begin shadowing Mr Murtha.

Before starting my investigation, I needed a cover story. Gerry was deeply immersed in work, as usual, but even he might notice if I suddenly went missing from our bed without explanation.

I rang Fiona, catching her at a bad time.

'Guess who's been here, clearing out my fridge?' she fumed. I didn't need to guess. Only one person could trigger such rage in Fiona. Her sister Una. Una is the runt of the Riley litter. A surprise baby who arrived ten years after Fiona's mum had given away the pram and the drop-sided cot and enrolled in an evening class for conversational French to help fulfil her ambition to retire to rural France when her hubby got the pension. But instead of the much anticipated French *gite*, they got a surprise baby. Una. And possibly because Mrs Riley was mistakenly treated for early menopause during the first trimester of her surprise pregnancy, Una was born middle-aged.

'She threw everything out. Except for a couple of bottles of orange juice. And a sun-ripe melon. She's sixteen. Why can't she be out doing drugs like any normal teenager? Being baton-charged at antiglobalisation demos? No, she has to come here and upset me. Ranting on at me about what she calls "the inadequacies of my diet".'

'Terrible,' I said, feeling cowardly.

'I mean, I accept that sometimes my fridge is a bit top-heavy with calorie-rich food. And maybe it is a little overstocked with double cream. But what does she expect?'

'Well . . . ?'

'My husband is a chef, for God's sake! Does everyone forget that? And of course I'm fat! I'm eight months pregnant! Anyway, that little poisoned dwarf can talk! She has thighs like a heifer. And she had the nerve to bring *me* a calorie counter? I told her where to stick it. And guess what she said?'

'No idea.'

'She asked if I'd been drinking! Now you're my witness, Annie. Have I had more than a single glass of white wine since I became pregnant?'

'Not at one sitting.'

'Exactly. And that little fascist thinks she can come here and lecture me? I'm convinced that Mum took the wrong child home from the hospital. Don't laugh. Nobody else in my family has such bulbous legs. And where did she get that one continuous eyebrow of hers? She's a changeling. When I told her I've only put on two pounds in the last week, she called me a liar. To my face. Have you ever known me to lie?'

'Never,' I whispered.

She calmed down. 'Thanks, Annie. No wonder I love your calls.'

'Actually, I rang to ask you a favour.'

'Name it,' she said eagerly.

'Would you cover for me with Gerry? Give me a key to your house? Fib about my whereabouts if he rings?'

'Of course! Oh God, I have to pee again.' She was gone.

Two minutes later she was back on. 'Now where were we? What's all this about you and Gerry?'

I explained my plan for the Murtha case. She listened to the whole story without once interrupting.

'Fiona?'

'Em?'

'Are you eating?'

'Oh, for God's sake. It's just a bit of leftover salami. I took it out of the bin when thunder-thighs left.'

'The bin?' I was horrified.

She chuckled wickedly. 'It was wrapped in silver foil, you dope. What do you take me for? Besides, eating is one of the few pleasures left to me at the moment. I can hardly go skiing in my state. Or horse riding.'

'You *never* went skiing. Or horse riding.'

'I know. But I could have if I wanted. Right now my choices are pretty limited.'

'You're the one who thought you'd never become pregnant,' I laughed.

'Yeah. But I didn't realise it would last *this* long,' she protested.

'Count your blessings. Elephants gestate for two years.'

'Oh, that reminds me, there was a brilliant documentary on the Discovery channel last night. All about this tribe in West Africa who use animal placentas to accelerate labour. What they do is cut out the . . .'

'Sorry, Fiona, someone has just come in. Does that account have to be tackled right now, Sandra?' I asked the empty office. 'It does? OK. Duty calls, Fiona. Talk to you later.'

4

I hadn't realised it could get so cold in a Honda Civic at two-thirty in the morning. But then the heater was playing up and my choice of outfit wasn't helping. I was wearing a gossamer-thin top, light pants and classy open-toed slingbacks in case I was required to follow Mr Murtha into some fancy late-night club, or even a posh restaurant.

No such luck. He checked into his hotel then slipped out almost immediately to hail a passing taxi. Following him through the busy city was no problem: the Civic slipped in and out of tightly packed traffic lanes like a ferret through a rabbit warren. The taxi finally dropped him at a newish apartment block on the Quays. Before I could get the camera out he had disappeared into the vestibule. I left the Civic on a double yellow and ran to check the names on the doorbells. Scribbling them in my notebook, I kept a wary eye on the door, then hurried back to the Civic, moving it to a spot marked 'Loading bay' from where I had a perfect view of the comings and goings.

Over the next few hours dozens of people went in and out of the building. Mr Murtha wasn't among them – he and his lady love were clearly having a cosy night in. More discreet, I suppose. Practically essential when you're having an illicit relationship in a town as gossip-hungry as Dublin. By six a.m. I was having trouble staying awake. Then a noisy black cab pulled up and Mr Murtha came out of the apartments and got into it. He was looking a bit worse for wear, I noticed, as I took shot after shot with the long lens, thirty-five millimetre, Nikon, an all-time favourite of Gerry's, which was recommendation enough for me.

The traffic being sparse, we were back outside his hotel in ten minutes. I took several shots of him going in the main door, his shirt-tail blowing in the wind. For my final shot I took care to angle the camera to include a huge overhead clock. Another old trick of Gerry's; camera timers aren't always accepted as evidence. Declan once had his evidence thrown out of court because a grumpy judge said his photos of a betting scam carried no legal weight. His honour said the blurred photos of money being put down could have been taken well before the off. They weren't, but nobody could prove the contrary. The legal team who lost the case never used Declan again.

Well pleased with my night's work, I drove to Fiona's, showered, changed and crept out again without disturbing her or the hideously snoring Pino. Given the early hour, I was first into the agency. A particular bonus. It meant I could start typing the first part of my report without fear of interruption. By the time I finished, I was practically euphoric. Couldn't recall when I'd last felt so good. I had lost a whole night's sleep, yet my energy levels were amazing. I couldn't wait to see Gerry's face when he was confronted with the evidence that I could handle an investigation as well as any trained detective. All that was left for me to do now was . . .

My mobile purred. 'Thought I'd give you a wake-up call. I missed you.' Gerry's voice was heavy with sleep. It was one of the many things about him I found irresistible – that low, testosterone-riddled growl first thing in the morning. Some of our more memorable sessions had been triggered by that early morning growl. But I had more practical matters on my mind today.

'I'm at my desk, sleepy! I didn't need a wake-up call. You need to get out of bed and help Barney sort out that shoplifting mess. It's taking *far* too long.' I couldn't contain my exuberance.

'But what are you . . . ?' he sounded puzzled.

'See you later.' I cut our conversation short. Gerry was smart. It wouldn't do to have him figuring out what I was up to *before* I solved the case.

Sandra arrived at nine. Brought me steaming hot coffee, ginger-nut biscuits and a prize piece of gossip about the handsome optometrist who had opened an office in the building next door. We both found him fascinating. Watching him arrive was guaranteed to liven up even the dullest morning, mainly because he was dropped off at his office by a succession of beautiful people. Of both sexes. He seemed to be on very familiar terms with all of them. Sandra decided they were all blood relatives, all of them being almost equally attractive in a head-turning, siblingesque kind of way.

Then one morning he was dropped off by an enormous black guy driving a brand new Lancia. And no matter how eagerly she watched out for him, Mr Beautiful Black Guy never appeared again.

'He's a male slut,' she categorised.

Maybe. But the big question remained unanswered. Was our slutty but handsome optometrist an AC or DC slut? We had a running bet on it.

'He's definitely one of them! I caught him eyeing up Barney.'

'Are you sure it wasn't the Harley? Men are always . . .'

'Nobody looks at a motorbike like that!'

'Men do.'

'Maybe. But he was definitely eyeing Barney.'

'Well, I'm not paying out because of a look. He has to openly state his preference or make an actual move on a man before you win,' I said.

'You can't bear to lose, can you?' She was disgusted. 'Plus you didn't see the *way* he was looking at Barney. Barney was fiddling with his motorbike and yer man comes out, and next thing you know he's practically drooling an' . . .' She looked out the window. 'Jesus, here's Mags and that effin' dog.' She was gone, leaving me still wondering about the popular optometrist.

I got stuck into work. Sorted my post, took a call from Mrs Green about her missing Yorkie, then rang Mr Murtha's hotel to verify his checking-out time. I wanted pictures of him checking out. Definitive proof that he had paid for a hotel bed that he'd never actually slept in. According to his wife he usually caught the one o'clock train home.

'City Cabs here. Can you confirm a Mr Liam Murtha's checking-out time. I have a booking here in his name for twelve noon. Destination Heuston Station.'

'There must be some mistake. Mr Murtha isn't leaving until tomorrow,' a cold voice said.

'Sorry. Dispatch obviously boobed.' I cheered silently and hung up.

I couldn't believe my luck. Now I could have another go at catching him with his lover. No nail-biting wait for his next trip up to town. This was perfect. But why hadn't he stayed over at her place? Did he go back to his hotel to recuperate? To ring his wife? Not that I cared. I wasn't one to look a gift horse in the mouth. All I had to do now was leave the office early and snoop around his lover's apartment block. If my luck held, I might even get her name from a chatty neighbour. Then I could hang about. Pray that he'd arrive back with her. The way my luck was running, I'd probably get a brilliant shot of them locked in an X-rated clinch and wind up the case tonight, shock the whole agency with my brilliance. I could picture the scene. Gerry bursting with pride as he told me not to touch another account book because I was a born detective. Well able to handle even the most difficult cases. I was so excited I could have gone without sleep for a month.

At eleven-thirty Sandra found me curled up at my desk.

'Annie?' She shook me awake.

'Sorry.' I sat up yawning. 'Late night,' I mumbled. 'You know how it is. Maybe I *should* get an espresso machine in here,' I said drowsily, referring to a heated meeting we'd recently held on the subject.

She gave me a murderous look. Wide awake now, I realised my gaffe. The mere mention of an espresso machine was enough to put Sandra in a funk for the rest of the day. She *liked* making coffee. *Liked* carrying it up to the offices. What might appear to others to be a thankless chore was a perk of the job to Sandra. How else could she freely walk in and out of other people's offices all day? And get to overhear even the most confidential information.

'I'd miss the craic,' she sulked.

'Sorry, Sandra. I don't know what I was thinking. I wouldn't swap your coffee and chat for a million espresso machines.'

Beaming, she put the coffee on my desk without spilling a single drop.

I was alone in the office again when Fiona rang to ask how the investigation was going, this time her voice bubbling with excitement as even she got caught up in the spirit of the whole thing. I suppose it got her mind off her pregnancy.

'Perfect,' I reported. 'Couldn't be better. But I'll need you to cover for me again. Tonight, if that's OK with you?'

'Another night? Poor Gerry. That's the second night in a row he'll be sleeping alone in that big brass bed,' she mocked.

'What about all the nights I spend alone when he's working a case? And in answer to your next question – no I won't miss the sex. That isn't high on my list of priorities right now. Besides . . .' I paused . . . 'it's only been thirty-four hours and . . .' I checked the clock . . . 'twenty-one minutes and three and a half seconds since we last . . .'

Her laughter drowned out the rest.

I noted the time. Four-thirty. I filed away any loose paperwork. Tidied my desk, grabbed my coat and geared myself up for a quick sprint through reception. It wouldn't do to give Sandra a chance to quiz me about my plans for the afternoon. She was an expert interrogator, which made her an invaluable receptionist, but she passed all information on to Gerry. Couldn't keep anything from the beloved *boss*.

My luck held. By the time I got downstairs she was too engrossed in a phone call to even notice me. 'If I can't find the right turquoise and leather belt to go with my new patchwork skirt, I'll kill myself,' she was promising someone.

'See you tomorrow, Sandra.' I darted past, only to crash into Gerry as he arrived, with Barney in tow.

'Where are you off to?' He steadied me.

'I . . . I . . . er . . .'

'Is it Fiona? Is she in labour?' He became alarmed.

It was so sweet of him, my heart melted. So sweet I was almost sorry for choosing the Possibility of Premature Labour story as a cover. But needs must. Barney once told a client they couldn't meet up because he was burying his grandmother that afternoon, when in actuality she was playing nine holes up in Craddockstown Golf Club.

'No, no. Fiona's fine,' I assured Gerry. 'Well, actually she's . . . feeling a bit down,' I amended quickly. 'And you know she likes having me . . . with her.'

A little smile tugged at the corner of his mouth. 'I like having you with me.'

Our eyes met, held and sparked, and his grip on my arm tightened. Gerry has the most amazing eyes. The darkest blue imaginable, and deep with promise. Compelling enough to suck you in, like warm quicksand. Set your pulse racing before you've even exchanged a word. Yet he's the least vain man I've ever known. Keeps his hair cropped short, not because of any fashion concerns but because he'd never remember to comb it. And I can't recall the last time I saw him *really* clean-shaven because he has stubble that seems to defy the strongest razor. But one look from those dark blue eyes can send your blood rushing to all sorts of embarrassing places. And he has a mouth made for kissing. That's the trouble with Gerry. Whenever I'm really peeved with him and try to put some distance between us, he gives me one of those looks and I turn to mush. Start wishing we were alone. Up close and naked.

That image was enough to have me blushing now. Reconsidering my sex ban. So he had played the stern boss when we were in the office with the rest of the staff. So? He could be doing a lot worse. Maybe I should tell him what I was up to? Confess that Fiona was happily eating her way through a four-pound box of Orange Creams, and I was investigating the Murtha case, and I'd be home in the morning to waken him. The way he likes to be woken. Which coincidentally is my favourite way as well.

His thumb was now pressing against my inner arm. Moving ever so gently up and down. Gerry has magical fingers. Even his thumbs are . . .

'Gerry, I . . .'

Barney nudged him. 'Gerry? I've been thinking about what you said earlier. About the possibility of it being an inside job. I know Williams dismissed the idea, but would it hurt to have a closer look at those security tapes? There has to be something we're missing.'

Gerry's grip on my arm loosened. A familiar look crossed his face. I wouldn't have been surprised to see one of those cartoon light bulbs suddenly start flashing above his head. He let go of my arm and turned to Barney. 'Did that last body search definitely come up with zero?'

'Yeah, but can we trust the gardai who did it? Maybe they were in a hurry to finish their shift? You know what they're like.'

Gerry frowned in displeasure.

'Sorry, boss. No disrespect. But you know how it is. Everyone's in a hurry,' Barney gestured.

A quick nod of agreement. 'OK. Let's take another look at that CCTV footage. There was something about those suspects as they left the shops. Their . . . Annie, did you want to tell me something?' He waited, but his mind had already left the building.

'No. At least, nothing important. I'll see you tomorrow.' I moved away, torn between relief and annoyance at this timely/untimely interruption.

He gave me a brief smile. 'See you tomorrow. Tell Fiona I hope she feels better.' He was gone, stepping into the lift with Barney, their heads practically stuck together as they discussed the shoplifting gang that was outwitting one of the biggest security firms in Dublin.

I went out to the Civic. With a bit of luck the heater might work tonight.

The chubby little woman was turning a worrying shade of purple as we neared the top floor of the apartment block. But using the stairs was her choice. When I'd mentioned the lift she had shaken her head in horror. 'Oh no, dear. I'm claustrophobic.'

I tried not to grimace as her heavy bags almost tore my arms from their sockets. I thought my offer to carry them up from the vestibule was inspired. Actually congratulated myself on it. Until we began climbing. To be fair, she did thank me for most of the first flight, then had to save her breath for the rest of the nightmare climb.

Only when we sat down in her small apartment did she manage to get her breathing under control again and begin answering my questions. In fact she was happy to, and clearly delighted to look at a photo of Mr Murtha. 'Oh yes, I recognise him. He visits Miss Manning quite a bit. She lives down the hall. Travels a lot, I think, because she's not there much. Even when she is, she keeps to herself. Not exactly friendly,' she puffed.

From the moment I'd spotted her struggling in the door with her three laden shopping bags, I'd known she'd be a talker.

'He's a regular visitor, this chap.' She tapped the photo with a plump finger. 'Stays overnight. If you know what I mean. Is he married?' Her eyes widened with curiosity.

'Are all the apartments on this floor one bedroom?' I sidestepped the question, using yet another technique I had gleaned from Gerry.

'One bedroom.' Her plump face crinkled up in a knowing smile.

She gave me the number of Miss Manning's apartment, plus a full description of her. 'She's tall. Elegant. Wears expensive clothes. None of your chain-store rubbish. And she's attractive. More elegant than pretty, if you know what I mean? Are you sure you won't have a cup of tea, love? A nice Marietta biscuit? I'll have my breath back in a second,' she said, her face regaining its near normal pink.

'Another time,' I thanked her. 'I have to get back to work.'

Hanging around the draughty stairwell I had more than enough time to mull over her description of Miss Manning. What made it interesting was that she could have been describing *Mrs* Murtha. Wasn't that just typical? A middle-aged husband starts hungering for a little variety in his life, his eye begins roving, and nine times out of ten it settles on a replica of his wife. Just a newer vintage. None of our business, Gerry would say. Just get the evidence. Well I already had that. The only thing I didn't have was a shot of Mr Murtha with his partner in adultery.

The top stairwell was lively as a morgue. Everyone except my plump witness opted for the lift. Half the apartments on the top floor seemed to have absentee tenants anyway. I was beginning to regret turning down the offer of tea and biscuits when I heard the lift doors clanging. I took a cautious peek around the corner.

Mr Murtha was stepping out of the lift, a brightly wrapped parcel tucked under his arm. It was tied with a large pink bow. A gift for his lady love? Despite my unfamiliarity with the camera I got two perfect shots of him letting himself into number twenty. Flushed with success I sat back on the stairs to congratulate myself, content to wait for my next big photo opportunity. I was beginning to feel like a real detective now. The lads were forever complaining about having to spend long periods of time hanging around draughty stairwells in search of photo evidence. Barney's favourite story was about the long hours he'd once spent waiting to get an incriminating shot of a sleazy drug dealer emerging from an inner-city flat. In his exhaustion he had sat down hard – on a turd. Danger comes in all guises to private detectives.

It seemed like for ever before the door of number twenty opened again. But this time I had the camera all primed. Through the long lens I watched an attractive woman, dressed in a midnight blue ankle-length dress, step into the corridor, her arms, neck and ear lobes glittering with jewellery. Enough gold to make me wonder what she did for a living. But then she was clearly dressed for a formal do, and some women like to go completely over the top for a big formal occasion. Had some of her finery arrived in Mr Murtha's gift-wrapped box? If so, he was a good shopper. Good taste. But where was he? She was already at the lift pressing the call button, and there was still no sign of him.

Come on, Mr Murtha. Get the lead out.

Miss Manning stepped into the lift. The doors clanged shut behind her.

I almost wept. He wasn't going with her! I should have known this was all going too well. Nothing ever came easy to me. There were always gremlins waiting in the wings. Waiting to trap me the moment I became even half confident.

But why wasn't he going with her? Afraid to be seen in public, with her on his arm? She was good enough for overnight sex sessions, but not to be escorted in public? Oh, I was going to enjoy busting him.

I paced the stairwell, watching the door hopefully, willing him to have a change of heart. To rush out after her and take her arm, apologising profusely for his selfishness. No chance. After a long fruitless wait, I tiptoed to the apartment door and listened. From inside came the unmistakable sounds of a Gilbert and Sullivan operetta – *The Pirates of Penzance*.

Bloody *Pirates of Penzance*? While she went out to dinner on her own? I gave up and went out to the Civic. If the heater was working I might as well sit listening to Leonard Cohen in comfort while I waited for Miss Manning to get back. Maybe get a couple of good shots of her entering the apartment block while Murtha was still in there. That should do it. I already had the neighbour's evidence. She had even offered to give me a signed statement, if I needed one. Carrying someone's bags can pay off handsomely.

Despite my heavy coat I was half frozen by the time Miss Manning got back. It had started to rain, water pooling on the now frost-free streets. I took a couple of indifferent shots of her as she jumped out of a cab and raced indoors, handbag held high to protect her shining hair from the sudden downpour.

It was seven a.m. and I was becoming disenchanted with the whole sleuthing business when Mr Murtha came out and got into a waiting taxi. He was back at his hotel in fifteen minutes. At seven-forty-five, just as my eyes were refusing to focus, he came out of the hotel, carrying his suitcase. I followed him to

Heuston Station, hung around until he boarded his train, then headed back to Fiona's for a quick shower and change of clothes. I couldn't go to work looking like I'd spent the night in a Honda Civic. People might ask questions.

'My God, what happened to you? You look terrible,' Sandra greeted me. 'And Gerry is in a foul mood. He said you had your mobile switched off again. You know how he hates that. He made me ring Fiona's, but she wouldn't waken you, said you needed your beauty sleep. You couldn't have got much. You look like shite.' One of Sandra's less lovable traits was her inclination to be brutally honest.

'Thank you, Sandra. Any mail for me?'

'Yeah,' she laughed. 'You've won three million dollars – in India. All you have to do is send fifty pounds and a stamped addressed envelope to collect your winnings.'

'Oh shut up, Sandra. It's too early for lame jokes.' Her perkiness was irritating. And the back of my neck was starting to ache. I hoped it was just the after-effects of hanging around a draughty stairwell and not a budding migraine.

'It's nearly ten o'clock!' she chuckled irrepressibly.

'Is that all? God, I feel rotten. Are the lads out?'

'Yep. I was just having my tea break. Coffee?'

'Yes please. And then will you drop this film over to Michael in the photo shop.' I put the reel on the desk. 'Tell him we need it like . . . yesterday.'

'He hates that.' Sandra claimed to know everyone's likes and dislikes.

'Tough. It's what he gets paid for.' I massaged my neck with one hand as I waited for my coffee, forgetting for the umpteenth time that drinking coffee in reception is guaranteed to set the phones ringing. Today was no exception.

'It's Mrs Murtha.' Sandra put the caller on hold. 'She wants to talk to Gerry.'

I took the phone. 'Mrs Murtha? Annie McHugh here. Yes, his partner. You'll be glad to know that we are making real headway with your case. Absolutely. You'll be getting a full report any day now. Well, I really shouldn't . . . yes, I know you've been patient. I appreciate that, but we have been exceptionally busy. I'll go so far as to say . . . your suspicions were justified.' It came out in a rush. 'I can't say any more until we have the full report. No, you don't have to thank me. I just wish we had better news for you.' I hung up, my heart pounding with a mixture of exhilaration and sympathy.

Sandra stared at me open-mouthed. 'Why did you say that to her? Gerry hasn't even looked at that file yet! He told Barney it was to be kept on the long finger. Why did you tell her it's sorted? Gerry will flip!'

I picked up my bag. 'Who owns this agency, Sandra? If you have any doubts, go check the sign on the door. I think you'll find it says *McHugh* Dunning.'

I headed up the stairs, leaving her dumbstruck, which was an event in itself. I couldn't wait to get my report typed up and see Gerry's reaction to it. There are times in life when, despite mountainous opposition, you just know you're on the right track. That you should carry on, regardless. This was one of those times. I hurried to my office, dismissing the mild crick in my neck and the pangs of tiredness from two whole nights of sleep deprivation. I began typing, ignoring the slight tickle at the back of my throat. It would all be worth it in the end. I knew that with absolute certainty.

5

Three-thirty p.m., and Gerry and Barney were high-fiving each other like rappers on speed. And with good reason. They had finally solved the baffling shoplifting case. Barney was so chuffed he high-fived the surly engineer, who had only come in to fix the lift. For the third time in a month. Sandra darted up and down the stairs with endless offers of coffee and biscuits, determined not to miss out on the celebration. The air was heady with success. We'd had a jubilant call from the Garda to say that every one of the culprits had been charged. Including two that nobody had even suspected in the first place. Except Gerry.

'What a scam!' There was a hint of admiration in Barney's voice as they post-mortemed the case.

'It wasn't all *that* original.' Gerry was as pragmatic as ever. 'I'm only surprised someone didn't spot it sooner.'

'Oh, come on. It took the maestro.' Barney raised his coffee mug in a dramatic salute.

'It took serious teamwork,' Gerry said.

'Teamwork my arse. We were all fumbling in the dark until you took over.'

Barney was right. Two of the biggest jewellery stores in Dublin were being robbed blind until Gerry broke the case. What incensed the owners was that their in-store security claimed to know who the culprits were. Hadn't they got them on tape? Acting suspiciously? Skulking close to where the jewellery went missing from? Yet two body searches came up with nothing. The jewellery continued to go missing. The suspects were barred from both shops, refused entry at the doors. Still the jewellery disappeared. A different shoplifting gang had taken over, this new lot laughing openly at the security cameras as they fingered the jewellery, blocking vital camera angles teasingly. Again, body searches came up with nothing. Gerry decided it had to be an inside job.

The security boss was livid. He'd found it humiliating enough having private detectives brought in over his head, but to be told he was looking at the wrong suspects? 'We have the bastards on tape! We *know* they're doing it! We just can't figure how they're getting the stuff out of the shops.'

Gerry took the tapes back to his office. Played them endlessly. Studied them until he was bleary-eyed. He had called Barney in. 'Watch their faces as they pass security,' he instructed. 'They're not carrying stolen jewellery. They're far too relaxed. And it's not an act.'

Despite the owner's misgivings he had waited until both shops were closed for the weekend, then brought in a specialised team to take them apart. Keeping even trusted staff in the dark, and using only expertly trained gardai, he found what he had suspected. Ingeniously fitted false bottoms to several well-placed jewellery trays. The missing jewellery hadn't left the shops. It was all there, but cleverly hidden, just waiting to be shifted.

All that was needed now was to identify the real culprits, not just the well-known shoplifters who had played out a charade for the cameras. But that was a job for the Gardai. Only they could take suspects in for questioning. Although Barney said he knew a quicker way to get results. 'A few smacks around the head and I'll have them singing like canaries.' Barney watched far too many Mafia movies.

Gerry went with the law. Hence his delight at the phone call. Two senior salespeople were charged with masterminding the robberies, one of them the nephew of the bigger store owner, a godson who had been thrown out of university for growing marijuana in a science lab and only got the managerial position in the jewellery store because his mother begged her brother to save her only son from a life of crime.

The shoplifters were charged as accessories. 'Accessories to what?' one of them bellowed angrily. 'We got feck all! That skinny little shagger promised us loads of money when he fenced the jewellery. What'll we get now?'

'Six months!' the gardai promised.

Gerry and Barney were still laughing at this when I dropped the Murtha file on Gerry's desk. 'Sorry to interrupt, lads,' I said modestly. 'But here's something you may find interesting.'

'What's this?' Gerry turned it around to read the name on the cover.

'Another success story for the McHugh Dunning Detective Agency.' I dimpled.

He looked puzzled. 'This is the Murtha file.'

I blushed with pride. 'Yes. I got Mrs Murtha her evidence.' It took huge amounts of self-discipline for me to hold back from doing a wild jig around his desk.

He looked at Barney, then at Sandra who was backing away towards the door.

'I thought I told you to put this file to one side, Sandra.' Gerry stopped her midstride.

'I did,' she squirmed. 'I put it at the very back of the cabinet. The one you . . .'

'I asked her to get it for me!' I cut in, and was rewarded with a grateful smile.

Gerry pushed the file away, touching it as if it had teeth.

Completely mystified, I looked at Barney. He shifted his gaze. I turned to Gerry. 'Aren't you going to look at it?' I asked in disbelief. 'I went without sleep for two nights to get that evidence.'

His head shot up. 'When was this?'

I posed, hands on hips. 'You didn't *really* believe I was staying with Fiona, did you?' I laughed. 'Come on, Gerry? If she went into premature labour all she'd have to do is whistle and half the Italian population of south Dublin would stampede to her doorstep. With cauldrons of boiling water, and . . . *zuppa di pesce*.' I waited for him to laugh.

Instead he turned to Barney. 'Sort out those tapes for the gardai, will you? They'll need them as evidence.'

'Sure, boss.' Barney picked up the tapes, giving me a curious look before leaving.

Sandra was jigging up and down now, her eyes darting from my face to Gerry's.

'Have you nothing to do, Sandra?' His voice was perilously soft.

'No,' she boasted. 'I finished the filing, and cut out all those pieces you marked in the papers. I've left the machine on. I can check the incoming calls any time.'

He glared at her.

'Or . . . I could take calls now?'

'If it's not too much trouble.' His expression had her fleeing.

I waited until the door closed behind her. 'What's going on here, Gerry? I got great photos for Mrs Murtha. More than enough evidence of her husband's adultery. Evidence that will stand up in any court. I followed him to an apartment on the Quays . . .'

'Telmore Buildings?'

'You knew?' I was shocked.

He picked up the file. Took out the photos. Flicked through them carelessly. 'This the lot?'

'Isn't it enough? I couldn't get one of them together, him and that woman he's seeing, but I recorded all their comings and goings. The times are on the photos. The first night he stayed with her until morning. The second night she went out for a few hours. Alone. She came back about two. That's her picture there,' I pointed. 'They were together until six. I doubt they were playing bridge?' I chuckled.

'I told Barney to put this case to one side.'

'You were busy,' I said generously. 'And I know you didn't consider it a very pressing case, but I had the time. OK I lost a couple of night's sleep. But I didn't mind.' I smiled. Then watched in disbelief as he threw the pictures on the desk and crossed to the big window to stand looking down into the street. What was he doing? Checking the traffic? After all my work? All those long, tedious hours of surveillance? Wasn't he going to . . . ?

Temper rising, I followed him. 'You're not going to say well done?'

He half turned, changed his mind, and went back to surveying the slow-moving traffic.

Deep inside me a little ball of fury ignited, became a roaring flame as I stared at his rigid back. 'I'm sorry if you're put out, Gerry! Sorry I didn't ask your *permission* to take the case!' I was trembling now, barely able to contain my anger. 'What was I thinking of? Solving a case all on my own? On the day of your *big* success? Silly me, thinking you'd be pleased. Appreciative of me trying to lighten your workload.'

He didn't move, just stood there, his face impassive. I wanted to hit him. Lash out to provoke some kind of response. Anything rather than be ignored like this. 'The woman has a right to know what her husband is up to!' I spat.

He swung around. 'You think so?'

'Of course I bloody do!' I was winning. It was written all over his face. I know a look of defeat and confusion when I see it. I've seen it often enough in the mirror. 'Every woman has the right to know when a man is cheating on her,' I said.

'He's not cheating on her.' He sounded weary. 'At least, not in the way you think.'

'What do you mean?' My stomach tightened.

'Murtha is a cross-dresser.' His voice was a dull monotone. 'Keeps a flat in Dublin. Comes up every couple of weeks or so. Dresses in female finery. Goes to a club. Has a few drinks. Then goes back home to his wife and family. The people he loves.'

I felt like I was drowning. Trying to communicate underwater. 'But . . . w-why? Why would he . . . ?'

'I don't think that's any of our business, do you?'

Dizzy with shock but still not prepared to back down, I said, 'It is, when his wife engages us to collect evidence against him.'

He shook his head. 'The man is a transvestite,

Annie! He has some deep-seated need to dress as a woman. Or maybe he does it for kicks. Whatever. He comes up to Dublin to play at being a woman.'

'No! You're wrong,' I was adamant. 'I *saw* his mistress. I spoke to a neighbour of hers.'

'I don't care if you spoke to the Pope. This man hasn't got a mistress. He has enough to do, coping with his existing problems.'

I knew he was telling the truth, I just didn't want to face it. I didn't want to believe that I'd spent two nights shadowing two people who turned out to be one. Didn't want to believe I'd sat in a freezing Civic hour after hour, risking pneumonia, to get more pictures of a man I already had on two rolls of film. Someone who, on reflection, had severe difficulty walking in high heels and had a hairdo as outdated as Peggy Mitchell's. How could I have been so stupid?

Gerry was watching me closely now, gauging my mood. 'It was a mistake anyone could have made, Annie.' He went to his desk and began putting the photos back in the file, pausing to take one last look at them. 'He makes a fine-looking woman.' His mouth twitched.

Was he laughing? I was on the verge of tears. Big, humiliating tears that I knew would choke me if I swallowed them, and he was standing there looking amused? I gritted my teeth. 'Why did you take the case if you knew . . . ?'

'Because I knew I could put it to one side. It's a tactic. You put it aside and hope the client will either cool off or lose interest altogether. It happens.' He closed the file, giving it a resounding slap with his long, slender hand.

'Wouldn't it have been simpler to refuse it?'

'And let her go elsewhere? Have another investigator report back to her? Last time that happened to the wife of a cross-dresser, the subject killed himself. A family lost a good husband and father. Don't look so worried, Annie.' His face softening, he reached out to touch me. 'There's no harm done . . .' he cupped my face in his hand . . . 'this time. I'll just . . . I'll lose the file again.' His smile became warm.

'Oh my God!' My hand shot to my mouth.

'Jesus! You didn't speak to his wife, did you?' He paled. 'You didn't tell her?'

'Not exactly,' I squirmed. 'I . . . I just told her her suspicions were . . . probably well founded?' I winced.

'Sweet Jesus, Annie. Why in the name of Christ didn't you talk to me first?' Enraged, he picked up the phone. 'Sandra?' His voice was a terrifying bellow. 'Get me Mrs Jane Murtha. I don't care *who* has the fucking file! You should have the number on your database. Is everybody around here witless?'

6

'Stop laughing, Fiona. It's not funny.' I covered my face in shame.

We were in the Café Naturalle, where I had gone to escape Gerry's wrath. Fiona had answered my call for help without hesitating. She had leaped – well, struggled awkwardly – into her silver BMW and arrived at the café wearing outsize dungarees and sandals that looked like St Francis of Assisi cast-offs. And she hadn't once complained about her swollen feet and ankles.

She was now doubled over with cruel giggles, clutching her massive bump as she hooted at my humiliating foray into the quagmire of private investigations.

'Not funny? You spent two nights trailing around after a man dressed as a woman. Took loads of photos of him. And still you couldn't tell it was a man in drag?'

'He wasn't in *drag*! As such.' I kept my voice low, desperate to retain my last vestiges of pride in a café renowned for its popularity among high-flyers. 'And I didn't *trail* around after him. Anyway, it was dark. And raining!'

'Raining?' Fiona looked at me in disbelief. 'In the apartment block?' She struggled to keep her face straight.

'Whose side are you *on*?' I slammed my brimming cup into its big, ostentatious saucer. Then cringed as two large drops of my latte splashed the sleeve of a passing Karl Lagerfeld suit. Worn, I was prepared to bet, by an eighteen-year-old money trader who probably drove a Lexus, had a penthouse apartment overlooking the river, and would never, even on his worst, most humiliating day, mistake a man for a woman.

'Even her – even *his* – neighbour thought he was a woman,' I defended myself to Fiona.

'The neighbour was a nutty old granny. *You* want to be a detective!'

'Not any more. I'm sick of being the butt of everyone's jokes.'

'Oh, don't be such a wuss. What did Barney say?'

'When he stopped laughing? He made me promise never to fix him up with a blind date,' I admitted reluctantly.

She got the giggles again. 'See, I was right. Everyone *is* laughing it off.'

'Not Gerry! You didn't see him. He's livid. I can never go back to the agency again.'

'Don't be melodramatic. You practically run the place.'

'Run it into the ground, you mean. I've now lost him *two* valuable clients.'

'These things happen.' She patted my hand. 'Remember that time I threw up on the dessert trolley in La Chisterna? I bet that lost Pino some customers.'

'It wasn't *your* fault you had morning sickness.'

She frowned. 'It was nine o'clock at night.'

'Well, like I told that snotty woman at the next table, it was morning somewhere in the world!'

Even in the depths of my misery the memory of that night could still bring a smile to my face. It was such an unforgettable scene. Sophisticated diners leaping to their feet in revulsion. Pino rallying the dumbstruck waiters, offering free wine or a liquor of their choice to anyone who had witnessed Fiona's unfortunate mishap. He had everything under control in a blink, moving between the candlelit tables with the grace of a six-stone flamenco dancer. Soothing, placating, making even the most sensitive diners comfortable again as the ruined trolley was whisked out of sight, to be replaced by a vomit-free one. But it was his loving support for Fiona that had impressed me. His non-judgemental acceptance of the mess she had made of his *pignolata strufoli* and all his other delicately crafted desserts. Why couldn't Gerry react like that to my phone call to Mrs Murtha? Why did he have to lose the head and bellow at everyone? Even at poor Sandra, who hadn't done anything wrong except temporarily misplace Mrs Murtha's phone number.

'Being a working detective *and* running the agency has to be unimaginably stressful. I don't know how Gerry does it,' added Fiona, anticipating my question. 'Even with your help,' she added quickly. Then looked me straight in the eye. 'Sometimes I think you expect too much of him.'

'What?' I couldn't hide my disgust at such flagrant disloyalty. Whose friend *was* she anyway? She was here to listen to *my* troubles. Not to voice her concerns about Gerry's stress levels.

'That's what Sally did,' she said quietly.

That was enough for me. I nearly walked out. If I hadn't been midway through a chocolate eclair, I might have, because the one person whose name I didn't want to hear mentioned right now was Sally – Gerry's *perfect* ex-wife. A woman who never raised her voice in anger. Who never complained or interfered with his work. Who could make a cordon bleu meal out of three potatoes, an Oxo cube and a lump of cardboard. A woman so saintly Gerry gave her permission to take his two little sons to live in the dry heat of Arizona, because her new husband, previously a top army athlete, was convinced that Ireland's damp climate was wrecking his hip joints. Although a more cynical person than me might suspect that the real reason he wanted to move was because even he noticed the way she sometimes still looked at Gerry, as if she was wondering if *his* hip action was as good as it used to be. I could have told her that in that department I had no complaints. It was only when it came to providing support for my emotional needs that he was as useful as a eunuch in a sperm bank.

My mobile shrilled loudly, making three of the nearby traders reach into their pockets.

'Annie? You won't believe who's here!' Sandra's voice was an excited babble. 'Mr Boucher! He just walked in. No appointment! Nothing. He's up in Gerry's office. Barney is with them.'

'Oh my God.' It was as if the sun was breaking through after a terrifying thunderstorm – everything around me suddenly took on a golden hue. Smiles became the order of the day. Even the ultra-cool waitress with the cadaver-white skin and deep purple lipstick, who normally treated me like a plague carrier, gave me a warm smile and a free refill.

'Boucher is back,' I told Fiona, explaining my sudden mood change. 'We must be getting the security contract.'

'No!' Sandra shouted in my ear. 'That's not why he's here. I listened at the door. Well, I was passing by, and . . . you know how sound carries in this building. It must be the brickwork,' she accused. 'So don't start lecturing me. Anyway, if people don't want you to hear them, they shouldn't talk so loud . . .'

'*What did you hear?*' My yell startled cadaver girl.

'No need to shout.' I could almost see Sandra's lip curling. 'Boucher's daughter has gone missing. He wants Gerry to find her. I bet he was *never* going to give us that security contract! He was just sounding us out. The sly bugger. But at least he came back. Anyway, I heard him rabbiting on about the need for discretion. Then he said something about Gerry's reputation superseding even that. Whatever that means. And you wouldn't believe the money talk out of him. Jesus, he must be worth trillions. Anyway, you'd better get back here. Gerry is in his element. He rang down twice asking where you were. Now don't tell him I told you, but I'm *nearly* positive I heard Boucher saying he'd like a female operative on the case.'

I was out of my chair, pushing cadaver girl aside. 'I have to go, Fiona.'

'What? You haven't even finished your éclair,' she said, her jaws bulging with choux pastry.

'You have it.' I kissed the top of her head. 'She's only allowed decaf,' I reminded cadaver girl. 'She's pregnant,' I warned, just in case she mistook Fiona's enormous bulk for a severe case of dropsy.

I ran, my heart soaring.

Sandra was busy in reception, the phone glued to her ear. 'Hold on, Annie,' she called.

I didn't. I did give her a grateful wave as I dashed past to take the stairs two at a time. I was midway up the third flight when I heard the heavy footsteps coming down. Simon Boucher appeared, looking strained and preoccupied. Then he saw me. Hesitated, as if he was about to say something hugely important, changed his mind, and hurried on. But not before giving me a serious nod of recognition.

Did I read too much into that simple nod? Surely not. It was definitely friendly. Well, not unfriendly. He certainly seemed to have forgiven me those few awful seconds when Fred refused to stop humping his leg. I floated up the last steps and knocked on Gerry's door.

'Where were you?' He was in his shirtsleeves, cuffs rolled up to his elbows as usual, looking very pleased with himself.

Barney, however, was scowling. Sitting way over by the window, his face a sullen mask. Barney *hates* missing persons.

'You saw Boucher?' Gerry rewound an audiotape.

'We passed on the stairs.' I smiled with relief. Clearly the Murtha case was behind us. We were on speaking terms again, back on an even keel. But then Gerry never held a grudge. That was more my department.

'OK. So here's the situation.' Gerry ran the tape, listening closely. He replayed it back and forth at top speed until he found the section he wanted. 'Boucher was here because his daughter is missing. He wants us to find her.' He stood, one hand poised above the machine. 'He gave us all the information he's going to, I'd guess. You'd have to dig a lot deeper to find out what makes that man tick . . .' He became pensive. 'Anyway, it's his daughter who interests us. So what do we know about this case so far, Barney?'

'That it's a missing persons?' Barney's sulk deepened.

'Well spotted.' Gerry refused to be drawn. 'We know that Caroline Boucher disappeared over a week ago.'

Barney shot me a sideways glance. 'And her old man waited till *now* to start looking for her.'

'Not true!' Gerry became irritated. 'He reported her missing within twenty-four hours. Went straight to his local Garda station.'

Barney made a face. 'Yeah. An' I bet *they* had him twigged in seconds.'

'Let's hear the interview tape. There may be something we've missed.' Gerry rang reception and told Sandra to hold all calls until further notice.

The tape crackled slightly, then Boucher's deep voice came on. 'I went directly to my local police station. Found myself dealing with Neanderthals. Being advised to go home and get a good night's sleep! As if I were reporting a lost puppy! Idiots!'

'So what did you do?' Gerry's voice.

'I *went* home. Waited patiently. Oh, perhaps I did phone them a couple of times during the night! What father wouldn't? That hardly excuses their lack of civility when I returned the following morning. That's when I found them increasingly antagonistic. Unhelpful to a worrying degree. I was shunted between a surly desk sergeant and a plain-clothes ignoramus who repeatedly got my name wrong. A detective who can't remember your name? It beggars belief. I warned him, telling him their chief superintendent is an acquaintance of mine, and I will not tolerate inefficiency, or bolshie, policemen. No need to look like that, Mr Dunning! I was *more* than patient with them. And never less than civil!'

There was a low *huh* of disbelief. Barney.

Then Gerry again. 'Tell us about the circumstances of your daughter's disappearance.'

'But I have already . . . !' Boucher's voice rose.

'If you don't mind. Please?'

A sigh of annoyance. 'As I have already explained, she disappeared into thin air. On the night of the seventeenth.'

'St Patrick's Day?' Barney's voice. 'Were you cele-brating St Paddy's Day?'

'We were having dinner together. It was a celebra-tion of sorts, I suppose. A year since I had bought her Big Leroy, a magnificent gelding, the envy of every . . .'

There was a low cough.

'I opened a special bottle of Beaune. Ms Lynch had cooked partridge. Partridge calls for a robust wine. Caroline surprised me by drinking almost two glasses. We were finishing dinner when she comp-lained of a headache. Possibly triggered by the rich wine. But it was a mild headache. Nothing of inter-est to you, Mr Dunning. Anyway, she left the table, saying she needed some fresh air. She threw on a warm coat, a fur hat – there was a serious frost that night, if you recall. She went out and . . .' A long pause. 'Since then – nothing. Not so much as a phone call. Nothing. My secretary contacted everyone we could think of. Any place she was likely to stay overnight. Even a couple of hotels that . . . that she might be familiar with. Nothing. Nobody has seen or heard from her since that night.'

'Did you part on good terms?'

'Did we . . . ? What are you suggesting?'

'Just trying to get the full picture.'

'I have given you the full picture. Twice! What more do you want? And yes, we did part *on good terms*. On excellent terms, if you must know. I love my daughter, Mr Dunning. She loves me. We don't have . . . differences.'

'Ever?' Gerry sounded surprised. 'She *is* seventeen.'

'A very mature seventeen. Don't mistake my daughter for some scatterbrained little nonentity. She attends a private college. Is doing particularly well in first-year Economics. She takes her work very seriously. She's an excellent student. Lives at home with me by choice. You are welcome to come and see how we live, Mr Dunning. I doubt any girl would turn her back on that lifestyle. Besides, her clothes are still there. Not a single item missing. Except for what she was wearing that night. Her passport is in the house safe, with whatever pieces of jewellery her mother left her. We can't find her credit cards, but then she would have had them on her person. Yet not a single cent has been drawn from her account since the seventeenth,' his voice cracked. 'Find her, Mr Dunning. Hire all the help you need. Money is not a consideration. Find my daughter. Please.'

'What about friends?' Barney's voice. 'Have you spoken to her friends?'

'Friends?' Boucher sounded surprised.

'She must have friends. Every seventeen-year-old has friends.'

'Caroline keeps to herself.' He sounded boastful. 'She's a studious girl.'

'What about this phone call your housekeeper overheard?' Gerry again.

'I wouldn't pay any heed to that. It's of no importance.'

'Your housekeeper heard her mention a pub.'

'Yes, but . . .'

'What was it called?'

'I have already checked that out, Mr Dunning. You can disregard it.'

A long silence. Then, 'What's the pub called?'

'Caroline wouldn't set foot in such a place.'

'The name of the pub, Mr Boucher?'

'The Dimmer. But . . .'

Gerry switched off the tape and got to his feet. 'So who's for a drink in The Dimmer?' He rolled down his sleeves.

'That place has a reputation,' Barney warned.

'So?'

'So we'd better go armed.'

'That's OK. We're taking Annie.' Gerry grinned wickedly.

'Oh, ha ha.' I pretended to be offended, but secretly I was chuffed to be included in what was, after all, the start of an investigation. 'Don't you want to check out the girl's room first? Find out what she's really like? Devoted dad's aren't always the best judge of a daughter's character.' I tried to sound knowledgeable.

He nodded. 'That's why I want to have a look at The Dimmer. Besides, it's gone eight, and I could do with a drink. Kill two birds with the one stone?' He picked up his keys.

7

'Christ, what a dump.' Barney shifted uncomfortably on the torn pub seat. 'How low are we expected to go in the service of our clients?'

He was in no mood for pleasantries. Too busy glaring at Gerry, who was over by the poorly lit bar getting our drinks. Gerry caught my eye and smiled, clearly untroubled by the thick cloud of cigarette smoke whirling around him.

'Like the feckin' cat that got the cream,' was Barney's comment.

But he was right. Gerry was looking extremely pleased with himself, but then nothing made him happier than the chance to solve a *missing persons*. Everything else would now be swept aside, put on the back burner. To be asked to investigate the disappearance of Simon Boucher's only daughter was a dream come true for Gerry. And not just because Boucher was rumoured to be richer than the Sultan of Brunei. Gerry would have taken this case for nothing. It had all of his favourite ingredients – a missing girl, no leads whatsoever and a half-demented parent pleading with him to find his missing child.

Hence Barney's foul mood. He reckoned we were already paying the price for Gerry's fascination with the case, sitting in this filthy pub on a miserable

Friday night because Caroline Boucher *might* have hung out here. Which, realistically, seemed pretty unlikely. If it were true, it would be the most intriguing aspect of the case. Everything else about it was run-of-the-mill. Caroline was hardly the first teenager to go AWOL without telling a parent. And missing teenagers tend to turn up again without any professional intervention. But what were the odds against someone from Caroline's background socialising in a place where half the customers sported greasy mullet hairdos and the other half were minus at least one front tooth. What could possibly attract posh Caroline Boucher to a place like this? Even the age group was wrong. The mullet-heads all looked like geriatric Bay City Rollers. One of them even flaunted tartans below his black hoodie. And something told me he wasn't on the way home from the Royal St George Golf Club. Or if he was, he was probably in illegal possession of its silverware.

Gerry brought us our drinks, the surly barman having better things to do than carry them a whole six feet to our table.

Barney drank his beer moodily. Downed his whiskey chaser as if it was in danger of being stolen from under his nose. It was that kind of place. Even our table had graffiti scrawled on it. *Billy Sucks* it said amid a plethora of cigarette burns.

'So we're not getting the security contract, then?' Barney seemed intent on riling Gerry.

Gerry wouldn't play. Too busy checking out each new arrival.

'This job will be pretty lucrative,' he said, his eyes following three leather-jacketed scruffs.

'Until you tot up the wasted man-hours,' Barney

grumbled. 'The time it takes to trace some spoiled rich bitch who's probably only out to get Daddy's attention anyway. I *hate* missing persons.'

'Just as well I'm handling the case, then.' Gerry was still intent on the trio at the bar.

'Aw, there's a shock. Why did you ask me to sit in on the interview if you'd already decided?' Barney griped.

The newly arrived leather-jacketed trio were now surrounded by mullet-heads, and even I could tell that money was changing hands. Judging by the mullet-heads' eagerness to part with their cash, they weren't just chipping in for a round.

'I'll get us another drink.' Gerry was gone again.

Barney watched him go. 'Talk him out of it, Annie.'

'Why? You look like you could do with another,' I said, deliberately misunderstanding. I sat back as if being surrounded by dentally challenged mullet-heads didn't trouble me.

'I'm talking about the Boucher case! Everyone knows missing persons aren't worth it! You know what'll happen. Gerry'll disappear off for days at a time. Spend weeks searching for a girl who probably doesn't want to be found. Then win or lose he'll come back ratty as hell. Boucher will hate us. Oh, don't look so shocked. You know we always get the blame for uncovering stuff the client doesn't want to know. Everyone will end up feckin' miserable. Gerry will be in the rats for days. And two months later, the girl will leg it again. Can you name *one* missing person's case that turned out well for us?'

'Gerry found my birth mother,' I said quietly.

'That was different! All he had to do was *trace* her. She wasn't missing!'

'She was to me.'

He shifted awkwardly. 'I don't want to appear mean, Annie, but even that hardly led to a happy reunion. She was a . . . well . . . your half-sister turned out to be a right bitch. Remember the way she dumped Declan?'

'Yes, but Penelope was kind,' I defended. She was the only worthwhile person in a family I hadn't known existed until my adoptive parents died. 'We got along fine.'

'Yeah? And how often have you seen *her* in the past three years? Twice? Three times?'

Once would have been a more accurate count. Although we do exchange Christmas cards. Still, it was far from the relationship I had dreamed of having with my birth mother's family. Although *she* had left me a surprise gift in her will. Her house.

'My birth mother left me her house!' I focused on a crack in my vodka glass.

'Which you sold to buy into the agency!'

'Yes! Wasn't that a happy ending?' I felt my lip quiver.

He was instantly contrite. 'Sure it was. You're the best thing that ever happened to the agency.' He slid along the torn seat to give me a rib-crushing hug.

I wriggled free and went back to examining my glass.

Barney reverted to his usual teasing self. 'Give me a nice clean assault case any time.' He seemed determined to cheer me up. 'A bit of actual bodily harm. Robbery with menace! The prosecutor hires you to get additional evidence. You crack open a few heads, get the names, justice is done. Chummy does his time. And you can go out on the pull without wondering if some nut is hiding in the bushes, waiting to stick you because you found his wife, or girlfriend, or daughter shacked up with someone he hates. And she's refusing to go home. So who does he blame?'

'No idea.' I found myself smiling.

'The PI, of course. Everyone wants to shoot the messenger. Something wrong with your drink?' He pointed to my untouched vodka.

'No. It's Smirnoff all right. But there's a big crack in the glass.'

'And the boss didn't spot it? Some detective!' He grinned cheekily. 'Give it here.'

I handed it over. He drained it in one go.

'You stole my drink,' I gasped.

'Don't worry, I'll have Gerry replace it. As soon as he stops acting as if we're here on a *murder* investigation.'

The gang of men at the next table fell silent. Put their pints down. Barney didn't seem to notice. He was too busy trying to attract Gerry's attention.

I told myself I was being hypersensitive about the sudden silence at the next table. The drinkers there could have simply run out of chat. But they didn't look like people who chatted. More the type that carried knives. My first view of The Dimmer and its patrons had had me cowering in the jeep. Only the very real possibility that Gerry might consider cowardice a major drawback in a budding PI had me following him into the pub.

'Maybe we shouldn't be discussing work in here,' I whispered to Barney.

But downing three drinks in quick succession had clearly degraded his hearing.

'You know what'll happen if Gerry continues with

this case, Annie.' His voice sounded like thunder. 'Declan and me will end up double-jobbing. And with Declan still working that smuggling case, guess who'll have to investigate every under age, penny-ante, drug dealing . . .'

There was a sudden mass exodus from the bar. The door didn't get a chance to close until the leather-jacketed trio and a massive gang of mullet-heads had left.

Gerry was left standing there like Custer, holding up a photo of Caroline Boucher. The barman put a whiskey in front of him, leaned across to say something to him. Gerry responded by tapping the barman's barrel chest with his index finger. He didn't look happy.

'The barman seems friendly enough.' It was sometimes hard to tell if Barney was being sarcastic.

'Sure,' Gerry growled. 'He'd slit your throat for a tenner. I put his brother away when I was on the force, and people around here tend to have long memories.'

'Well, thanks for sharing that with us.' If I wasn't already terrified, that did it. 'Should we leave now, or wait until they start breaking our legs?'

'Relax, Annie,' Barney laughed. 'You're with two fearless detectives, remember.'

'I dunno about that.' Gerry was edgy. 'Drink up and let's get out of here.' He swallowed his Scotch in one go.

'Give us a chance,' Barney complained. 'I can't throw back a pint in a single gulp.'

'Then you shouldn't be in here, blondie,' a voice behind us boomed. 'This pub is for real men.'

Barney turned slowly, his eyes cold.

Gerry blocked him. 'Leave it,' he said quietly.

But Barney was too pumped up to listen. Totally irritated now, he was looking for an outlet for his frustration.

'Jaysus, what a complete hole. Do you do functions?' he called to the watching barman. 'Cos I'd like to book a party for my pot-bellied pig. He likes drinking with his own kind.'

'Barney!' I looked around for the emergency exit.

'Let's go,' Gerry said.

We had almost made it to the door when a metal ashtray came flying through the air and almost parted Barney's scalp.

'Jesus!' he swivelled.

'Aw. Spoiled yer nice hairdo did I blondie?' the deep voice boomed again. 'Sorry about that, darlin'!' He made loud kissing sounds.

Gerry had to manhandle Barney out the door.

In the street Barney was incandescent with rage. 'I don't care how much fuckin' money Boucher has, his daughter must be some slapper to drink in a hole like that. And you're going to waste agency time looking for her? If I were her father, I'd *pay* her to go missing if that's the kind of filth she hangs out with.'

Gerry's face tightened. 'We're not the morality police, Barney! We're detectives for hire. As long as you work for McHugh Dunning you'll remember that!'

'Oh yeah?' Barney tossed his floppy hair out of his eyes. 'Well, McHugh Dunning isn't the only agency in Dublin. And word on the street is that Jim Nolan is headhunting sharp young investigators right now.'

Gerry smiled. 'They can't be all that sharp if they'd work for Jim Nolan.'

'At least he isn't fixated on bloody missing women!' Barney stormed off.

Gerry stood looking after him. 'Don't you want a lift?'

'You can shove your lift.' He was gone.

Gerry turned to me in exasperation. 'What the hell was that all about? Two drinks and he turns into Rambo?'

'Three,' I said quietly.

'What?'

'Three drinks. He drank my vodka.'

'So?' Still puzzled, he peered at me. 'What has that got to do with that stupid crack about missing women? Are you laughing, Annie?'

It would have been hard not to. Everyone was aware of Gerry's obsession. Except Gerry. But then he had also been the last person to know that his saintly wife was playing away. She was packing her case before he twigged that she was leaving him, according to Fiona. I never heard Gerry's version. He refuses to discuss the past; considers it a waste of time. Even when he opened the birthday cards his boys sent him from their new home in Arizona, he kept his feelings to himself. Just smiled, then took that long cold drive down to Kerry. Still, he had driven all the way back again that same night. To please me.

'What are you like?' I linked his arm and leaned my head against his shoulder. 'You and Barney? Two kids competing to see who can pee the highest?' I laughed.

'Don't be daft, Annie,' he looked severe. 'You know

I can pee higher than anyone.' His face broke into a sly sideways grin.

We laughed our way back to the Cherokee. When I held out my hand out for the keys he barely hesitated, then spent the journey homewards nuzzling my neck. Giving it little mock bites. 'I love your neck,' he said, tracing its lines with his tongue.

Fortunately, I'm the most law-abiding driver in Dublin. Well. I didn't break the speed limit. Not until we came within sight of our house. And that was only because by then Gerry seemed to have forgotten that my neck ended at my shoulders.

Gerry left the landing light on when he came to bed. I'm not afraid of the dark, just not overly fond of it. He used to enjoy teasing me about this until I pointed out the clear advantages of making love with the light on. He slid in beside me now, and went straight for my neck.

'Where were we?'

'Well, I was hoping you were going to tell me what that ugly barman said about Caroline.'

'Now?' He was surprised. Which was fair enough, because usually I'm the one who bans work-related topics from the bedroom.

I smoothed the rebellious sprout of hair that refuses to sit down on the crown of his head. 'Don't you want to talk about the Boucher case?' *Or if not the actual case, how about Sandra's insistence that Boucher said he would like a female investigator working on it?*

'Not now,' he grinned, and ran a finger across my shoulder and under the strap of my silk nightdress, pushing it outwards.

82

'Why not? You're the one who said we should discuss things more.'

'I said that?' he sounded puzzled.

'Well, when I said it, you didn't disagree. You were packing for Kerry, and I said it was time we started being more open with each other. More upfront about our individual needs.'

'When did I ever hide my needs from you?' He bit my neck gently and slid the second strap off my shoulder.

I wriggled with pleasure, but refused to succumb. 'No . . . listen, Gerry, be serious. We should discuss . . .'

'Aw, not now, Annie,' he grimaced, and disappeared under the sheet.

'Then when? How often do we get a chance to talk alone any more?'

'We're alone now.' The nightdress slid below my breasts.

'Yes. That's why I'm trying to avail myself of this opportunity.'

'Me too.' He ran his tongue between my breasts. I tried not to groan. Gerry knows exactly how to please me. In bed.

'No, listen . . . are we equal partners or not?'

'Definitely equal partners. Definitely.' He slid the nightdress towards my hips.

'Then . . . how about if *we* investigate the Boucher case? You and me? It needs two people. And Barney hates missing persons. And I could . . .'

'What?' he mumbled thickly.

'I know I made a botch of the Murtha case,' I said quickly. 'But I've learned from it. And if we worked together, you could keep an eye on things. Guide me?

Like a mentor? You'd make a great mentor. And I bet *Boucher* would be pleased to have a woman working on the case.' I played my trump card.

Silence.

I arched my back to allow my nightdress free passage. Give and take. That's what defines a good relationship. Fiona said she read that in *Cosmo*. And she has a brilliant relationship with Pino. Anyway, where would be the sense in me impeding Gerry's progress, now that his hands were doing intensely pleasurable things to me under the sheet. I lifted it to call down to him.

'Gerry?'

'Yeah. OK. OK,' he panted and threw my nightdress on to the floor.

'No. You have to promise.' I tried to hold him off. It wasn't easy, because we were now both panting heavily enough to power a steam locomotive.

'I promise,' he gasped, and was inside me before I could exhale. And everything else became irrelevant. I was now free to concentrate on the moment. Sort of like a Buddhist. To move rhythmically with him. And against him. Increasing his pleasure. Well certainly mine. The two of us were now making enough happy noise to waken the dead. Or at least the Great Dane next door, who began howling at the moon.

Not that I cared. I was on the brink of ecstasy with the man I loved. Multiple orgasms could well be on the cards tonight. Maybe even for him. *And* I had just made a major career breakthrough. Gerry had agreed that we would work the Boucher case together. Gerry never broke a promise. His whole professional reputation was based on that one immovable premise. He moved faster and deeper into me until my whole being melted with love. And searing desire. I raked his thrusting back with my nails and tried not to yell like a cowboy.

8

I stretched languidly and reached out to touch Gerry. He wasn't there. I sat up, checking the room sleepily. The clock said nine-fifty. The blinds were open, the alarm switched off.

I hurried downstairs. Found a note stuck to the fridge with a magnetic raspberry. One of Gerry's less endearing habits. Almost on a par with his ongoing failure to ever, ever put the toilet seat down.

The scribbled note was brief. *Got an important call. See you at the office.*

I dashed into the shower. Washed and conditioned my hair at top speed, ignoring the contra-instructions on both bottles. I was blow-drying it into a semblance of sleekness when a thought struck me. If I was starting work on the Boucher case, how come Gerry hadn't turfed me out of bed at seven? He always insisted that with a missing persons case time was of the essence. Did he forget to reset the alarm? He never forgot when he needed our tax returns completed on time. I dumped the blow-dryer. My hair could dry by itself. Not prettily, but there are more important things.

I tore through the traffic in the Civic, the faulty heater veering from boiling hot to freezing cold with every gear change. Three miles of this and my hair took on a life of its own.

Barney's Harley was parked alongside the Cherokee in the narrow side street. I squeezed the Civic in beside them, taking up the last parking space. Cadaver girl from the Café Naturalle, who had been following close behind, shot me a filthy look and gunned her Mondeo back towards the busy road.

Hurrying round the corner I shrugged her a silent apology.

Sandra looked up, startled, as my hair preceded me into reception. 'My God, what happened to your hair?'

'It's no big deal.' I touched my still expanding frizz. 'It'll settle.'

'Into what?' she giggled. 'A giant Brillo pad?' She flicked back her newly styled, silken mane with its recently acquired pink highlights.

I dived into the lift.

'Watch out upstairs!' she called after me. 'Bullets are flying.'

'What?'

Before she could reply, the lift doors closed between us.

I was still ten feet away from Gerry's door when I heard the rising anger in his voice. I slipped in quietly. Looking more agitated than he'd been since the Murtha debacle, he was barking into the phone, gesturing at the pacing Barney to keep quiet.

I sidled up to Barney. 'What's up?' I mouthed silently.

He shot me a warning look.

'Surely you could send me a *copy* of the file?' Gerry said. 'Yeah, I know that. But I need this favour. Boucher is . . . hey, how many times have I stuck my neck out for *you*? OK, OK. Then just copy the relevant bits. Send *them* over. Oh, for Christ's sake . . . I'm not asking you to break the bloody official secrets act. It's not . . .'

I looked questioningly at Barney. He stared back. At my hair.

'Thanks, Tom. Yeah. I owe you one.' Gerry hung up. 'Christ, I'd kill for a cigarette. I don't suppose . . . ?' Catching my look of disapproval his voice trailed off. Or maybe it was my hair. But Gerry's battle against nicotine is the stuff of legends.

Before I could say a word he was on to reception. 'Sandra? There'll be a courier arriving shortly with some papers. For me!' he bellowed impatiently. 'I want them on my desk, asap. Got that?'

He hung up. Turned to me, his eyes wary.

Of course they were. A few hours ago he had promised that we would work the Boucher case together. Then what does he do? Muffles the alarm when it rings? Creeps out leaving me to sleep in? Hardly the actions of someone eager to form an investigative partnership with me. He was obviously regretting his promise. Trying to keep me out of the loop . . .

'OK, Annie, here's the state of play on the Boucher case.'

Or maybe not.

'Barney called me early this morning. He met a man in a club last night . . .'

'Congratulations,' I grinned at Barney.

He didn't even smile. 'One of Nolan's wankers,' he said.

'This wan— chap . . . he gave him an important piece of information about Caroline Boucher. Information which the Gardai have just confirmed.'

Barney was still muttering, wearing out the floor-boards.

'For Christ's sake, Barney, sit down. You're making me dizzy.'

'What's this new information?' I asked.

'Simon Boucher hasn't been totally upfront with us.' He made a quick notation on his desk pad. 'It seems that Caroline ran away from home when she was fourteen. There was a major fuss about it at the time. And the thing is there may have been other unreported incidents.'

'Incidents?'

'She's a persistent runaway,' Barney said. 'A "small" detail which Boucher kept from us.'

'He's known to be paranoid about his privacy,' Gerry defended.

'Then how come that wanker who works for Nolan knew Caroline's history?'

'He has a brother in the Garda,' Gerry said.

'You have mates there!'

'Yes. That's why we'll soon have a copy of their file on Caroline.'

'What use will that be? An outdated three-paragraph report telling us she ran off, worried her father, and came home with her tail between her legs?'

'Boucher never mentioned that she had run away before?' I asked nervously.

Gerry shook his head.

'Lying bastard,' Barney said.

'He didn't lie, he . . .'

'Withheld information? Yeah, you told me.'

Gerry gave him a look. 'He's not the first client who's tried that. I'll sort it.'

'Will you drop the case?' I asked.

He didn't reply.

Barney was pacing again. 'I knew he was lying from the outset. In that whole interview he never once made real eye contact. That's always a dodgy sign.'

Before joining McHugh Dunning, Barney had taken a correspondence course in criminal psychology with an American college in Wyoming. After three months' hard study they gave him a degree, probably would have given him a Masters if he'd reregistered for the second trimester and paid the extra six hundred.

Gerry ran an anxious hand through his hair, ruffling it until it resembled a baby porcupine.

'I *knew* he was lying!' Barney repeated.

Gerry's face hardened. 'Knew it in your water, did you?'

He opened our Boucher file. Flicked through it as if this might magically divulge some previously hidden information. Barney watched him, fingers drumming impatiently on the desk.

Gerry finally gave up on the file. 'Tom O'Neill says that three years ago the Gardai pulled out all the stops for Boucher, yet managed to keep the investigation hush-hush. Boucher was then spending more time in Switzerland than in Dublin, but remained so influential here they were ordered to put huge manpower on the case. Ransom was uppermost in everyone's mind. Four days later a commis waiter in the Shelbourne Hotel rings up to say a girl answering Caroline's description is staying in their most expensive suite. And if it is her, will there be a reward? It *was* her. Living it up on caviar and champagne. She had run up a bill for several thousand. Had room service run ragged.'

'And this time you thought we might find her in The Dimmer?'

He gave me a look he usually reserved for Barney. Progress of a sort, I suppose.

'She's seventeen now. Less likely to be playing childish games. And don't forget, I had information that she was overheard planning to meet someone in The Dimmer. The very day she disappeared.'

'Aw, come on, Gerry, even her old man didn't believe that. He said his housekeeper got the name wrong.' Barney perched on the edge of the desk.

'The barman recognised her from her photo.'

'That gunner-eyed gimp? He wouldn't recognise his own mother if she was breastfeeding him.' Barney spat out his chewing gum in disgust, aiming it straight at the waste-paper bin.

'I believe him . . .' Gerry paused. 'The gardai don't.'

'I'm with the gardai,' Barney said quickly.

'They're not infallible!'

'You're still convinced her disappearance is suspicious? She's not just slumming it in some five-star hotel? Sunning herself in Barbados? Jet-skiing in the Maldives?'

'Her father has her passport.'

'So you're going to continue with the case?'

'That's what I do. I'm an investigator, remember? A PI?'

Barney scrambled to his feet. 'Well, if it's OK with you, this PI will get back to chasing up those witness statements on Mick Kelly. That piece of filth has been living off the proceeds of heroin dealing for years, yet still manages to evade the law because no one will give evidence against him. Too fond of their kneecaps. Even his ex, who hates him, won't talk to the gardai.

The public prosecutor thinks she *might* talk to me. If I ask nicely.' He pulled a face.

The fax machine hummed into life. Gerry reached for the incoming paper.

'You go ahead, Barney. But take care, OK?'

Barney didn't move. 'Er . . . any chance Annie could come with me? Kelly's ex is a bit of a hard nut. She . . . I might have a better chance of loosening her up if . . . if I have a woman with me?'

My heart skipped a beat. Barney was inviting me to work a drug case with him? Drug cases were mega. If I got to work a drug case, even for a single day, everyone would have to take me seriously. Even Gerry.

He concentrated on the fax. 'Sorry. I need Annie here,' he said without looking up. 'I have an important job for her.'

This time my heart skipped two beats. For months now I had been dropping broad hints that I'd dearly love to handle some investigative work. Anything at all. Big, small. Schoolyard pilfering? Tips going missing in a hairdressing salon? Nobody paid the slightest heed. Now two detectives were competing for my assistance?

Barney scowled with disappointment. 'You're the boss. I'll have to do my best to get some key *judiciary* evidence alone. Get that dangerous scum locked away.' He opened the door. 'Oh, good luck with finding your little rich girl. That should make our streets a lot safer.'

Gerry nodded, his mind clearly elsewhere.

I wanted to hug him. And wipe the worried frown off his face. Assure him that he could trust me with any type of investigative work. I wanted to promise that if it was concern for my personal safety that was making him hesitate, he could relax. I had taken a six-month self-defence course, last winter. Attended nearly all the classes. Well, three.

'So what's this *special* job you have for me, Gerry?'

'What?' He seemed startled.

'The job.' I pointed to the fax.

'Here.' He handed it over. 'Take care of that, will you. It's right up your street. They seem kosher. Sean over in Prestige Estates has already checked their bona fides. Done the groundwork. Try to get it sorted today, will you, Annie?'

I read the fax eagerly. It said the directors of a company called Dreamland Interiors were on their way to view our two vacant floors. Experts in interior design, wallpapers, and Eastern wall hangings, the two ladies would be arriving shortly, and as Sean from Prestige Estates was unavoidably detained, he would be eternally grateful if we would afford them every courtesy until he got here.

9

I locked myself in my office and told myself that killing my partner would be a bad career move in anyone's book. Having a major row with him right now would serve no purpose either. Not when our prospective tenants could arrive at any second. No point in having them walk into the middle of a brawl. Not when we needed to rent those two floors asap.

And I needed to present a positive front to them. Let them see that we'd make attractive business neighbours. I checked my reflection in my little handmirror.

'Christ!' I did a double take.

I had forgotten about my hair. No time to smooth that now. The most I could hope to achieve on the appearance front was to tone down my flaming red cheeks. Try camouflaging them with a little or even a lot of beige foundation, a proven standby for just such embarrassing occasions, according to its maker. Although I doubted that the House of Revlon had ever encountered a situation quite like this.

My office door handle rattled.

'Why is this door locked, Annie? What's wrong?' Gerry sounded puzzled.

'Nothing! Not a single feckin' thing,' I yelled. 'As long as you keep well out of my way!'

'What?' I could almost hear the wheels turning in

his brain. Picture him replaying the scene in his office. Him handing me the fax, me reading it, turning puce, and sweeping out without a word. 'Open the door, Annie. This is childish. Open the door and talk to me!'

Talk? *Now* he wanted to talk? The master of *Not now, Annie* wanted to *talk*?

Beige foundation in place, I outlined my lips with a new collagen-enhanced lipstick Sandra had convinced me to buy. Apparently all the cool people were wearing it. Collagen-enhanced lipstick was in, right now. Sandra always knew what was in. And out.

'Collagen plumps up your lips,' she had coaxed. 'Makes you look like Lara Croft. Irresistible.'

May as well use it. It couldn't make me look any worse than I already did.

Yes it could. The door handle continued to rattle as I scrubbed furiously at the long red slash that used to be my mouth. A final rub with a wet wipe removed the offending lipstick. And one layer of my epidermis.

The phone shrilled.

'Annie?' Gerry. Using his mobile directly outside my door. 'The people from Dreamland Interiors will be here any minute. Are you going to open this door?'

'Screw you,' I shrieked through burning lips. 'And screw Dreamland Interiors!' I slammed down the receiver.

It rang instantly. 'Screw you! And . . .'

'The directors of Dreamland Interiors are here, Annie,' Sandra sounded nervous. 'And Gerry's not answering his phone.'

'I'm on my way.' I gave my flaming lips a final soothing pat and unlocked the door.

Gerry blocked my path. 'Annie? What are you . . . ?' He stared. 'What happened to your mouth?'

He could talk – he looked like a vagrant. His loosely rolled up shirtsleeves were unravelling sloppily, his finger-worried hair stood on end. His usually attractive five o'clock shadow was bordering on the six-thirty.

'Tidy yourself up,' I ordered, and swept past him and into the lift. 'The *ladies* from Dreamland Interiors will probably want to view the whole building. We don't want them thinking we have squatters.'

He stood looking after me, his face the colour of new putty.

Even if I had been looking my best, my first sighting of the directors of Dreamland Interiors would have had me cringing. They both looked like they had just walked off the set of *Sex and the City*. With glorious, sun-streaked hair, impossibly perfect figures and make-up that enhanced rather than covered their flawless skin, they were living proof that thirtysomething *was* the new twenty. Clad in stunningly cut, figure-skimming outfits in toning shades of khaki/subtle tans/olive greens – possibly the new black? – they also looked every inch the stylish design experts they were reputed to be.

I greeted them as warmly as I could. It wasn't easy.

Naomi Lawlor Billings was clearly the alpha female. And a complete cow. She looked at me as if I ate dung, winced openly at my hair, and rattled off a list of faults she had already noted about our building.

(1) It was in a deeply unfashionable area.
(2) Consequently, difficult to find.
(3) It had no off-street parking.

(4) It had no display windows – to speak of.

(5) The biggest fault of all. It faced the wrong way.

'Feng shui recommends an east-facing entrance,' she said accusingly.

I glanced helplessly at Sandra, who cravenly ducked behind the reception desk. Clearly the four minutes she had spent in Naomi Lawlor Billings's company had been three too many.

'There's handy parking in a little side street around the corner,' I began. 'We find it very convenient. There's always space enough for at least—'

'You mean opposite that filthy building site?' Naomi was horrified.

Pathetically eager to please, I nearly pointed out that all the building site entrances faced east, then caught myself in time. Mentioning that could result in an own goal. In a couple of months that very building would be competing with us for the rental market.

I hit the button for the lift instead, deciding to show them the second floor first. The one with a superior view.

'Is this lift faulty?' Naomi watched as I punched the call button for the third time.

'No! Just extra busy today. Loads of people coming in and out. Viewing our vacant floors,' I lied sweetly.

She pulled a metal tape from her Louis Vuitton handbag and brandished it like a bull-whip.

'Your offices are on the *third* floor?'

'Would that . . . be a problem?' As if I had to ask.

'It could be.' The tape crackled. 'If the lift is unreliable. We couldn't possibly have *your* clients walking past *our* floors,' she said, as if she suspected all our clients of being muggers and rapists.

'We like to leave our doors *open*.' Tudi Gilligan,

her fellow director, spoke for the first time, her voice a gentle whisper. 'Essential if the chi is to flow freely.'

'The chi?'

'Exactly! My door *must* face east!' Naomi commanded. 'I'm a committed feng shui practitioner.'

Our popular IT consultants had been Belfast Presbyterians. I couldn't recall them ever forcing their beliefs on us. Something told me things would be different with Naomi.

Her Louis Vuitton bag suddenly rang.

'Yes?' She flicked open a minuscule phone. 'Well, Bono will just have to wait. Yes! I am fully aware of the importance of his side entrance. Micheal Flatley didn't complain when I strip-lighted his! Absolutely not!' She threw the phone back in her bag.

Tudi's grey eyes met mine. They gave nothing away.

Naomi was first out of the lift. She marched ahead of us, dropping names like confetti. I didn't catch all of them, but the few I did were seriously impressive. She appeared to be on intimate terms with at least two of the Corrs, several international supermodels, and a government minister who was being tipped for the EU presidency.

I longed to mention Simon Boucher. Let her know we weren't rubbish. But in McHugh Dunning we had to practically take an oath of secrecy when it came to naming our clients.

'Em? A detective agency directly above us?' Naomi wrinkled her perfect nose in distaste. 'I'm not altogether sure our clients would be comfortable with that. We have a reputation to consider.'

She glanced at Tudi, who seemed to have taken a vow of silence. Tudi was every businessperson's dream: a genuinely silent partner.

I tried directing my sales talk at her. 'You'll be happy to know that the lease includes full use of our spacious and well-designed reception area.' I quoted our half-page ad in the *Irish Times*. 'And *both* these floors offer panoramic views of the city. An added bonus is the unbroken view of Dublin Bay, with it's crystal-clear and sun-dappled waters.' *If you stand on a chair, twist your head to the left and wait for a break in the clouds.*

Tudi spoke. 'Two full floors, Naomi . . . a lot more square-footage than in our other premises. Extra space for your new minimalist displays . . .'

'Huh.'

'An office each? Separate floors?'

I imagined a hint of desperation in Tudi's soft voice. 'And all this . . . natural light.' Arms outstretched, as if to embrace all around her, she suddenly gasped, 'Oh my gosh, Naomi! This door faces east.'

'I should hope so. At what they're asking for the lease.' Naomi was now grimacing as if she could smell something putrefying under the floorboards. 'Don't tell me there's no air conditioning?'

I was on the brink of telling her that there wasn't a big demand for air conditioning in rain-drenched Dublin when Gerry walked in. He had clearly made an effort to tidy himself up – washed his face, splashed water on his hair, pulled on a jacket. Gerry's idea of a makeover.

Both women were impressed. Hugely taken with him. Tudi actually began speaking in full sentences after I introduced him. But Naomi was the real shocker. Dropping her major bitch persona, she greeted him with such kittenlike eagerness I wouldn't have been surprised to see her rub herself against his ankles.

'So *you're* the owner of the detective agency?' she pouted attractively. '*And* a working detective? A dangerous occupation, *n'est-ce pas?*' she twinkled. 'How on earth does your wife cope with the worry of that?'

Before Gerry arrived she had inferred that private detectives were the scum of the earth, not fit to breathe the same air as her millionaire rock stars and wannabe Euro politicians. Now her kohl-rimmed eyes were all but devouring him, her manicured hands fluttering as if they ached to touch him.

His discomfort at all this sudden female attention inspired me. I saw a way to pay him back for the cavalier way he had just treated me.

'Gerry hasn't got a *wife*,' I gushed. 'He's still looking. Ha ha.'

They swooped. Smothering him in Chanel No. 5.

The look on his face was payback enough for my earlier distress. Gerry's life had once been threatened by a knife-wielding thug whose wife he was assisting. He hadn't looked half as frightened then as he did now. Knife-wielding thugs he could handle. A couple of man-hungry interior designers terrified him.

'Annie?' he appealed.

I ignored him. We badly needed to rent out these two floors. Our once-friendly bank manager was starting to make seriously threatening noises regarding our growing overdraft. And here we had two perfectly respectable prospective tenants. Both of them looking extremely interested now. Especially Naomi, who was no longer searching for flaws or behaving as if she was viewing the Amityville building.

'I think one could easily draw yang energy into this place.' She gave Gerry another blinding smile. 'Overcome its lack of chi by the appropriate use of greenery.'

'. . . greenery,' Tudi agreed.

Naomi drew air pictures underlining her vision of what these basic offices could look like with the help of a genuine talent. Hers.

Tudi looked on admiringly, every now and then echoing Naomi's suggestions as if she also wished to emphasise just how well feng shui could enhance a property. Even one as sadly lacking as this one.

'All it takes is time. I'll explain it to you, Gerry. In simple terms,' Naomi cooed.

'Annie?' he appealed again.

I kept my eyes on the floor.

'People assume that it's a difficult philosophy. A common misconception, I assure you.'

'. . . misconception,' Tudi smiled.

'In fact,' Naomi caught his arm, her talonlike nails gleaming deep purple, 'I could teach you the principles in a single evening!'

'. . . single evening.'

'The most essential thing to keep in mind is that the area to your left is the dragon side. This represents male energy.'

The blood drained from Gerry's face.

'And the area to your right is the tiger side. Signifying female energy. Now in business, as in all areas of one's life, one should constantly strive for an unequivocal balance between the two. So my *first* suggestion to you would be . . .'

I slipped away quietly.

I was stepping into reception when Sean from Prestige Estates hurried in from the street, leaving a paper trail in his wake. 'Sorry, Annie,' he panted, his huge bulk heaving with the effort. 'Damn auctions. How's it going with Naomi?'

'Oh, she's being sweet.' I helped him pick up his fallen papers.

'Sweet? The woman is a bloody nightmare. If Dreamland Interiors didn't have all that cash, I wouldn't touch them with a bargepole. Has she mentioned feng shui, yet?'

'Er . . . I . . .'

'You're lucky then. Once she starts on that, you'll never shut her up!'

'Really?' I smiled.

'But Dreamland is no fly-by-night company. If they sign a lease, you're quids in. If Tudi likes a property, she'll meet your price. *And* you'll have no problems getting a six-month advance. It's Naomi that's the problem,' he sighed. 'She's viewed everything on our books and hasn't once seen anything she likes.'

'Oh, I think she has now,' I grinned.

'You sure?' He mopped his balding temples. 'I'll be honest with you, I don't think I can take much more of her.'

'Then brace yourself for the good news. Gerry is handling the viewing! He'll give you a shout when the papers need signing.'

'He's . . . he *wants* to show them around?'

'Insists on it.'

'Ah, I don't think I can . . .'

I pushed him towards the door. 'Course you can! Get back to your office. Pour yourself a large Scotch and wait for the call. You'll still get your commission,' I promised.

'Thanks, Annie. You're a doll,' he wheezed, and legged it.

'What's going on?' Barney came downstairs, swinging his crash helmet like a bowling ball.

He waved to Sean, wincing as he watched him lose more papers to the rain-spattered wind.

'Jesus, if ever there was a candidate for a coronary.' He cringed.

'What are you doing here?' I ignored the hapless Sean who was now being berated by a bullying traffic warden. 'I thought you were out getting evidence on that drug dealer – what's his name?'

'Kelly. I've been trying. Spent the last half-hour on the blower. Kelly's ex has scarpered again. Gone to ground. My snitch said we had more hope of finding Bin Laden.'

'So you're scuppered?'

'I didn't say that,' he grinned. 'I've managed to trace her to Curracloe. In Wexford.'

'I know where Curracloe is. But what's she doing there?'

'Living in a caravan. On the beach.'

'In this weather?'

'Her choice. All I have to do now is get down there and hope she'll talk to me. Wish me luck.' He turned to go.

'Barney?'

'Yeah?'

'Want me to come with you?'

'I thought Gerry had a job for you?'

'That's all done and dusted.' I gritted my teeth.

'Well, if you're sure . . . ?'

'I'll get my coat. Leave your helmet with Sandra. I'll drive.'

His face fell. 'Aw, I'd rather . . .'

'What?' I bristled.

'Nothing. Sandra, take care of this, will you?'

Intrigued, Sandra put a caller on hold and dropped the helmet behind the desk. 'What's going on? I thought you were showing Dreamland Interiors around Annie?'

'Well I'm not,' I snapped.

'She's assisting me with an investigation,' Barney said.

'We're going down to Wexford to help crack an important case,' I answered her baffled look. 'But it's a secret. So whatever you do, don't tell Gerry. OK?'

'What do you take me for, Annie?' she looked hurt.

I knew we'd only just be out the door when she'd be on to him.

Perfect.

10

'He was screwing a young one all the time we were living together.' The wind rocked the caravan as Mick Kelly's ex told her story into the Voice Operated Recorder.

She'd been reluctant to talk at first, eyeing us and the VOR with deep suspicion. Then I made three coffees from a jar of instant I found on the sink, and Barney tipped a warming dollop of whiskey into each mug. That's when she began to relax. Even more so when Barney said he'd leave her the rest of the Jameson's.

She was sobbing now. Blowing her reddening nose into a succession of tissues I kept passing her. 'She was still in school when it started. Can you believe that? A fuckin' schoolgirl?' she looked at me with sunken eyes.

I gave her my last tissue, watching as she dabbed at the river of black mascara that was running down her gaunt face. If she didn't stop crying soon, we'd be in big trouble. The caravan was so lacking in even the most basic comforts, I knew there would be little hope of finding a spare box of tissues here. Such genuine poverty made me uneasy, guilty for ever complaining about our business over-draft.

Still, I couldn't help noticing that the baby sleeping

on the nearby bed was as fashionably dressed as Romeo Beckham. I hadn't realised they made Reeboks that tiny.

'Like a bleedin' little skeleton she was. Except for her big tits. They all have big tits now, don't they? No matter how skinny they are?' Mary gave me a questioning look. As if she expected someone with a seemingly endless supply of coloured tissues to have the answer to all of humanity's major questions.

I gave her what I hoped was a knowing nod.

Satisfied, she continued. 'He bought her clothes. A stereo. A DVD player. Anything she wanted. Spent all the money on her, he did,' she sniffled, her anger helping to dry her tears.

Barney tried to steer her back to the subject we were here to discuss. 'But he definitely sold drugs from your mother's house? You saw him hand them over? Receive payment?' He waited, pen poised above his little black notebook as if he didn't trust the VOR either.

'Amn't I after telling you? There used to be queues out to the feckin' back gate. Halfway down the lane on dole days.' She searched her pockets furiously for her cigarettes before realising she was sitting on them. Bypassing Barney, she offered the squashed pack to me. 'Smoke?'

'No thanks. I gave them up,' I lied. I had never smoked. Well, only when I was fourteen and in convent school. Never for actual pleasure.

'I'm giving them up as well,' she nodded in approval as she lit up. She inhaled deep and long, drawing comfort from the battered cigarette.

Calmer now, she sat back and blew out a thin trail of smoke. 'Anyway, when the Gards came snooping he hid the gear under me mother's mattress. She was bedridden. From a stroke,' she explained. 'God rest her soul.' She crossed herself respectfully.

'So they never found any evidence of hard drugs in your mother's house?' Barney's voice was almost gentle.

'Of course they bleedin' didn't! They weren't going to lift a dying woman, were they?'

'And you didn't tell them there were drugs in the house?'

Again a look of scorn. 'I have three kids.'

I glanced over at the sleeping baby.

She saw my look. 'The other two are in school,' she said proudly. 'I make sure they go every day.'

I gave her an admiring nod.

'Kelly is their father?' Barney was scribbling like mad.

'No. Well, he's Dylan's father. The others are . . .'

'Your husband's?'

'One of them is.' She shot him a defiant look. 'But they all call Mick Daddy. The bastard,' she sniffed, threatening to cry again.

'You'll give evidence against him? In court?' Barney emphasised.

'Feckin' right I will. Him and that little tart. She's no better than a prostitute. Do you know where they're living? Tempelogue! In a private house with a carport. Variegated ivy on the end wall. You know that yellow kind?' She had clearly done some investigating of her own. 'Imagine how much a place like that costs? Little tart! I had to move down here when me mother's neighbours started picketing our house. Called me a drug dealer, they did. Threw stones at the windows. I never sold drugs in me life.

Ivy on the feckin' walls!' She drew hard on her cigarette.

Barney glanced at me before asking firmly, 'So Mick Kelly is the father of one of your children?' He checked his notes.

'Maybe two.' She blew out a long trail of smoke. 'He doesn't give me a penny for them either. Spends it all on that little tart.'

'You are entitled to maintenance,' I said sympathetically. 'Even while he's waiting to go to trial. I could check that out for you. If you want.'

Barney shot me a warning look.

'Oh would you, love? Even a few bob would make a difference. Do you know how much kids' shoes cost?'

I glanced at the tiny Reebocks. 'No idea.'

'. . . and trying to feed them?' She pointed to the Coco-Pops on the sink.

'We have to get back to the office.' Barney practically dragged me out the door.

'What did I do wrong?' I pulled my arm free of his grasp. 'She's entitled to maintenance, isn't she?'

'*If* the kids are his. And there's no proof of that. And if we drop him in it with Social Welfare we could be opening a whole can of worms. Back taxes, dole fraud, rent fiddles.'

'I thought we wanted to drop him in it?' I puzzled. I had assumed that the whole purpose of this interview was to get evidence on this toxic pig and drop him in it with as many state agencies as we could.

'Not yet. And not for Social Welfare fraud. The prosecutor wants to nail him for drug dealing. He's building a huge case against him. He doesn't want him getting a warning slap on the wrist. Something that might send him legging it to the Costa Del Boy to buy himself a new identity and a villa with a roof solarium before we can get him to court. Right now Kelly thinks he's safe. He knows people are too frightened to talk to the Gards. He doesn't know about us. Yet. So we keep shtum. No phone calls to Social Welfare, OK?'

'But what about Mary? What does she do in the meantime? She has three kids to feed. She must be going through hell.'

'She didn't complain when she was living off his drugs money,' he said coldly.

'She said he gave her nothing!'

He gave a dismissive shrug. 'Yeah. Right.'

'I believe her. She seemed honest.' I meant it. She was too distressed to be lying.

'Honest enough to stand by while he sold heroin to half the kids in her old neighbourhood?'

My stomach lurched. I had heard enough horror stories of heroin abuse not to know what that meant. Then I thought about Mary's ravaged face.

'But . . . what could she have done about it? She was as much his victim as the kids who were buying the stuff.'

'Are you kidding, Annie? She let him hide heroin in her dying mother's bed!' His voice dripped with disgust.

I swallowed hard. Then pictured the flimsy caravan. The bed where Mary's three children slept. Her look of utter dejection. 'Maybe she had no choice?'

'There's always a choice.' He was adamant.

I unlocked the Honda, muttering angrily to myself.

'Have you a problem with this investigation, Annie?'

'No,' I lied smoothly. 'I . . . I was just thinking how great it must feel to be like you. So positive. Always so sure of yourself.' I waited for him to deny it.

He didn't. Just smiled and slid into the car. 'Detectives have to be positive. As well as smart. And sometimes impossibly agile,' he grinned as he wound himself into the cramped seat. 'Otherwise we'd never get the job done.'

I hit the accelerator so hard the Honda took off like a rocket.

'Jesus, Annie, slow down. I haven't buckled my seat belt yet.'

'Really? I'd have thought someone as positive as you would have done that before I got the key in the ignition.'

Tyres squealing, I swung the Civic round to head back to Dublin. At least the rain had cleared, which meant I could put my foot down.

Barney was so quiet I looked to see what was up. He was leaning back, his hands clutching the seat, his knuckles showing stark white against the dark upholstery.

'For God's sake, Barney, relax. We're barely moving. Sit up nicely and I promise we'll stop off at The Randy Goat for a drink.'

'You'd better, because I'm going to need one. Maybe even a change of underpants if you don't slow down.'

It was after midnight when I got home. Gerry was in bed. Not exactly snoring, but doing a funny mouth-breathing thing he sometimes does when he sleeps on his back. Which was exactly how he was positioned now, deliberately stretched across the bed so I couldn't get in without waking him.

You have two chances of that tonight buster. I whispered, looking at him. *Zero and none*.

I filled a hot-water bottle and went to sleep in the spare room. A place I don't particularly like because it's north-facing and chilly. And hasn't got Gerry in it. But there was a principle at stake here. I had to take a stand. I was a full partner in McHugh Dunning. My financial input had made it possible for us to move out of the condemned building where Gerry had first set up the agency. And today I had proved that I was as good a detective as any. Well I would be, if I got enough practice. I hugged the hot-water bottle and tried to sleep.

I was out of bed at six.

Before hurrying into the still dark and chilly street, I left plenty of evidence that I *had* come home. *And* slept in the spare room. I wasn't going to have Gerry taking the moral high ground, complaining that I had sneaked down to Wexford behind his back. Well I had, but that was his fault for raising my hopes then dashing them so cruelly. Forcing me to act like a bloody estate agent. As if I didn't handle enough mundane crap for McHugh Dunning without having to listen to a litany about bloody feng shui. From a woman who probably spent more on her false nails than I did on food.

Feng shui my arse.

11

Gerry came into my office looking like he hadn't slept for a month. I knew better. He wasn't exactly snoring when I left the house, but he wasn't lying awake fretting either. He probably slept better in our big warm double bed than I did in that bloody spare room.

I kept my eyes on my computer screen, concentrating on getting the monthly account sheets to balance.

He stood behind me. Watched me struggling with the pallid-looking figures.

'Dreamland Interiors are taking the lease,' he said quietly. 'Trudie signed it.'

'Tudi,' I corrected him, my fingers busy at the keyboard.

'What?'

'Her name is *Tudi*.' I double-checked a couple of inflated-looking figures on Declan's expense account claim, decided they were bogus, and erased them without pity. When I suffered, everyone suffered.

'Whatever. She signed it.'

'Good.' I readjusted the total, which would now leave Declan a lot lighter in pocket than he'd been hoping. His own fault, anyway. He should know better than to fictionalise his expense account when a trained bookkeeper owned forty per cent of the business.

Gerry edged closer. Limping slightly, I noticed. He had an old knee wound which sometimes troubled him in cold weather. It had been serious enough to catapult him out of the Garda, but I sometimes suspected him of playing the old soldier. Especially when he limped on the wrong leg. And it hadn't escaped my notice that even in sub-Arctic conditions he could leap behind the wheel of the Cherokee like an Olympian on speed, leaving me with the ten-year-old Civic.

I hit 'print'. My faithful OKI hummed into life, spewing out page after page of neat columns of figures. I found this part of the job almost pleasant. It was the one area where I had total control. Nobody ever challenged me when it came to balancing the accounts.

I could feel Gerry's breath on my neck as he leaned across me to pick up a page. He checked the figures. As if he could tell a debit from a credit.

'I have an appointment for twelve noon,' he suddenly announced. 'With Boucher's housekeeper. She's agreed to go through Caroline's things with me. To show me her diaries, letters, all that sort of stuff. All the things Boucher has been so reticent about.' He paused. 'You can go in my place, if you like. You might get a better sense of Caroline from her personal things. Cut through the smoke Boucher is blowing up our . . . noses. I'll go down to their place in Wicklow. See what I can find out there.'

'Fine.' I brought Barney's expense account up on the screen. If Gerry was expecting me to throw my arms around him in gratitude for his offer, he had another think coming.

There was an uneasy silence.

'You don't *have* to go at twelve,' he said. 'You can go later if you like. Whatever time suits you. After lunch if you want,' he waited.

I didn't reply. He wasn't getting off the hook that easily. I checked the screen. Barney's figures were spot on. Not a cent out of place. I totalled them again anyway, before moving on to profit and loss.

'I'll tell the housekeeper to expect you, then?'

'Fine.' I hit 'print' again.

'Annie?'

'Yes?' It came out sharper than I intended.

'Don't forget to . . . Take plenty of notes, won't you?' He was gone.

I waited until the door closed behind him before leaping to my feet in delight. Yes! Yes! I did a victory lap around my desk. *You did it, Annie.*

Giddy with excitement, I went back to the computer and brought up Declan's expense account sheet again and carefully reinstated his claim to have used enough petrol to travel to the Arab Emirates and back. In a helicopter.

It may be the duty of a bookkeeper to scrutinise the expense accounts of the investigators for anything untoward or iffy. Detectives, on the other hand, should stick together. Unable to control my enthusiasm, I shut down my computer with a flourish and headed out to begin my very first bona fide investigation.

Sandra watched me scribble my name and intended destination in the big diary in reception.

'You and Gerry sorted, are you?'

'What?'

'Well, he was hanging around my desk first thing this morning. Had me sweating bricks. I thought he was doing one of them time and motion studies. Seeing if he could downsize? That's the buzzword in the café these days. Half the traders are being downsized. But Gerry just wanted to ask about you. Wanted to know if it was you or Barney who decided that you should go down to Wexford together. I didn't tell him!' she said quickly.

I gave her a look.

'Well he'd guessed anyway!' she gave in. 'He knew you were in a temper. This morning he asked me if I knew what time you got back.'

I buttoned my coat, feigning indifference to all this unsolicited information.

'Don't you want to know what he did then?' she called after me.

'No. But I bet you're going to tell me,' I chuckled, knowing nothing she could say could spoil this day.

'He rang Fiona,' she said archly.

I swung around. 'This morning? Did you listen in to their conversation?'

'No! I swear I didn't.' She shook her head so hard I pictured her teeth loosening.

'Shame,' I mused. 'I'd love to know what he said to her. Now I'll have to text her, and this is her day for the antenatal clinic. She'll be in there for ever. Incommunicado. No mobiles allowed,' I said in disgust.

She smirked. 'So did you and Gerry have a big fight?'

'No. We don't fight. We're not children.'

Our eyes met, held until neither of us could quite keep a straight face. She pointed to the diary. 'You're going to the Boucher's house?'

'I am.' I turned up my collar proudly.

'Like an investigator? Jaysus, you should fight with Gerry more often.'

'No argument there,' I agreed.

'Me and Jimmy fight too. Well, not really fight. More row. Mostly when he tramps muck into the house. Or brings his messy seedlings in to escape the frost. Making up is pretty cool though, isn't it? And anyway a good row always leads to great sex, it says so in the new . . .'

I stopped listening. Turned away to text Fiona instead. RU4E2TALK?

Whatever Boucher paid Ms Lynch, his housekeeper, he should have doubled it. The woman was beyond price. On the surface she was polite and open, even friendly, while cleverly managing to avoid giving away any real information about the private life of the Bouchers, no matter how cannily I framed my questions.

'What a beautifully kept house,' I said, trying to sweeten her up, and was rewarded with an offer of tea.

The Boucher kitchen had a wider selection of teas than the Café Naturalle. I passed on the Earl Grey, Lapsang Souchong, and Green herbal, and asked for Lyons Gold Label. With lemon, in case asking for milk might cause her eyebrows to disappear altogether.

Ms Marie Lynch had worked for the Bouchers for five years and clearly loved her job. Understandable when you realised that not only did Boucher have a weekend place in Wicklow, he was also known to spend great chunks of the year in Switzerland.

'Not too much housekeeping here in Dublin then,' I smiled.

She froze me with a look.

'Have you been to the house in Switzerland?' I tried again.

'More tea?' Her mouth tightened.

She was happy enough to confirm Boucher's story of the seventeenth, even down to the single bottle of classic French wine she had decanted for dinner that night. She even remembered Caroline drinking most of her second glass of the rich red burgundy, and finally unwound enough to admit that, yes, it was perfectly understandable that Simon Boucher would be so close to his only child.

'He dotes on her.' She nearly smiled.

He clearly wasn't the only one who doted on her.

'You probably know her better than her father does.'

Her face tightened again. 'What do you mean?'

'With her father being so busy, away so much. His business interests are pretty widespread, aren't they?'

'He's here a lot more than people think. He'd never neglect her. She's the apple of his eye.'

I sipped my tea. 'But it was you who heard her planning to meet someone in The Dimmer, wasn't it?' It felt almost sacrilegious mentioning a place like The Dimmer in such a beautifully kept house.

Clearly Ms Lynch felt the same. She was outraged. 'As I told Mr Boucher, I can't be completely sure she mentioned that . . . that place.'

'He seemed confident enough about it,' I lied, 'when he spoke to us.'

'Did he?' She looked worried.

'Can you think of any reason why Caroline would run away?'

She froze. 'Absolutely not.'

I drained my cup. 'Could I see her room now, please?'

Caroline didn't have a room, more of a presidential suite. Half of the top floor of the big house was her personal domain. This *was* the girl who had everything: her own private study, a dressing room bursting with designer clothes, a trillion cuddly toys and a sound system that a professional DJ would swap a kidney for. She even had a grand piano. Not much used, by the look of it. But still.

The only thing missing was the pony. Ms Lynch wasn't slow to tell me that Boucher had bought Caroline a thoroughbred hunter for her seventeenth birthday. To keep her other pony company. They were stabled at the family manor house in Wicklow.

My heart began to race. 'Would Caroline . . . ?'

'No! She hasn't been down there for months. Hasn't hunted since she had a run-in with that awful Saab crowd.'

'Hunt saboteurs?' My ears pricked up. 'When was that?'

'A . . . a long time ago.'

She threw open the doors of an enormous walk-in wardrobe. 'Just press the bell when you're finished,' she said, and left.

I went through the clothes with little enthusiasm. Ms Lynch was so happy to leave me to my own devices, I guessed someone had already scoured the wardrobe for anything that might give away any secrets or embarrass the Boucher family. A little stash of grass? Condoms? A vibrator? What did seventeen-year-olds get up to nowadays? Since passing thirty I'd had little connection with them.

I was right about the wardrobe: clean as a whistle. Not a hint of anything untoward; not a clue as to why Caroline might have disappeared. My painstaking search only confirmed what I already knew: Caroline Bouchard was extremely rich, spoiled rotten and had far too many clothes for one small, size ten girl. A look through her diary proved just as fruitless. The few sporadic entries mentioned nothing more personal than exam dates, a couple of tutorial references, and notes on books she needed from the library. If these were the main focus of her life, you'd wonder why she needed all those expensive clothes. Especially that double drawer of exquisite underwear, some of which I considered a bit dubious. More Ann Summers than the huntin', riding and shooting set. But then what did I know about teenage fashions? Fiona was the only one I knew who came even close to having that many pure silk panties, but that was because she claimed any lesser fabric gave her thrush.

Ms Lynch arrived back in time to catch me sighing over the diary.

'Find anything?' Our eyes met. She looked away first.

'Could I borrow this?' I held up a small photo album.

'Of course. Anything that will help you find her.'

Intent on leaving everything exactly as I'd found it, I knelt to lock the diary away in a low drawer. 'So there's nothing more you can tell me about Caroline? You have no idea why she might have disappeared? No clue as to her . . . ?'

There was a weird choking sound. I turned to see her hunched over Caroline's bed, sobbing as if her heart would break.

Embarrassed, I said the first thing that came into my head. 'Don't upset yourself. She'll turn up safe and sound. You'll see.'

She looked up at me with brimming eyes. 'Oh, thank you. You can't imagine how comforting it is to be told that by a professional investigator.'

12

'She's devoted to Caroline and totally in awe of Boucher,' I reported back to Gerry over a steaming cup of coffee and two hideously fattening cream cakes, which I'd stopped off at the café to buy because I'd missed lunch.

'What about this run-in with the anti-hunt protesters? What happened there?'

'Nothing much. They exchanged all the usual insults. *Bloodthirsty pigs! Work-shy layabouts!* It only lasted a couple of minutes. Oh, one of them did feed vegetarian sausages to the hounds. That was it.'

'No consequences?'

'A little diarrhoea.'

'I meant Caroline,' he laughed.

'Oh.'

He picked up the little personal photo album. 'She looks even prettier in these candid shots,' he said. 'But she has . . .'

'Everything!' I bit into my cake. 'You should see her *room*! And there's not a hint of misbehaviour. No drug taking, drinking or any kind of rebellion. She's the perfect daughter. Everyone's darling.'

It wasn't what he wanted to hear. He needed clues as to why she had gone missing, not more evidence of how happy she was. He studied the photos closely. In one of them Caroline was sitting on a beach, obviously in Ireland because she was wearing a big woolly sweater and looked pinched with the cold.

'Are you eating that cake?' I asked.

He shook his head, pushing the plate towards me. 'I got pretty much the same story in Wicklow.' He watched me eat. 'Except that no one mentioned the Saabs. The staff there did all agree that she's a nice, uncomplicated girl. Adores her daddy, seldom drinks, never smokes and shows endless patience with the horses.' He looked up as Declan came in.

'Sounds like my perfect woman.' Declan threw himself into a chair. 'Who is she?'

'Our missing person.' I wiped cream from my mouth.

'Caroline Boucher,' Gerry said.

'Jesus. Boucher Investments? The Boucher we were chasing for that security contract?' He picked up the album.

'None other.'

'A kidnap?' Declan's face lit up.

'No.'

'Aw.' He was disappointed. Then hopeful again. 'You positive?'

We didn't get many kidnapping cases in McHugh Dunning. Well, none, to be exact. But the lads lived in hope. There was always the possibility that a real biggie was just around the corner. And that Jim Nolan and his pack of inept wolves wouldn't get their hands on it first.

'It's been ten days,' Gerry explained. 'We'd have heard by now. Kidnappers don't hang about.'

'What if it started out as a kidnapping, then took a turn for the worse?'

'What do you mean?'

'Suppose someone kidnapped her and . . . she died?'

'What?' I nearly choked on my cake.

'It happens,' he said calmly. 'We've all heard of such cases. An accidental smothering. Neck gets broken in a fall. An overzealous hardman gets carried away. He—'

'Oh, come on!' Gerry rebuked.

'Just pointing out the possibilities,' Declan said. But then nothing was ever so grim that he couldn't make it sound worse. He put me off my cake, forced ugly thoughts into my head.

My heart pounding in dread, I asked, 'You think something like that could . . . might have happened to Caroline?'

'Always possible.'

I felt sick. And not because I had eaten the two cream cakes on an empty stomach, but because I couldn't bear to think of someone as sweet and vulnerable as Caroline being hurt. I had spent two hours going through her personal things. It had left me feeling that I knew her, almost intimately. And maybe because her clothes were so tiny, they brought out a protective streak in me. Unlike those times in communal changing rooms when I wanted to strangle anyone who could slip into a size ten without a struggle.

'Nobody would hurt that girl. Everyone loves her,' I insisted.

'Everyone?' Declan was increasingly sceptical.

'My guess is she ran away. Things got on top of her. That happens a lot to teenagers. They can't cope. People expect too much of them. At home. In school. So they run off. For all sorts of reasons.'

'And hers would be . . . ?'

'How should I know?' I snapped. 'I'm just hoping she ran away.'

'Annie was at the Boucher house today,' said Gerry as he looked up from examining the photos. 'She went through the girl's things. Trying to get a sense of her.'

Declan nodded in approval. 'What made her tick.'

'*Made*?' I was horrified.

'What?'

'You said *made* her tick! As if she's dead.'

He looked at me, his flat eyes emotionless. 'Sorry. I didn't mean to upset you.'

'We don't have a single lead,' Gerry cut in. 'Everyone I've spoken to has said she had no reason to run away. The Gardai are playing it close to their chest, as usual. Mick Henessey is in charge, and he's not exactly sweating it.'

'What's your take on it?'

'I'm not sure. But . . . something about it stinks. I can't explain. It's just . . . too many people are falling over themselves to tell me how happy she was. How content with her lot. Then she disappears into thin air? Without a hint of foul play?'

'How is Boucher taking it?'

'Hard to say. He's upset, but . . . I think he's holding something back. He's a *very* powerful man. I'd have expected him to have had heads rolling by now. In his position any other parent would be close to hysteria.'

'Simon Boucher doesn't strike me as being the hysterical type.'

'Yeah. But . . . why come to us?'

They eyeballed each other.

'Our reputation?'

Gerry made a face.

'Your reputation alone is—'

'Yeah, yeah.' Gerry dismissed the unspoken compliment. 'The man has millions. He could have half the police forces in Europe working for him. But he comes to us? If one of my boys went missing I'd be on to every news-rag in the country, yet I had to promise him there would be no publicity. I'm beginning to wonder about this girl. Nobody can be as squeaky clean as she's supposed to be. She's seventeen, not twelve.'

'Absolutely,' Declan agreed.

'My God, you two are so cynical,' I said angrily. 'Is this what happens when you get stumped on a case? You end up suspecting everyone of something? Especially teenagers. You forget that we're only called in when things go wrong in people's lives. What about all the millions of decent teenagers who never even *encounter* a wrongdoing?'

Declan looked at me. 'What planet is that on, Annie?'

Gerry started to laugh, and immediately turned it into a cough. Then he did something even more hurtful. He reached over and patted my hand. 'And she wonders why I don't want her out there playing detective.'

'*Playing* detective?' I exploded. 'Is that what you think I've been doing for the past two days?'

'No! I didn't mean it like that. It's a figure of speech. Just . . .'

'. . . an expression.' Declan, who had spent a third of his life in a wordless drunken puddle, tried to help out. If *he* wasn't such a good detective he'd be in the gutter.

'Who asked you?' I turned on him. 'And why are you still here, anyway? Are all the pubs closed?'

Gerry's eyes flashed with anger, and I knew I had gone too far. And the awful thing was, I didn't mean it. I had supported Declan whenever he'd fallen off the wagon. Knew how difficult life could be for anyone with a drink problem. And he did try. I had just run off at the mouth now because I was sick of their bloody know-all attitude. What did Declan know about Caroline? Or this case? I was the one who had gone through her things, yet the second he walks in Gerry starts consulting him?

The familiar little tic danced in Gerry's cheek. 'I think you should apologise to Declan.'

'What for?' I asked stubbornly.

'It's OK. She was just kidding. Weren't you, Annie?' Declan threw me a beseeching look as if he feared the wrong word might tip us all on to the brink of thermonuclear warfare.

'I was kidding,' I said gratefully.

'Told you,' Declan relaxed.

'Well, in future I'd be grateful if you'd think before you speak, Annie.'

'Me?'

'Yes, you. It gets wearing having to constantly walk on eggshells around you.'

'Walk on . . . ?' I practically catapulted out of my chair.

Declan beat me to it. He was on his feet and heading for the door. 'I'm off to get a good night's sleep. You have my report on that cross-border beef smuggling, Gerry. You were right about those poor animals – they do a quicker turnaround than Ryan Air crews.'

Getting no response, he made another attempt to

lighten the atmosphere. 'Don't know how anyone sleeps in the feckin' country, though. Shaggin' dawn chorus? I couldn't wait to get back to the big smoke. Get me a lungful of carbon monoxide.'

Gerry's smile was as genuine as a two-pound note.

I didn't even try. 'Explain what you mean – walking on eggshells?' I asked him.

Declan disappeared.

'Gerry?' I waited.

'Calm down,' he sat back. 'Nobody is attacking you. You're just too . . . too thin-skinned these days. Always on the defensive.'

The phone rang. 'What?' he snapped into the reciever. 'Oh yeah, put him on. Seamus? I hear you're still lecturing in that private college in Leeson Street? Robbing the rich? Yeah, I bet,' he laughed. 'Listen, I need some information on a girl who's doing first-year Economics there. Of course I'll keep it confidential. Have you ever known me to run off at the mouth?'

I slammed the door behind me.

Declan was standing by the lift.

'Annie?' He turned. ''Man loves you. Go easy on him. He's trying.'

'He certainly is.'

I reached past him to hit the button. Changed my mind and hit the stairs instead. I wasn't going to stand there and let Declan lecture me on how to conduct a relationship. Every relationship he'd ever had had been scuppered by either his fondness for the drink or his habit of choosing to play above his weight. He only ever fancied women way out of his league. All it took to turn him on was a plummy accent and real pearls. Weird. Hardly surprising that he had a string of failed relationships behind him. All of them short term. Plus he could be monosyllabic to the point of rudeness. Compared with him, Gerry was Anthony Clare.

So where did that *walking on eggshells* crack come from? The cheek of Gerry. I always tried to see his point of view! I was endlessly understanding about his ex-wife. Had never once admitted to hating her. Out loud. I had invited his two little boys to stay numerous times. Not my fault that their overly possessive mother kept finding reasons to keep them in America. This year alone she had already used up measles, mumps and two varieties of viral flu. Gerry didn't complain. He never said he had to walk on eggshells around her. Just made his weekly phone call to his sons from his office every Friday evening. After which he'd come out whey-faced. In need of a stiff drink.

So maybe I did cross the line with that pub crack. But whose fault was that? It was his remark about *playing* detective that triggered it. Figure of speech my arse. Still. Gerry wasn't usually nasty. He could be tough, but that went with the territory. And he did have a lot on his mind. In my own defence, I was premenstrual. And concerned about Caroline. But then so was Gerry. Concerned about Caroline.

I touched up my make-up, fixed my hair and went down to reception to wait for him.

He stepped out of the lift looking even more strained than he had upstairs. I waited until he came close, then stepped out from behind the reception desk.

'Hi!'

'Jesus Christ, Annie.' He grabbed his chest. 'I thought you'd gone.'

'No. I waited for you. We have things to discuss.'

'Like?' He sounded weary.

'Your attitude to me. The way you dismissed me in front of Declan. As if I were some kind of flaky dimwit.'

'Let's get a couple of things straight, Annie. If I thought you were some flaky dimwit we wouldn't be standing here together. But I'd like you to remember something. Declan is one of the best detectives I know. He's also a man trying to cope with a major drink problem, so slagging him off about it isn't acceptable.'

'*You* said I was *playing* at being a detective!' I accused.

'I was trying to keep the mood light. If I offended you, I'm sorry. You did a good job today and . . .'

I flushed. 'You really think so?'

'Absolutely. Now can we close up here and go home? Or is Sandra waiting to leap out from behind the postal tray and put the heart crossways in me?'

'No. She's gone.'

'Good.' He went around switching off lights, setting the alarm, throwing Sandra's discarded emery boards in the bin.

I checked the answering machine. Straightened the desk diary.

'Ready?' he asked.

'Ready for bed.' I faked a yawn.

The look he gave me was indecipherable.

Walking to the door he limped slightly. This time on the right leg. I trailed guiltily behind him, wanting to throw my arms around him. Wanting to tell him I loved him, and that he'd never, ever have to walk on eggshells around me again. That from now on I'd be as thick-skinned as any detective. Once he kept me on the Boucher case.

'Sorry if I was being supersensitive before, Gerry. I . . . I'm anxious about Caroline. I know it's stupid to care about someone you've never even met, but I can't help it. I keep thinking about her. Wondering if she's lying somewhere, hurt. Trapped in some dark, scary place. Calling for help, knowing nobody will hear.' A big lump blocked my throat.

He swung around and pulled me close. I buried my face in his chest, wiping my nose on his shirt front, and before I knew it we were kissing. I never meant it to go any further than that. But Sandra could be right. Maybe a row does ignite the flames of passion. I suddenly remembered that we were standing in the middle of a glass-fronted reception area.

I took my hand off his zipper and tore myself from his arms. 'Let's go,' I panted. 'I'll drive.'

He let go reluctantly. 'I'll give you a million euros if you can get us home in under ten minutes.'

'You're on!'

We tore out to the car.

We were almost home when my mobile shrilled.

'Don't answer it,' Gerry groaned.

'It could be important.'

'Annie?' It was Fiona.

'What do you want?' I shot through an amber light.

'What do I want? You texted me, remember? What the hell is going on with you and Gerry? He was on to me first thing this morning. Practically grilling me.

Asking if you were here last night. I didn't know what to say. You didn't prep me! I had to improvise. I said I was in the middle of a severe Braxton Hicks and he'd have to ring back after I'd completed my first-stage breathing. Then I tried to get you. But as usual you were uncontactable. Why do you have a mobile if it's never on? I had to leave my phone off the hook to stop Gerry getting back on to me. Twenty minutes later Pino comes dashing in. Practically hysterical because he couldn't get through, and you know him, he always thinks the worst.'

'Fiona, could you make this short? I'm on the dual carriageway!' I could have added that Gerry had his tongue in my ear, but decided that might require an even longer explanation.

'Oh are you, Miss Snappy? Anyway, Pino put the receiver back and Gerry comes on again and Pino bawls him out and Gerry hangs up. Not because of Pino, but because Sandra had walked in. So I don't know where you were last night, but it had better be worth all the trouble you caused me.'

'It was,' I laughed, as Gerry made frantic throat-cutting signs at me. 'I was working a case with Barney, in Wexford. We stopped off for a drink on the way home.'

'You worked with Barney? I thought it was Gerry you wanted to . . . ?'

Gerry put his hand up my skirt. 'No,' I giggled.

'So it wasn't?' Fiona was puzzled.

'Er . . . look . . . I've got to hang up, Fiona. I'll get busted for using a mobile while . . . driving!'

'Don't hang up! I want to know what's going on with you and Gerry? I got your text message. So what's the craic?'

'I'm working the Boucher case with him.'

Her scream of delight almost deafened me. 'Tell all!'

'Can't. Not right now.'

'Can't? Who made it possible for you to follow that nutty transvestite around? Who was there for you when you needed a friend? Now when I want to talk . . .'

'It's not a good time.'

'Fine . . . in future I'll make an appointment to speak to you.'

'Fiona . . .' I wailed.

'Are you going to tell me what's going on?'

'Yes. First thing tomorrow.'

'Now! I'm bored.'

Gerry tried to grab the phone. *Get away*. I mouthed at him.

'Isn't there something you could watch on TV? What about that new programme – what's it called? *Parenting in the Twenty-first Century*?'

'That rubbish? Who the hell wants to watch a twiglet-sized woman interviewing a million-dollar-a-year fund accountant, who claims she breastfeeds baby Leticia while driving little Phelim to nursery school, *after* she's given her husband a blow-job and made pasta ragu for twenty-eight impending dinner guests? I haven't even had the kid yet, and it's all I can do to get out of bed in the morning. Blow-jobs are definitely a thing of the past.'

'Better not let Pino hear you saying that.'

'As if he cares. He's treating me like a vestal virgin these days.'

The image of the hugely pregnant Fiona being treated like a vestal virgin had me laughing so hard I almost dropped the phone.

'Annie!' Gerry whispered.

'Sorry.'

'It's not your fault,' Fiona said. 'You know, I could go right off the idea of having this baby.'

'Bit late now, Fi! Anyway, don't be silly. You know you're blissfully happy.'

Hang up. Gerry was mouthing silently. *Can't.* I mouthed back.

'I wonder if you can get post-natal blues in advance? Can your hormones sort of invert and . . . ?'

'Look, I'll call over to see you in the morning.'

'No chance of a quick visit now?'

I glanced at Gerry. 'First thing in the morning, I promise.'

'I suppose you're exhausted after your long exciting day at being a detective,' she sighed.

'Well . . . yeah. And . . . my shoes are killing me,' I moaned as Gerry bit my neck.

'You sound like you're in pain, all right. Are your shoes new?'

'Er . . . I have to go, Fiona.'

'What's the rush?'

'Gerry is waiting for me,' I said truthfully.

'Tsk. You were born lucky. Working with the man you love,' she said dreamily. 'Pino sees more of his sous-chef than he does me. And that damn television crew, they're all he talks about.'

'Pino adores you.'

'Yes, but . . . the only one showing any interest in *my* pelvic floor these days is my ob/gyn man. And he's a misogynist. Do you know what he said at my check-up?'

'Gerry is waiting, Fiona.'

'Oh go on, rub it in.'

'He wants to discuss a case.' I peeled Gerry's hand off my groin.

'I'll bet. The case of the horny detective, is it?'

I choked back a laugh. 'Go and turn on Channel Four. You're bound to find something interesting on that.'

'I don't want to watch *other* people having sex!' She hung up in disgust.

13

'Caroline isn't a natural rider.' The burly head groom spoke in clipped tones, as if he owned the Boucher stables instead of just working there, slopping out the stalls.

He was leading a huge stallion across the wet cobbled yard, making no allowances for me as I tried not to slip in my stack-heeled boots. Gerry had no trouble keeping up with him, but then he had been here before. Today's visit was a follow-up. Gerry was keen to interview all the loyal Boucher staff, and the head groom had gone missing the last day he'd called.

'She found it difficult being around horses,' the groom continued. 'But she's a Boucher. She persevered. Fair play to her. I take my hat off to anyone who overcomes a genuine fear of horses.'

I jumped as the stallion flicked his enormous tail in my direction.

'Don't spook him!' The groom turned in annoyance.

'About Caroline?' Gerry said coldly.

'What can I tell you? She's a poor rider. Nervous. Took a bad fall once. She's awkward in the saddle. Lacks control, even with the mares. They sense it, you know. Don't like nervous people.' He gave me a reproving look before reaching up to pat the gigantic horse on the neck. 'Take Big Leroy here. He likes a relaxed rider. Don't you, handsome lad?'

Big Leroy whinnied in agreement.

'Yet her father bought him for Caroline?' Gerry frowned.

The groom shrugged. 'So? She conquered her fear. It took time and patience, but she did it. Her father is very proud of her. We all are.'

'Does she bring her friends down here a lot?' I asked.

'No.'

'No? But it's such an amazing place. An exquisite setting for a house. I'd have thought any girl would be dying to show off a place like this to her mates.' I looked back at the long, ivy-covered house, admiring the way it seemed to grow, almost organically, out of the gently rolling hills that backed up behind it, its long windows affording what had to be spectacular views of the valley below. The stables alone would probably make a million if they went on the Dublin property market as 'bijou residences'.

The groom gave me another scathing look. 'Caroline doesn't show off.'

'Not even to her boyfriend?' Gerry asked quickly.

'What boyfriend? She comes down here with Mr Boucher. Rides out with him. Just the two of them.' He backed Big Leroy into his heated stable.

'So she never once brought a friend here?' Gerry frowned.

'I've never seen her with a friend. I have work to do.' He clearly felt he had given us enough information.

Maybe he had. We had driven the fifty miles to this rural idyll with a definite picture of Caroline in mind; we were leaving with a slightly different impression of her. One definitely at odds with the constantly smiling, overindulged rich girl in the photos.

'Do you think pictures can lie?' I asked Gerry as we walked back to the jeep.

He took his time answering. 'I think most people have different facets to their personalities.'

'You mean we're all two-faced?'

'No. If I asked ten people to describe you, do you think they'd all give me the same answer?'

'God, I hope not,' I laughed, and climbed into the jeep.

'There you are, then. Why should Caroline be any different?' He turned the ignition.

'Did yer man look a bit funny to you when you asked about a boyfriend?'

'No.'

'Maybe it's just me, then.'

He looked pensive, as if he was trying to recall something the groom had said.

We were driving out of the electronically controlled gates when I had an idea. 'Why don't we try talking to their family doctor? Sometimes women tell their doctors things they wouldn't dream of sharing with anyone else. Things . . . you know . . . secrets.'

'Secrets? You cheeky bugger!' He swerved to avoid hitting a wandering fox. 'What kind of secret would Caroline share with her doctor?'

'The obvious one. She's seventeen. Nearly eighteen. Her father insists that she's pure as the driven snow. I wouldn't be surprised if she's on the pill. If fact I'd be surprised if she isn't.' I thought of the drawerful of neatly folded silk underwear.

'And I need to hear this because . . . ?' he waited.

'You need a prescription for the pill,' I said smugly. 'And if her repeat prescription ran out, she'd either have to find another doctor, or . . .'

'. . . contact her old one.' He beamed. 'Ring Boucher. Tell him we need the name of their family doctor.'

Ringing a billionaire like Simon Boucher was a complicated business. First you got his secretary. When she finished quizzing you, asking you everything from your mother's maiden name to when you shed your wisdom teeth, she passed you on to his PA. And the whole rigmarole started all over again.

'Mr Gerry Dunning needs to speak to him *now*!' I finally exploded.

Boucher wasn't happy to be called out of a business meeting, especially when he heard why he was being called.

'Why do you need to speak to our doctor?' The phone line bristled.

'In cases like this it's advisable to explore every avenue.' I looked questioningly at Gerry, who gave me an encouraging nod. 'There could be certain . . . if she had to renew a drug prescription, for instance, we could try tracing it. Naturally we'd have to know what it was for first.'

'My daughter doesn't use drugs! Prescription or otherwise.' I baulked at the naked contempt in his voice.

Gerry pulled over and took the phone. 'Do you *want* us to find your daughter?'

The GP was called Murphy Dillon. That was his surname; Boucher didn't tell us his Christian name. Maybe rich doctors don't need one. We had difficulty finding his house. It was tucked away in a leafy enclave in outer suburbia where practically every house had the ubiquitous ivy on the gable wall and well-tended gardens of at least half an acre. Only a discreet plaque distinguished the doctor's house from its neighbours, as nothing as common as numbers was allowed to vulgarise the sedate close.

Murphy Dillon greeted us at the door, claiming, in one breath, to be late for a golf game, semi-retired and borderline deaf. And totally shocked that Caroline was missing.

'Such a beautiful girl. Always smiling,' he boomed.

He assured us, in deafening tones, that she was in excellent health. Definitely not on the pill.

'Why do you ask? She doesn't have a boyfriend, does she?' He peered at me over steel rimmed bifocals. 'Thought not. She's an innocent girl, extremely close to her father. He's overprotective, of course. Not surprising, given the family history. Losing her twin was a dreadful shock for Boucher, and then of course that business with his wife, some years later. Sad. Sad.'

He saw our mystified expressions.

'Oh yes,' he yelled. 'Very sad indeed. Given that he always wanted a son.'

We stood watching him wheel his golf bag out from under the wide staircase, neither of us as shocked by what he was saying as by the sheer duplicity of Simon Boucher. Gerry had made it clear to him from the outset that he only took a missing persons case on the proviso that the client was prepared to be completely honest with him, because there had been cases in the past when something hurtful and very personal had been revealed too late for Gerry to help prevent the pain and distress its exposure eventually caused.

'Caroline's twin died within days of their birth. An inoperable heart defect!' the doctor bellowed as he pulled on his golfing cap.

'Sad case . . .' He searched about for his gloves. 'Watching, powerless, as that little life ebbed away. Nearly destroyed the man.'

'And his wife? Caroline's mother?' Gerry yelled back.

'Lucinda? Stunning woman. German blood, of course. Skilled horsewoman. Magnificent seat. Great golfer. Played off scratch.' He nearly forgot his golf bag in his enthusiasm. 'But life goes on. Hope the rain holds off this afternoon. Want to give that bloody Hayes chap a good trouncing.' He chuckled. 'He's a virologist, you know.'

'What happened to Boucher's wife?' Gerry asked as we were hustled out.

'A good life?' the doctor yelled. 'It is indeed. If the bloody rain holds off.'

Sandra came in as I was typing up my interview notes. Always hungry for gossip, she took her time setting my coffee and biscuits on the desk.

She picked up a photo of Caroline. 'Poor Caroline. Poor little rich girl. First her brother dies. Then her mother,' she said sadly.

I knew I'd made a mistake chatting to her when we got back. But Gerry had driven back from the doctor's in silence, reluctant to discuss the twin business until he had spoken to Boucher. And Sandra was dying to know how we got on. And I wanted to talk. And Sandra *is* a trusted member of our staff.

'Imagine losing your *twin* brother.' She leaned against my desk.

'She wouldn't have any memory of him.' I concentrated on my notes.

'I dunno. I saw this film once where these twins were psychically linked. They could pass messages to each other, even when they were in different countries.'

'Caroline's twin is dead,' I snapped. 'He's not passing messages to anyone. Except maybe through a medium.'

'But that's exactly what happened in this film. The girl in it, well, she was only a kid really . . .'

'Sandra, I have work to do.'

I was depressed enough without hearing about sad movies. Caroline's life was full of tragedies. The poor dead twin. The talented mother who hadn't lived to see her only daughter grow up. I was in no mood to hear about crappy movies that exploited people's need to feel that death wasn't the end. I had buried my beloved parents. I knew how painful that was.

Gerry rang through to ask me to speed up. To get over to his office before bloody Boucher arrived. And I thought *I* was being grumpy?

I worked too fast and made loads of mistakes, which meant I lost the time I'd saved, because I had to retype half my work all over again.

I arrived in Gerry's office to find him in mid-conversation with Boucher. I slid the notes on to his desk and took a seat well out of Boucher's eye-line.

'I had no reason to think you needed to know about something that happened nearly eighteen years ago!' he was saying. 'What possible relevance can that have to your investigation?'

'You were told at the outset. For an investigation like this to succeed, I have to know *everything* about the missing person.' Gerry's expression was steely.

'It was nearly eighteen years ago. She was an infant! How is it relevant?'

'I decide what's relevant here.'

Boucher's neck flushed. He sat back. 'Her twin died within days of his birth. He was a weak baby.'

The look Gerry gave him would have had ninety-nine per cent of the population running for the hills. Simon Boucher was made of sterner stuff.

'Caroline has no memory of him!' he blustered. 'He only lived for two days.' He made it sound as if the baby had let everyone down by dying.

And Caroline? Had she let him down by running away?

I was now convinced that was exactly what had happened. She hadn't fallen into a hole in the ground or been abducted by aliens, snatched by evil kidnappers. She had run away from this cold, domineering man. I would have. Of course, I would have packed some of those beautiful clothes first. Taken a couple of those Prada suits with me. And at least one pair of the exquisite Jimmy Choo shoes, which were still in their boxes. I certainly wouldn't have left that BMW Z3 car behind. A red convertible. Was the girl demented?

'You may not like my questions, Mr Boucher, but I'm afraid you'll have to answer them,' Gerry was saying. '*If* you want me to continue with the case.'

'I'll answer your questions.' Bouchard folded his arms. 'If I think they have any bearing on your investigation.'

They eyeballed each other frostily.

'Anything else you've . . . withheld from me?' Gerry picked up my carefully typed notes.

'Withheld . . . ? What is it you want, Mr Dunning? Intimate family details? Let me see now? I have a pet name for my daughter, used it since her infancy. I call her . . . Bunny. Is that enough for you?'

'Anything else?' Gerry studied the notes.

'She ran away when she was fourteen.'

'Go on.' Gerry didn't blink.

'I didn't mention it before because . . . she was fourteen . . . concerned about schoolwork. Her exams were looming. She was terrified of failing. Has some ridiculous notion that the world would end if she failed her exams. Besides, she came home. Passed her exams with flying colours. The whole thing was a storm in a teacup. Not worth mentioning.'

'Anything else you didn't think worth mentioning?' Gerry was writing in his notebook. He never used notes. He's one of very few people who have total recall. When he wants. Besides, he tapes his interviews. The little black notebook was a prop, something he used to overawe certain witnesses. The ones he suspected of lying.

'I can assure you, Mr Dunning, Caroline has no dark, hidden secrets. She's just a normal teenager.'

Normal? Her twin died within days of their birth. Her multitalented mother died before she was thirty. Her father is a rampant billionaire. She stands to inherit a couple of hundred million. That's normal? I yelled.

I didn't really. Just sat there, quiet as a mouse. Not daring to interrupt. I didn't even get to my feet as Boucher was leaving. He shook hands with Gerry, then turned to offer me his hand. It felt surprisingly warm.

'I'm relying on McHugh Dunning to find my daughter.' He gave me a long, penetrating look.

Gerry walked him to the door, quoting number three on the list of Private Investigators' Hoary Old Platitudes. 'We'll let you know the moment anything breaks.'

Boucher left.

I sat there, trying to make sense of his sudden about-face. Ten minutes ago I wasn't deserving of a hello. Not even an acknowledgement. Then he shakes my hand? Behaves as if he's entrusting me with finding his daughter?

'What did you make of that?' Gerry was just as puzzled.

'No idea.'

'Me neither. Can you imaging him calling anyone *Bunny*?'

I woke from a bad dream to find myself alone in bed. It was four a.m. and Gerry's pillow felt cold. I threw on a dressing gown and padded downstairs, my bare feet recoiling from the chill of the floorboards. Next year I was going to shag-pile this whole house from top to bottom, style faux pas or not. I might even ask Dreamland Interiors to do it, just to annoy Naomi.

Gerry was in the living room, sitting in the dark, the heavy window drapes wide open so he could see out into the starry night. A half empty bottle of malt whiskey was on the table in front of him. To the best of my recollection that bottle that had been full when we went to bed.

I sat down heavily. 'Any chance of a drink?' I indicated the whiskey.

'Malt whiskey gives you a headache,' he reminded me.

'I'll put soda in it. That makes it practically medicinal.'

We drank together. 'Do you think she's dead?' I asked fearfully.

It seemed like for ever before he answered. 'I don't know. The Gardai don't know. Nobody seems to know anything.'

'How can someone so cosseted disappear without trace? Lots of people knew her. OK she doesn't appear to have any friends, but she has classmates. Someone must know something.'

'If they do, they're not telling me.'

'God, the world can be a shit place.' I curled up beside him, putting my head on his lap.

'Tell me about it.' He tucked my bulky dressing gown tighter around me and held me. I closed my eyes for a second.

When I opened them again, the sun was up. The wall clock said eight-fifteen. I shook Gerry awake and we raced about, making coffee and toast. Showering. Getting ready for work. Or another day in paradise, as Barney might put it.

The phone call came out of the blue.

'Hi. My college tutor tells me you're looking for Caroline Boucher?'

'Who are you?' I asked cautiously.

'Lou Donaldson. I'm in Caroline's year.'

'Yes?' The last thing we wanted was bored students offering to put up posters of Caroline in their favourite pub. Boucher had been adamant about that. Low-profile he had instructed.

'I saw her last Saturday.'

I was on my feet. 'Saturday?'

'I'm just back from Belfast. Up visiting the folks. Doing a bit of skiving, to be honest.'

'You saw Caroline?' I tried to stay calm.

''Did. In the bar of the Europa hotel. In Belfast. I was going to go over and say hello, but . . .' He chuckled . . . 'I was with this wee girl . . . about to get lucky.'

'You're sure it was Caroline?'

'She's in my year! We see each other every day. What's going on?'

'Oh, nothing major. You know these doting fathers. They like to keep tabs on their daughters.'

'Tell him he doesn't have to worry about Caroline,' he laughed. 'Miss goody-two-shoes. If you tried it on with Caroline she'd freak.'

'Who was she with in Belfast?'

'How should I know? A gang of people. They were having a right laugh.'

My heart pounding, I rang Gerry. He was due back from a meeting with a residents' association in Glasnevin. A small community there was living in fear of a gang of thugs who were preying on elderly mourners in the nearby graveyard, mugging them for a few euros. The association had grown disenchanted with the Gardai, and decided to hire a private detective. With time to spare before he met with an ex-employee of Simon Boucher's, Gerry had gone to see them.

He caught his breath now. 'Belfast? Is he positive?'

'You can ask him yourself. But he's pretty sharp.' I gave him the student's name, his mobile number, the address of the Belfast hotel.

'He's convinced it was Caroline?'

'Absolutely. They're in the same year. He knows her well.'

'Bloody Belfast? No wonder we kept coming up blank in Dublin.'

Before I could comment he had swung the jeep around and was heading back up the M1 en route to Belfast. 'I'm on my way. Should be there in an hour and a half. I'll ring you.'

'What about your appointments? The case meeting? And I need that information on the cemetery muggings, plus you'll need a change of clothes. You haven't even got a razor!'

What I wanted to say was, come back and get me and we'll go to Belfast together. Investigate this tip-off as a team. Instead I wimped out, listed a whole pile of other reasons why he should come back to the office first. He wasn't interested.

'You take the case meeting, Annie. I'll fax you the information on the cemetery muggings and pick up a razor en route. And don't worry about my clothes. If I spot the fashion police approaching, I'll dive for cover,' he said dryly.

'Talk to you later.' I swallowed my disappointment.

14

Sandra was in seventh heaven, practically levitating with delight. Not only was she able to keep her mobile on because the *boss* was away, but the sort of people she always dreamed of working with were now marching through our reception.

Dreamland Interiors were moving in. Ultrachic furniture and bedding of the type most of us had only seen in magazines was being ferried upstairs, most of it dazzling white. Even the few unwrapped rolls of fabric I spotted were bleached white. Yet the people carrying all these exciting items were the antithesis of all this paleness – they were all shades and colours. Sandra and I watched as a seemingly endless throng of these glamorous people paraded past us, some of them heading for the lift, others carrying strangely shaped artefacts up the stairs, one of these being a marble statue of a couple doing something that couples don't normally do in public. Jigging with excitement, Sandra pointed out what looked like a small black twig in what I guessed was a priceless Chinese vase.

She was so taken with the glamour of it all, she forgot to put the address on a set of incriminating photos we were sending a wronged wife.

The courier waiting to pick them up didn't mind the delay.

'Deadly,' he kept repeating as yet another perfectly

shaped girl swanned past, only to be outclassed by the next exotically clad creature.

Declan held his forehead. 'Jesus. Hitler's troops marched into Paris with less fanfare.'

Outside, two huge removal vans blocked the traffic, the drivers unperturbed by the delays they were causing anyone hoping to reach the Financial Services Centre down the road.

'When God made time, he made plenty of it,' a whistling removal man reminded a protesting motorist.

'Time is money, you stupid arsehole!' the taxi driver retorted, trying to out-cliché him.

The latte drinkers in the Café Naturalle risked being judged uncool by gathering to watch the unfolding drama. The builders on the corner ate their ham sandwiches and looked down from above.

Not everyone was impressed. 'Who in the name of Christ would buy that?' Declan asked as a glass *Venus de Milo* sailed past reception.

'I would.' Elbows on the desk, Sandra openly drooled.

Barney arrived, demanding to know who had given those effin idiots permission to block the whole effin street? Then he spotted the microskirted crew coming down our stairs and rushed to join the rest of us behind the observation desk.

'You're right, Annie. This is better than the pictures.'

Even handsome optometrist was out on the street for a better look, triggering another debate as to whether it was the butch removal men or the microskirted girls he wanted a closer look at.

Our IT tenants had taken less than an hour to

move out of the building. They had wheeled heavy filing cabinets, computers, printers, desks and an assortment of chairs and packed them, without fuss, into a single removal van which whisked them away without incident. Dreamland Interiors moved in like Barnum & Bailey.

'Just as well Gerry's away. Man, he'd lose it if he saw this,' Barney said as things became increasingly chaotic.

A reed-thin Asian boy walked past, screeching hysterically into a red mobile. 'What do you mean, no problemo? Of course there's a problem! I said ten yards of six-inch tulle! Not six yards of ten-inch tulle, you Latin ignoramus.'

Naomi floated in, wearing a red silk kimono. An embroidered dragon curled around where her hips would be, if she had any. With every step the side-split kimono parted to reveal her endless tanned legs as she conducted operations with her slide rule, her high-pitched voice putting the fear of God into everyone who heard it. Except Declan.

The moment he heard her speak, he was lost. Immobilised with lust. Only his eyes moved, tracing her every gesture.

'Jaysus!' Barney nudged me.

I was concerned that Naomi might be directing too many people into the always-temperamental lift.

'What'll we do if it breaks down?' I asked Barney. 'Run?'

'Should I give them a hand? Help speed things up?' Sandra asked as the whole reception area threatened to hit gridlock.

'Go ahead, I'll see to the phones.'

'And could you ring my friend Rosaleen? Tell her

I can't make it for lunch. Tell her I'm moonlighting with Dreamland Interiors,' she giggled.

'Sandra!' I yelled after her.

'What?' she slumped.

'What's your friend's number?'

For the next hour she endeared herself to everyone connected with Dreamland Interiors. No job was too big or too small for her. She ferried boxes that even the semi-macho boys baulked at. Tore up and down the stairs faster than anyone else, retrieving fallen objects, rescuing carelessly dropped scarves and ribbons.

'Why doesn't she work like that for us?' Barney puzzled.

'Because we're not beautiful,' said Declan, watching Naomi.

Barney nudged me again.

'You're welcome.' Sandra was bowing to a grateful elfin-like chap whose bleached hair was styled like a meat tenderiser. He had thanked her for retrieving a fallen feather duster.

'Wasting your time there, Sandra,' Barney winked, reducing her to choking giggles which became uncontrollable when the attractive little elf approached him to ask in a pronounced lisp, 'Where ith the head, dude?'

Barney and I collapsed behind the reception desk.

Sandra was in her element. Her only gripe with the agency was that we didn't attract enough glamorous clients. She once got the hump with Gerry because he turned down a request to provide protective escorts for two visiting American models.

'It's not what we do.' He remained adamant.

There was enough glamour flitting past this

morning to satisfy the most star-struck receptionist. No actual bona fide models, as Barney discovered, but tons of wannabees. Naomi had roped them in with the promise that there were bound to be photographers sniffing about to record such an important occasion. In fact not a single one arrived to snap the hopefuls, who were as thin as hairpins and wearing clothes that wouldn't decently cover a ten-year-old.

'I can't believe all these glamorous people will be working here. They *will* be working here, Annie?' Sandra looked hopeful.

I was loath to burst her bubble. 'What do you think, Barney?'

'No idea.' He picked up his crash helmet.

'They're not all staff, are they?' Sandra looked gutted.

'Probably just friends helping out.' I patted her shoulder.

'Thank God for that,' Barney said. 'Our plumbing couldn't have taken it.'

'What?'

'All that bullshit!' he laughed, and hurried away.

The big vans finally drove off, the flashy cars following close behind. Watching them go, Sandra was practically in tears, but she pulled herself together and kept busy by sweeping up the debris that littered our previously clean reception area.

'Cheer up, Sandra,' I said. 'Here comes someone else who's bound to liven up our day.'

Mags was at the door, holding it open to let Fred in ahead of her. He stood there and shook his filthy wet coat all over the clean floor.

'Oh for feck's sake! Annie?' Sandra wailed.

★ ★ ★

If Sandra was finding it hard to settle back into her routine after the excitement of the morning, Declan was finding it impossible. If I didn't know better I would have suspected him of being back on the drink. Back to sending the profits of The Randy Goat soaring.

He wasn't. He was in love.

I had seen it all before. At Sandra's wedding, when he met my posh half-sister, he decided he'd found his soulmate. As if she'd give up her life among the jet-setting horsey crowd to settle down with a private detective who didn't know his bit from his bridle? After a few days – and nights – of torrid sex, she had replaced him with a jockey with calloused hands and a penchant for the short whip. She liked them rough, Francesca. I suspected Naomi, his new crush, liked them handsome, smiley-eyed and with a startling likeness to George Clooney.

I decided to rescue Declan by organising a case meeting. Keeping him busy was a sure-fire way of keeping him out of trouble. He liked hard work, and when I had finished assigning cases he would have little time for lusting after someone so far out of his league. Depending on which case he'd be working on, he would either be spending the next week hiding in a graveyard waiting for a mugger to strike, or he'd be hanging out in packed science labs, choking on formaldehyde as he waited to get the name of the poison responsible for the death of a Persian cat, a glorious Rhododendron, and a red beech.

'Holy shit!' Barney gasped as he read the long list of complaints our new client had taken out against his neighbour. 'This bastard poisoned a cat and left it on our client's doorstep?'

'I'll take that,' Declan said quickly-grabbing the file. He liked poisons.

'OK.' Barney looked grim. 'I'll take the graveyard case, Annie. I'd like to get me hands on the muggers who are robbing those OAPs.'

'But take care, Barney. The report says there's a gang of them, and those kids can be vicious.'

'We'll see how vicious they are with my boot up their arse!' Barney began reading.

'You're not to tackle them! The minute you see anything happening, you're to ring the Gardai.'

'OK. And I'll ask the muggers to hang around until they get there. The guys who did this to an old lady?' He held up a picture of a woman with a broken nose and two black eyes. 'I'm not to apprehend them? I'll definitely keep that in mind.'

'Gerry said . . .'

The phone rang. 'Annie? You'd better get down here.' Sandra sounded panic-stricken. 'There's people here from a garden centre. They're putting two big plants out at the front door. And you know how Gerry feels about pot plants.'

'What kind of plants are they?'

'Who gives a shite. All I know is Gerry will go ballistic. And you know who he'll blame. I'm supposed to be in charge of the reception area. But Naomi won't listen. They're like bloody big trees. Six feet tall, if they're an inch!'

'Don't exaggerate!'

'I'm not. The men are riveting the containers to the pavement. Making them thiefproof, the guy said. Get down here, Annie. Please.'

'What's wrong?' Barney was on his feet.

I put the phone down. 'There's a row brewing in

reception. Something about plants. They sound like bay trees. Naomi is apparently insisting on putting two—'

'I'll sort it.' Declan moved like Road Runner.

Watching him dash out, I knew who would win this battle. Naomi's bay trees would be safe. At least until Gerry got back.

15

With Gerry in Belfast, I got sucked back into the old office routine. Everyone seemed to feel they had a call on my time. Declan wanted my help to research some ancient by-laws that might prove useful to his battling neighbours case. Barney needed encouraging to remain at his post in the rain-lashed graveyard because the muggers hadn't appeared for days. Gerry rang, asking me to pick up some additional photos of Caroline – full-length shots this time. He wanted them faxed to Belfast asap.

And someone had to answer client inquiries. While Sandra checked her horoscope.

'This is shite.' She swung around, her pink fingernails blending seamlessly with her new pink coffee mug. 'Look at this, Annie.' She held up her favourite tabloid. 'Isn't this shite?'

'Absolutely. So why do you buy it?'

'Be serious. Listen to this: *Watch out, Gemini. You could be heading for a rough patch. As the sun makes its way out of your sign there is a chance that you may be facing disappointment in both your personal and professional life. Finances are uncertain.* How would you feel if that was your horoscope?'

'My horoscope?' I tried not to sound bitter. 'It sounds like a rerun of my life.'

Bang on cue, my *bête noire* surfaced. Our bank

manager was on the line, requesting an immediate meeting. I managed to convince him that I was tied up until Gerry got back, then promised him that we would strive to be in the black by the end of next month at the very latest.

'Not good enough, I'm afraid. Your overdraft is becoming a major concern to us. You may need to trim your sails somewhat,' he said sternly.

A weekend sailor, he was addicted to nautical metaphors. At our very first meeting, when I was entrusting him with money from the sale of my birth mother's house, he said he liked the cut of my jib. Now he clearly regarded me as a bit of a shipwreck.

Sandra eavesdropped shamelessly on our brief conversation. 'He's a Taurus,' she whispered. 'I can tell. They're obsessed with money. It's all they think about.'

I ended the call with a flurry of promises, then turned to her. 'Fax these photos to Gerry, please.' I handed them over and retreated to the relative peace and quiet of my office.

My bum was barely on the seat when Naomi came barging in. She marched to my desk, waving a list of complaints.

'I want these sorted.'

Top of her list was the noise from the nearby building site. Number two was a new one on me – *A worrying rattling emanating from radiators*! And down among a trillion other complaints was a demand that *we* provide safe parking for *her* clients. Or else.

'Leave it with me. I'll see to these.' I forced a smile.

'Without delay!' she commanded.

'I'm right on it.' I winked.

She looked satisfied, and left. I was dropping the

list in the bin when the phone rang. Sandra again, wondering if I would be interested in checking out a possible tip-off.

'It's about the Boucher case.'

I was out of my chair like a missile.

My only concern about the tip-off was its source. Mags.

She had apparently arrived in reception as Sandra was about to fax Caroline's photos to Gerry. 'What are you doing?' she'd asked curiously.

'None of your business.'

'I only asked.' Mags craned her neck to get a better look.

Later, Sandra swore to me that she had only left the photos out of her hand for a second to take a call from Mrs Green – Flopsy was on the loose again – and that when she turned to get them, Mags was examining them closely.

'Get your filthy hands off those photos!'

'I'm only lookin'.'

'Give them here.' Sandra grabbed them.

'I know that girl.' Mags tapped at the top photo with a grimy finger. 'Let me talk to Gerry.'

Sandra ignored her. She remembered Mags claiming to know George Bush after seeing his picture on the front page of the *Irish Independent*. But this time Mags persisted. 'I want to talk to Gerry. I might have information about that girl.'

'Get out of here, Mags!' Sandra faxed the photos to Gerry. Looked up to see Mags still standing there, watching.

'I'm not moving until I talk to Gerry.' She folded her arms.

That's when Sandra rang my office.

'Not her!' Mags protested when she saw me step-ping out of the lift. 'I only give information to Gerry. I'm his *snitch*.'

I took a calming breath. I had warned Gerry that giving Mags a TV set for her room was a mistake we'd all live to regret. Plus I was in no mood to indulge her wild fantasies. When Gerry had rung earlier he'd ben grumpy as hell, bemoaning the fact that his trip to Belfast had been a complete waste of time so far. Nobody in the Europa hotel recalled seeing Caroline there. Not on Saturday or any other night. That's why he wanted the full-length photos. 'A different shot of her might jog someone's memory.'

'Gerry's in Belfast,' I said to Mags. 'You either talk to me or leave.'

'Gerry pays me for information.' She pursed her non-existent lips. 'He gave me a colour television.'

'Goodbye, Mags.' I turned on my heel.

'I know the girl in those photos,' she said quickly. 'Is she missing?' She watched me, her little raisin eyes alive with cunning.

I tried to see beyond them, to plumb the depths of her bobble-hatted little head. It wasn't easy. She looked harmless enough, but she was a practised con artist. That's how she had survived on the streets for so long, by using her wits. Well, basically lying. Still, if there was even the slightest chance that . . . ?

'Why do you ask?' I ventured.

'Well, I haven't seen her around lately.' She gave me a canny look. 'Is there a reward?'

'Get out of here, Mags.'

'I know her boyfriend,' she said quickly.

My heart jumped. 'Her boyfriend?' Of course I

didn't believe a word of it. Only a fool would trust Mags. She was a world-class schemer.

'Haven't seen him around lately either.'

'Dropped out of your social scene, have they? Haven't been spotted lunching lately?' I forced a smile, when what I wanted to do was shake her until her bones rattled. *If you're lying to me I'll—*

'Lunching? Huh! They won't let me into McDonald's any more.' She edged closer, her body odour practically forcing me to my knees. 'I used to see them going in and out of his flat!' she boasted. 'Up near Christchurch.'

My heart began to pound so loudly I was convinced that even Sandra, now happily encouraging one of her phone friends to have her hair highlighted, had to notice. The thing was, there were tons of new apartments in the Christchurch area, some of them bordering on the fashionable. It was entirely possible that Caroline had a boyfriend living in one of them. Boucher might insist that she didn't have a boyfriend, but how many fathers are privy to their teenage daughter's love lives? Someone as beautiful as Caroline was unlikely to be spending her *nights* in lonely solitude.

'Could you . . . show me where the flat is?' I tried to sound nonchalant.

'Course.' Mags became smug. 'It's in St Martin's Lane. Behind the big corpo car park. Where they're going to build all them new offices.'

Disappointment knifed through me. I wanted to kick myself for being so gullible, dumb enough to let her raise my hopes even for a nonosecond. While it was always possible that a friend of Caroline's lived in a relatively modest apartment in

Christchurch, the likelihood of anyone living in that long-neglected street behind the temporary public car park was laughable. That whole terrace of Georgian houses had been in the throes of being demolished when a row over some murky building permits brought the work to a standstill. The place now resembled war-torn Beruit. Half the houses were boarded up, and the remainder were in such a poor state of repair you'd be lucky to get two feet along the terrace without getting your head split by falling masonary.

'Get out of here, Mags.' Sick with disappointment, I hit the button for the lift, then opted for the stairs instead. If I had to stand looking at that wizened little face for another second, I might strangle her. She was an incorrigible liar.

'What's her real name, anyway?' she called after me. 'Her boyfriend calls her Bunny!'

Sitting on the damp street bench outside McDonald's, I questioned Mags again. 'Are you sure you heard right? He definitely called her Bunny?'

She munched her way through her Big Mac. 'I'm not stupid.' She picked up her Coke, her mildest movement sending a wave of killer BO in my direction.

I tried not to inhale as I waited for her to finish. She chewed each skinny chip endlessly.

'How about dessert?' I asked sarcastically.

'Oh no. I don't want to ruin me dinner. It's at one.'

I checked my watch. Five past twelve. We had been sitting here for twenty minutes, closely observed by Fred, who missed no opportunity to assault my leg. I slapped him away for the umpteenth time.

'The nuns serve dinner at *one*?'

'On the dot.' She gave Fred the last couple of French fries, and threw the remaining crumbs to some foraging pigeons.

'Ready to show me the flat?' I tried again.

I was becoming excited now. Pictured myself ringing Gerry. Telling him the case was solved. Or at least that I had photos of the flat where Caroline had been hiding with her secret boyfriend. Imagine the buzz that would cause.

'Ready?' I stood up, sending the pigeons scattering.

'All right. All right. What's your rush?' Mags folded the McDonald's wrapper carefully. Filed it away in her pocket. Packed the Big Mac carton into her carrier bag. 'I have to be at the nuns at one. What's *your* hurry?'

After pointing out three different houses in the long-neglected terrace and then changing her mind, Mags finally settled on number twenty-four. 'That's it. I remember it now. It has a hole in the roof.'

I looked up. Every house in the terrace had a hole in the roof.

She directed me to the basement of what had once been a beautiful Georgian building. It was now a dump. Even the steps leading down to the basement looked like they'd collapse if the wind changed.

Mags waited in the safety of the street above, watching curiously as I knocked on the weather-beaten door. When there was no reply to my third knock, I called up to her, 'Are you sure this is the place? You definitely saw her going in here? With a man?'

She sniffed. 'I saw her.'

I unwound my scarf, spat on it and tried to clear an inch of grime from the narrow window by the door. A waste of effort and a good scarf, because a blowtorch couldn't have shifted that gunge.

Mags was growing uneasy, looking over her shoulder, glancing towards the tower block that overlooked the lane.

'I'll be late for me dinner!'

'Are you sure this was where you . . . ?'

'I saw them,' she insisted. Then gave me a sly look. 'I can get you in.'

I hurried up the crumbling steps. 'You can get me in? Then why didn't you . . . ?'

'No . . .' She spoke with an irritating slowness. 'I said I know *how* you can get in.'

'Jesus, Mags, if you're messing me about . . .' My head beginning to ache, I wiped my now filthy hands on my even filthier scarf. 'How *do* I get in?'

'It'll cost you. People don't do things for nothing.'

It was starting to rain. Big soft drops landed on my head, which I could have protected with my scarf if it hadn't been squashed into a filthy ball in my bag. 'What do you take me for, Mags?' I snarled.

She backed away. 'It's not for me! I know someone who can pick the lock. But he'll want paying. Loads of money! At least . . . twenty euros?'

I gave her ten. 'I'll give you the rest when he gets me in.'

'Euros! I hate them!' She pocketed them swiftly. 'Not like real money. You stay here,' she ordered, adjusting her bobbled ski-hat and marching off, chin held as proudly as if she had just closed a major deal with the Bundesbank. Watching her squat little figure disappear down the street, I wondered if her

163

lock-picker was just another figment of her fertile imagination.

'There you are, miss.' The wiry little tramp swung the door open. It had taken him five seconds to pick the intricate lock. He stood aside to let me pass.

'Thanks, Mickey. Get yourself something hot to eat,' I said, slipping him two fives, although Mags had warned that he wasn't to be trusted with money.

'He's a loser,' she had whispered. 'You better pay me, in advance.'

Mickey grabbed the notes and disappeared.

I took a hesitant step into the old building. No need to rush, I assured myself. Besides, it was pitch-black inside. Well, pitch-grey. I couldn't see beyond two feet. I paused, while my eyes became accustomed to the darkness, and tried to ignore the unpleasant smell that permeated the whole place. Dampness? Or something more sinister? I drew my sleeve down over my hand and felt for a light switch. Some hope. Holding the door open to allow daylight in, I was able to make out an old sofa in the corner of the room. Beside it stood a mound of gutted candles and a plastic garden table that might once have been white but was now grey, and coated in what I hoped were only mouse droppings. Directly ahead, about twelve feet from where I was standing, was another door, this one covered in crude graffiti, the wall surrounding it jam-packed with drawings. Fortunately it was too dark to make any of them out.

The place had clearly been used as a squat. But not recently. The industrial-strength lock would have seen to that. The question was, would Caroline Boucher have squatted in a place like this? In every picture we had of her she gleamed like a new pin. She was definitely a three-showers-a-day girl. Deodorised to the hilt. I couldn't picture her walking along this run-down street, let alone living in this hellhole. The ultimate clue was the carpet of cigarette butts on the floor. Caroline was a fervent anti-smoker. Wouldn't even sit in a room where people lit up, according to her father.

I backed out into the fresh air and took a cleansing breath. Mags had conned me. Taken me for a ride. If the lads found out about this, I'd never live it down. They'd give themselves hernias, laughing. And Gerry? Well, my detective career could be over before it had begun if he heard I gave Mags twenty euros to get me into this dump.

I pulled the door closed and left. I was halfway up the steps when something swift and furry darted across my foot. I screamed and stumbled awkwardly, skinning both my knees on the filthy steps.

Wincing in pain and humiliation, I hobbled back to the Honda.

16

Fiona put three spoonfuls of sugar in my tea and a Finger of Fudge in my hand, as if I were five and recovering from a fall in the playground.

'Eat that!' she ordered. 'And drink your tea. Sugar is good for shock. And chocolate raises your seratonin levels. And that's what you need, right now. Do you know what all serial killers have in common?'

I chewed my fudge miserably.

'Low seratonin levels!' she answered herself. 'It's a proven fact. I watched a two-hour documentary on serial killers last night. Excellent. Well worth taping.'

The day her pregnancy was confirmed, Pino got her a satellite dish. Understandable, I suppose. She already had everything else. A sensational home, an eight-week-old foetus, a Volvo estate, and more money than she could handle. But the moment her doctor hinted that she might have to keep an eye on her blood pressure, Pino ordered a satellite dish. His plan was to get her to relax. Put her feet up. I'm almost sure it didn't include her becoming an expert on serial killers.

But then, as Gerry says, life has a way of turning around and biting you on the arse.

She checked the plasters on my grazed knees. 'I still think you should have an anti-tetanus shot,' she worried. 'I know the rat didn't bite you. Or pee on your leg. That's how you get Weil's disease, you know. When they pee on you. You'd have been in big trouble then.'

'What do you think I'm in now? Wait till Gerry sees these.' I looked at my torn knees. 'It'll be the Murtha case all over again.'

'Maybe this happened for a reason, Annie,' she consoled me.

'A reason?'

'To make you rethink this whole detective lark.'

'Lark?'

'Will you give over sounding like an echo. You know what I'm saying. You don't seem to be having much luck with this career plan of yours. If I were you, I'd have a long, hard think about it.'

'I have done,' I sulked. 'I like being a detective.'

'Like it? Breaking into derelict houses? Falling into rat shit?'

'You can't be sure that was rat shit on my tights! You just guessed.'

'Well, I've never claimed to be an expert on rat shit, but whether it was or not, you could have been in serious danger in that place. You hadn't a clue what you were walking into. It could have been a drug den. A . . . the . . . the lair of a . . . a demented rapist!'

'How would a demented rapist have got in there? I had to pay Mags' friend to pick the lock.'

'Well you should have had better sense than to listen to Mags!'

I shrugged.

'That's how people get killed.'

'By listening to Mags?'

'By being naive enough to trust someone who lives on the fringes of the law.'

'Oh, for feck's sake, Fiona. She's just a homeless old woman. Not Donna Corleone!'

'She's not homeless. Didn't Gerry get her a flat?'

'He got her a room. And OK she tricked me into going to St Martin's Lane to worm a few bob out of me. It's not a capital offence. And you'd better not tell Gerry.'

'As if I would. But I wish you'd *think* before you act. If you'd waited for Gerry to get back before rushing off, he'd have . . .'

'Done exactly the same thing as I did. The minute he heard the name Bunny he would have been down to St Martin's Lane in a flash.'

She turned away in disgust.

Why was *she* so annoyed? I was the one with the bleeding knees. And for someone who preached to me about personal safety, she wasn't above taking a few risks with her own. She was planning on giving birth in her living room, for God's sake! With mad Maeve in attendance, a woman who shouldn't be allowed near a blunt instrument, let alone given access to a birth canal.

She topped up my tea. 'I hate to see you being made a fool of, Annie.'

I sipped my tea without comment.

Not so Fiona.

'All I'm saying is that maybe you should back off. Leave the investigating to real detectives. And . . . don't tell them about this little episode with Mags.'

'What is your problem, Fiona?' I slammed my cup down. 'Friends are supposed to encourage each other. All you've done since I got here is tell me how stupid

I am. Well thanks for having such faith in me. Do you want something else to worry about?' I got to my feet. 'I'm going right back out to find Mags, and this time she won't get away with just pointing to a house and running. She must have heard the name Bunny somewhere.'

'You're not going back to that dangerous . . . ?' Fiona was horrified.

'I'm not a quitter.'

Her face tightening, she marched across the room, reached under one of her immaculate silk cushions and pulled out a folded newspaper.

'Read that,' she said, throwing it at me. 'I saw it first thing this morning. Meant to ring you about it later. Then you appeared, all upset and bleeding and . . . read it, and you'll see where Mags got the name Bunny from.'

It was just a small article tucked away in the financial section. A weekly colour piece on the young and rich. This week it featured Caroline Boucher. Gave a sketchy outline of her life. Where she had attended school, what she was studying in college, her hobbies. How much she'd be worth when she reached twenty-one. Heading the article was a picture of her – shining blonde hair, sweet face, triple string of pearls. Underneath it said Caroline (Bunny) Boucher.

'Mags!' I fumed. 'The old . . . bitch! The conniving old . . . !'

'Now do you see the sort of people you end up mixing with when you get involved in this detective lark? It's not like sitting in a nice safe office, answering the phone. Having the craic with the lads while you balance the books.'

I reread the article, my head pounding, with a

mixture of embarrassment and fear. Embarrassment because once again I had made a total fool of myself. And fear because if Simon Boucher saw the article . . . But, hold on, there was no reference in it to Caroline being missing. I checked it more closely. Nothing. In fact it read like a press handout, which it probably was, written ages ago by someone in his employ when it suited Boucher Investments to have the beautiful Boucher daughter gracing the financial pages. It was sheer coincidence that it had appeared just as we were searching for her.

But Mags had pulled a masterly stroke, seeing Caroline's photos and putting two and two together. Even waiting until I was walking away before mentioning the name Bunny. And I fell for it. Bought her a Big Mac. Let Fred hump my leg while she finished her French fries.

'It could be worse,' I turned to Fiona. 'At least the press aren't on to the real story. Gerry would go ballistic if they were. He promised Boucher we could keep this whole thing low-key.'

She pushed me back down on to the big squishy sofa. 'And you obviously have. So forget it. Drink your tea and relax.'

'Any more fudge?'

Going to fetch some, she tripped over my bag. She bent to pick up my mobile, where it had slid out on to the floor. 'Shouldn't this be on?'

'I suppose.' I flicked it on without enthusiasm. It rang instantly.

'See! That's what happens,' I grimaced, then realised the call was from Gerry.

Fiona tore the wrapper off another Finger of Fudge and offered me a bite.

'Gerry?' I chewed. 'I . . . was just about to ring you.'

'You've seen it?

'Just now,' I said nervously.

'How the hell did Sandra miss it? She's supposed to check the papers.'

'Well . . . not necessarily the financial section,' I defended her.

'Why not? Do we work in a financial vacuum?'

'There's been a lot happening. Dreamland Interiors moved in. They're . . .'

'Boucher has been on, from Zurich. He's in bloody Zurich and he can respond quicker to an article in an Irish paper than my own staff?'

This definitely wasn't the time to tell him about Mags. Of course it might never be. Gerry's tolerance levels could sink to subterranean levels when it came to people who botched things. Twice.

'There's no great harm done,' he sighed. 'It's just a colour piece. But Sandra should have spotted it. You'd better talk to her. On the plus side, it might even jog someone's memory. But warn Sandra to be careful. Tell her to give out no information whatso-ever. She's to refer all calls to you. If she can't spot a newspaper article about a client, she can hardly be trusted to recognise someone trying to scam us. Now, what's all this about Mags?'

My stomach tightened. 'Mags? I never . . . ?'

'Sandra said something about Mags.'

'You've already spoken to Sandra?'

'I wouldn't have to if you'd keep your mobile on.'

'Mags . . . she was just messing.' I held my breath.

'I guessed as much. This case is the pits. One of the senior managers has just come on duty here. He said they have a regular guest who quite resembles

Caroline. There's a picture of her on his office wall. Taken at a Christmas party.'

'And is she . . .'

'Oh, she looks a bit like Caroline all right. But she's about thirty-six. That college mate of Caroline's needs his eyes tested. I've been on to him and he admitted that from thirty-odd feet away, and in soft lighting, maybe he wasn't in the best position to identify anyone. Bloody time-waster.'

'It happens.' I swallowed.

'Yeah, well we've got to be more zealous in future. Spot the time-wasters before they lead us up the garden path.'

'Definitely!'

'I'm beginning to wonder if this whole case is . . .' He paused.

'What?'

'Nothing. I'm just wrecked. I hung around the hotel till all hours last night, clocking everything that moved. By two a.m. even the barmen were beginning to look like Caroline. And security were starting to give me some very funny looks. I felt like jacking the whole thing in.'

This was so unlike Gerry, it totally rattled me. He was known to see things through to the bitter end. That's what kept him in his failing marriage for so long, hanging on until his wife joined an aerobics class, lost nine pounds and ran off with the guest instructor, a top army athlete. That's when Gerry finally admitted that his marriage was over.

I tried to cheer him up, but the words came out wrong.

'Your knee is probably giving you trouble. It's all this rain. Everyone is complaining.'

172

'My knee's fine. I'll talk to you when I get back.'

'Today?'

'Tomorrow morning.' A pause. 'I wish it could be today.' His voice deepened.

I felt a huge rush of love. Of longing. A sudden need to hear him say he was missing me.

'I miss you, Gerry.' I waited.

'I . . .'

'Yes?'

'I . . .'

Say it, you bastard.

'I'll see you tomorrow.' He was gone.

Fiona watched as I fired the mobile into my bag. 'Everything OK?'

'Sure. He says he loves and adores me. Can't wait to get back and make mad passionate love to me. Says he can't sleep for missing me.'

She nodded solemnly. 'Let me guess. He said, "See ya."?'

'Correct. But how did you . . . ?'

'Pino does that when he's with other people.'

'You serious?' I was surprised. I always took Pino to be the embodiment of the passionate Latin male. Only a slap away from making love to her in public.

'You think Pino whispers sweet nothings down the phone when his staff are lined up waiting to hear which wine they should recommend with the Tuscany casserole? I'm lucky to get a *ciao*.' She chuckled.

That made me feel miles better. And another Finger of Fudge perked me up completely. We sat there, chewing companionably, wishing men were more like women, but with their dangly bits still intact.

'I'm not going to tell Gerry about today's fiasco,' I decided. 'But how can I hide these bloody knees?'

'Wear support tights?' she twinkled.

'Support tights?'

'Yeah. If you get them in a dark enough shade they'll hide the plasters. Keep them on day *and* night.' She gave me an arch look. 'I guarantee he won't notice your cut knees.'

'He may not notice my knees, but I'm pretty sure he'll notice a wedge of heavily elasticised rayon getting in his way, when we . . . when we . . . I'll have to take them off sometime.'

'Not necessarily.' She looked smug.

'Not . . .'

'Here's what you do. You keep them on, but minus the gusset. You get some sharp scissors and cut the gusset out. That's what I've been doing. My pregnancy support tights are like chain mail, but so comfortable, I often keep them on in bed.' She leaned close, her attitude becoming confessional. 'They work so well, Pino forgets that I'm pregnant.'

I stared at her enormous bump. 'He forgets . . . ?'

Our eyes met and I began to giggle. Quietly at first, then I cracked up so completely, she joined in. We ended up rolling on the sofa, laughing helplessly.

I was first to recover. 'You expect me to believe that?' I mopped my eyes.

'Cross my heart and hope to die,' she said. 'Of course he would have downed several glasses of Burgundy before we stared. Just the same.' She beamed.

I still wasn't convinced.

'For God's sake, Annie, he's a man! And so is Gerry! The day we can't outwit one of them is the day I'll hang up my thong.'

'Your thong?' I gaped at her huge girth as she lay

belly-up on the pale sofa, her weight making its squishy cushions sag almost to the parquet floor.

'Don't ask. You have enough sad images to be going on with.'

We were both convulsed again. Laughing so hard, Fiona clutched her bump protectively with both hands.

17

Barney and I were putting the finishing touches to his brilliant old age pensioner disguise when Gerry arrived back from Belfast.

He was way behind schedule, thanks to rush-hour gridlock on the Swords Road. But that wasn't why he burst into my office, his face like thunder. 'What the hell is going on here, Annie? What are those yokes doing out at our front door?'

'What yokes? Oh, you mean Naomi's bay trees?' I feigned innocence.

'Bay trees. Apple trees. I don't care what the hell they are, I'm not having them outside our door. This is a detective agency, not a fecking nightclub. I want them out of there before some moron starts stringing lights on them.'

'You mean the lights aren't on them yet?' Barney grinned.

An elbow in his solar plexus had him wincing like a girl.

'Never mind the bay trees, Gerry,' I said. 'What happened to "Hello, Annie. Good morning, Barney. Nice to see you. Forgive me if I appear somewhat stressed this morning. I have been on the road since daybreak, and the traffic from Belfast is a nightmare."'

'Yeah, yeah, all of that,' he said impatiently. 'Now, can someone please get those bay trees out of there.

Barney, would you . . . ?' He noticed Barney's outfit for the first time. The baggy Oxfam shop suit and kipper tie. 'Why are you dressed like a superannuated pimp?'

'Annie thinks the graveyard muggers are keeping away because they spotted me patrolling the place. She suggested I dress like an old codger.'

'Oh.' Gerry was contrite.

'You make a very attractive old codger, Barney,' I said. 'In fact . . . if I were forty years older I'd be trying to shift you.'

'Cor. Thanks, missus.' He pretended to grope me.

'Hey! Remember where you are, you dirty old git.' Gerry sounded ratty, but his eyes were smiling. 'Now get your superannuated arse up to the graveyard and trap those muggers before they top some poor old pensioner. Have you got everything you need? Pepper spray? Mobile? Truss?'

The phone interrupted our laughter. 'What is it, Sandra?'

'Mags is here. She saw Gerry coming in. She wants to talk to him.'

Christ. She'll blab about my visit to the squat. Maybe try the Bunny scam on him.

'You still there, Annie?' Sandra sounded worried.

'Yes,' I snapped.

'Fred is outside. Peeing on the bay trees. What'll I do?'

'Get rid of Mags,' I hissed.

'What?'

'Get . . . rid . . . of . . . Mags,' I mumbled as Gerry came to stand beside me.

'What's going on?' he asked.

'Fred is peeing on the bay trees. I'm telling Sandra

to give Mags the papers and get rid of her,' I smiled.

'Jesus Christ, when I left forty-eight hours ago this place was a professional investigative agency. What the fuck happened?' His expression darkened.

'Dreamland Interiors moved in.' Barney pulled on a flat cap to cover his too pretty blonde hair, and stuck a heavily gummed Stalinist moustache under his nose, checking both for effect in a big handmirror.

'Right.' Gerry was tight-lipped. 'You get on up to the graveyard. I'll put that Naomi Billings one in her place.'

'Careful, Gerry.' Barney adjusted his moustache. 'She eats men for breakfast. She already has Declan wrapped around her little finger.'

Gerry shot him a filthy look. 'Has she now?'

I dived in. 'And remember, if Mags says anything at all to you . . . she's an incorrigible liar. You can't believe a word she says!'

He looked back at us from the doorway, his expression puzzled. 'Is anyone around here normal?'

I was securing Barney's cap with a hatpin when he jerked sideways.

'Sorry, did I stick you?'

'It wasn't that. Look down there.' He pointed out the window.

Three stories below Fred was positioning himself to pee on a bay tree. Gerry was trying to lift its twin, struggling manfully with the big container. He straightened up, took a breath, then had another go. The container didn't move.

'Didn't anyone tell him those containers are riveted to the pavement?' Barney winced.

'I've been busy,' I said guiltily.

'He'll give himself a hernia!'

I was turning to ring reception when there was a sudden flurry of movement below. Naomi had joined Gerry. Well, she was standing over him, looking like the cover of a glamour magazine in her gossamer-thin skirt as she tapped him on the shoulder. He looked up just as a sharp gust of wind caught her skirt, blowing it practically waist high, giving him a close-up of six inches of smooth golden thigh exposed between white silk stocking tops and brief oyster silk knickers.

And there wasn't a single plaster on her perfect legs.

I nearly jumped through the window. Would have if I thought I'd land on her well-groomed head. How could anyone keep their hair that smooth and shiny in our weather? Or look that perfect at eight-fifty-five on a windswept April morning. And was it just coincidence that she happened to stand windward of Gerry when every weatherman had forecast gales?

He was standing beside her now, smiling. *Smiling?* What happened to *I'll put that Naomi Billings one in her place?*

When the wind threatened to lift her skirt again, they laughed together and he helped her hold the skirt down. *Laughed!* Then Mags was there. Pushing between them.

Go for it, Mags! You show her.

'Uh-oh.' Barney made a sound like a Teletubby as Naomi elbowed Mags aside, all the while smiling at Gerry. Then he was leading her indoors, by the *elbow!*

'Oops, there goes the skirt again.' Barney leaned against the window for a better look.

'Barney!'

He shrugged. 'Sorry.'

'I thought you couldn't stand her?'

'Can't. But she has wicked legs,' he grinned.

'She's an exhibitionist!'

'True,' he smirked under the heavily gummed moustache. 'But then legs like that deserve to be exhibited. And those suspenders?' He sucked in his breath lasciviously.

'Aren't you supposed to be up in the graveyard?'

'On my way.' He backed off and picked up my keys. 'Honda in its usual spot?'

'Where else?' I rang reception.

'Don't fret, Annie,' he said. 'Gerry's too smart to be seduced by a pair of magnificent legs . . . OK, OK, I'm going.' He grabbed his old git carrier bag and left.

I dropped the phone and raced back to the window. There was nobody at the door below, just the disputed bay trees swaying in the wind.

I counted to a hundred before dialling reception again. This time it was picked up immediately.

'Sandra? Get me Gerry's office.'

I checked my hair while I waited. In the short walk from my car to the agency the wind had played havoc with my carefully straightened locks. It was now curling wildly around my shoulders, bouncing cheekily instead of sitting all sleek and shiny like Naomi's.

'Sorry, Annie. He's not there. He's probably in Dreamland Interiors with Naomi. They went . . . hold on a second. *Shut up, Mags. She isn't his fancy woman! She owns Dreamland Interiors. No, you can't talk to him!* Sorry about that, Annie. Do you want me to try Naomi's office?'

'No. Don't do that. I'll . . . talk to him later.' I bloody would. How many times had Sandra and I tried to brighten up the agency with a few pot plants? And every single time Gerry had gone ballistic, saying he was running a detective agency, not a garden centre. But uberbitch Naomi could put a forest of bay trees – well, two – around our front entrance, flash her knickers and sleek hair at him, and he caved in? What would it be next? A big neon sign out front saying Dreamland Interiors?

'It's not like it's a big *neon* sign,' Gerry said, dismissing Barney's grumbles.

'It may as well be! It's twice the size of ours! So I say no. Why should they have a bigger sign than us.' Barney paced the office unhappily. 'They're only a sublet. They don't *own* the building. Brian and Niall were happy with their sign.'

'They were IT consultants.' Declan chewed his thumbnail.

'So what do Naomi and Tudi do that's so special? Sell fancy wallpaper? Help some poncey prats to choose between bleached cotton and Thai silk pillow-cases?'

'They're interior designers.' Declan spat out his nail.

'And that's why they need a bigger sign than us?'

'It's only marginally bigger, and expertly planned so it *won't* be detrimental to our main aspect . . .'

Barney and I exchanged glances. Detrimental? Main aspect? Someone was putting words in Declan's mouth. He hadn't spoken like that since he gave up the drink.

'. . . so why do you have a problem with it?' he finished.

'Well, for a start, I think Naomi is a complete wagon,' Barney admitted. 'She barely acknowledges me when we share the lift. If we bump into each other in the street, she looks at me as if I just crawled out from under a rock.'

'Maybe if you didn't dress like a vagrant.'

'Maybe if you weren't hoping for a leg-over!'

'That's enough!' Gerry lost patience. 'I thought we'd sort this in minutes. If you two continue squabbling, we'll be here for ever.'

'It's not me. It's him. Trying to curry favour with Naomi so he can get into her knickers,' Barney muttered.

'What did you say?' Declan growled.

'You heard me.'

'Shut up, the pair of you! I don't have time for this. I only asked your opinion out of courtesy. Now show some decorum. Or shut the fuck up!' Gerry cleared his throat. 'Sorry about that, Annie. But you'd need the patience of Job here.'

'Can I say something?' Declan asked.

'Keep it short!'

'Dreamland Interiors aren't trying to take over. They view a large sign as part of *their* overall marketing strategy. Its no skin off our nose.'

He definitely had the hots for Naomi. Before she arrived, his only contribution to staff meetings were low grunts. Now he was talking marketing strategies?

'Marketing strategy my arse.' Barney wasn't impressed. 'They just think they're better than us. This isn't a shopping mall. We have a sign out there to let people know they've found us. It's not a feckin' ad. If we let them do this, what's next? Will we have to put up a bigger sign? Saying what? Is your wife becoming the village bike? Do you suspect her of having it off with the vicar? Is your old mum being flashed by Mickey Dwan in number seven? Let McHugh Dunning sort your . . .'

Despite himself Gerry started to laugh.

'Dreamland Interiors isn't a detective agency,' Declan said icely. 'They're . . .'

'Selling a service? Same as us. Same as that bent optometrist next door. I don't see him putting up a sign saying 'Going blind? Groping a granny by mistake? Come and get your mince pies sorted'.

Gerry didn't even smile. Clearly past being amused.

'And if anyone needs a big sign, surely its an optometrist? Am I right, Gerry?'

'What do you think, Annie?' As usual Gerry threw me in the deep end.

This time I was prepared. I had seen this coming from day one. Certainly from the morning Naomi got to leave her bay trees out front. She was never going to be satisfied with being on an equal footing with us. It wasn't in her nature. Naomi considered herself to be something special. Dwarfing our sign was only the start of her campaign. Her next move might be a lot more ambitious. And personal.

I looked at Gerry. 'I think this is the thin end of the wedge. Dreamland Interiors have taken advantage of us since day one. They're already taking up more of Sandra's time than we do. She's now ringing their suppliers. Delivering their post first. They have three phone lines, yet they've started giving *our* number to some of their special clients.'

'What?' Barney and Gerry were shocked.

'You mean why? Because *their* clients are too posh

183

to redial. Instead they get our Sandra's friendly voice, first time.'

As Gerry's face darkened with anger, Declan began making inroads into his remaining thumbnail.

'Do you know why Sandra isn't here now?' I was on a roll. 'She's delivering a parcel for them. *Our* receptionist is delivering goods to *their* clients.'

'Hold on, Annie,' Gerry cautioned. 'Let's not blow this out of all proportion. This morning's delivery is a one-off. I knew about it.'

'Me too,' Declan chipped in. 'Naomi needed to send a book of fabric samples asap to a certain VIP client.'

'What Naomi needs is a good kick up the A.R.S.E.,' Barney said.

'Why can't she use a courier service like the rest of us?'

'Because they charge extra to deliver kicks up the A.R.S.E?' Barney had a low boredom threshold. Hated formal meetings unless he could turn them into a cabaret.

I tried to remain businesslike. 'When Naomi appropriates our receptionist, it leaves our front desk unmanned.'

'Wide open to terrorist attacks,' Barney chuckled.

'We have a buzzer,' Gerry said.

'We pay Sandra's salary,' I said.

'OK. You talk to her, Annie. Now back to why we're here. Who thinks Dreamland need a bigger sign?'

His sheer chutzpah left me speechless. *You talk to her, Annie.*

'Not me!' Barney said.

'Or me,' I hissed, still smarting from Gerry's unbelievable cheek.

'What difference would it make to us?' Declan had run out of thumbnails to chew. 'What about Sandra's vote?' he added. 'I'll take that if . . .'

'Over my dead body!' I interrupted him. I was sick of him and his pathetic crush on Naomi. I hated Naomi. Well, hated the way she flirted with Gerry. The way her skirts seemed to be shrinking daily. OK, it *was* bordering on summer, but even the rising temperatures didn't explain her need to elevate her hemlines to pelmet levels. Only one reason why she wore skirts that short. She saw the effect they had on Gerry. Because, hard as he tried, it was pretty obvious that he couldn't help looking at her legs, which were longer than anyone's – except a giraffe's. But the sight of their cellulite-free perfection rushing up and down the stairs brought out the worst in me. And how come she only used the stairs when Gerry was around? The sound of his voice in reception seemed to be the signal for her to appear, all flushed and girly, asking him to fix one of the machines in her office. As if he could tell one end of a laser printer from the other. Or knew anything about computer screens. We haven't been able to watch Channel Four since he adjusted our horizontal hold.

'OK,' he decreed now. 'Sandra isn't here, so Annie will take her vote. She knows her best. Now, who's for Dreamland putting up a bigger sign? Hands.'

Declan's hand shot up, followed by Gerry's, moving a lot more slowly.

'Where's Sandra's vote?' Declan turned to me.

'She's voting against.' I gave him an evil smile.

'She wouldn't . . .' he began.

'Against?' Gerry called.

I put up both my hands.

Barney could hardly hold his up, for laughing.

Declan went puce. 'That's cheating! Sandra wouldn't . . .'

'Oh, for Christ sake!' Gerry got to his feet. 'The no's have it. Now get back to work.'

Declan scowled but said nothing. Barney said he'd probably used up his quota of big words anyway.

18

The queue at the off-licence moved at a snail's pace.
The dopey girl who double-checked every single price
with the even dopier night manager was on the till.
Her regulars were wise enough to choose only cans
or bottles with price stickers on them. Tonight there
were a lot of strangers in.

'Price check on Rocco Valpolicella D.O.C.,
aplease?' she called loudly.

Another wait while dopey night manager looked
up his price list.

The couple queuing in front of me bickered non-
stop. Having accused her weary-looking mate of
everything from mass murder to being congenitally
lazy, the thin woman moved on to what was clearly
the root of all her dissatisfaction – money.

'Just tell her we can't afford to pay any more. She's
only minding two small children.'

'*You* tell her. You yap to her about everything else.'

'I'm not discussing money with her. That's your
job.'

'You picked her!'

'How was I supposed to know that she'd raise her
rates the minute the kids settled in.'

The queue suddenly lurched forward and the bick-
erers put three bottles of wine on the counter.

'Price check on Chilean Santa Monica, aplease?'

While I waited I checked that the sticker on my bottle of Chateauneuf-du-pape was still intact. I had chosen this bottle specially. Not just for the sticker, but because I wanted a special wine to go with the meal I was cooking for Gerry. I was hoping for a romantic night in, and not just for my own selfish pleasure. Gerry was totally frustrated with the Boucher case. Despite putting in horrendously long hours, he was getting nowhere with it, mainly because Boucher refused to budge on his demand to keep the investigation low-key. Determined to cheer Gerry up, I was planning a really special supper for him.

The bickering couple left, and I handed my wine to dopey girl, taking care to present the bottle with the price sticker facing her.

'I'm in a bit of a rush.' I put the exact amount in her hand.

'Price check on Chateauneuf-du-pape . . .' she began.

'No! The price is *on* it. See.' I pointed to the sticker.

'That's last week's colour. This week's is blue. Price check on Chateauneuf-du-pape, aplease,' she yelled.

I made it home with my sanity intact. Most nights Gerry and I cooked dinner together, except for when we ordered a takeaway, which was becoming all too frequent these days. Tonight was going to be different. Tonight we were going to set aside all work matters and share a leisurely meal, listen to our favourite music and discuss our lives and dreams, the way couples did in fictional TV movies.

Overhearing the bickering couple in the off-licence had reminded me, if I needed it, of how fortunate we were not to have kids. We didn't have to worry about the cost of childminders or shelling out for expensive school uniforms. Although Gerry did send a tidy sum to Arizona every month for child support. I slugged down a large vodka.

He was barely in the door when I handed him a Scotch, ice cubes clinking merrily.

'What's all this?' he smiled.

'An aperitif. Now sit down and relax. I don't want you to do a single thing tonight, except chill out.'

He didn't object. Seemed glad to put his feet up and watch the news while I cooked, although it's no secret that I'll never win any culinary awards. Still. I dashed about grilling steaks, steaming vegetables and making a hideously complicated salad from a recipe Pino gave me. I hadn't known you could *cook* lettuce. I spent so long trying to arrange the now slippery leaves artistically, I forgot about the steaks until a plume of blue smoke alerted me, but as they were still this side of charcoal, I knew Gerry wouldn't complain.

'As long as it's dead and not cold, I'll eat it,' he once assured Pino when he quizzed him about how he liked his meat.

I covered the steaks with a rich pepper sauce. Served them with a trio of green vegetables. Then rearranged the limp salad in a more open dish so I could surround it with tiny triangles of toasted brown bread to perk it up.

'No chips?' Viewing the table, Gerry's smile was a tad strained.

'Ta-ra!' I uncovered a plate of fat, golden chips.

'Ah, you're my dream woman, do you know that?' He piled a mountain of chips on to his plate. 'What did I do to deserve this?'

'Don't worry.' I filled his glass to the rim. 'I'll think of a way for you to repay me.'

'Em . . .' he munched happily. 'Are we talking a threat or a promise here?' His eyes smiled at me.

'Drink your wine,' I said huskily.

The steaks were surprisingly tasty, if bordering on the carcinogenic. The pepper sauce disguised their burned edges perfectly. The wine didn't need disguising, it was superb. Between us we made short work of it. The gods smiled on us because the phone didn't ring once, and neither of us mentioned the Boucher case. The background music was courtesy of Gerry's favourite CD, and by the time Van was singing lovingly about a brown-eyed girl, Gerry was looking more relaxed than he had in weeks.

'How was your steak?' I finally asked.

'Perfect.' He gave me a lazy smile.

'Not *too* well done?'

'It was perfect.'

'Good.'

'What happened to your curls?' he drained his glass.

'My curls?'

'Yeah. You came into the office one day with your hair all curly and . . .'

'*Curly*? You liked it . . . *curly*?' I had major problems with the word frizzy.

'Course I did. You know how I like it when you get all flushed, and . . . your hair gets all tousled . . . and wild and . . . the way you look when you're in the bath, and you're all soapy and soft and . . .' He leaned over to touch my wrist, his slim fingers curling around it making my pulse race.

Yet part of me was still trying to figure out those

comments about my hair. Were they for real? I spent great chunks of my life straightening my disobedient mop. Forcing it into decreed fashions. Trying to protect it from getting damp and out of control. Now he tells me he prefers it *tousled*? The way he was looking at me, his eyes so warm and inviting, I knew he had to be telling the truth. He honestly preferred my wild hair to the sleek, elegant manes we were surrounded by lately.

Thrown by the unexpectedness of this compliment, I reached out to the empty wine bottle. 'It's . . . it's all gone,' I said dumbly.

He put down his napkin, came around the table and, taking my chin in his hand, tilted my head back gently. 'Show me your tongue.'

I did as instructed. He took the bottle, tilted it and drained the last few drops of wine on to my waiting tongue. 'Swallow,' he instructed, his eyes on my mouth.

He called it savouring the last of the vintage. I called it foreplay. I was right. We were entwined on the carpet before the last drop slid down the back of my throat. Unwilling to lose precious seconds by going upstairs, we undressed each other speedily without unlocking our mouths. Van was still growling, and my best panties were airborne when the phone shrilled.

'Ignore it,' I groaned against Gerry's mouth.

A deep, familiar voice filled the room. 'Tom O'Neill here, Gerry. If you're there, will you pick up, please? We've had a reported sighting of a body in the bay. Just been confirmed. A woman. Blonde hair, they think. And a long dark coat. You'll need to get down there fast if you want . . .'

★ ★ ★

Speeding along the quays we were overtaken by two Garda cars. An ambulance shot past at breakneck speed. We had little need of Tom's directions – the trail of flashing blue lights led us to the scene. At the sea wall Gerry parked the jeep and hurried into the gathering crowd. I held back. He stopped to exchange words with a young garda before turning to call me. And still I hesitated. The water's edge might be a magnet for all these uniformed men, but I found it repellent.

There was small talk going on all around me. A gruff voice remarked on the weather. Said it was a mild night. Bright, which was helpful in these situations.

'Grim work,' one of the Gardai commented as they stood watching a motor launch set out across the water.

Several people were talking into mobiles, then the ambulance backed up noisily, edging as close as possible to the water.

'You think it could be the Boucher girl?' I heard Gerry ask.

'Hard to say.' The tall spare garda stamped his feet as if the night were cold instead of April-mild. 'General description fits. But if the body has been in the water any length of time, we'll have to wait for the post-mortem. You know what the sea can do to a body.'

Terrified that I might disgrace myself by throwing up in front of all these seasoned professionals, I moved further back, regretting that I hadn't stayed in the jeep when Gerry gave me the choice. But as his co-investigator I couldn't shy away from such scenes for ever. I'd have to learn to cope. Looking at Gerry, I wondered if anyone ever really did. He looked grey. As if he were also feeling the non-existent cold.

A sudden call from the cruiser galvanised the watchers. They surged forward as I hesitated. I had no wish to see a drowned body.

A hand on my shoulder made me jump. 'Annie?' A long-time Garda friend of Gerry's was standing beside me. Malachy Egan, once a humble desk sergeant, now wearing the lighter blue uniform of a chief superintendent. 'What are you doing here?'

'I'm working the Boucher case with Gerry.'

'Oh.' He was surprised. 'Well, you're wasting your time here. There won't be a positive ID until after the PM,' he babbled on in Garda shorthand. 'She's been in the water quite a while, and there's an amount of facial trauma. One of the divers thinks it might have been caused by a ship's propeller. Not something you'd want to leave your fireside to see.'

The ground began to tilt. Then Gerry was beside me, putting a supportive arm through mine.

'It's not Caroline,' he said.

'You can tell?' Malachy was surprised.

He nodded. 'It's not her. She has black roots. Caroline is a natural blonde.'

'Thank God.' I slumped against him in relief.

'She's *somebody*'s daughter,' he said bleakly. 'Somebody's child.'

'I'll see you, Gerry. Night, Annie.' Malachy put his mobile away and went to join the group by the launch. As they parted to let him in, I got a clear view of the stretcher. A thin wrist hung over the edge, ending in a small, almost childlike hand, the nails painted blood red and dripping with seawater.

★ ★ ★

We drove home in silence. Turning into our road you could pick out our house from the rest, because in our rush we had left the lights blazing. It didn't make our return any less grim. The messy living room didn't help. It looked like a wild, raucous party had come to a sudden halt there, the festivities abandoned without warning. Even my scattered clothes had a forlorn look about them. I had taken such care in choosing them for this special dinner. Determined to cheer Gerry up. And I had, until the phone call came.

I picked up my clothes glumly, collecting Gerry's shirt and tie, which he had abandoned when the call came to throw on a sweater instead. You don't hang about buttoning up a shirt when there's a body to be identified. Trying to blot out the image of those scarlet nails, I began clearing the table. Threw the empty wine bottle in the bin, on top of the unused condom.

Gerry came into the kitchen, reaching past me to put the kettle on. He took out two mugs with comical Darby and Joan faces on them. A gift from Fiona for his birthday.

'I don't want tea.' I pushed away the Joan mug.

'I'm not making tea.' He splashed whiskey into the mugs.

Ignoring my protests, he forced a hot whisky into my hand. 'Drink it. It'll help you sleep,' he promised.

It didn't. I lay in bed wide awake, listening to his even breathing. Whenever I closed my eyes I saw that pathetically small hand with its scarlet nail varnish, dripping with sea water.

I finally did sleep, but fitfully, and only after convincing myself that I had to put aside that terrible image, block it from my mind, otherwise I would never make a detective.

I woke to find myself pinned to the bed by a dead weight. Gerry had managed to wrap his arms *and* legs around me in his sleep, and was lying across me, his head buried in my armpit. When I tried to make myself comfortable, he groaned in his sleep.

'Shhh.' I smoothed his hair. Tried to flatten the stubborn little bit that poked up on the crown, defying all efforts to curb it. Some day I was going to get some scissors and get rid of that anarchic little tuft.

'Annie?' he mumbled. 'You asleep?'

'Yes.'

'Good.' His whole body relaxed, and he began to breathe evenly again. Watching him, I wondered how many years of detective work it would take before I reached that level of professionalism. Then I kissed the top of his head and went back to sleep, comforted by the feel of his warm body against mine.

19

'Do you believe that bloody man?' Gerry slammed down the phone. 'He gets his PA to ring me? His only daughter is missing, and he gets his bloody PA to check on our progress?'

'Maybe he . . . ?'

'Gives a shit? I doubt it!' He tapped a name into his computer. 'If it wasn't for the girl, I'd drop this case right now.'

'If it wasn't for the girl, there wouldn't be a case,' I said.

'OK, Pollyanna,' he said, giving me a sly grin, 'let's get moving. I want you to go through the list of people we've interviewed so far. Print out the names and addresses of everyone I put a black mark against.'

'A black mark?' I smiled. 'Isn't that a bit melodramatic?'

'A biro mark, then. I need to talk to them again. Reinterview everyone she spoke to in the week leading up to her disappearance.'

'That's a lot of people, Gerry.'

'Did you think this job would be easy?'

I shrugged.

'Print out that list. There has to be something I missed. Some tiny clue staring us in the face. I don't believe a seventeen-year-old can cover her tracks as well as she has, not without help.'

'You think someone is hiding her?'

He stared at me for a second. 'I'm saying there's always a clue. It's just a matter of finding it. Let's start with the housekeeper, and work backwards.'

'What about Boucher? He was the last person to speak to Caroline as far as we . . .'

'Forget him. He's busy with the gnomes.'

'Gnomes?'

'Zurich?'

'Oh. Yes.'

The phone rang at his elbow. When he ignored it, I picked it up. 'Gerry Dunning's office.'

'Annie?' Sandra said. 'Barney's back. He's on his way up.'

I smiled at Gerry. 'Barney's back.'

Even he had to grin. We already knew that Barney had caught the graveyard muggers. It was practically on the news. One surprise, though. There *was* no gang. Only one fleet-footed teenager. Still, the old git disguise had worked a treat. Convinced that he had a frail old age pensioner in his sights, the mugger had attacked Barney viciously, from behind, only to find himself flying through the air courtesy of a well-honed judo throw.

He was probably even more shocked to find himself being kneed in the groin and told to 'Shut the fuck up' when he pleaded for mercy. Barney has his own, very idiosyncratic, investigative techniques. He dragged the hooded mugger to the Honda Civic, handcuffed him to the door and practically threw him at the Gardai when they arrived. By then a small crowd had gathered. And word spread like wildfire. In the short time Barney spent giving evidence to the Gardai, he became the hero of the combined residents' groups. Lauded by blue-rinsed matrons, and given an open invitation to their Sunday tea dances, he had signed two petitions for the restoration of capital punishment for anyone who mugged an OAP, before he excused himself and headed back to the agency.

'Wahay!' Barney strode in like a conquering hero, his kipper tie in ribbons, his moustache hanging out of his top pocket.

'Next case,' he rubbed his hands. 'Come on, Annie. Line them up. Superdetective is here!'

I didn't dare look at Gerry. But fair dues, he congratulated Barney whole-heartedly.

'Well done. We're already getting calls offering you similar work.'

'Naturally! I'm king of the world, I am. Only kryptonite can stop me.' He stuck the moustache back on and strutted around. 'Who am I, Annie?'

'Supergit?' I asked.

He made a run at me. I ducked behind Gerry, and the three of us almost ended up on the floor in a laughing heap.

Then Barney went and spoiled everything.

'So what's happening with the Boucher case, Gerry? Any progress there?'

After that, everything went downhill. Even my faithful printer packed up, refusing to print out the list of required names no matter how hard I thumped it.

I was giving it one last warning thump when Declan came in to announce that he had wrapped up his feuding neighbour case. With excellent results. He had presented his bereaved cat owners with irrefutable clinical evidence that their beloved pussy had died from a virulent strain of cat flu, not a mysterious poison administered by their neighbours. He then showed them even clearer evidence that their beech tree had succumbed to canker. An old enemy in that particular neighbourhood. He also passed on photographic evidence that it was a frequently trespassing mutt that had done for their award-winning azaleas, not their neighbours' beloved German shepherd. And peace broke out in Lilac Grove.

Declan handed me a nice fat cheque to deposit in our bank account.

'It's strangely satisfying, reuniting battling neighbours.' He nearly smiled.

I was handing him his next case when Gerry arrived. Fresh from reinterviewing Caroline's college tutor, it was patently obvious from his body language that this had been another wasted trip.

But Declan obviously never sat the body language exam.

'How's it goin', Ger?' he asked. 'Things finally moving on the Boucher case?'

'Everyone hits a bad patch,' I consoled him as we tried to eat the worst takeaway that had ever masqueraded as real food.

He pushed his plate away. 'Where did you get that vindaloo? It's poisonous.'

It was. But I finished mine. When I'm premenstrual, I'd eat a horse.

'I could make sandwiches?' I offered as I cleared the table.

He didn't reply. But it *was* Friday. His stalled case aside, Friday is always a bad day for Gerry. It's the day he makes his weekly phone call to his sons. Before leaving the office he had made his call, and, as usual, came out afterwards white-faced and silent. Even stopping off at our friendly local hadn't improved his mood. We had one quick drink, listened to the local bore explaining how manned space flights were to blame for all this mixed weather we were having this spring, and headed home. Then, of course, I went and bought the vindaloo from hell.

We were getting ready for bed when I made a last-ditch attempt to cheer him up, aware that it might show me in a very poor light, but willing to risk it if it helped wipe that look of defeat off his face.

'Mags made a right fool of *me* the other day,' I confessed, then told him the saga of St Martin's Lane, explaining how Mags had tricked me into buying her a Big Mac and French fries. How Fred pumped my leg. The way Mags had raised my hopes by leading me to, not one, but three dilapidated houses before finally settling on number twenty-four.

'And that turned out to be a rat-infested dump,' I laughed.

'But she said she saw Caroline there?' He wasn't smiling.

'Yes. Can you imagine?' I waited for him to laugh.

'You think she was mistaken?' He was as serious as the grave.

'She wasn't mistaken! That's my whole point, Gerry. I was such a gullible fool. I believed her, but it turned out she made the whole thing up after seeing that article in the morning paper. The woman missed her vocation. She should be writing fairy tales.'

'You reckon?' He frowned.

I changed tack. 'How about these beauties?' I uncovered my knees. 'I got these running out of that dump of a house. I haven't had scabs like this since I was eight.'

His frown deepened. 'I did wonder about them.'

'You did?' Bloody hell, he *had* noticed them. So much for doctoring the stretch-tights.

'Are you positive Caroline wasn't in that flat?' He wasn't interested in my knees.

'Flat?' I sulked. 'It wasn't a flat. It was a derelict squat! Filthy. Cigarette butts everywhere. Even the rats were leaving the day I was there! Caroline Boucher wouldn't set foot in a place like that unless she had a gun to her head. Oh no! Don't give me that look. The whole point of Mags's story was that she saw Caroline going in and out on a boyfriend's arm.'

'Have you spoken to Mags since?'

'Spoken to her? She's lucky I didn't throttle her.'

'Has she approached you?'

'Of course. You know Mags, persistence is her middle name. Her new scam is pretending she got the house number wrong.'

I went to the bathroom to fetch my knee ointment. No need for subterfuge now the cat was out of the bag. I sat on the bed and started lashing the antibacterial on to my knees.

He watched me. 'Mags said she got the house number wrong?'

'Yeah. Claiming dyslexia. What next? She's a stigmata?' I laughed.

Not a flicker of a smile.

'Shit.' I squeezed the tube too hard, sending a white oily blob shooting on to the dark blue duvet I had paid a small fortune for at a pre-summer sale.

'Give me that.' He took the tube. 'So there *was* a

number on the house?' He smoothed the ointment across my knees. So gently my eyes began to close.

'Was there a number, Annie?'

'What? Oh, yeah. Number twenty-four.' Gerry's hands could soothe a saint. I leaned towards them as he made small circular movements with his fingers. 'Trust me, nobody was living in that house. Except rats.' I gave an involuntary shiver.

'Did you check out number forty-two?' He put the cap back on the ointment.

'Why would I check forty-two when Mags said it was twenty-four?' *And even more important, why did you stop rubbing my knees?*

'Where are my jeans?' He was running around like a headless chicken.

'The ones you just . . . ? In the linen basket. Where are you going?'

He was in the bathroom, dressing. 'If you want to come with me, throw on something dark. And get a move on.' He pulled on his shoes, not bothering with socks.

'We'll never get this open.' Gerry leaned against the big door in defeat.

We had made a dozen attempts at prising open the door of number forty-two, without success. The door was old, but rock solid.

'What would happen if you took a run at it?'

'I'd break my shoulder. Maybe just my collarbone.' He stepped back.

'We need Mags's friend, Mickey.'

'I'd settle for a grappling hook.' He looked up at a tall first-floor window. 'Is it my imagination, or is that window gaping slightly?'

'You're not thinking of climbing up there?' I was horrified. If he tried that and slipped, he could fall forty feet into the street area below, where we were now standing. Even worse, he might land on the spear-tipped iron railings that surrounded the place.

He was now intent on the window. 'I bet I could force that. It looks rain-damaged. If I got my hand underneath I could ram it open.'

'Who do you think you are? Arnold Schwarzenegger?'

The moment I said it, I knew it was a mistake. It sounded too much like a challenge. Now he'd have to prove he could do it. I had spent three years in close proximity to three tough detectives and still hadn't learned when to keep my gob shut.

'That drainpipe looks safe.' Gerry was spoiling to climb it.

Safe? It looked as if a puff of wind would send it crashing to the ground. Along with anyone fool enough to be straddling it.

'If I can get to the top there,' he pointed, 'I could reach across to the window. It's definitely ajar. Swollen by rain would, you say?'

'Yeah! Swollen and rotten. Ready to collapse, like this whole building.' I kept picturing what those spiked railings could do to a falling body.

'Where's your sense of adventure, Annie?' Gerry was back on form again. 'It's a way in, isn't it?'

'That window is nearly forty feet above the . . .'

'Don't exaggerate. I could drop back to safety if I had to.' His mind made up, he was already moving, finding perilous toeholds in the brickwork, pulling himself up the shaky drainpipe. Playing bloody Spiderman.

'Please, Gerry!' I pleaded with his blue-jeaned behind. 'Wait till morning. I'll have Mickey pick the lock first thing. We'd be inside the house in seconds. With no risk.'

The word risk seemed to spur him on. He was almost there now, reaching across to the window. One hand clutching the swaying pipe, the other stretching . . .

'Careful, Gerry! That pipe is loose.'

He looked down, gave me a devilish smile and, gripping the drainpipe with his knees, deliberately waved both hands. 'Look, Ma! No hands!'

I screamed. He grabbed the drainpipe. 'Annie! You put the heart crossways in me.'

Afraid to make a sound now, I chewed my lip half raw, watching in silence as he used his body weight to force the window open. Then he was gone.

'Gerry?' I whispered.

A muffled yell. 'I'm OK.'

I almost wet myself with relief. And pride. All sorts of hazards could have been waiting in that dark, boarded-up house. Anyone else would have held off until daylight. Not Gerry. A born detective, he just got on with the job. Any second now he'd be down in the basement, searching for clues. Of course, he *could* have waited for Mickey to pick the lock. I dismissed such a disloyal thought. He was in now, and if he was right about Mags mixing up the house numbers, we could be halfway to finding Caroline before daylight. This was what real detective work was all about. Not sitting around waiting to snap adulterous husbands in flagrante.

There was a sudden crashing sound from inside the house.

'Gerry?' I screamed.

A cloud of dust shot out the open window. There was a shout. I held my breath.

'*Aaaaaagh!*'

'Gerry?' Almost petrified by fear, I called again, louder this time. '*Gerry?*'

Nothing.

I moved without thinking. Fear of heights forgotten, I was up the drainpipe like an alley cat. Ignoring the way the rusty pipe tore at my scabs, I was at the open window in seconds.

'Gerry?'

I thought I heard a faint cry. I swung inside, dust choking me, clogging my nose and throat.

'Gerry?' I peered into the dark.

The voice was even fainter. '. . . floor's collapsed . . . don't move!'

Of course I moved. Galvanised by fear, I crawled across the creaking floorboards, coughing up dust until I reached the edge of a gaping hole and called down into the utter blackness. 'Gerry?'

'*Aaaaaaaaagh!*'

'I'm coming.' The floorboards swaying beneath me, I was crawling again. Except this time I was going backwards.

20

The casualty team said Gerry was lucky. A tiny Filippino nurse with a dazzling smile said he had angels by his side. I hadn't seen any, just a bunch of sweating firemen and a ginger-bearded paramedic who deserved canonisation. The firemen smashed the heavy door down and got him out at warp speed as the remains of the two ceilings creaked ominously above them.

Watching him being stretchered out, torn and bleeding, was enough to have me parting with my vindaloo.

'You were very brave.' A dust-covered fireman handed me into the ambulance.

Brave? Screaming like a harridan? Throwing up on a fireman?

'Is he going to die?' I asked the casualty team. Repeatedly.

They banned me from the emergency room. Possibly because when I heard someone listing his suspected injuries, the remains of the vindaloo hurtled up my throat before I could stop it. Someone escorted me to the bathroom, where I lost all track of time. The next thing I knew I was listening to Barney's voice as he wiped dirt, snot and blood from my face, telling me that Gerry was going to be OK.

'OK?' I echoed. 'Didn't you hear his list of injuries?

206

Broken ribs, a dislocated knee, a fractured something or other. And all that blood. He's going to die, isn't he?'

'He's not going to die! What you heard was a list of possible injuries. Anyway, broken ribs don't kill you.'

'They can pierce your lungs.' I was inconsolable.

'Nothing pierced his lungs. What he has are lots of contusions. That's where all the blood was coming from.' He dried my face, his own milk white with anxiety. 'Gerry has a hide like a rhinoceros. You're getting yourself in a state for nothing.'

'Then why won't they tell me what's happening?'

Out in the corridor I spotted a man in a white coat. Recognising him from the A&E team, I ran after him, tugging at his starched sleeve. 'Is he going to die?'

He frowned at my bloodstained clothes. 'Those lacerations need seeing to.' He tried to check my badly torn hands.

'They're nothing.' I stuck them behind my back. 'Is he going to die?'

I knew I was behaving badly, but I was consumed by fear. Sheer overwhelming terror at even the faintest possibility that I might lose Gerry. The fear was a giant fist squeezing the air out of my lungs and all rational thought from my brain.

'He's a very lucky man,' White Coat said calmly. 'We can fix broken bones.'

'Thank you,' I moaned, slumping against him in relief, leaving a trail of blood and snot on his immaculate white coat.

I made a deal with the casualty doctor. If he let me see Gerry for a couple of minutes, I'd be quiet.

And I'd have my own cuts seen to. He gave in. But the sight of Gerry lying on the bloodstained table had me reneging on my promises. He looked like he had fallen into a threshing machine.

The ambulance driver came in to have a quick look at him. 'Amazing! When I got the call, I thought for sure I'd be picking up a DOA. And here he is, looking robust.' He glanced, curiously, at Gerry's chart. 'Fell through both floors? Christ he's lucky. Tell him to buy a lotto ticket.'

'He's in bits,' I protested, furious at this lack of respect for someone on the verge of death.

'Superficial,' he said, dismissing Gerry's wounds, and hurried away to answer another emergency call.

That's when I finally accepted that Gerry *wasn't* going to die.

An Indian nurse cleaned my knees. Dug splinters out of them. I didn't make a sound until she mentioned the tetanus shot.

'An injection? Oh no. I can't stand needles.'

She glanced around helplessly, the syringe dangling from her gloved hand.

Barney appeared and took me by the shoulders. 'Squeeze my hand and look at the wall chart.' Squeezing his hand helped, but looking at the wall chart was a bad move. Or maybe I looked at the wrong one. The one I chose had a healthy looking man on it with his pink innards showing, so I was already feeling queasy when the smell of antiseptic hit me, and everything went black.

Declan arrived in time to see me being revived by two nurses.

'Jesus! Annie as well?' He was shocked, his hand

shaking so badly it rattled the hospital trolley when he tried to touch me.

Feeling better now, I was able to reassure him. Explain that I was fine, just needlephobic. 'And Gerry has nine lives. He's going to be all right.'

I became the comforter, covering his hand with mine, my heart going out to him even though he fancied Naomi and I could smell whiskey on his breath.

Next morning Gerry was sitting up, demanding his clothes.

'My ribs will heal,' he insisted. 'And a dislocated knee never killed anyone. That knee survived a gunshot wound, remember?' He indicated his hugely plastered knee.

'Yes, but it has to be kept immobilised. That's what the plaster is for. And they want to keep you under observation for a few days.'

'No chance.' He pulled a monitor tag off his chest, grimacing when it took several dark hairs with it.

'You had a very bad fall, Gerry! You lost so much blood, the ambulance driver thought he'd be picking up a corpse!' I tried to scare him into behaving. His face was so bruised and swollen it was difficult to tell if it worked.

'You do know that you fell through *two* floors?' I emphasised.

'I wasn't counting,' he growled.

At least his brain was still intact.

They moved him from Accident and Emergency into a little side room, and that's when things got totally out of hand. Half the Garda force in Ireland came to see him, some of them straight off shift, still in uniform, all of them wanting to know exactly what happened, if he had been set up by some blackguard.

'Are you sure it was an accident?' one of them asked as I walked him back to the corridor.

I was still trying to convince him when Fiona arrived. A quick hug for me, and she bustled into the little side room, her huge bulk forcing everyone else out. As the gardai filed out past me, Pino tiptoed in carrying a large basket of fruit. And *wine*?

Sandra arrived in tears.

By mid-afternoon half of Dublin seemed to know about the accident. Naomi and Tudi drifted in on a cloud of Chanel No. 5. A get-well card arrived from handsome optometrist, an email from our ex-tenants, the IT consultants.

Sandra ate Gerry's grapes and told him she had banned Mags from the agency for life.

'She'll never get past our door again. Not even if there's a mountain of newspapers cluttering up my reception.' She spat pips into a plastic sample cup.

Gerry said nothing.

I stood in the doorway, watching him. Knowing that all this kindness was wearing him out. I knew how he felt, because I was in receipt of the overflow. Barney and Declan kept offering to stay over in the house with me until Gerry was discharged. Fiona invited me to stay with her and Pino. Even Naomi tried to be nice, telling me to stop worrying because it was making me look old and haggard.

The hospital staff said I shouldn't be afraid to ask questions. 'We're here to answer them,' the consultant said, before flying off to Tenerife for a golfing weekend.

Everyone was being supportive.

'He's doing very well. Lucky he was so fit. Still, we'd like to keep an eye on him for a few days, watch out for any opportunistic infections. His ribs are badly bruised and some of those cuts were filthy.' The big red-faced house doctor looked as if he should be out turning the sod. Maybe even dragging him back from Tenerife.

'What about his knee?' I voiced Gerry's main worry. 'How long will that have to remain in plaster?'

'Oh, no more than four or five weeks,' he said happily.

When I gave Gerry the good news he flipped. 'Four weeks? I can't hobble around on a crutch for four weeks! I have work to do.'

I told the nurses it was a mistake reducing his medication. Mildly tranquillised, he *might* stay in bed. With his head clear, he'd have to be stapled to the mattress. They thought I was joking, a second little Filippino nurse barely able to control her giggles, until the ward sister caught him using his mobile, making calls from under the sheets. She tried to confiscate his phone. 'You know the rules, Mr Dunning. No mobiles allowed. They interfere with our machines.'

There was a short, undignified struggle before she was called away to a code blue or pink or something.

'She's a fascist,' Gerry complained. All his complaints were channelled through me, as if I were some kind of freelance medical interpreter.

'You'll be home soon, you can make all the calls you want then,' I humoured him.

'And in the meantime, how do I talk to my boys in Arizona?'

His saintly ex-wife had sent flowers by Interflora – a huge bunch of hothouse blooms that dwarfed every other bouquet in the hospital. The accompanying card was signed by her and his two young sons, with an unbroken line of kisses underneath which I found very unsettling.

But of course he had to phone them. I agreed to keep an eye out for roving nurses. I listened to him chatting to his sons, downplaying his injuries. 'A couple of minor scratches,' he laughed. 'I bet you guys get a lot worse playing American football.'

I pictured them laughing, sitting in the lovely dry heat of Arizona. I wondered what they would think if they could see him. Apart from his other injuries, he had six stitches in his forehead, and there wasn't an inch of his face that didn't have some deep cut or scrape on it. His eyes were turning black, and the slightest movement caused him to grimace in pain.

'OK you guys, I have to go. I'll talk to you tomorrow. If Nurse Ratchet isn't about.'

As he slipped the phone into his pyjama pocket, he caught my look of reproach. 'You didn't expect me to scare them, did you? They're just kids.'

'Finished with that mobile?'

'Sure. I wouldn't want to get the nursing staff in trouble. It's off for the day now.'

Impressed by such thoughtfulness, I put my head gently against his chest, and whispered, 'I love you,' then jumped when the mobile rang in my ear.

Ten minutes later he was still pleading innocence. I finally kissed his torn hand in forgiveness, making him smile. He was still smiling when he suddenly looked over my shoulder, his bloodshot eyes widening in surprise.

I turned.

Simon Boucher was standing in the doorway.

Maybe it was the sneaky way he crept up on us, or maybe it was because I needed someone to blame for Gerry's accident, but seeing him standing there like a model for a Saga cruise, I was suffused with a rage so powerful it almost frightened me.

Completely oblivious to my fury, they shook hands like two business colleagues before a dull shareholders' meeting, both of them behaving as if Gerry wasn't lying there looking like he'd been chewed by sharks.

To be fair, Boucher did look slightly uneasy.

'Your receptionist told me what happened. You were working on Caroline's case when this . . . ?'

'Yes.'

Boucher sat down, hard. 'It *was* an accident?'

'Oh yes. I had information that she was seen in a certain place. I went to investigate and . . .' Gerry's casual shrug ended in a wince.

'How did you . . . ?' Boucher stared at his injured leg. At the white plaster cast resting above the crisp hospital sheets.

Gerry hesitated for a second. 'I . . . I fell through a floor. The boards were rotten.' He made it sound like an everyday mishap. As if falling through two floors and ending up in a hospital emergency room was all part of the daily ritual of any private investigator.

Boucher looked unhappy. In a manicured, expertly coiffed, Armani-suited way.

'My injuries are mostly superficial,' Gerry reassured him.

'What about your leg? That looks serious.'

'Dislocated knee. I had an old injury there which possibly weakened it.'

Weakened? I'd had enough of this macho shit.

'He went into that house a superbly fit man!' I burst out. 'You can see for yourself the condition he was in when he came out! That knee will never be the same again! Plus he has cracked ribs, abrasions all over his body, stitches in his head! He was concussed, unconscious, practically comatose . . .' I ran out of complaints, then remembered the ambulance driver's remark. 'The ambulance nearly headed for the morgue!'

Boucher paled. 'I had no idea. But it *was* an accident?' His brow furrowed.

'Well, nobody pushed him, if that's what you mean. But he did incur life-threatening injuries while working on *your daughter's* case.'

Gerry shot me a furious look, but I wasn't going to pussyfoot around Boucher any longer. He had only paid us our usual advance, it wasn't like he was paying us in gold nuggets.

'I honestly didn't think there would be any great risk involved, Mr Dunning. On the contrary . . .'

'Risks are all part of my job.'

'Gerry!' I nearly choked.

'What about your hospital bills?'

'They'll be enormous!' I jumped in before Gerry could stop me.

'Leave it, Annie,' he said.

'Don't tell me to leave it!' I hissed. 'I'm the one who has to balance the bloody books. This case already has us out of pocket. Now our insurance will shoot up. All we need now is for the developer who owns that property to sue you for breaking and entering.'

Boucher seemed startled.

'Don't act so shocked, Mr Boucher. You're a banker, aren't you? Are you really surprised to hear that property developers are a litigious lot?'

'That's enough, Annie.' In between the cuts, Gerry's face was turning the shade of his bed sheets. In fact, not so much white as colourless.

I shook his restraining hand off my arm.

'Because of *your* case we may have to file for bankruptcy!' I hissed at Boucher, and left.

The hospital steps were swarming with covert smokers. For the first time ever, I envied them. Wished I shared their filthy, antisocial habit. Wished I had something to stick in my mouth and put a match to. Chewing my lip borderline raw hadn't helped calm me down. Watching the girl next to me inhaling blissfully, I almost snatched the cigarette from her mouth.

'Miss McHugh?' A burly man in a dark suit approached me.

'Yes?'

'Mr Boucher says will you wait, please?'

I remembered this muscle-bound idiot. Barney called him Odd Job. He was Boucher's driver. I had puzzled over his peculiar body shape, wondering why he had bigger muscles on one side than the other, until Barney enlightened me. Pointed out that the enormous bulge near his left armpit was a gun. That people like Boucher invariably employed ex-SAS men as their drivers-cum-bodyguards.

The horrifying bulge was less than three feet away

from me now. I was staring at it when Boucher came down the steps.

'Thank you, Trevor.'

Odd Job slipped away.

'I'm sorry about . . . Gerry's accident, Miss McHugh. I hope this will help.' He held out a cheque.

I snatched it from his hand without a glance.

'I'll match that when you find my daughter.'

His big shiny car pulled up beside us, a sombre Odd Job at the wheel. Boucher stepped in and it drove away soundlessly.

21

It was May Day. The first day of summer, and the temperatures seemed all set to prove it. Gerry's four days of hospital observation were up. He was due to be discharged at the weekend, maybe even earlier. I hummed along with the radio as I drove to work. The lads were solving cases at the rate of knots, and Boucher's cheque was nestling in our bank account, a large enough sum to keep the bank manager off my back for months. On impulse I pulled over and rang Fiona. She hadn't been to see Gerry yesterday, which was unusual, though not surprising. She was finding the final weeks of her pregnancy tiring. She was huge – at least two Hindenbergs wide now. And depending on her mood, she was accusing the baby of either pressing on her bladder, or squashing her lungs, or giving her a hiatus hernia. Her *joie de vivre* was dwindling by the hour.

Pino answered her mobile. He sounded tense. 'She's not feeling well, Annie.'

'What is it this time? Bladder? Lungs? Hernia?'

'No. Nothing like that. She's feeling . . . heavy . . . listless. And her back hurts.'

'She *is* pregnant!' I tried not to laugh. His naivety about the whole business *was* laughable. He was a well-travelled man, spoke five languages, could charm a restaurant full of diners with a flick of his olive-skinned wrist, cope with staff tantrums without turning a hair, produce a five-course gourmet meal for eighty in a kitchen criss-crossed with electric cables, semi-hysterical sound men and burning hot television lights. But let his pregnant wife give a mild grunt of discomfort, and he collapsed like a poorly baked soufflé.

Watching the morning traffic speed past, I had a sudden terrifying thought. 'She's not in labour is she?'

'Maeve says no. But she is feeling strange. Dizzy. Maeve says for her to have a long, relaxing, seaweed bath. But Fi says the smell of seaweed is making her nauseous. Could you come offer, Hannie?' His accent thickened. A sure sign of rising panic. 'She would lick you to be here.'

'I'm on my way.' Risking the ire of my fellow motorists, I made an illegal U-turn.

All the way to Fiona's I kept praying she wasn't in labour. She was my best friend and I would do anything for her – except watch her give birth. I couldn't ignore her request to come over, but at the first hint of a contraction I'd be out of there like a rocket. Where the hell was mad Maeve, anyway? Shouldn't she be there? Holding Fiona's hand, humming mantras? Telling her she was at one with the great mother universe? She was the one who had talked Fiona into a home birth. Then again, the baby wasn't due for another two weeks. Maeve obviously knew the difference between real and false labour – Pino was panicking unnecessarily. He'd had plenty of practice at that lately. When Fiona had had severe heartburn one night, he'd got on the blower and insisted that Maeve drive over and deliver the baby immediately, only to discover that what he considered second stage labour was just the after-effects of the two chocolate eclairs Fiona had gorged after supper.

This morning's rumpus was probably a three-eclair panic.

Even before Pino opened the front door, I could hear screaming. In the centre of the big, open-plan living room, Fiona was lying naked on a mattress, her modesty protected by a light cotton sheet which was sticking to her huge bump, which was in turn caked in sweat. Along with her hair and face.

'Wait till I get my hands on that bitch Maeve,' she puffed.

'You OK?' I swallowed hard.

She stopped puffing. 'Oh yeah. I'm perfect,' she snarled. 'Except for being in excruciating agony. Don't worry, it comes and goes. Bound to be false labour. Maeve said early contractions are like gentle ripples on a calm seashore. These are more your fucking tidal waves hitting the rocks,' she spat.

'Is Maeve on her way?' The word contraction was enough to have me dry-retching.

'We can't rich her.' Pino was quivering like a half-set jelly.

'Her line is busy. She's probably talking to some other gullible fool. Telling *her* to listen to the whale song. To enjoy the little rippling contractions that . . . Oh sweet Jesus . . . sweet Jesus . . .' Fiona was screaming again.

'Should I . . . ball something? Ball water maybe?' Pino's eyes were deep pools of terror.

Fiona was almost convulsing on the bed. She had been rehearsing for this baby's birth for months, even took yoga classes to help her deal with the more severe contractions when they eventually came. Surely at this early stage she should be coping better?

'I think my waters just broke,' she panted. 'Will you have a look?'

Oh God and His holy mother, help me. Please. I took a deep breath. Told myself it was only water, the fluid of life that we all float in before our entry into the world. I lifted the sheet a millimetre and took a peek. A silent scream started somewhere around my toes. but before I could let it out, another emotion took over. I was overcome by such a surge of protectiveness for Fiona that I somehow contained my dread of what was happening. My friend was in big trouble here. Even a medical ignoramus like me could see that. Knew that she shouldn't be lying in a widening pool of dark red blood.

I grabbed Pino so hard he yelped in pain. Only fair.

'Ring an ambulance. Quickly.' I swallowed my own panic. 'Tell them it's an emergency. Quick!'

'What the hell are you whispering about,' Fiona bellowed as he half ran, half staggered out of the room.

I sat on the bed and gave an Oscar-winning performance. 'Nothing for you to worry about, kiddo. I just wanted to give him something to do.' I smiled and took her hand. 'Bloody men. This is woman's stuff, kiddo.' I tried to keep both our hands from shaking. 'You're going to be fine. You *and* the baby. Now take a nice calming breath and show me how well you can do all those exercises you've been practising for months.'

'Fuck off,' she growled, her face glistening with sweat.

'Now, now. No call for that kind of language. You're having a baby. And I'm here to help. I'm here, Fiona,' I chanted as if I were speaking to a child.

'No drugs . . .' she yelled as she twisted on the mattress.

'Don't worry, no one is going to force you to take drugs.'

'I *want* drugs, you stupid bitch,' she screamed. 'I want a feckin' epidural right now! And I want gas and air and pethedine and *oooooooh* . . .' she yelled, her face contorting in pain.

Forty minutes later, Calum Marco Molino came into the world, serene as a buddha and with a belly to match. Oblivious to the fear and hysteria he had triggered in those who loved him, he stretched, yawned, gave a little cry and went back to sleep. His father looked as if he might never sleep again – he had almost succumbed to a fatal coronary en route to the hospital as the wailing ambulance sent traffic scattering so the waiting medical team could beat the world speed record for Caesarean deliveries.

Maeve didn't make it. She was busy elsewhere. Listening to the whale song, I suppose.

I paced the waiting room, anxious for news, doubling over with sympathy pains every few seconds. When Pino finally came to tell me the great news, I threw up all over him. Then we both cried.

I was finally allowed in to see Fiona. She was dry-eyed – a radiant, shimmering Madonna, nursing the only person not traumatised by the whole birthing experience.

I stood there, afraid to breathe.

'Look at him, Annie. Ten pounds four ounces,' she

boasted. 'And everyone said I was carrying water. Huh! They weren't being kicked in the bladder by a size nine foot. Were they, my precious?' She gazed in wonder at her sleeping son. Then turned to ask, 'Does anyone get a smell of sick in here?'

'We owe you, Annie.' Pino stood there in his ruined Armani suit. 'Without your quick thinking, I could have lost both of them.' He was crying again.

'Rubbish,' Fiona giggled, high on happiness and whatever was being dripped into her arm. 'I flew through it. Hardly felt a thing. And nothing could have stopped my boy. Look at the size of him. He's a giant.'

'Like his papa,' Pino sobbed.

'Not really,' Fiona said amiably. 'I think he looks more like my Aunty Cecilia. He even has her hairy back.'

Twenty-four hours later the pain from Fiona's Caesarean section kicked in. Either that or her doctor had cut her medication. She called me at the office, sobbing bitterly.

'I'm in agony, Annie. I can't move. Can't bend. My nipples are like boils. The baby can't feed. And I haven't had a proper bowel movement since Monday. And that wagon of a nurse won't give me another painkiller. She says I'm overprescribed. Bitch. I'm in hell, Annie.'

I tried to calm her. Promised to assure the ward sister that Fiona would be the last person on earth to become addicted to painkillers. Of course I'd have to go to the hospital to do that. And I already had a horrendously busy day ahead of me. Mrs Green's Flopsy was missing again, and an old client of Gerry's had been beaten up in the marital home. I advised him to call the Garda. Especially when I heard that this time his wife had knocked out his front teeth.

'No cops.' He was adamant. 'My missus doesn't know her own strength. Ask Gerry to have a word with her. She'll listen to him. I don't want her charged. How would I manage without her? I found me teeth behind the gas cooker, anyway. The plate isn't even damaged. Tell Gerry to come over. Or maybe you could come yourself?'

Not if I was to get to Fiona. *And* drop in to see Gerry. I wanted to talk to him about the Boucher cheque.

I went to the maternity floor first and found Fiona's door closed. Decided that there was probably a doctor in there doing medical things to her. I chanced a quick peep through the high glass porthole anyway. She was alone. Sleeping like a baby. Her *and* Calum.

A movement by the cot caught my eye. I stood on tiptoe for a better look.

Gerry was leaning over the cot like an unshaven guardian angel. A pretty ferocious one, with his stitched forehead and bruised face. But the tenderness in his black eyes as he offered a slim finger to the baby made my throat constrict. The baby grasped his finger and clung on, and I remembered when I had last seen that look in Gerry's eyes. It was the day before his sons had left for Arizona. We had taken them swimming, sat watching them race each other in the big indoor pool, the younger one making Trojan efforts to overtake his brother. The way Gerry had looked at them that day, his heart in his eyes, had haunted me for weeks. Then they were gone to

America and we were back at work, and life moved on.

A maternity nurse came bustling up behind me. Recognising me from the birth morning hullabaloo, she was extra friendly.

'Is he still in there? He said he only wanted to see Fiona and the baby for five minutes. Time up, Mr Dunning.' She pushed open the door.

'Annie?' Gerry was delighted to see me. 'Come and check this out,' he whispered gleefully. 'This little guy won't let go.'

'Oh yes he will.' The nurse snatched the baby's hand and tucked it under the blanket. 'Now back downstairs with you, Mr Dunning. Mum and baby need their rest.'

'Who trained you? The Waffen SS?' Gerry whispered in disgust as the baby gave a little whimper at being disturbed. Fiona grunted, but didn't move. She was out for the count. Someone had caved in and given her extra painkillers.

'Oh, Mr Dunning, you're just what we need on the maternity floor,' the nurse said sharply. 'Another comedian! Back to your own floor, please. I bet the nurses there are lining up to give *you* a bed bath.'

'A bed bath?' Gerry missed the sarcasm in her tone.

'Nothing like a brisk bed bath, I always say.'

'Jesus.' Gerry moved with extraordinary speed for a man on a crutch. 'She is kidding, isn't she, Annie?'

I shrugged and followed him into the corridor.

'I want my clothes,' he sulked.

'Oh, stop grumbling. Think about that lovely big cheque Simon Boucher gave us. And don't forget, he promised to match it when we find Caroline.'

'Yeah. How did you wrangle that out of him?'

'Wrangle? I used perfectly acceptable business methods. Don't you remember?'

'Not really,' he frowned. 'I was still pretty groggy that day he came in. You didn't . . . ?'

'Would I lie to you about money, Gerry?'

The question hung between us for a second. Gerry and I have a chequered history in that particular area. But he knew that, while I was capable of *bending* the rules with my fee-collecting methods, I would never resort to anything unsavoury.

'Excellent. Now all I have to do is get out of this hellish place. Get the investigation up and running again.' He hopped into the lift, using the crutch as if he'd been practising all his life.

22

Barney and Declan were arguing loudly in my office. Nothing unusual about that, except that they stopped the second I walked in.

'Thanks, lads.' I took their reports. 'Sorry I haven't been around much for the past couple of days. Maybe I should have just moved into the hospital full time.' I laughed.

They didn't respond.

'Problems?' I looked from one solemn face to the other.

Barney cleared his throat. 'We're both more than willing to continue splitting the outstanding cases between us, Annie. Anything to keep the pressure off Gerry.'

'But?' I knew there was a *but*.

He fidgeted.

'What? What is it?'

Declan dropped the bombshell. 'The Boucher case has to go, Annie.' His flat eyes were as emotionless as ever.

'It's come to a dead end.' Barney was uncomfortable.

Declan wasn't. 'It's been nothing but trouble from day one.'

How could I argue with that? The case had caused us endless trouble. It had nearly cost Gerry his life.

Left us short-handed in the agency. It was even giving rise to cruel gags in The Randy Goat, a favourite watering hole of both gardai and private detectives. *Heard the one about the PI who fell through the roof when he climbed up a drainpipe to see if number twenty-four looked like forty-two from another angle?*

'I suspect even Boucher doesn't want her found,' Barney said.

I unlocked a drawer and took out a slip of paper. 'This is the lodgement receipt for a cheque Simon Boucher gave me the other day.' I held it up for viewing.

Barney whistled. 'That's more than we've made from our combined cases in the last six months.'

'Precisely. He says he'll give us the same amount again when we find Caroline. Do I have to remind you two how generous Gerry can be when it comes to sharing a windfall?'

'Should we drop everything else and . . . ?' Declan was almost out of his chair.

'No! You can stick with your own cases, just keep an ear to the ground for anything that might advance the Boucher case. I'll do the same.'

Barney rubbed his hands in glee. 'Sounds good to me.'

'Will Gerry be working it full time when he gets back?' Declan asked.

'Of course! Having to use a crutch for a while won't stop him. So you go ahead with that animal cruelty case. That warehouse owner definitely left those guard dogs without food or drink for a week. And he expects people to believe his story about a scavenging fox?'

'Slime!' he agreed. 'I'll find that missing CCTV

footage if it kills me. That'll put him in the dock for sure. The telephonist in the opposite building says she won't rest till he's in prison.'

'We all know that's not going to happen,' Barney said.

'Maybe not. But we can at least shame him. Get his picture in the tabloids when the case comes up?'

'Good. You'll keep following the judge's wife, Barney?'

'Do I have a choice?'

'No,' I laughed. 'His Honour is getting impatient. And the case can't be as boring as you make out.'

'Care to try it? Swap jobs for a day?' He looked hopeful.

'OK. Here's my schedule for today. I have to meet with our bank manager. Get him to clear that cheque a bit faster. Then go and talk to a college mate of Caroline's. *Again.* Come back here to make sure that, in my absence, Sandra hasn't managed to double-book appointments for us. She's trying extra hard to be helpful. Then I have to talk to Naomi. Convince her that the builders across the road have every right to use pneumatic drills to tear up the cement pathway they put down last week. Then I have to hassle the building engineers, tell them our lift is playing up again. Find a new plumber because our old one has decamped to Spain and Naomi is complaining that the heating in her office still isn't working properly. Which makes me wonder why she persists in wearing skirts that barely skim her pubic bone? Then I have to meet Gerry's doctor and find out how soon he can put weight on that injured leg, because if I don't have an actual date Gerry will probably insist on walking on it straightaway, crutch or not. Then . . .'

'OK. Point made. I'll follow the judge's wife.' Barney got to his feet.

'Naomi doesn't wear skirts up to her pubic bone.' Declan had a faraway look in his eyes.

I waved a hand in front of his face. 'The dogs, Declan! The dogs!'

My working day finally over, I raced to the hospital to see Gerry and found myself nodding off in the lift. I was so exhausted I would have happily crawled into bed beside Gerry and – a first for me – fallen asleep.

I gave him a quick rundown on the day, up to and including Naomi's complaints about the noisy builders.

'Anything on Caroline?' he asked.

'No-o-o. Her college mate was too busy admiring his reflection in a windowpane to give me a straight answer. No pun intended.'

'What?' he frowned.

'He was wearing eyeliner.'

'You took notes?'

'Right here.' I handed them over.

'That night we broke into the house, Annie? Did you see anything to make you suspect Caroline *could* have been in there?'

'Hang on!' I raised my hands in protest. 'You were buried in a mound of rubble. You were concussed and gushing blood, and you're asking if I spotted any clues as to Caroline Boucher's whereabouts? Well, I hope you'll forgive me, but I was sort of concentrating on . . . saving your life?'

'Yeah, and don't think I didn't appreciate what you did.' He caught my hand. 'But I hate loose ends.'

'Tough. I'm going home. I'm exhausted. Fiona will

be down to see you later when she pops the baby into the nursery for the night.'

'Aw no, not again. She was here for an hour last night giving me the latest World Health Organisation data on the benefits of breast milk. And something really strange.' He lowered his voice. 'She gave me a graphic description of the state of her nipples.' He shuddered. 'Said she's going to try *nipple clamps*? What the hell is going on there?'

I nearly choked, 'Nipple *shields*, you fool.'

'Oh. I did wonder.'

'Consider yourself lucky. She told me about her plans to eat her placenta.'

'Eating her placenta? What kind of hospital is this?'

'One that possibly saved your life?'

'Did you bring in my clothes?'

Damn. I knew I had forgotten something. 'Er . . . no need. Just ring me when they discharge you.'

'When will that be? Christmas? That drainpipe out there is beginning to look very appealing,' he grinned wickedly.

'Gerry!'

'Well, I don't know if I can take another hour of Fiona and her leaking breasts. In all the years I've known her, I can't remember her ever bringing up the subject of breasts before!' He looked miserable.

'She's never had a baby before. She's not trying to be provocative. Breasts only mean one thing to her right now.'

'What's that?'

'Baby-feeding implements. And pretty sore ones at that!'

He frowned. 'I don't remember Sally having that sort of trouble.'

Course not. Saintly Sally would never have experienced anything as vulgar as sore breasts. Or anything even borderline nasty. Blood, sweat and episiotomies were for normal women, not living saints.

'There's a lot of things about childbirth you don't know,' I accused him.

'Well that's that then. We're never having kids.'

I froze. 'I wasn't aware that was up for discussion.'

'Isn't that what I've just said?' he grinned.

'Yes,' I eyed him narrowly. 'But *before* you said it, I didn't know it was up for discussion.'

'What?' He was confused. 'Why are you looking at me like that? Where did this come from?' He inched away from me.

'You're the one who brought up the subject! You started talking about childbirth. Funny topic for a man. Are two children not enough for you? How many were you planning on having? Three? Six? A baker's dozen?'

'I never said I wanted more children.'

'Doesn't mean you weren't thinking it!'

'I wasn't thinking about feckin' kids. All I did was tell you about Fiona.'

'No need to swear. Some role model you'd make for a child, swearing like a trooper.'

'Christ, Annie, what is it with you tonight? Where did this conversation come from?'

'You! You started it.'

'Jesus. Sometimes I think we're living on different planets.'

'Well there's a coincidence! Because that's exactly how I feel right now! I'm on planet *keep it all together at all costs, Annie*, while you lie there thinking how sweet Fiona's baby looked. How nice it might be to have a dear little baby of our own. Why *were* you hanging around the maternity unit?'

'Hanging around the maternity . . . ? I went up to see Fiona. You told me to.'

'Well you'd better get something straight right here and now. It will be a cold day in hell before anyone convinces me to breed like a rabbit. Here's the books you wanted.' I threw his thrillers on the bed, missing his injured leg by inches. 'Surprised you didn't ask for a book of nursery rhymes.'

He watched me leave, his mouth agape.

'Doing well, isn't he, Annie?' Imelda called as I passed the nurses' station.

'Huh!' I marched out.

Crossing the hospital car park I saw Pino approaching, laden with flowers and fruit. A picture of parental joy. I tried to duck. Too late. He had spotted me.

'Annie!' Impossible as it seemed, his smile widened. 'Been up to see Calum, have you? Is he not the most beautiful baby? And so strong. One day he'll play centre forward for Juventus!'

'Oh, shut up! I've had as much baby talk as I can stomach for one day. There must be some other subject people can discuss. There's more to life than babies, you know!'

I sat in the Honda and hung my head in shame. I had just accomplished something that even the squabbling producers of Pino's upcoming TV food show couldn't. I had wiped the smile off his face. Sent him on his way, looking downcast. In the three years I had known him, he had never been less than courteous to me. I had just repaid him by snapping his head off. Sending him in to his nursing wife looking hurt and bewildered. And all because I imagined Gerry was fostering a secret longing for a child. Shame on you, Annie McHugh, I castigated myself as I started the car.

I drove to a nearby florist's. Came out staggering under the weight of a bouquet I couldn't possibly afford.

Fiona looked startled, when I burst into her room and handed it over. 'For me?' She could barely see over the flowers. 'But you brought me flowers yesterday.'

'I know.' I reddened. 'These are just a little extra. Well, a lot extra.' I threw a quick glance at Pino, who was standing by the baby's cot, his eyes wary.

'They're beautiful, Annie. But they must have cost a fortune.'

'Friendship has no price,' I smiled.

Pino watched as she put down the flowers carefully and threw her arms around me. 'You're so special, Annie. Isn't she, Pino? Have you ever seen such an *enormous* bouquet?'

'Never,' he said, his expression still guarded.

'Sorry, Pino.' I felt myself filling up. 'Forgive me?'

He reached out to hug me. 'It's an emotional time, *cara*. For all of us,' he said generously. 'My mama is hysterical for days now. Crying. Laughing. And she's thousands of kilometres away. It's the nature. A new life! It brings all emotions close to the surface.' His brown eyes welled up.

'Oh, you two are not going to start crying again, are you? And will someone please tell me what the hell is going on? Has something happened that I don't know about?'

'Yes. I've come to my senses. That's why I brought

the flowers. The last thing I'd want to do is hurt either of you. You're my best friends!'

'*Both* of us?' Fiona eyes popped.

'Both of you. And Calum,' I laughed.

'So you *would* like him to play for Juventus?' Pino asked slyly.

'Only if Man United pass,' I grinned.

I left Fiona staring after me. Pino was beaming from ear to ear. I knew he'd explain. Unlike Gerry, he *enjoyed* big emotional scenes.

Instead of heading home for some much needed sleep, I drove to the agency. There were two messages on the machine, the first from Mrs Green. Flopsy had come home. For this Mrs Green was eternally grateful to McHugh Dunning, and the cheque was in the post.

The second message was from the judge. His wife was planning on spending a long weekend in Emerald Waters, a luxury health and beauty spa noted for its upmarket clientele. Money alone couldn't gain you access to Emerald Waters; you had to have that indefinable something. Maybe it was class. It was rumoured that the spa had turned away a wealthy first division footballer and his wife because they didn't have it. Yet Pierce Brosnan, who came from Navan, was said to have recuperated there after the stresses and strains of filming his last Bond movie. Apparently he was shaken and stirred for five whole days amid the spectacular scenery and soft rolling mists of the Galway hills.

'I've made a booking for your investigator,' the judge boomed. 'Recommended him. Said he was a top lyricist. Tell him to keep my wife in view at all times.'

I hoped Barney appreciated his good fortune. There was little danger of him sitting on a turd in the exquisite Emerald Waters. Except, of course, if he specially requested it.

23

Gerry's face was wreathed in smiles as he waved goodbye to the hospital nursing staff. In the Civic, however, it was another story.

'Why didn't you bring the Cherokee?'

I changed gear. 'How could you climb into a jeep with your knee in a cast?'

'I'm not a cripple!'

'You grimace whenever we turn a corner.'

'Maybe if you didn't take them on two wheels.'

'What?'

'Sorry. It's just . . . this damn knee . . . it's . . . awkward.'

His knee wasn't the real problem. He just hated being driven. Hated not being in control. Mostly he hated the way the hospital had kept him in until Monday. Complained that his specialist only did so because he was a megalomaniac.

Smiling to myself, I deliberately swung the Civic around the next corner, but he didn't flinch. That was Gerry for you. Just when you thought you had him sussed, he surprised you by acting against type. Or maybe he didn't mind me being in control. Maybe under the tough, and sometimes cranky, detective there was a new man trying to break out. I reached over and caught his hand.

Instead of telling me to keep my eyes on the

road, he kissed my fingers. Sweet.

We were now approaching a busy junction. 'Go straight to the agency,' he instructed.

'Are you insane?' I almost ran the red light.

The look he gave me said arguing would be futile. At the hospital he had promised the megalomaniac that he would do exactly as he was told for the next few weeks. He would take his medication, not overdo things, and, most important of all, ring our GP as soon as he got home. Now he wanted to go straight to work?

'You promised to go home,' I said.

'I lied,' he laughed. 'So would you if you were trapped in that house of horrors. Take a left here. That way you'll miss the traffic coming in from the motorway.'

I took a left. Why not? I had been using this route since he'd been hospitalised. And always took the left turn. I was pulling up outside the agency when he said, 'There, wasn't I right about that left turn? See how much time it saved?'

'Yes. Thanks for pointing it out to me.'

He gave me a sceptical look.

I patted his good leg. 'Know what, Gerry? I don't know how I manage to get out of bed in the morning without your guidance.'

Gerry was clearly surprised to find the agency still standing. Definitely disgruntled to see cases being solved, life going on. He flicked through the day diary. 'Fine. Fine. Good. No progress on the Boucher front, then?'

'We do have a sizeable cheque in the bank,' I reminded him.

237

'Oh, how could I forget that.' He gave me one of his inscrutable looks.

There was a tap on the door. 'In,' he yelled.

Naomi swept in, a bunch of long-stemmed tulips resting in the crook of her permatanned arm. I might have been invisible for all the notice she took of me as she honed in on Gerry.

'Sandra said you were back! These are for you,' she cooed. 'You were *sorely* missed. This place was a shambles without your guiding hand at the helm.'

'What?' I steamed.

'There was a cold atmosphere.' She shot him a coy look from beneath her lashes.

'That was the radiators, Naomi. They needed bleeding,' I snapped.

She fingered Gerry's stubble. 'Now you take care of yourself, big man. No more heroics, thrilling as we may find them.' She went doubly coy, leaning so close to him she almost squashed his tulips. He didn't object. She was still wittering on when Declan came in.

He looked surprised. 'Naomi? I didn't know you were here.'

'Didn't I just wave to you as I came in?'

I'd never seen Declan blush before. And the whole thing became totally nauseating, Naomi making eyes at Gerry, offering to drive him to a genuine Chinese healer (in Beijing?) touching his forehead where one of his deeper cuts was forming a rather dashing scar, and Declan watching her hungrily, practically salivating at her every utterance.

When the phone rang, Gerry grabbed it like a lifeline. 'Fiona? Yeah. Thanks. Where else would I be? Nah, I'm OK. Yeah, she's here. Cracking the whip.' He handed me the receiver.

'Hi! No, he's OK.'

Tudi came in. I returned her wave, then watched her and Naomi compete to be the first to sign Gerry's cast. They took so long wittering over what they should write that Gerry actually became embarrassed. Still, he didn't exactly fight them off, I noticed.

'What's going on there? Annie? What's happening?' Fiona became curious.

'Hold on a sec, Fiona. I'll transfer this call to my office.'

'So you left Gerry with the Dreamland vultures?'

'He didn't look too upset. I think Naomi is growing on him. Anyway, I have an important question for you. Do the super-rich dress for dinner after having colonic irrigation?'

'Is this a quiz?'

'No! Barney is going to spend a long weekend in Emerald Waters. He'll be there on a case, silly. You must know Emerald Waters? That ridiculously expensive health spa?'

'Of course I know it. But why Barney? He's hardly the Emerald Waters type.'

'That's why I need your help. I'm supposed to tell him what to wear. What clothes should he take?'

'Very few, if the rumours are true,' she laughed. 'The hanky-panky there is supposed to be on a massive scale. So my source says.'

'Hanky-panky? Who is your source? Mary Poppins?'

'Close,' she laughed. 'It's Maeve.'

'Maeve goes to Emerald Waters? I thought she belonged to the Let's-all-sit-around-hugging-a-tree-while-eating-a-warm-placenta school?'

'That too. But she used to give weekly talks at Emerald Waters when it first opened. What did she call them? Oh yes – "Nature as God's Nutritionist". She's a great believer in nettle soup.'

'She's also deranged. I want to know what normal – well, normal *rich* people – wear there. Barney has to blend in.'

'Tell him to shag the tennis coach, then,' she giggled. 'Apparently that's de rigueur in Emerald Waters.' There was a soft cry in the background. 'Oh, is Mummy's darling boy awake? Who's the most booful boy in the whole world? And did he have a fwightening, fwightening dweam?'

'Hello? Earth calling Fiona!'

'Oh, Annie, you should see my little precious. He's just waking up and he's all warm and rosy and cuddlesome. Even his jobs smell like strawberry muffins.'

Strawberry muffins? If pregnancy had knocked Fiona slightly askew, motherhood was trying to finish the job. I hoped there was an antidote. Before the real Fiona disappeared altogether.

'Maeve was here yesterday. She fell in love with him. Said she could just eat him.'

'Well, I'd take that as a serious threat. Don't leave her alone with him for a second.'

'Oh, is Aunty Annie being howible about Aunty Maeve?' she cooed happily.

'Fiona, just tell me if the rich and famous keep their Gucci tracksuits on for dinner at Emerald Waters? Cos if they do we're going to have to buy one for Barney.'

'Well, I've been told that people have trouble keeping their clothes on at any time in that place. Yes, Calum, Mummy's heard naughty, naughty stories

240

about that funny-wunny place. Pity that naughty Naomi won't go there. Dwown herself in the whirlpool bath,' she laughed.

'What are you saying?' I became irritated.

'You've just said Gerry's chatting to her. Since when does Gerry chat?'

I had a long think about this. And I didn't like what I was thinking.

'Annie? Are you still there?'

'He's not chatting! He's just being polite,' I snapped.

She chuckled. 'That's all right, then. Isn't it powecious? Unky Gerry is just being polite, and not trying to get another look at naughty Naomi's legs.'

'Give over, Fiona. I'm sorry I ever told you about that.'

'Oh, has Mommy's poweecious got windy-poo?'

'Fiona, do you really think . . . do you think Gerry might . . . fancy Naomi?'

'. . . pat your booful back and get rid of all that windy poo.'

'FIONA!'

'Itsy bitsy spidey climbing up the spout . . .'

I hung up and went back to Gerry's office.

Naomi and Tudi had left, Gerry was putting down the phone, and *Declan* was advising him not to be foolish. 'You need to rest. I think you should go home.'

'He *is* going home,' I interrupted. 'I'm driving him right now.' I picked up my bag.

'Good.' Declan sounded relieved. 'You can do those student interviews another day, Gerry.'

'What student interviews?' I turned.

Gerry looked guilty. 'I need to catch them today, before they break for . . .'

'Over my dead body, Dunning,' I said. I meant it. This was one argument he was not going to win.

The tutorial room in Caroline Boucher's college was surprisingly cramped. Surprisingly, because this private college was known to charge half a king's ransom per term. Along with being cramped, the room was so badly ventilated that by the time Gerry and I had interviewed four students, the single window was almost completely steamed up.

We put aside our cups of instant coffee and continued trying to prise information out of yet another reluctant student. This one being the worst of the bunch.

Gerry began again. 'Was there anything at all about Caroline's behaviour that made you think she might . . . run away?'

The girl played with her pitch-black gothic curls, rolled a piece of gum between her tiny white teeth and gave him a blank stare.

The first student we'd interviewed had stared at Gerry's leg cast as if it was contagious. The next one had accused us of being the drug squad. Gothic girl clearly harboured the same dark suspicions, no matter how strenuously we denied them. Feigning tiredness, she deliberately yawned in Gerry's face, rubbing her heavily kohled eyes with black-varnished nails.

'Late night?' He outstared her.

She straightened up defensively. 'No!'

'He meant swotting,' I lied.

'Oh. Well, yeah.' She almost relaxed.

'We're not the police, Bettina. We're not here to grill you,' I said.

242

'So I can go then?' She picked up her cigarettes.

'We're here because Caroline's dad is out of his head with worry. All he wants to know is that his daughter is safe. If she said anything of significance to you before she . . . before she went off, we'd like to know, so we can reassure him.'

She looked at Gerry. 'Like I told *you* last time, I hardly know Caroline. Sharing a tutor doesn't make us friends. Anyway, she'd never confide in me. Little Miss Perfect.' Still chewing gum, she tore open the cigarette pack.

Gerry pointed to the no smoking sign.

She gave a bored sigh.

'If I tell you something, will you feck off and leave me in peace?'

'Promise.' I nudged Gerry into silence.

'Right. Now I'm not saying this means anything, but the last two days before she . . . whatever . . . she was buzzing. She wasn't on anything, you understand. She doesn't even smoke.' She looked amazed. 'But for a couple of days, she was . . . kind of . . . up . . . smiley. You know . . . friendly. Almost sticking her love letters in people's faces.'

'Love letters?' I gave Gerry another warning nudge. I didn't want him scaring her off.

'They must have been. Why else would she carry them around with that cheesy grin on her face?'

'Any idea who they might have been from?' I dared.

She rolled her gum in her teeth again. 'No. They were foreign. Airmail. Funny stamps. I have to go. I have a class.' She got up.

'Bettina?'

She turned.

'Thanks.' I smiled.

She paused at the door. 'The stamps might have been . . . I think they were Australian.'

Gerry ordered me to drive straight to the Boucher house. It would have been pointless to argue. A complete waste of time. Anyway, he seemed to have boundless energy, didn't look to me like someone who needed to rest. He stood with his hand leaning on the Boucher doorbell, his fingers tapping impatiently. 'Couldn't you just shake them sometimes?'

'Who?'

'Teenagers. That little witch in the college. Love letters from Australia? She could have told me all that three weeks ago.' He pressed the bell again.

'She thought you were the drug squad.' I tried not to smile.

'She did in her arse. She was just strutting her stuff.'

'You're wrong. She was genuinely afraid you'd bust her.'

'She was strutting her . . .'

The door swung open and a furious-faced Ms Lynch stood there. Gerry took his hand off the bell and leaned hard on the crutch instead, the perfect picture of a wounded hero.

Ms Lynch's irritation evaporated. She welcomed us into the house with profuse commiserations over Gerry's accident. Then she was her brisk self again, ushering us across the big hall and into the drawing room, offering her usual wide selection of teas.

Gerry declined for us both and went straight to the point of our visit. 'Was Caroline receiving any overseas mail in the weeks leading up to her disappearance?'

'No.'

'You're positive?' He couldn't hide his surprise.

Her eyebrows shot up. 'I handle the post.'

'Could she have hidden her post from you?'

'She leaves for college long before it arrives.' She looked curiously from his face to mine.

'Is there . . . any post here for her now?' he asked.

'Well, yes . . . but . . . I don't think I can allow you . . .'

'I have her father's permission to look through her things. I imagine that includes her post . . .'

There was nothing of significance in the little bundle of letters Ms Lynch handed over with tight-lipped reluctance. Nothing even mildly personal, except for a party invitation to a twenty-first that was now ancient history.

'Has she friends in Australia?' Gerry was blunt.

'Not that I know of.' Her eyebrows almost met her hairline again.

'That was hardly worth offending the housekeeper for,' I said as we left.

'No,' he agreed. 'Did you see her face? She looked as if she was itching to box my ears for ringing the doorbell. That's it!' He grabbed my arm as I started the jeep.

'What?'

'A post office box. What would you do if you didn't want your overbearing father to see your post? If you wanted to keep it a secret?'

'I'd get myself an email address.'

'OK. But Caroline's not you. What if you were a sweet, old-fashioned girl?'

Leaving me to mull this over, he took out his mobile. 'Brian? Gerry Dunning. Yeah. Long time no see. I was, but I'm fine. I need a favour, Brian. Isn't your department in charge of post and . . .' he laughed. 'No, it's not quite life and death. OK, talk to you later.'

'If she has a post office box, he'll trace it,' he said smugly.

'You sure about that? I thought civil servants lived strictly by the rules?'

He laughed. 'Not when they owe you a favour. Remember that double-glazing chancer who conned all those elderly women out of their life savings? Brian's mother was one of his victims.'

'So? Just because you got his mother's money back doesn't mean he'll give out information on something that's essentially . . .'

His mobile purred. 'Brian? Thanks for getting back to me. Tell you what I need, a girl called Caroline Boucher has possibly been using a PO box number to . . .'

Gerry could call in more favours than a Mafia Don.

He was still on the mobile as I drove into the big supermarket car park. He put it away and stared out at the big 'Prices Slashed' sign as if he had never before seen a 'Two for One' special offer. 'What are we doing here?'

'We need food. There's nothing in the house.'

'You're not going shopping now? I'm tired. We can order a takeaway later.'

I was swamped with guilt. He'd been so full of energy, so Gerry-like all day, it had actually slipped my mind that he'd only left hospital that morning. Even using the crutch hadn't slowed him down. Well, not so that you'd notice.

'Sorry, Gerry. I should have thought.' I reversed out of the parking space and headed for home.

'It's OK, babe.' he said, stroking my arm forgivingly.

I rang Sandra from the house. Promised I'd be back shortly, that I was only home for a minute to drop Gerry off.

'Hurry up, will you, Annie,' she said. 'Barney has me scourged about what clothes he should pack for that posh spa. When I said he should ask Naomi, he flipped. Wouldn't it be a good idea to ask her? She's probably been there.'

'Having a toxic clear-out?' I asked.

'Why does everyone hate her?'

'No idea. She's such a sweet, lovable person.'

'Will you hurry, Annie?'

'Yep.'

I swallowed two asprin to counteract an ominous neck tension that was threatening to become a full-blown headache, and went upstairs to tell Gerry I was leaving and to see if he was OK.

'Gerry? Do you need anything before I go?'

He came out of the bathroom draped in a towel, water dripping everywhere. Only the gleaming plaster was miraculously dry. He came towards me, Clooneyesque eyes gleaming wickedly.

'Oh no!' I held up my hands. 'You can stop right there. Forget it! You're only just . . . And I'm needed back at the agency . . . Sandra is already . . .'

He came closer. Still smiling.

'Oh, play fair Gerry.' I backed away.

'How long has it been? Six years?'

I got the giggles. 'Six *days*!'

'Same difference.' He took my hand and ran it along his wet stomach. 'Emmmm . . .'

I groaned. 'I have a trillion things to do. Sandra needs . . . !' My hand began moving of its own accord.

'We all have needs,' he smiled as the towel hit the floor.

'So I see.'

Balancing himself against the bed he began to unbutton my jacket.

'Oh well.' I used my free hand to speed things up. 'I suppose another . . . three minutes . . . won't . . .'

'You cheeky . . .' He laughed and pushed me on to the bed without once using his hands.

24

Two weeks passed in a blur of happiness. Everyone was finally starting to treat me as Gerry's assistant investigator. Barney and Declan both eased off on asking me to do things which a non-investigator could easily handle. I.e. Sandra. Although you had to ask her several times. And then remind her again a few days later. Gerry and I were amassing huge amounts of information on how Caroline Boucher had spent the days leading up to her disappearance. It could be only a matter of weeks, possibly even days, before we found her. Declan was handling a land fraud investigation, his three years of law studies making him the most suitable person for that particular job.

Gerry and I were comparing notes on the Boucher case when Barney arrived back from Emerald Waters looking like Bob Marley. Except that his dreadlocks were light blond.

'Jesus, what happened to you?' Gerry was horrified.

'Got myself a tan, didn't I?' Barney grinned with delight, his teeth gleaming luminously white against the dark mahogany of his skin.

'A tan? You're black!'

Barney shrugged. 'Might have overdone it a bit. But it was all in the line of duty. Mrs Judge Regan spent half the weekend in the tanning room. And I was told not to lose sight of her. What do you think, Annie?' He bared his arm. 'Is that smokin', or what?'

'Smokin'?' I laughed.

'Smoked ham.' Gerry frowned. 'And what's with the hair?'

'Mrs Regan having hair extensions, was she?' I guessed.

'Correct.' He high-fived me with glee. 'Have you any idea how much time it takes a woman to get hair extensions?' he asked Gerry.

'Get to the point,' Gerry said.

'It's all in my report, mon.' Barney adopted a sing-song Jamaican accent. 'You know, mon, I could get used to this look.' He fingered his dreadlocks lovingly.

'Tough.' Gerry picked up the phone. 'Sandra? Get up here, will you. And bring that hairdryer you keep behind the desk. Sandra, this is me you're talking to. Do you think I haven't seen you straightening your fringe? Yes, *that* blow-dryer. Bring it up here.'

Sandra and Barney came out of the small toilet tittering like twelve-year-olds. But to give her her due, Sandra had worked wonders on Barney's hair – he was practically his old self again. Except for his startling tan. He checked his reflection in Sandra's handmirror for the tenth time. 'Aw, shame. I liked the Rasta look. It didn't half pull the la-a-a-a-dies.' He gave his reflection a come-hither smile.

'You weren't there to pull women. You were there to do a job,' Gerry said.

'I had to protect my cover, didn't I? I was Rod Hunt, award-winning writer of rock lyrics. Mega in the music world. Putting it about was all part of the image. The receptionist asked if any of my co-written albums had gone platinum. I told her I was big in Bucharest. Massive in Moldavia. She was impressed. The scary thing is, so was Mrs Judge Regan. She's a bit of a vulture, that one. *And* she likes her meat young. There were a couple of hairy moments in that tanning room, I can tell you.'

Gerry tried not to laugh.

'Not funny. Wait till you read my report. Sunday morning I had to hide out in Colonic Irrigation.'

'Ugh,' Sandra grimaced.

'You can say that again. The nurse in there, built like a sumo. Course she'd have to be. Do you know how much people pay to have a rubber hose pushed up their . . . ?'

'Enough!' Gerry said.

'Colonic irrigation is just a fancy name for an enema.' Sandra looked sick.

'Sure. But those people aren't *normal*.' Barney air-signed inverted commas. 'They *like* it. Not Mrs Judge Regan, I'm happy to say, although she does have her own little addictions.'

'Is she on drugs?' Sandra loved hearing scabrous tales of the rich and famous.

Barney gave her a look. 'My lips are sealed.'

'Ah, go on. Tell us.'

'Have you nothing to do, Sandra?' Gerry asked.

'No.'

'Find something.'

'Everyone else gets to hear the stories,' she muttered as she stamped out. I might have felt sorry for her if I didn't know that she'd stand outside the door listening and end up knowing more about the case than I did.

'No eavesdropping!' Gerry shouted after her. 'OK, Barney. Give me a brief outline. I'll read your full report later.'

'Well, over the weekend Mrs Judge Regan availed herself of most of the facilities. She had her chakras balanced, lay in flower-perfumed waters, was reflexologised, used the tanning room, the gym and the yoga master. And as far as I could tell, every other professional instructor from the tennis coach down.'

'Are you saying she . . . ?'

'I counted five.'

I stared at him in disbelief. 'He's kidding, Gerry.'

''Not.' Barney grinned and held up his pocket camera. 'Got the evidence.'

'I don't believe it! You must have tailed the wrong woman. Mrs Regan is sixty.'

'I know. I double-checked her file. Found the receptionist very cooperative there.'

'I bet.'

'*And* the assistant hair stylist,' he grinned.

'What? One tart wasn't enough for you?'

'Annie, will you let him speak.'

'No. I saw those photos of Mrs Regan with her husband. She loves him. She could hardly keep her hands off him.'

'She can hardly keep her hands off anyone,' Barney chuckled.

'You sure about this?' Gerry leafed through the report.

'Positive. She wasn't exactly discreet. She staggered out of a *private* gym session on Sunday looking as if she'd been put through a mangle.'

'Step aerobics makes *me* look like that,' I snapped.

'Do they also give you a big hickey on your neck?'

Gerry turned away. 'Thanks, Barney. I'll read this later.'

'Lighten up, Annie,' Barney pleaded. 'Don't shoot the messenger. I only report what I see.'

'Not what a slut of a receptionist tells you?'

'Aw, be nice, or I won't tell you who I saw there.' He leaned into my face. 'In the steam room. Buck naked. Think movies. Think big. Very, very big.' His eyes widened dramatically.

'Pierce Brosnan?' I fell into the trap.

'No! He's never been there. That was just a rumour. But who is that other, sort of fat Dub actor who's now working in Hollywood? Well, he was there trying to shed a few pounds. Too ashamed to be shedding the blubber stateside, I bet? He was putting the moves on some old bird doing qigong. He was well into her. She signed in as Marianne Faithfull, but I don't believe it. Everyone there uses an alias.'

'Wow.'

Gerry was more interested in checking the instant prints. 'Good quality. You got plenty of Kodaks to back them up?'

'Tons.' Barney picked up a picture. 'She has a great body for someone her age. Great boobs. But then they should be. The judge paid top dollar for them.'

'How do you know?'

'Receptionist.'

Gerry nodded. 'Did she . . . was she involved with any of the clients?'

'Na. Though like I said, there was one near miss in the tanning room. Apart from that she stuck to the professionals. The tennis coach being her

favourite. Apparently his volleys are unforgettable.'
He looked as innocent as a newborn.

'The receptionist,' he answered Gerry's silent inquiry.

'OK. I'll pass on the bad news to Judge Regan. I have another couple of calls to make, then I have a small job for you two. Meet me downstairs in fifteen minutes.'

'A small job?' Barney was curious.

'Fifteen minutes. OK?'

Gerry climbed awkwardly into the Cherokee, throwing his crutch into the back seat. 'OK. Go to St Martin's Lane.'

'What?' Barney and I chorused.

'I want to have another look at number forty-two,' he said brightly.

'You're not serious?' Barney gawked in disbelief.

'Just a quick look. Satisfy my curiousity.'

'You're going back into that death trap?' I asked fearfully.

'No,' he smiled. 'Barney is. And you.'

'OK!' Ignoring Barney's expression, I pulled away, tyres squealing.

Outside number forty-two Gerry gave us a brief lecture. 'Just poke around a bit. The firemen said both ceilings are completely gone, so there's no danger of any fallout. At least in the basement,' he grinned. 'Which is where I want you to look. But avoid the stairs, just in case. No heroics now. Just look around. Here, take these.' He pulled two hard hats from behind his seat.

'I thought you said it was safe?' Barney became worried.

'The hats are just a precaution. Do you think I'd let Annie near the place if I thought there was any danger?'

'Course not,' I said. 'Everyone knows if you had your way I'd never leave the office.' I grabbed a hat.

'You'll have no trouble getting in.' Gerry pressed it down on my head a little too forcefully. 'Someone stole the door. Probably flogged it to a tourist. Told him James Joyce signed it. Have a good look around. I want that basement checked out before the wrecking crews get here.'

'I thought you said just poke around.'

'Just do it, Barney. If you find anything interesting, give me a shout.'

'And you'll be?' Barney pulled on his hard hat.

'Sitting here in the jeep, listening to Van the Man. I'm still convalescing, remember?'

Barney peered uneasily into the rubble-strewn building. 'Maybe you should wait out here, Annie,' he worried.

'On yer bike.' I elbowed him aside and clambered over a mound of wood and plaster to get into the dilapidated house.

Inside, it didn't at all resemble number twenty-four. Well, it had no ceilings, for a start. And no smell.

'Careful.' Barney was behind me, flashing a powerful lamp at where the ceiling should be. 'Jesus! Look at that! Did he really fall through the two floors?'

I refused to look. Or even think about it. 'We're here to search,' I said, needing no reminder of how close I came to losing Gerry.

'Man, he was lucky.'

'I wish people would stop saying that. Lucky would

have been never to have heard of this damn place.'
I kicked viciously at a piece of wood.

He shone the torch along the walls. 'No graffiti.
This wasn't a squat, then. And there hasn't been a
fire in that grate for years. Just as well you had the
sense not to follow Gerry up that drainpipe.'

I stiffened. 'What do you mean?'

'Well, if you hadn't had the wit to stay on the
ground that night, the two of you could have ended
up in a pool of blood right here. Nobody knew where
you were. Your bodies would have lain undiscovered
for months. Nothing but putrefying corpses by the
time the demolition workers got here.'

'I had my mobile!'

'That would have got smashed in the fall.' He began
searching the rubble. Stopped to pick up something
white, becoming excited before throwing it away in
disgust. 'A bloody sweet wrapper,' he hissed.

'What exactly are we looking for?'

'A note telling us Caroline Boucher was here?' He
turned over another clump of wood.

There was a shout from the doorway. 'Hey! What
are youse doing in there?'

Two curious little faces appeared. 'Is that your jeep?'

I was beside them in a flash. 'Don't you touch that
jeep,' I warned the grinning kids. Barney had said
this was a notorious joyriding area. He'd know. He
had once been searching for a stolen motorbike
behind the high-rise flats opposite and came back to
find his car missing. He was reporting it stolen when
it tore past him with a ten-year-old at the wheel. This
pair looked about that age. Which meant they were
probably twelve. The bigger one had a tipped cigarette hanging from his lip.

'Ah, who'd want that jeep?' he said cheekily. 'What is it? A 3.7 V6, the 16-valve? Or is it the 2.5?' he frowned.

'What's it to you?' I asked.

'Huh! Jeeps are crap, anyway. Can't do a proper handbrake turn. They corner wide as well.' He stared hungrily at it. 'And that pinion steering? Tsk. Airbags are shite as well.' He tore his eyes away from it. 'What were youse doing in that house?'

'None of your business.' Barney was beside me, blinking in the bright sunlight. 'What are you doing smoking? Don't you want to grow up?'

'Not like you, yeh big lank.'

'Charming,' Barney grinned. 'Why don't you take a leaf out of your friend's book. He's not smoking.'

'He's not me friend. He's me brother, and he has asthma. Fags wreck his tubes.'

'But not yours, huh? Do you know who used to live in that house?' Civilities over, Barney was the probing detective again.

'Yeah.' The kid blew a perfect smoke ring.

'Who?' I asked eagerly.

'Me Granda. So if you want to go back in there, youse'll have to pay me.'

I turned away. 'Let's go, Barney.'

He didn't budge. 'When did your Granda live here?'

'I dunno. Years ago. But it's still his house,' he reminded us.

'Seen any strangers hanging around it, have you?'

'Yeah.'

'When?' I asked.

'Now,' he smirked. 'Hey, give us a go of your jeep, will you?'

Barney was trying not to laugh. 'Apart from us, did you see anyone else coming in and out of here?'

The boy was too busy checking out the jeep again. 'What can she do?'

'A hundred and thirty,' I lied, and turned to the smaller boy. '. . . did you see a girl coming in and out of . . . ?'

'He can't talk,' his brother interrupted. 'Would you give *him* a go in your jeep?'

'What's going on?' Gerry yelled down at us.

'Who's that?'

'Our boss,' Barney said. 'The slave driver.'

'Come on, Liam.' The bigger one legged it up the steps, his brother following more slowly. As if his lack of speech wasn't burden enough, Liam also had a pronounced limp. I hoped Gerry wouldn't notice. He was a complete sucker for . . .

'Let's get back to work.' Barney hit the torch and we went back inside.

We continued our search of the ruined house with little enthusiasm. After twenty minutes of half-heartedly turning over bits of rubble and finding nothing more exciting than a second sweet wrapper, we agreed to pack it in.

'Oh God, Barney, look at the jeep,' I warned as we climbed the steps.

He looked up warily. Three pairs of eyes were watching us through the windscreen.

'Aw, shit! What the hell is Gerry playing at?'

'Just to the end of the road,' Gerry was saying as we got in. 'And only if you fasten your seat belts.'

'What happened to your leg, anyway? Did you crash?' The bigger boy blew out a long trail of smoke, stinking out the whole jeep.

'Something like that. Annie, this is Tomo. And that's Liam. Tomo likes cars. He's going to be a racing driver when he grows up.'

'I didn't know they had a racing circuit in Mountjoy?' Barney muttered. 'Give me that cigarette.' He tried to grab it.

'Buy your own.' Tomo ducked beyond reach.

'Put it out,' Gerry ordered.

'Jaysus.' Tomo threw the lighted cigarette out of the window.

'Just to the end of the road, Annie. OK?' Gerry sat back.

I turned the jeep and drove it hard over what was little more than a network of potholes. With every comfortable bounce, the kids hooted with delight. I took a sharp right, heading into a long straight stretch of road, and sheer luck had us hitting a break in the traffic. I sped along the wide street, Tomo now breathing hard on my neck. After a quick glance at Gerry for the go-ahead, I took another right and headed back to St Martin's Lane, this time taking a slightly longer route.

'Annie!' Barney reprimanded.

'Put the boot down!' Tomo was practically spitting on my neck with excitement.

Back at St Martin's Lane, I braked so hard only the quality seat belts kept us from flying through the windscreen.

The kids were reluctant to leave.

'Aw, just one more go, Gerry?' Tomo pleaded.

'Sorry. Annie has to get back to her day job at the speedway.' He leaned over and opened the door.

Tomo drummed his feet on the back of my seat.

'Out,' Gerry ordered.

'Will youse be coming back here?' Tomo waited.

'Oh yeah.' Barney spoke sarcastically. 'We'll be back here on a weekly basis.'

'Will youse give us more goes in the jeep then?' Tomo asked.

'Sure,' I answered.

'Thanks,' he said, and pushed his brother out the door.

Driving away, I glanced in the rear-view mirror. The two boys were standing close together watching us depart. Then Tomo lost interest, focusing instead on lighting the cigarette he had already stuck in his mouth. I hit the throttle and they disappeared from view.

25

We dropped Barney off at the agency and doubled back across town to meet Gerry's friend Brian. I had never met Brian, so it was a major shock to see an anorak-wearing nerd nod to Gerry from the pub doorway before rushing to join us.

He was an hour late, but sat down without a word of apology, wiping his skeletal hands on a big cotton hanky and checking out the pub as if he expected armed officers to leap out from behind the beer pumps.

'I'm not happy, Gerry,' he said through the thinnest lips I had ever seen. 'I could be jeopardising my pension, giving you this information.' He wiped the rim of his glass with a paper tissue before gulping his waiting drink.

'For feck's sake, Brian, will you relax,' Gerry said. 'If I were still a Garda detective I could get a court order like that,' he snapped his fingers. 'I'd have the information on my desk within the hour.'

'Just the same.' Brian threw a furtive look over his shoulder.

'Oh, come on. It's only information about a bloody PO box. It won't bring down the government.'

'Just the same.' Another nervous look around.

It took three double Jameson's before Brian felt relaxed enough to part with his precious information.

'She has a PO box all right.'

'I knew it.' Gerry was gleeful. 'What about her post?'

'It wasn't easy getting that information. First I had to contact Foreign . . .'

'Just tell me.'

'All the post directed to her box came from New Zealand. Just a few letters really. The last one she picked up arrived on Friday the fourteenth of March.'

Gerry and I exchanged glances.

'Three days before she disappeared,' I murmured, feeling like a real detective.

'Nothing at all since then?' Gerry pressed. 'Are you sure, Brian? There isn't anything in the . . . ?'

'I said she picked up the last one.' Brian wiped his hands again.

'And you're absolutely positive that it arrived on the fourteenth?' Gerry double-checked.

'Well, if you're not going to take my word . . .' Brian was offended.

'I'm just . . . this is important to us, Brian!'

'My pension is important to me.' Brian looked as if he might wipe his hands again.

'OK. Thanks.' Gerry sat back. 'Give my regards to your mother.'

Brian's bony face lit up. 'She always asks about you,' he beamed. 'Says if you're ever in Maynooth you're to call in. She won't forget what you did for her.'

'It was nothing.'

'Just the same.' He was gone.

We mulled over Brian's information.

'So she got the final letter that Friday? And the following Monday she went missing.'

'You think she went to meet the letter writer?'

'Maybe,' he worried.

'And then . . . ? Oh God, you don't think . . . ?'

'Now don't *you* go all neurotic on me. This isn't the first time she's disappeared, remember? And all those other times she arrived home safe and sound. So let's not get our knickers in a twist.'

His calm act didn't fool me. I'd seen his expression when Brian had mentioned the date: he'd jumped to the same conclusion I had. Caroline had been communicating with an unknown man. Gone to meet him that last night. Love letters, the goth girl had said. A big grin on her face . . . smiley . . . as she carried them about. A perfect description of a girl in love. She goes to meet this unknown man – and disappears? I felt a sudden chill. A terrible foreboding.

Gerry pushed aside his empty glass, a frown rucking his forehead. 'Her tutor checked her computer for anything untoward. He's positive she only used the Internet for research. Study references only. He insists she's no Internet junkie.'

'Oh my God. What if she met one of those psychos who hang around chat rooms? The ones who trick young girls into meeting them? Older men pretending to be teenagers so they can . . .'

'Then why would he use snail mail? If his hunting ground was chat rooms?'

'Because . . . she became suspicious? Uneasy? He reverted to letters to gain her confidence. Make her feel safe. That's probably why he chose New Zealand. Think of the image. All those pure green pastures. New Zealand Lamb. And he probably guessed she'd open up more to him if she thought there were thousands of miles between them. When in reality he was probably right here, in Dublin. Just around the corner from her. It's not difficult to get someone to post your mail in another country. All he had to do was continue writing her love letters. It's called grooming, isn't it? That's what these sickos do, they . . .'

Gerry tried to calm me.

'You're getting ahead of yourself, Annie. Worrying unnecessarily. The first rule in any missing persons case is, keep your head. The second is, look close to home. That's where the real clues are. And don't forget that in every single missing person's case I've worked, the outcome was . . . pretty mundane. We'll check out the New Zealand connection, but keep in mind that Caroline is no wild child. You heard what her college mates call her – Little Miss Perfect. She's not likely to have run off with some Internet nut. A girl like her who never takes risks? Who only goes horse riding with her father? The most outrageous thing she ever did was run up a bill in a five-star hotel. That's the most daring thing our investigation has turned up on her.'

'There is one small thing I didn't tell you, Gerry. Something about her room.' I sat back.

He waited, his eyes giving nothing away.

'You know the way her room is sort of . . . childish? Soft toys on the bed?'

'Yes. But that fits in with everything we've been told.'

'She has a drawerful of sexy underwear,' I said quickly.

'What do you mean sexy?'

'What do you think I mean?

'Is it . . . over-the-top designer stuff? Ultramodern . . . a bit daring . . . ?' He became rattled.

264

'Not really.'

'What then?'

'Well, it's . . . sort of provocative.'

'Provocative?'

'Open-crotch panties? Bras with the nipple area cut away?'

'And you never thought to mention this to me?'

'Don't yell at me. Lots of girls buy things like that for a laugh. They don't necessarily wear them.'

'Jesus, Annie, we're looking for a missing seventeen-year-old and you didn't think a drawerful of provocative underwear was worth mentioning?'

'I didn't think . . . It's not *that* provocative,' I backtracked, at a loss to explain my reluctance to expose Caroline's private . . .

'Bloody right you didn't think! Maybe it's time you started.'

I was back at my desk, sorting out paperwork, convinced that Gerry would never again let me within a mile of a case. Any case. He was on his way to the Boucher house. Alone. Preferring to sit in a minicab rather than be driven by me.

The more I thought about what he called my lack of judgement, the angrier I got. What had I done that was so terrible? Just tried to leave Caroline with a modicum of privacy. After all, her taste in knickers was hardly likely to lead us to her, unless she was working as a lap dancer.

Jesus! How could I have been so dumb? Of course I should have mentioned the knickers. Left it to Gerry to decide if . . . OK now, hold on . . . Gerry is an expert at sussing out clues. One look at that underwear drawer and he'll know exactly what it means.

Sandra came in unannounced. 'Thought you could do with this.' She put a mug of coffee on my desk and held out a folded copy of the *Evening Herald*.

'Look at your horoscope, Annie,' she instructed. 'It says your career is on the up.' Before I could take it, she began reading. 'Your bright ideas will prove illuminating to others, leading to next week's extraordinary revelations. And with Jupiter about to cross the pivotal point of your chart, you can look forward to even bigger and better victories. It says partnerships are particularly well-starred. Isn't that brilliant?'

'Deadly.' I sipped the coffee. It tasted like poison. Or maybe that was just wishful thinking.

'Mine is shite,' she said cheerfully. 'But who cares. Jimmy got our tickets for the Witness festival. I can't wait for that. Plus we're going clubbing every night this weekend. One of his best mates is home from England and wants to go on the razz. So don't expect me to be in early on Monday. Or fit to make anyone's coffee until at least midday. You'll all have to grind your own beans,' she chuckled. 'Oh, I nearly forgot. Gerry said not to expect him home for dinner tonight. And . . . something else . . . but I can't remember what it was. Anyway, he'll be late. You're not to wait up for him.'

I woke from a bad dream. It was three a.m. and I was alone. At first I thought Gerry hadn't come home, then I heard the faint sound of music coming from downstairs.

I opened the living room door quietly. He was lying on the sofa, smoking.

'What are you doing?' I was horrified.

He didn't look remotely guilty. 'Trying to put the

puzzle together. Make connections. The answer to Caroline's disappearance could be in those letters, but something about St Martin's Lane keeps niggling at me.'

'I meant, why are you smoking?'

'Oh, that.' He tapped ash into a saucer. 'It helps me think.'

'After all you went through to break the habit? All those patches?'

He popped open a can of beer, took a mouthful and grimaced in disgust.

'Why start smoking all over again?' I sat beside him.

'Let me think, Annie. I have sore ribs, a banjaxed knee and a case that's doing my head in because it's going nowhere. Would you consider all or any of those reasons enough to crave a cigarette?' He took a long, blissful drag.

'Where did you get it, anyway?'

'Tomo,' he grinned.

'Tomo? You took a cigarette from a child? A twelve-year-old kid?'

'I didn't *take* it. I *paid* him for it. He made a fair profit.' He looked pleased.

'You *paid* a child for a cigarette? I don't believe it.' I did, of course, but I wanted to emphasise my disgust at such irresponsible behaviour.

'You're not a smoker. You wouldn't understand,' he said.

'I thought you weren't a smoker either. Not any more.'

'Well, you thought wrong. I'll always be a smoker. Just one who manages to stay off the weed from time to time.'

'Gerry!' I couldn't hide my disappointment.

'Ah, don't do that face. All I did was smoke one little cigarette.'

I glared at him.

'Well, OK. Two. It's not a hanging offence, is it?' He nudged me with his good knee. An action usually guaranteed to have me nudging him back. Not tonight.

'It's not like I'm chain-smoking!' he pleaded.

'Smoking kills. You know that. My father coughed his lungs up because of those damn things.'

'Your father died in a car crash, Annie,' he frowned.

'Yes, but . . . he had that terrible racking cough at the time. That could have affected his concentration.'

He caught my hand. 'Smoking doesn't cause car crashes, Annie.'

'Prove it.' I pulled my hand away petulantly.

'OK. Let's agree that smoking causes everything from bad breath to war and pestilence and . . . have a beer,' he offered.

I brushed it aside. 'I don't drink beer.'

'I don't suppose . . .' He held out the cigarette.

'Not funny.'

'Don't be angry.' He nudged me playfully again. 'Smoking helps me think, livens up the receptors in my brain.' He inhaled deeply.

'Really? Funny how it makes you look stupid, then. Almost like Tomo with that yoke hanging from your lip.'

He became thoughtful. 'Poor little bugger. You know, I'm convinced there's some clue to Caroline's disappearance in that street. Why would Mags come up with a story about seeing her there if she hadn't?'

'Because that's what Mags does! She makes up stories.'

'Yeah, but something has to trigger them.'

'Yes. In this case it was that newspaper article!'

'No. Before that. She saw something before the newspaper piece. That's what made her notice Caroline's picture in the paper. She gets things muddled, but she's not stupid.'

'Did you talk to her?'

'Yeah.'

'And?'

'You know Mags. She asked me for money, said Fred needed to see the vet.'

'You're such a soft touch! No wonder she comes whining to you.'

'Something about that street,' he insisted.

'Maybe the fact that you nearly died there?'

'I'm missing something, I know I am.'

'Functioning taste buds, if you can drink that swill.' I indicated the beer.

He frowned. 'It is horrible.'

'Where did you get it, anyway? Buy it from Tomo, did you?' I laughed.

'Barney left it in the jeep.' He took a long gulp. 'Christ, it's brutal,' he shivered. 'But . . .'

'Don't tell me. It helps you think?'

'Actually it dulls the brain, probably kills off hundreds of brain cells per second, but what the hell, everything is a risk.'

'Brilliant. So between the beer and the cigarettes, you and I can probably look forward to a contented future together. I can't wait for you to be both emphysemic and gaga, wetting yourself three times a day.'

'Aw, but you'll still love me, won't you?' He ran a finger across my breast.

'What did you think of Caroline's underwear?'

He withdrew his finger as if he'd been burned. 'You don't pull your punches do you?'

'It's just a simple question.'

'What can I tell you?' He put the beer can to his lips, changed his mind and left it back on the table.

'What you're *really* thinking. For once.'

Our eyes duelled for a second before he looked away. 'OK, I'll tell you. I think she's a very unhappy little girl. More mixed up than we were led to believe. On the surface she appears to have everything. You saw that house. *Houses.* The horses. The clothes. Everything we're told a teenage girl needs to make her deliriously happy?' He shook his head. 'Then you look closer. And you see enough clothes to get three girl bands through a year. And a pile of underwear that a stripper might hesitate to wear. Now, I could be wrong, but I don't believe that happy and fulfilled seventeen-year-old girls buy themselves obscene underwear.'

'Maybe she just bought it out of curiosity?' I defended her – or was it myself, for not mentioning it to him after my first visit to the house.

'It's possible. If she was as sheltered as we've been told, and then suddenly thrown into the student world of goths and some of those other nutters we met, she could be having some real adjustment problems. All those mixed messages? Tricky enough for an adult, but for a sheltered seventeen-year-old?' He shifted uncomfortably.

'Maybe she just likes pretty underwear?' I said.

'Pretty?'

'Colourful. All that red satin. Those gold lamé panties.'

'Crotchless? And some of that other stuff?' He tried the beer again, this time managing to swallow a whole mouthful before shuddering.

He obviously thought a proper detective would have mentioned Caroline's more erotic underwear immediately. But not *all* her stuff was questionable. And who decides what's questionable anyway? Fiona has underwear that I wouldn't be caught dead in, and vice versa. White aertex isn't to everyone's taste.

He stubbed out his cigarette. 'What time do you reckon it is in Arizona?'

'What?'

'Arizona. I wonder what time it is there?'

I'd heard him the first time. It was hearing him say it out of the blue that took me by surprise. How would I know what time it was in Arizona? I had no interest in Arizona. I was still thinking about Caroline. Gerry was the one with an ex in Arizona. And why did Arizona suddenly enter his head? One minute we're knee-deep in the Boucher case, then suddenly his mind is on Arizona?

'Surely you know the time difference by now?' I didn't hide my irritation.

'Yeah.' He looked at his watch. 'They're eight hours behind us, so . . . anyway, it doesn't matter. I'll hang about. Stay awake until . . . they won't be back from the game yet. I was afraid that I'd fall asleep and end up ringing them far too late, disturbing the whole household when they were in bed.' He looked sheepish.

Well God forbid he'd disturb saintly Sally's sleep. It was OK to disturb me, though. Waken me with his loud music. And then, midway through a conversation about a case that was upsetting the whole agency, suddenly start talking about bloody Arizona. Bad enough that he had me worrying about Caroline and her kinky underwear. Now he had moved on to his wife. Well, ex-wife.

'I'm off to bed.' I managed a tight-lipped smile.

'Night.' His lips grazed my cheek, his mind clearly far away. In Arizona?

I gritted my teeth and planned my revenge. I couldn't wait till he came to bed and tried to disturb me. I'd show him. I gritted my teeth.

I could have spared myself the angst. When he did come to bed, he didn't even waken me.

26

Next day Gerry was in the rats. All day. He had emailed our information on Caroline to the police in Auckland and was waiting to hear from them. It was a long shot, but he said it was worth it.

To keep him occupied, I collected a pile of papers that had been waiting for his signature and took them to his office. He wasn't there. Sandra was, hunched over his desk, fiddling with what looked like a new paperweight.

She jumped guiltily when I walked in.

'What are you up to?' I asked suspiciously.

She pointed to the cut-glass paperweight. 'What do you think?' she asked warily.

'Very nice, if you're into paperweights.'

'It's not a paperweight.' She spoke in hushed tones. 'It's an ashtray.'

I dropped the papers on the desk. 'Where is he?'

'Talking to Barney. Or maybe Declan.' She ducked out, almost colliding with Gerry in the doorway.

'Coffee's on your desk, Gerry.' It sounded like a coded warning.

'Thanks, Sandra.' He came in, his eyes wary.

'No word from New Zealand?' I asked.

'No.'

'So you're definitely back on the dreaded weed?' I indicated the ashtray.

'Oh, that. Naomi gave it to me. It's for . . . emergencies.'

Emergencies? I knew that before the day was out, the damn yoke would be brimming with butts. Still, I tried to give him an out.

'Is the knee troubling you?'

'Not much.' He scribbled his signature without bothering to read a single line of the papers I put in front of him. He could have been signing away his kidneys for all he knew.

'Gerry?'

'Yeah?'

'Those expense account sheets are looking good, aren't they? Well within budget?'

'I noticed that,' he lied. 'We're on the road to recovery, then?'

'Well, yes. Unfortunately you've just signed away all your body organs to a clinic in the Philippines. They quoted me five grand for your lungs.'

He gave an uneasy laugh.

I picked up the papers. 'Of course they won't want them now. Now that you're a hard-core smoker again.' I swept out before he could start claiming that the glass ashtray was an ice sculpture.

I was as concerned about Caroline as he was, and I wasn't smoking. And nobody was giving me presents of lead crystal ashtrays. There was one other problem with having a confirmed smoker in the agency. They might lead others astray. This wasn't my personal fear, it was our insurance company's. The one I had recently assured that McHugh Dunning ran a strict non-smoking policy in order to get a discount on our premiums.

I consoled myself with the thought that nobody

else knew that Gerry was back on the fags.

Barney and I met in the corridor. 'So Gerry's back on the fags?' He grinned. 'It wasn't just a momentary aberration then?'

'What?'

'The other day in the jeep. You didn't really think all that smoke came from that kid's cigarette? You can be such an innocent, Annie.' He mock punched my chin. 'What about that fancy ashtray Naomi gave him? He must have been slipping up to her office for a sly one on a regular basis. Dropping ash all over her top-notch designs,' he chortled. 'So she gives him a designer ashtray. Declan is mad jealous.'

And people say the *wife* is always the last to know?

Still I defended him. 'It's his leg,' I said. 'It hurts like hell.'

'He'll need to smoke something a bit stronger than tobacco, then.' Barney gave me his butter-wouldn't-melt look and went to find Declan.

I hurried outside to find Mags. There was something I needed to clear up with her. Something extra pressing, now that I was worried that some psycho might have Caroline in his clutches. The thing was, Gerry couldn't shake off his uneasy feeling about St Martin's Lane. And while he might be weak-willed when it came to cigarettes, he had an invincible radar when it came to tracing missing people. If his gut reaction told him Mags was hoarding some information about the case, it was worth checking out.

Since Gerry's accident she had been avoiding the agency, but I knew the alternative route she took to the Financial Services Centre. I stood in wait, watching out for the filthy bobble-topped ski-hat to appear round the corner. And there it was, moving along at a steady pace.

She spotted me, and turned to run. As if she could outpace me? I tore after her, grabbed her by the arm, and half pushed, half pulled her across the road and into the Café Naturalle.

'Sit there and don't move.' I went to order coffees.

If the staff didn't want Mags and Fred stinking out their megacool café, there was little they could do about it, given my mood. And the fact that they all fancied Barney, who normally accompanied me here, didn't hurt. He was the only one they ever gave *three* free refills to.

The café was practically empty, the prework rush over, the elevenses crush yet to come.

I put a milky coffee in front of Mags. 'Now listen, I have something to ask you. And if you lie to me, you'll be the sorriest woman who ever walked the streets of Dublin. Do you understand me?' I narrowed my eyes, hoping it made me look menacing.

It worked. 'Yes.' She was a frightened little mouse.

'Good. You know Gerry could have been killed in that terrible fall?'

'I never sent him to that house.' Her lip quivered.

'I know that. But you did lie to me about seeing Caroline in St Martin's Lane, didn't you?' I menaced again, this time giving it all I had.

'I . . .'

The cadaver-like waitress was whispering to her even skinnier workmate, giving her a push in our direction. I turned and gave her my menacing look. She stepped back, taking refuge behind the high counter as she twiddled her skinny plaits nervously.

I turned back to Mags.

'You lied to me about seeing Caroline, didn't you?'

'I . . . maybe.' She considered for a second. 'Maybe I did. But I *thought* I saw her.'

'Did you or didn't you?'

'What?'

'See Caroline?' I nearly lost patience.

'Sometimes I think I did.'

'Jesus, Mags, you're not stupid.'

'No,' she agreed.

'So did you see her? Or not?'

'In St Martin's Lane?'

'Where else?' I gritted my teeth.

'Maybe I did see her somewhere else. Near the big corpo flats?'

'Not in St Martin's Lane?'

'No. I think it *was* near the corpo flats. Across the way from St Martin's Lane.'

'Think hard, Mags,' I pleaded. 'Was it in the lane or near the corporation flats?'

'I'm nearly sure it was . . .' She paused to think. '. . . in both.' She gave a pleased smile.

I dropped my head in my hands.

'Or they might have been . . . different people?' She was anxious to help.

'Then why did you tell me it was her?' My voice rose, attracting another flurry of interest from behind the counter.

Mags squirmed unhappily. 'I dunno. I saw her photo in the paper.'

'Caroline's photo?' I so needed some clarity.

'Yes. I was putting the pages down for Fred. He'll only go on the big papers. Won't shit on them cheap tabloids.'

'Fred will only poo on the broadsheet financial

pages?' We were entering the realms of the surreal here.

She smiled proudly. 'You didn't know he was trained? Well, he is. He never ever . . .' She began a long preamble about Fred's bowel habits.

My head began to throb as the awful possibility hit me. Was it Fred's penchant for pooing on the financial pages that had led to me following a false trail which had culminated in Gerry almost losing his life? I was so angry I could hardly bear to look at Mags. Yet I owed it to Gerry to clear up any lingering hope that she could lead us to Caroline.

'. . . Sister Margaret says he's the best-trained dog she's ever . . .'

'Shut up about Fred!' I leaned across the table and shook her. 'All I want to hear from you is if you *ever* saw this girl anywhere near St Martin's Lane?' I slammed a photo of Caroline on the table.

'I . . .'

'If you lie to me, I'll . . .' I lowered my voice. 'I'll cut your tongue out!'

'Oh . . .' She pursed her little lips in fright.

'The truth now!' My yell had the café staff gasping.

'Just interviewing her.' I smiled at them and brushed some loose grime from Mags's coat, like I had once seen a slick detective do in a popular TV series.

Mags looked as if she might make a run for it. 'What did you ask me again?'

'Have you seen this girl in St Martin's Lane? Ever?'

She turned away. 'No.'

My anger dissipated in one long outgoing breath. 'Jesus Christ, Mags. You have no idea how much pain and trouble your lies have caused so many people.'

'Sorry.' Her thin lips quivered.

I got up to leave.

I was walking away when she said. 'I *might* have seen her coming out of the corpo flats. Is she bald now? With a ring in her nose?'

It took immense will power not to run back and land one on *her* snub little nose. Instead I stepped out into the street, where the wind caught my hair, whipping it into a wild tangle of curls.

There was a sudden scream from the café. Fred was humping cadaver girl's leg at warp speed.

'Deal with it,' I muttered under my breath, and hurried back to the agency.

I was barely in the door when Sandra yelled, 'Gerry got an email from New Zealand!' Sandra loved to be first with the big news.

Too excited to wait for the lift, I took the stairs two at a time.

'What's the news, Gerry?' Breathless from my mad sprint, I fell into his office.

He looked up, startled.

'From Auckland?' I panted. 'What's . . . ?'

'No news.' He frowned. 'They just acknowledged my email.'

27

It was mid-June. Dublin was on the brink of a heat-wave and we were still no nearer to finding Caroline Boucher than we had been in freezing March when she'd first disappeared. We hadn't even come across a single genuine sighting of her. But everything else was moving along nicely. Gerry was finally free of the hated leg cast, fully restored to his normal robust health. And Naomi appeared to be finally tiring of her endless pursuit of him. Baby Calum was now a massive seven-week-old bouncer, which was why Gerry and I had been invited to dinner with Fiona and Pino. They were eager to discuss arrangements for his upcoming christening. Well, Fiona was.

Sitting on her squishy cream sofa, she reached into a mountain of baby clothes to pull out a tiny, doll-sized christening gown. 'See what I mean?' She held it up for inspection. '*This* wouldn't even fit Calum's right arm.'

We were trawling through a box of baby things that had arrived that morning from Italy. From Nonna Molino, Pino's doting mum, who had miraculously rallied from her death bed after Calum's birth.

Gerry and Pino were outside, having excused themselves after a sumptuous, wine-soaked dinner. Full to bursting, they both said they needed fresh air. Although my guess was that they were hoping to escape any further discussions on Calum's christening, an event which was turning into a three-ring circus, with Pino's close relatives flying in from as far away as Capri. The two of them disappeared out front, eager to examine a minor scrape on Pino's beloved Porsche, Pino being anxious to get a detective's opinion as to whether the scrape might have been maliciously inflicted or was just an accident.

'Don't forget to dust for fingerprints,' Fiona had called after them as they went out. 'We don't want Pino shooting the wrong suspect.'

She took several more baby clothes from the box, all of them ludicrously small when measured against the sleeping Calum, who, at less than two months, was roughly the size of a gluttonous two-year-old. Not a single item among the exquisite little nightshirts, vests and baby dungarees would fit him. Not even the glistening orange raincoat with the red plaid lining and matching hat, which was clearly designed for Paddington Bear.

Checking out the Paddington Bear outfit we began to giggle. Wine always had this effect on Fiona, and after all those months of semi-abstinence – including her allotted breastfeeding time – she was well into depleting Pino's private stock again. He, generous soul that he was, never hesitated to indulge her.

'Such a shame.' She smoothed a little embroidered nightshirt with loving fingers before giving me a soulful look. 'Its almost sinful, letting all these beautiful clothes go to waste. I don't suppose you'd consider . . . ?' She made a baby rocking motion.

'Doh! Well there's a bright idea, Fi! You have a box of teeny, tiny baby clothes, so why don't I have a baby to fit them? What a perfectly sound reason to have a baby.'

'Who's having a baby?' Pino came in shaking the rain off his jacket. 'Annie? You kept that very quiet.' He turned to Gerry who was following behind, growling into his mobile.

'What?' he looked at Pino.

'Annie's having a baby,' Pino chortled.

Gerry didn't even blink. Just continued his conversation with his caller, then looked at me and said, 'If she is, it must be an immaculate conception.' His attention on his caller again, he said, 'Yes. Any time. It doesn't matter how late. He has my mobile number. Tell him it's important.'

He followed me out to the jeep, dragging his heels like a child. 'What did I say that was so terrible?'

'You don't know? You didn't see Fiona's face?' I ran to avoid the heavy downpour. *Light, intermittent showers,* the jovial TV weatherman had promised less than five hours ago. *To be followed by a heatwave with temperatures reaching well into the thirties, and* . . . Could you trust anyone?

'If I knew what I said wrong, would I be asking you what it was?' Gerry splashed through a river of water and dived into the jeep.

'You practically told Pino I was frigid!'

'What?' he was incredulous.

'You told him we *never* have sex. Didn't you see the look of pity on their faces?'

'I never mentioned sex!'

'You were too busy taking an emergency call to know what you were saying.'

282

He braked sharply at a red light and turned to face me. 'What emergency call?'

'Exactly! What was so important about that call that you had to take it in the middle of our first night out in months?'

'As I explained to Pino,' he said carefully, 'that call was from Simon Boucher's PA. I had left a message saying we have to talk, this case is stretching out far too long. We have to get things moving again.'

'So you think his PA can help?'

'Not him. Boucher! His PA isn't allowed any input in the case.'

'Is he allowed to call his partner frigid?'

He was sighing in exasperation when there was a sudden loud bang and we were pitched backwards. Then forward again, only to be pinned to our seats by voluminous airbags. 'Jesus Christ!' Gerry rammed on the handbrake. 'Some stupid fucker ran into me.'

He had. But we had also run into something – the car in front. And it had all happened so fast even I couldn't tell which collision had occurred first. Not that either of them was life-threatening. There were no screams of agony or sounds of metal tearing metal. Not even a crumpled bumper. Just a lot of inflated airbags and three irate drivers leaping out to point accusing fingers at each other.

'It wasn't my fault,' a high-pitched nasal voice insisted. 'It was that jeep! Jeeps should be banned from city roads.'

'Jeeps aren't the problem. It's idiots like you who can't tell green from red who cause collisions. Is there a reason why you started moving and then stopped without warning? In the middle of a heavy traffic flow?'

'There was a bloody lake in front of me.'

'So you slammed on your brakes? Knowing I was close behind you?'

'Ah, you admit you were too close?'

'No I don't, you imbecile. Do you admit that you don't have the skill to manoeuvre a Renault 4 through a couple of inches of water? And just for the record, I was already breaking when I was pushed from behind. By this moron here.'

The moron stood there shivering. Even dripping wet he couldn't have weighed ninety pounds. 'I thought you were much further away from me. And moving faster. This rain distorts everything . . .'

'Rain my arse. I can smell drink on your breath. How many did you have?'

'Nobody got hurt.' Moron sounded close to tears.

'My wife may have whiplash,' nasal voice whined. 'Her chiropractor won't be happy.'

The argument continued, providing light relief for the lines of bored motorists driving past, some of whom slowed down for a better look, probably hoping to catch sight of a mangled limb or two. I sat back and let the after-effects of Pino's rich red burgandy mellow me out. This whole thing was just a storm in a teacup. My Honda regularly suffered more damage in the supermarket car park than any of these three cars had in this stupid collision, yet passing drivers were behaving as if they were viewing a scene from *Gladiator*.

I half closed my eyes, glanced idly down into a passing car. And nearly jumped out of my skin with shock.

Caroline Boucher was looking up at me. Then she was gone. Driving away in a big silver BMW.

I catapulted behind the wheel of the jeep. Yelled out the open window.

'Gerry? Gerry? Get in! I've just seen Caroline! I've seen her!'

I was already inching the jeep past the stalled Renault, forcing my way into the jam-packed left lane, when Gerry jumped in the passenger door, rain dribbling down his face.

'The reg?' he yelled. 'Did you get the reg?'

'No! But it's a silver BMW. You can see it from here. Six cars ahead. See?'

'Yeah. You sure it's her?' He clicked his seat belt.

'The window may have been steamed up –' I put the blower on high – 'but no one has ever challenged my eyesight. Damn this rain.' I wiped the windscreen impatiently. 'I'll try to get closer so you can get the reg.'

Easier said than done. The traffic was dense, and moving way too fast for such atrocious weather conditions, every car clinging jealously to its pack position. Short of ramming one of them, there was little hope of changing lanes. We were all wedged in like speeding sardines.

'Can *you* make out her reg?' I yelled as the road curved to the right.

'I'm not bloody Superman.' Gerry was practically on the dashboard, peering helplessly into the downpour.

'Christ, Gerry,' I suddenly remembered, 'I'm over the limit. If the Garda stop us we're . . .'

'. . . fucked. I know. But we can't change places now.'

285

We were approaching a major crossroads. The BMW was still six cars ahead.

'The road widens here, broadens into five lanes. Keep a sharp eye on her, Gerry.'

'Change lanes,' he ordered. 'Get into the right lane now.'

'But that's for right turns only. What if she . . . ?'

'It's our only hope . . .'

'But what if she . . . ?'

'*Change!*' he yelled. 'Try to get alongside her.'

I tried, bringing two other drivers to the brink of coronaries when I practically sheared the nearside doors off their cars.

'Can you see her?' I inched closer to the BMW.

'Jesus. It is her!' He opened the window, letting the rain lash in. 'Hit the horn! Hit the horn!'

I did as instructed. Caroline half turned, her eyes widening in fear.

'Flash the lights!' he shouted.

I did, and at first I thought she was swerving away from us in fright. When I realised what she was doing, it was too late. She took a left turn and disappeared into the rain.

Tightly wedged in by traffic, I had no choice but to continue straight on.

'Left. Left,' Gerry shouted as we sped past the junction. 'Take the next left. That road curves back around. We can meet her head on.'

A bad choice of words, given the circumstances, because to take the next left I'd have to cross two lanes of fast-moving traffic. A stunt best left to *Jackass TV*.

'There's a break! Go!' Gerry clutched the dashboard and closed his eyes.

Headlights on full, we made it. To a deafening cacophony of angry motor horns and possibly the ruination of several underpants.

'Keep left . . .' Gerry's voice was a squeak . . . 'and floor it. We can't let her get away.'

But she was gone, and no amount of driving round and round the sprawling housing estate we were now in could bring her back into view.

I slowed down and looked at Gerry. 'What do we do now?'

It was probably frustration that made him jump out of the moving jeep and check a carelessly parked BMW. I mean, visibility was bad, but this BMW wasn't even the right colour.

'Bloody rain. It does distorts everything.' He got back in the jeep.

Four more laps around the quiet estate, and it was time to admit defeat.

'You're right,' Gerry answered my silent inquiry. 'She could be parked in any one of a hundred – a thousand – garages around here.' He gave in.

We were speeding out of the housing estate when we heard the police siren.

'You don't suppose that's . . . us?' I asked.

'Course not! But take the back road home anyway.'

That's when I saw it. The big silver BMW coming out of nowhere. Heading straight for us.

'It's her!' Gerry cried. 'Block her! Block her!'

I swerved in front of the big car. It reversed smoothly into a laurel-hedged driveway. Before I could brake, Gerry was out, leaping across the hedge. I raced after him.

'Caroline?' he yanked open the car door.

A white-haired old man was sat behind the wheel,

his mobile phone raised like a weapon. 'I'm not afraid of you! The Garda are on their way!' he threatened. 'Bloody joyriders! I'm not afraid of you!'

The lights came on in the house. The door opened and a massive brown dog sprang out, teeth bared in readiness.

'Get them, Rusty!' the man ordered.

'Run, Annie,' Gerry said.

We were back on the dual carriageway when a Garda car tore past. Happily it was going in the opposite direction.

We sat in the kitchen in silence. Looking at each other. Wrapped in dressing gowns and all talked out, sipping the remains of our hot whiskeys – Gerry's cure-all.

He suddenly spoke, repeating the question we had asked each other a trillion times since we got home. 'It was her, wasn't it?'

'Definitely.' I clutched my glass.

'And no one was holding her prisoner in the car?'

I shook my head. 'She was alone. Looking very happy. Until I honked the horn and flashed the lights at her.'

'Right! So first thing tomorrow we go as planned. Forget Boucher's paranoia about going public. Once he has her back safe, he won't care how we did it.'

'Exactly.'

'We'll get Phil in the photo shop to run up a few hundred copies of the best picture we have of her. The one with her looking exactly as she did tonight. All big-eyed and fair-haired. That remarkable blonde hair, flicking up where it touches her shoulders.' He sounded pleased.

'We'll knock on every door in that housing estate.'

'Pull the others off their cases to help out. Put everything else on hold. This time we search aggressively. Stick her photo in people's faces. Force them to look! Tell them her poor father is distraught. Suicidal. That'll get a reaction. The lads can hit the pubs, discos, clubs, wherever youngsters hang out. Make a major fuss. Leave photos of her everywhere. Pin them to the walls of toilets if they have to. We came so close.'

'If only the traffic had been lighter.'

'That's water under the bridge now! Although in future you should remember to get the reg number first thing.'

I should? What about him? I was driving. And in such poor visibility, I was lucky to see the car in front of me. All he had to do was sit there. Why was it my fault we didn't get the reg?

'It's essential to get the reg! I know your first thought was to call me. Get the jeep moving. But . . .'

He saw my expression. 'But apart from that, you were great. Your responses spot-on. You'll make a good detective, Annie.' He touched my cheek.

I was only just short of melting into a dribbling pool on the floor, kissing his feet in gratitude, but mindful of my dignity I leaned over to kiss his lips instead. Our mouths were just about to meet when the doorbell rang.

I went to the window. There was a flashing blue light outside.

'There's a Garda car at the gate, Gerry.'

The Garda's deep voice echoed along the hallway. 'I mean, what the fuck were you doing, Gerry?'

'How did you know it was me?'

'How . . . ? Five irate citizens gave us your reg number. We didn't even have to run it. Everyone in the station recognised it. For Christ's sake, we have reports of your jeep hitting eighty in a thirty-mile-an-hour zone.'

'That's rubbish! The traffic was crawling. I couldn't have done eighty if I'd tried. And how the hell did all those people get *my* reg number, when I couldn't see three feckin' feet in front of me . . . ?' His voice trailed off.

'Christ, Gerry! I'm warning you. Try something like that again and you're in big trouble. People thought you were fucking joyriders!'

There was a guilty silence.

'I was on a case.'

'None of us is above the law. None of us.'

'I agree. Er . . . how's the new baby? He must be getting on for one now?'

'He's eight, Gerry.'

'God, doesn't time fly,' Gerry chuckled. 'Give Eilish my regards.'

'I'm serious now, Gerry. This is your last chance.'

'Night.'

I waited for the door to close before joining him in the hall.

'Are we in trouble?'

'Big time.'

'Oh God.'

'Well, not me, just you when I tell them you were driving. You'll be on *Crimeline* next week. Probably make the centrefold of the *Garda Review* the week after.' He chased me up the stairs.

★ ★ ★

I was diving into bed when his mobile rang. He tried to look uninterested, shrugging it off, but his eyes kept returning to it.

'Oh for God's sake, answer it. It's probably Boucher returning your call. May as well tell him the good news.'

He went out to the landing where the signal was always better.

The call seemed to take for ever. I was about to check that he was still alive when he came back in, looking like he'd been kicked in the groin.

I sat up. 'What is it? Is it . . . Arizona? Something happened to your sons?'

He shook his head, his eyes downcast. 'Boucher. He says under no circumstances are we to hawk photos of his daughter around a Dublin housing estate. He says if we do that, the press will definitely get hold of the story.'

'Does that still matter? We're so close, it will all be over in a flash.'

'He's halfway through a major deal with AOC, the big American bank. The negotiations are apparently at a very sensitive stage. He wants us to hold off until they reach an agreement. Until the final papers are signed.'

'But . . . did you tell him we saw her?'

'Of course I told him,' he snapped. 'He asked how she looked. If she appeared to be in any danger.'

'And . . . ?'

'Did she seem to be in any danger to you?' he asked angrily.

'Well . . . no. We were probably in more danger taking that turn-off.'

'So that's that. We're to do nothing until he gives us the go-ahead. Until he gets back to Dublin.'

'When will that be?' Incredulity draining me of all hope, I slumped on the bed.

'Two, three days?'

'So in the meantime, we . . . ?'

'We get some sleep.' He pulled back the covers and got into bed.

'We do *nothing*?' Temper rising now, I prepared to do battle.

'He's the client,' he said evenly.

I hissed in frustration. 'So . . . we can't make a move without his permission? How insane is that? Supposing . . . supposing we're wrong and she *is* in danger?'

He gave me a look. 'I've told you, we do nothing. He's the client. Do I have to keep reminding you that we're not the police?' he snapped.

Keep reminding *me*? It was Barney who needed reminding that he was a PI with none of the powers of the Garda. I *never* assumed . . . Even tonight I only drove the jeep like a squad car because Gerry told me to. Now he was telling me to roll over and go to sleep. Was this what my new career was to be like? Blindly obeying orders. Without question.

He pushed aside the duvet, pulling the sheet up around his shoulders instead. 'We're detectives for hire, Annie. Paid to do the client's bidding.'

So that was it, then? A phone call from Simon Boucher and all our plans had to be cast aside? Our well-mapped strategy thrown on the dung heap? We had risked our lives on that dual carriageway tonight. Given our all for the client. Now he'd ordered us to back off, and we had to obey.

Gerry was feigning sleep, his back turned to me. I reached over to touch his shoulder, then reconsidered.

Punching my pillow instead, I paraphrased Sandra: 'This is pure shite!'

28

Two days passed and we still hadn't received the go-ahead from Simon Boucher. But something else had arrived with a vengeance. Dublin was in the grip of the hottest heatwave in living memory.

'Better late than never,' Barney said, nudging Declan as they stood in Gerry's office staring down into the boiling street where every passing girl seemed to be showing more flesh than the women in the lap dancing club they were about to work undercover in. An old client of ours, a major investor in the club, had received a tip-off that his club manager was indulging in a little creative bookkeeping. Barney and Declan both volunteered to work there, Barney behind the cocktail bar, Declan on the door.

Gerry also had a new case, this one not quite so glamorous. He was hoping to trap a couple of cheeky villains who were swapping dead greyhounds for top racing ones, somehow managing to slip the dead mutts into locked kennels during the night, then legging it with the champion dogs. Three bereaved owners had mourned the sudden deaths of their champions before someone realised that all three corpses were ringers. Gerry guessed that the live dogs were well on their way overseas for resale.

Barney and Declan listened curiously as he gave me a list of numbers to ring. 'Get me all the information you can on dog tattooing. Someone was obviously duplicating the winners' tattoo numbers. All the ringers had them. And check out those two names at the top of the list. Tom O'Neill over in Donnybrook garda station will tell you if they have form.'

Barney laughed. 'I didn't know dogs were into tattoos? While you're at it, Annie, find out what the most popular dog tattoo is. "Rover loves Spot?" Or would it be "Blackie for ever"? And . . .'

'Sod off, Barney!' I marched back to my office, already irritated by having to sit around making phone calls when all I wanted to do was get out there and find Caroline.

I had almost completed the calls when Naomi came in. 'I have a problem,' she shrilled.

I put down the receiver, glanced heavenwards and waited. Apparently the sudden rise in temperature was causing her precious fabrics to wilt.

I counted to a silent ten. Very slowly. Clutched the receiver again until my knuckles shone white. 'What do you expect me to do about that, Naomi?'

'For the rent I'm paying, I expect you to supply air conditioning.' Her voice became even shriller.

I patiently explained that as our summers usually have the life span of a gnat, and can frequently be hard to distinguish from the other three seasons, air conditioning had never figured in our plans.

'I knew you'd say that, so I made my own arrangements. I've hired an engineer.'

'Good for you.' I unclenched my teeth.

'But I've come up against another problem.' Her face tightened.

'*Another problem?* Surely not?' I tried a little irony, knowing full well I was wasting my time.

'Follow me,' she ordered. I did. It was easier than arguing, and Gerry's final number could wait. It wasn't as if it would help us find Caroline or anything important like that.

Naomi grumbled her way along the corridor into the lift and on into reception.

'Tell her what you told me!' she ordered a sad-faced stranger, who turned out to be the engineer she had engaged to fit a top-of-the-range air-conditioning unit, to serve both her floors.

'To install it, I'll have to sh-shut the p-power off for the day.' He looked terrified.

'On both floors?' I was surprised.

'The whole building,' Naomi said.

'Are you nuts?' I nearly laughed. 'We can't be without power for a whole day!'

'But my designs are being ruined,' Naomi screeched.

'Sorry, Naomi. But there it is.' I turned to go.

Gerry came out of the lift with one of the greyhound owners, both of them smoking like chimneys, although the no smoking sign in the lift was gigantic.

'What's going on?' Gerry asked.

Naomi grabbed him. 'I'm glad you're here, Gerry. I need air conditioning.'

He looked puzzled.

'Her fabrics are wilting,' I explained.

'And you're telling me because . . . ?' He became increasingly puzzled.

'We need to cut the power to the building. Just for the day.' She clung to his arm.

'Out of the question.' He shrugged her off.

'Please.'

'Can you install it on a Sunday?' He turned to the engineer.

'I . . . I dunno. I'll have to check with the boss.'

'Then talk to me when you do. Maybe in a month's time. When things are calmer. Maybe some holiday weekend,' he reasoned.

'In a month's time I won't need air conditioning to keep my displays intact,' Naomi pleaded. 'I have a special Tropical Island decor week planned for then.'

'Gerry, we'll be late . . .' The greyhound man was becoming impatient.

'Hang on. You decorate tropical islands?' Gerry frowned at Naomi.

'She means a tropical island *theme*, Gerry.'

Naomi shot me a grateful look. 'So you see, heat and high humidity would be a positive bonus then. Right now it's destroying the effect of my crisp white backdrop. Even my bed drapes are wilting. My Arctic Winter theme is being ruined.'

'Gerry? They'll have moved the dogs.'

'I'm coming. Swop them around then,' he said to Naomi. 'Have your tropical display now, while the weather is hot and humid. Wouldn't that make sense?'

Naomi looked as if she might explode. 'How can you be so dense? My clients expect me to be in the vanguard of design. To show them the future today. Tomorrow *is* today in the design world. If I lose sight of that, I'm finished.'

Gerry looked at me. 'That makes sense to you, does it?' he asked, as the greyhound man fretted.

'Oh, for goodness sake, a ten-year-old child could understand it!' Naomi finally lost it with him. 'Apart from any marketing concerns, consider the time it takes for a layout design to make the transition from drawing board to scale model, and on to a person-alised version for any given client. And as all my clients are cutting-edge personalities and won't accept anything less, surely you can see my dilemma? Right now I'm exhibiting a futuristic seasonal mode, because fabric designers worldwide are presently thinking along the lines of an arctic, ecominimalist, almost barren – that is to say, nuclear – winter, look.'

I could tell she had lost Gerry somewhere around *futuristic seasonal mode*. He looked at the engineer, then back to her. 'Yeeeah. But apart from that, what sort of sad people want to see winter designs in this heat?'

Naomi touched her brow with a pink-taloned finger, and I knew, intuitively, that her one-sided love affair with him was over. Dead as a nuclear winter.

'I could get you a fan?' he offered.

'A fan? You expect me to put a cooling fan in the middle of an arctic display?' her voice held all the chill of her arctic snow scene – *before* the heat ruined it.

'It might stop those beautiful drapes wilting,' I tried.

'Air conditioning will stop them wilting!' she screeched. 'And I need it now, before I become the laughing stock of the interior design world. A photog-rapher from Irish Interiors is arriving first thing on Friday. If I don't have fully functioning air condition-ing by then I'm . . . ruined!' She waved her arms like a windmill, making everyone step back in fright and the sad-faced engineer look as if he might burst into tears.

'The whole building without power?' Gerry asked him.

'The whole b-building,' he blinked nervously.

'For how long?'

'One d-day. At least.'

'That's it, then.' Gerry toughened. 'We can't be without power. We couldn't even send a damn fax or pull information from a database. Out of the question. Are you trying to wreck *my* business, Naomi?'

There was a breathless hush as we all waited for her reply. Even Sandra waited, ignoring the ringing phones as she looked over with big, fearful eyes.

'Well?' Gerry demanded.

'Sorry.' Naomi paled.

'Right then.' Gerry left, the greyhound man running alongside him, trying to keep up with his long strides.

'S-so that's th-that then?' The sad-faced engineer hesitated for a nanosecond before scuttling off behind them.

Although she was fighting hard to keep her composure, it was obvious that Naomi was on the brink of tears. Losing was a whole new experience for her, and she didn't like it. For the first time since we'd met, I felt sorry for her. She was unbearably bossy, overly fond of lists and never stopped complaining, but she put in a longer working day than almost anyone I could think of.

Declan claimed to know that she frequently stayed back long into the night, working on her designs. He said you could often see her office light blazing at two in the morning. From across the street.

Gerry's reply to that had been a gruff warning: 'Stalking is against the law, Declan!'

'Sandra?' I called over to the reception desk now. 'Any coffee?' I rolled my eyes towards Naomi.

'Sure.' Sandra could be sharp enough when she chose. 'Just made a fresh pot.'

Naomi sipped her coffee gratefully. Neither of us spoke. Just sat there, side by side, almost like friends. I tried to think of a way to cheer her up, but short of telling her that every one of the builders opposite had dropped dead, I couldn't think of a single thing guaranteed to bring a smile to her beautifully made-up face.

'Look on the bright side, Naomi,' I finally said. 'It's almost July. We could have ground frost tomorrow.'

To my utter astonishment, she nearly smiled. 'What's happening to this country anyway?' she said. 'When you can't even rely on a miserably cold summer any more.'

'It's all this global warming.' Sandra offered us both a refill. 'Jimmy says the plants don't know one season from another any more. Our climbing roses were in bud last Christmas, and yesterday Gerry Ryan said it was hotter in Wexford than in Malaga. Oh, good morning!' She darted back behind the desk as a uniformed man arrived.

It was Simon Boucher's driver, his lop-sided body looking scarier than ever.

I got to my feet, my heart pounding.

'Is Mr Boucher here?' I glanced out at the big car.

'No. He's in Switzerland. He sent this. For Mr Dunning's eyes only.' He looked from me to Sandra and back again. Unsure which of us to entrust with the important looking manila envelope. Still undecided, he spotted Naomi.

'Ms Lawlor Billings?' He looked surprised.

'How are you, Trevor?' she said frostily.

'For Mr Dunning.' He handed Sandra the envelope.

Naomi sat there, rigid as a stone carving.

'Ms . . . Billings . . .' He gave her a curious look and left.

Naomi looked as if she might drop her coffee cup. I grabbed it, before it hit the floor.

'Are you all right?'

'You look like you've seen a ghost!' Sandra hurried over, her gossip antenna working overtime.

Naomi gave a weak smile. That was twice in one morning. 'It's . . . Trevor is the last person I expected to see in here.'

'Do you know him?' Sandra moved closer.

'Would it be rude of me to ask for another coffee?' Naomi put a hand to her forehead.

'One sugar?'

'Make it two. Three. Please.'

'You know Odd J— Trevor?' I half expected a rebuff.

'No . . . I mean, yes . . . I knew . . . the man he drives for.'

'You know Simon Boucher?' I squeaked.

'Know him? We were engaged to be married.' She gulped her coffee thirstily.

I nearly choked on mine.

We found a quiet corner in the Café Naturalle. My idea. Privacy could be hard to come by in the agency, despite its reputation for discretion, and there was so much I wanted to know about Simon Boucher. Certainly more than the meagre bits he was willing to share with us. I wanted to know everything, and not just out of curiosity. The Boucher case was causing a rare coldness between Gerry and I. I couldn't help it. Gerry persisted in his belief that the client called the tune, but I felt it was so wrong for Boucher to put his business interests before his young daughter's well-being that I would have . . . Well, I wasn't sure what I would have done, but I definitely wouldn't have sat back doing nothing. Or gone out chasing missing greyhounds.

As Naomi and I had already consumed enough coffee to keep our nerves on edge for the rest of our lives, we both ordered relaxing green tea. Then sat back and eyed each other warily.

'You were engaged to Simon Boucher?' I couldn't disguise my eagerness.

'For almost a year.' She nodded.

Why was I surprised? Ireland is a small country, and they were cut from the same cloth, her and Boucher. Well, the same background. Old protestant families. Landed gentry with beautifully rounded vowels, and all that came with that double-edged sword.

'We had six weeks to go to the wedding,' she said. 'Everything was arranged. The reception. The honeymoon. I was redecorating his houses. I had almost completed the manor house in Wicklow, transformed it beyond recognition,' a note of pride crept into her voice. 'Got rid of all that dark ugly furniture. Let some light in and . . .' She paused. 'Then Caroline ran away, and . . . everything fell apart.'

'How old was she then? Fourteen?' I pushed.

She nodded. Blew her nose into her designer hanky.

'But they found her ten days later. Why didn't you go ahead with the wedding then?'

'Have you met Caroline?'

'No. But I've seen her photos. She's a sweet little thing.'

She gave a bitter laugh. 'Sweet? She's a monster.'

The chill started somewhere in my lower back and began creeping upwards.

'She . . . she can't be that bad.' I faked an amused laugh.

'Let me put it this way – would you describe me as a shrinking violet?'

'Not exactly,' I said drily.

'Well, she had me in tears. Every day.'

'What about Simon? Her father?' I held my breath, dreading what I might hear. After all, Simon Boucher could be holding the future of the agency in his hands. A couple of greyhound owners or a partner in a lap dancing club, no matter how well meaning, weren't going to put the dent in our overdraft that Simon Boucher could.

'Simon? He's a saint!' Her eyes had a faraway look.

No ambiguity there, then. He was a saint and Caroline was a monster. And of course Naomi wasn't biased or self-centred. She wouldn't be bitter because Caroline had spoiled her plans to marry a multimillionaire . . .

'She's an evil little . . .'

'Hold on, Naomi. She may have wrecked your marriage plans, but she *was* fourteen. Fourteen-year-olds tend to inhabit their own reality. As Gerry likes to point out, their brains are wired differently. Plus she had lost her mother. Probably thought she was about to lose her father – to you! Or that she'd at least have to share his affections. That's a hard river to cross when you're fourteen.'

She gave me an icy look.

I refused to back down. 'Remember what it was like being fourteen? Your hormones all over the place. One day you're in love with a nun, next you're slobbering over a picture of a half-naked Arnold Schwarzenegger, trying to rub out his loincloth with the school ink eraser. No? That was just me, then? You never . . . ?'

'She killed my cat.'

Silence.

There wasn't a lot I could say after this. I did still wonder how unbiased her opinion of Caroline was. Relations tend to become strained in the run-up to any wedding, and it couldn't have been the most harmonious time in Caroline's life, having to face the prospect of Naomi for a stepmum. Still, a murdered cat is a fairly damning indictment against anyone. OK, I too had found Naomi hard going. Once I had even gazed longingly down the lift shaft as she stood there screeching about the faulty lift. But you can't just give in to your baser emotions. Well, not all the time.

She was becoming uncomfortable now, clearly regretting that she had unburdened herself to me. Possibly afraid that I might retell the story to Gerry. Nobody likes it known that they were jilted at the altar. Or even six weeks in advance of it.

I doubted that Caroline had deliberately killed her cat. She probably did what most teenagers do. Left a door swinging open. And the poor cat ran out and got squished. Sad. But hardly evil.

'I'm sorry your cat got run over, Naomi,' I said.

She looked startled. 'He didn't get run over. She choked him. Throttled him with her bare hands. Evil.'

I paid for both green teas and left. Naomi was too upset to look for her purse.

Gerry flatly refused to accept that Caroline was evil incarnate.

'She's a seventeen-year-old kid, Annie. So she caused trouble when she was fourteen? Who the hell didn't? If you knew some of the things I got up to at that age, you'd run a mile. What I do believe is that her father has shown endless patience with her. So when he asked me not to chance exposing their private lives to the press, to hold off until he gave the go-ahead, I felt he had every right. I wasn't happy with it, but I felt he deserved our loyalty.'

Now I started wondering if my coldness to him over his acceptance of Boucher's orders had been a little unjust. We had slept back to back for two whole nights now. That's how strongly I had felt. But Gerry had brought that on himself. Why didn't he explain his feelings more clearly that night, instead of just turning over and going to sleep? And even now he expected me to read his mind, just handing me the contents of the manila envelope Boucher's driver had delivered. Barely giving me a chance to flick through the neatly typed pages, he was asking what *I* thought of it.

It was a proposal for a highly desirable five-year security contract with Boucher International. Reading it, the phrase *money for old rope* flashed though my mind. I had assumed that this much-discussed security contract would require us to hire burly men in uniforms, to stand in doorways and refuse people entry to various Boucher buildings. I was wrong. This proposed contract would require McHugh Dunning to make background checks on all prospective employees of Boucher International. And for this we would be paid astronomical fees.

But it was just a proposal. Not an actual contract. That would be drawn up *after* we completed our present job – i.e. found Caroline.

'But he won't let us go ahead. So how *can* we complete the job? Boucher is the one ordering us to hold off.'

'Exactly. He's obviously testing us. Wants to see if we can obey instructions. To the letter.'

'God, he's Machiavellian!'

He shrugged. 'He's a businessman. Sharp. The moment I described how comfortable Caroline looked behind the wheel of that BMW he was satisfied she was in no danger. Possibly doing her own thing, all right. Annoying for him, maybe. But I think the BMW convinced him she wasn't on the road to self-destruction.' He sat back. 'We just have to be patient. Wait for him to give us the go-ahead.'

'And you're happy with that?' I was uneasy. There was something almost murky about a man like Boucher constantly dangling promises in front of us. Although this was a pretty tempting promise.

'Aren't you?' Gerry smiled.

I looked at him and our eyes met. Held. Two whole nights of sleeping back to back made him look doubly handsome. Twice as appealing.

'Come round here and tell me if you're happy.' He reached for my hand.

We were sharing his chair, our kisses becoming deep-down and dirty, when the phone rang. He hit the speaker button.

'Gerry, a man from the dog track wants to see you

asap. He said can he come over right now. He has major information for you.' Sandra's voice echoed around the office.

He reclaimed his tongue and tried to slow down his breathing.

'Tell him . . . I'll be here.'

'Gerry?' Disappointed, I slid off his lap.

He got up and locked the door. 'In that traffic, it'll take him at least twenty minutes to get here.' He tore off his jacket.

'Oh. OK, so . . .' I unbuttoned my blouse. 'Think you can show me what you can do in twenty minutes?' I smiled.

His shirt landed on top of his jacket. 'You'll be screaming for mercy.'

'Ha! Drop those pants, big boy!'

He was unbuckling his belt when Sandra's voice said, 'Er . . . maybe you should hang up now, Gerry.'

He thumped the speaker button. 'Fuck.'

'Well . . .'

29

I didn't mind having to shop for Calum's christening gift. As his prospective godparents it was only right that Gerry and I should buy him something really special. Maybe even memorable. It was having to shop alone that cheesed me off. Gerry had promised that we would choose the gift together, said he was looking forward to it. Then he gets a call from the greyhound club – another dead dog. This one in a kennel with a hidden video camera in the roof.

'I'll leave you the Cherokee,' he said as he dashed out. Like he was doing me a favour. As if I should find it endearing that he was taking the Honda and leaving me the big four-wheel drive for a shopping trip in the traffic-choked city in the middle of a heat-wave.

'What a sweetheart!' I stamped out through reception, not sure what was irritating me most – Gerry's sudden departure, the unbearably humid weather or the greyhound thieves.

Sandra giggled behind her hand, like a geisha, her latest habit since overhearing that embarrassingly intimate scene in Gerry's office.

It took me an hour to find parking near Grafton Street, by which time my cotton dress was stuck to my back with sweat and it was becoming blatantly obvious that my newest anti-frizz hair serum was anything but. I decided to give up the fight. Let the humidity do its worst. Let my hair curl unchecked. I even semi-resolved to throw away the blow-dryer when I got home. It would save so much time, and besides, Gerry had claimed to prefer my hair curly. As did the noisy builders, if their raucous yelling when I passed by was any indicator. In fact, everyone seemed to like my more natural look once the initial shock wore off.

The po-faced jeweller didn't. But then he didn't like me, period. I didn't have deep pockets. Or a moustache. He minced towards me as I peered into his beautifully lit display case. Stood preening his Village People moustache, gazing past my shoulder and on out into the sun-drenched street as if he were hoping Colin Farrell would suddenly materialise in his shop doorway.

When I asked to see a more extensive selection of his silver goods, he went all hissy. I persisted. Then wished I hadn't, because now I was trapped into examining row upon row of monstrously expensive solid silver spoons and traditional silver christening mugs, which were beyond hideous.

I was mid-sigh when my mobile rang.

'Sandra?' I waited for the giggles to subside.

'Sorry to interrupt your shopping, Annie, but some woman in Wexford wants to talk to you. She said you know her. Said she used to live with Mick Kelly. Isn't he that drug pusher who got nine years? The one who sold smack from that old granny's house? Anyway, I told her you were busy. Told her Declan and Barney would be here soon. She wasn't interested. She wants you. Says it's important.'

★ ★ ★

The drive to Wexford was a joy. Despite the heat, Dublin had been partly overcast, but two miles beyond the city the sky turned a cloudless blue, and a light breeze eased the awful humidity.

The beach behind Mary's mobile home was already packed with sunbathers and whole armies of laughing children splashing in and out of the sparkling surf.

Last time I'd been here, the place had been deserted, the sea shrouded in a grey mist as the rain beat relentlessly against Mary's flimsy home. Today she was sitting under a striped sun awning, perched at a white plastic table, wearing a minuscule bikini and an enviable suntan. Even her smile took me by surprise. It was hard to equate this glowing creature with the downtrodden woman who had sobbed on my shoulder a few months back.

She finished dishing out ice cream to her children. 'Go on, now, the lot of youse. Over to the towels. And if you go in the water, remember to hold Dylan's hand!' she warned, one eye clocking my arrival.

'Want some ice cream?' She held up the large tub.

'Er . . . I wouldn't mind.' I plucked a half-eaten sweet from a plastic chair and sat down.

She scooped out the remains of the ice cream. 'Kids! They eat like vultures.'

'You look fantastic.'

'Why wouldn't I?' she chuckled. 'He got nine years. You did a good job.'

'Oh, that wasn't me. I only helped collect evidence. It's the Garda you should be thanking. And the people in the DPP's office. You wouldn't believe the hours they spent on that case. The endless paperwork. People don't realise how many dedicated professionals it takes to get someone like him put away and . . .'

Seeing her eyes glaze over, I changed tack. 'This beach reminds me of a holiday postcard a colleague once sent me. From Barbados.'

She chuckled happily. 'I know. Great, isn't it?'

I sat back and kicked off my shoes, wriggling my toes in the warm sand, and savoured my ice cream. 'Mmmmm.'

'Nice?' She smiled.

'Perfect. I think I'll stay here for the day.' I held my face up to the sun.

She squinted over at me. 'Have you and some other detectives been hanging around St Martin's Lane? Looking for a missing girl?'

If she had pulled a gun out of her bikini briefs I couldn't have been more shocked.

I jolted upright. 'H . . . how did you know?'

'Me nephew. Tomo.'

'Tomo?' I gawked.

'He described you perfectly,' she chuckled. 'He's a cheeky little bugger.'

'Tomo?' I composed myself, remembering that I was here in a professional capacity. Even if I had been momentarily distracted by . . . everything.

'I knew it was you.' She was chuffed. 'He said you gave him a go in a big jeep.' She glanced over to where the Cherokee was half hidden in the sand dunes. 'He's a skinny little kid. Face full of freckles?'

'I know who he is.' Described me perfectly did he? Cheeky little fecker. Selling cigarettes to Gerry. What was he up to now? Selling arms to Iraq?

'I thought you'd remember him. He's a gas

character!' She chuckled. 'He was down here with me brother for a few days. Me brother is having a few . . . business hiccups. I told him to come down here for a while. Better than Spain.'

Before I could comment, she was talking again. 'Tomo got a right sunburn.'

I fanned myself with a paper hanky.

'He hates the beach anyway. All he cares about is cars. Cars, cars, cars. Can't keep his hands off them. Little bugger.'

So that's why I was here. Tomo was in trouble. Barney said he was a joyrider in the making. Already well known to the Garda. If that little . . . if he had knocked someone down, I wasn't going to get involved. I didn't mind helping Mary out, but if that little . . . God, it was hot.

'The other detective,' she was saying. 'Your boss? Gerry is it?'

'Yes.' I tried to think of an excuse to leave. My mobile was off, but I could always say it was on vibrate, that I had received an urgent summons. Had to get back to the office asap.

'He showed Tomo a photo of a girl youse are looking for.' She watched me closely.

'Really?' I feigned interest.

'Yeah. Tomo told me brother about it. Me brother says it would be worth your while to go to the International Hotel.' She gave me a knowing wink.

'The International Hotel?' Mobile forgotten, I sat forward so fast my back made a squelching sound as it came away from the plastic chair.

'Yeah. You know that big one on the corner of the green? About ten minutes from St Martin's Lane?'

'I know the hotel. But what do you mean, worth our while?' I frowned.

'What do you think I mean?' She was irritated. 'Look, I'm only telling you what he told me! If you don't want the information . . .'

'No . . . I mean, of course I do. Are you saying the girl we're looking for is in the International?'

'Listen.' She hunched towards me, her tanned face hardening. 'If my brother says you should look in that feckin' hotel, you better do it. There isn't anything goes on around there he doesn't know about. That's his patch!' Her eyes were angry.

'His patch? You make him sound like a drug dealer.' I smiled.

She turned to check the kids, who were now chasing each other in the surf, squealing in mock fright whenever they failed to avoid an incoming wave. With their healthily tanned little bodies and shining hair they looked like an ad for supervitamins.

'Mary?'

When she didn't reply my stomach tightened. All the way up to my scalp. 'Your brother sells drugs? After what Kelly did to you? And your mother?'

'He's not like Kelly!' She was livid. 'Anto only sells a bit of blow. A few dozen Es here and there. Maybe a bit of . . . we all have to make a living! He'd never push heroin. He's a born-again,' she boasted.

A born-again drug dealer? My head became too heavy for my neck.

Mary got to her feet and started calling over to her kids.

'Mary? Are you . . . ?'

'I'm just telling you what he told me! He's only

helping you because you gave his kids a go in your jeep. And you were decent to me.'

I tried to make sense of this new information. Yes, I did give the kids a go in the jeep. And after seeing how Mary was living, I had asked a social worker if she could do something for her. But . . .

'Tell the blond detective the money went a long way.'

'The money?'

She looked at me as if I were senile. 'The sixty he gave me! Last time you were here?'

'Oh, that.' I made as if it had slipped my mind.

Bloody Barney. He let me stew all the way home that day. Said I shouldn't be wasting my sympathy on Mary. To save it for the kids her pusher boyfriend got hooked on heroin. Then *he* slips her sixty euros? Behind my back?

I scrabbled for my purse.

'No!' She was affronted. 'I don't want your money. Me brother takes care of me now. I *told* you, he's a born-again Christian!'

'Sorry.' I ditched the purse.

She lowered her voice as a couple of leather-skinned sun worshippers strolled past. 'Now remember, it's the *International* Hotel. Top floor.'

'Top floor,' I echoed.

'Are you done with that?' She indicated the plastic dish.

'Yes thanks.' I passed it over.

'You better get going then. Before the traffic builds up.'

I was being dismissed.

She turned to call the squealing kids. 'Come on, you lot. Time to get dried off. Get Dylan, Britney.'

I picked up my shoes, hesitated. 'Mary . . . ?'

'The International Hotel,' she said, and walked away down the beach to meet her kids. She swooped the little toddler up in her arms. He was as fat as a butterball, his skin golden. The other kids clearly adored him, fighting to kiss his little bronzed feet as Mary swung him high in the air. Their loud laughter followed me all the way back to the Cherokee.

I drove like a fiend, ringing Sandra en route.

'Find Gerry. Tell him to meet me at the agency. Something major has come up.'

'Mega.'

At least she didn't giggle.

I parked the Cherokee on double yellows in open defiance of the approaching traffic warden who lived to make my life a misery. I didn't even stop to argue with him, which probably ruined his day. I was so wound up, so eager to share my news with Gerry that I even ignored the half-empty lift – after I spotted a chattering Naomi holding court in it – and raced up the stairs instead.

Everyone was gathered in Gerry's office. Even Sandra, who was doing her best to appear overworked as she collected the used coffee things. She paused to give me a covert thumbs-up, then continued to move the coffee mugs from A to B and back again, clearly determined not to miss a thing.

I didn't waste any time. 'I know where Caroline Boucher is!' I announced.

'*That*'s the big news?' Gerry looked disappointed. 'But we already know the area where she's . . .'

'No. I know *exactly* where she is,' I beamed.

That got everyone's attention.

'She's in the International Hotel!' I burst out. 'Top floor!'

There was a stunned silence.

'The . . . the International on the green . . . ?' Barney began.

Gerry waved his hand for silence. 'How do you know, Annie?'

I grinned. 'You're not the only one with a snout! Er . . . snitch.' I corrected myself.

'And?' he barked impatiently.

'Mary Kelly said her brother told her to tell us that we'll find Caroline on the top floor of the International!'

His eyes narrowed. 'And you believe her?'

'She didn't drag me all the way down to Wexford to spin me a yarn.'

'Is she saying Caroline has been there . . . all this time?' It was Declan's turn to question me.

'I don't know about that! But she's there now. Can we go, Gerry? We don't want to lose her!'

'Hang on,' he said calmly.

'She's in the International, Gerry!'

'Why is Kelly suddenly passing information on to us?'

'Who cares? Mary hinted that it's because we gave his kids a ride in the jeep, but I dunno. Maybe it's because Barney gave his sister money!' I babbled. 'Does it matter?'

Barney flushed. 'I gave her sixty euros, Gerry. That time she gave me information on her scummy heroin pusher boyfriend. That Kelly guy.'

'Are they all called Kelly?' Sandra asked.

'You still here?' Gerry turned.

'No! Nearly done . . . just a couple more . . . mugs.'
She ducked behind Barney.

This wasn't going quite the way I'd expected. I
thought we'd be halfway to the International by now,
preparing to smash down doors and lead Caroline
out in triumph, despite her father's orders to hold
off. But surely even he wouldn't want us to miss this
golden opportunity. So why was everyone standing
around asking dumb questions?

A coffee mug slid noisily along Sandra's tray.

'Will you leave those bloody mugs be, Sandra!'
Gerry yelled. 'Give me a quick rundown on this
brother, Barney.' He was on his feet, pulling on his
jacket, unlocking a special little drawer at the back
of his desk.

I froze. He wasn't dismissing my information after
all. On the contrary, while Barney gave him the man's
history, Gerry was doing something guaranteed to
put the heart crossways in me – slipping a little hand-
gun into his belt. The gun he always swore he never
used.

My dread of guns was no secret. A sick fear started
to gnaw at my stomach. I looked at the others to see
how they were reacting to Gerry 'tooling up', as
Barney called it. Nobody seemed at all concerned.
Not even Sandra. Barney was still talking, giving
Gerry a full biog of Mary's born-again brother.

'. . . small-time dealer,' he was saying. 'St Martin's
Lane is his patch. We're obviously interfering with
business. All that heat.'

'Heat?' I echoed.

'The night of Gerry's accident? An ambulance, a
fire truck and a cop car with four gardai in it? He
must have been shitting himself when that lot arrived.

Him *and* his customers. They're busy scoring, then suddenly find themselves in the middle of what looks like a law and order convention. And you'd already been spotted snooping around.'

'Me?' I said in disbelief.

'Oh come on, Annie! That's where Flynn conducts his business. A fly can't light there without him knowing. And then *three* of us arrive? Park the bloody jeep on his doorstep? Start questioning local kids? That lane is a dope dealer's dream. All he has to do is hang out on the corpo balconies and wait for the customers to show up. He nips down, does the deal, slips back into no-man's-land again. Perfect. Then all these nosy detectives start sniffing around. Remember the night we took a wander down there, Declan? Bad vibe! All those scumbags!'

Declan nodded.

'Annie.' Gerry caught my elbow. 'This guy wants us away from his patch. He'd break legs if that's what it took. Happily he's found an easier way, and we're the beneficiaries. I hope.'

'So . . . he's not helping us because we gave his kids a go in the jeep?' I swallowed.

He didn't reply. But to his eternal credit, he didn't laugh either.

Once, after I'd had a major row with Gerry about his lack of sensitivity and was threatening to leave, Fiona had said, 'But he's so fundamentally decent, Annie.' And, angry as I was that time, I'd been forced to agree. To admit that it was probably what made me fall in love with him. Well, that and his great body.

'Ready to hit the road, boss?' Barney was jigging impatiently.

'What about Boucher? Didn't he ask you to hold off?' Declan frowned at Gerry.

'Sod him,' Barney grinned.

Gerry slipped his old warrant card into his pocket. 'Boucher didn't want his daughter's picture plastered all over Dublin – his fear was that the newspapers would get hold of the story. Put it on the front page. He wouldn't object to us picking her up quietly. Sandra, I need you in reception. Go man the phones.'

She shot him a look of pure adoration before legging it.

I was now afraid to breathe. Please don't tell me to man the books, Gerry. Please. Not with the others listening. Not in front of everybody, when I'm the one who got the big tip-off. Please be fundamentally decent when I need it. Please.

I closed my eyes.

'Annie. Grab your bag. You and me are going to the International Hotel.'

For a split second I thought I might faint with emotion, or maybe even hyperventilate, but both feelings passed and I got my breathing under control again. I didn't even scream with delight. But it was a close thing.

'What about me?' Barney's face fell.

'Sorry, Barney. This needs a softly-softly approach.'

'I can do softly,' Barney pleaded.

'Well you'll get a chance to prove that later. Right now I want you to go to my house and wait. If this tip-off is kosher, I'm going to need you there.'

Watching us hurry out, Barney muttered to Declan, 'Softly-softly? I can break a door down softly. That time we were investigating the money-lending ring wasn't it me who kept things . . . ?'

We got into the lift. Gerry hit the button. 'Just follow my lead, Annie, OK? And don't look so worried. I've never had to draw a gun while working a private case. It's just a precaution. OK?'

'OK boss,' I dimpled. He was probably fibbing, but I didn't care. He had chosen me as his back-up. He could have had Declan, Barney, even phoned a friend. Well, half the Garda force. Instead he had chosen me.

He shot me a wicked sideways grin, his eyes crinkling up at the corners.

He'd never know how close that grin came to messing up the case. Because given the chance, I would have had him on the floor of that rickety lift right then and there, even if it had considerably lowered our chances of finding Caroline.

The hotel reception area was deserted except for a heavily made-up receptionist whose beige-blonde head was buried in the latest edition of *Cosmo*.

The International used to be the queen of hotels. Rooms there needed booking months in advance. Then the lucrative American market collapsed, and the once great hotel was reduced to offering even its most luxurious rooms at sinfully low rates. And still the uptake was slow.

The hall porter clearly thought it was still the good old days. He was officious to the point of rudeness. Until he saw the colour of Gerry's money. Then he took a long, hard look at Caroline's photo.

'Emmm. Maybe.'

Gerry flashed another crisp note.

'Well, yes, I think she is staying here. Looks a bit different from her photo, though. If I give you a room number, it didn't come from me.' He threw a furtive look over his shoulder, like a ham actor in a B movie.

Gerry made a mouth-zipping motion.

'Top floor. One-oh-two.'

We were on our way. The lift was Rolls-Royce smooth. It deposited us, and one blue-haired, flinty-eyed matron, on the top floor in seconds. Gerry signalled for me to wait until the thickly carpeted corridor was clear before checking the room numbers.

'That's it.' He pointed. 'One-oh-two.'

He rapped briskly. 'Room service,' he called.

The door opened a crack. 'Must be a mistake, I didn't . . .' a woman's voice said.

Gerry put his weight against the door, preventing her closing it.

An anxious blue eye peered out through the opening. 'Go away! I didn't order room service.'

'Didn't you, Caroline?'

'What?'

One push and we were in. Before she knew what was happening, Gerry had the door locked behind us and was ordering me to block the only other possible exit, a narrow bathroom door.

We were finally face to face with Caroline Boucher. And we hadn't even raised our voices, let alone used the gun that was still safely tucked into Gerry's belt.

I was both euphoric *and* sweating with nerves. Definitely incapable of clear thought. But remembering Gerry's instructions – *Follow my lead* – I watched him, and when he scanned the big room, I followed suit, doing my best to appear professional.

Caroline stood there looking terrified. Wearing a huge fluffy white bathrobe that was way too big for her, and an even fluffier towel that was wrapped round her head like a Hindu turban. Even so, there was no mistaking her. This was Caroline Boucher all right. The girl whose image we had been living with for over three months. There was no mistaking that perfect little oval face with its neat features, creamy skin and clear blue eyes that were so like her father's.

She cowered away from us in fear.

'It's all right, Caroline.' Gerry reached out to reassure her.

'Get away from me!' she yelled. 'Get away! Don't you touch me!'

'Don't be afraid. We're not here to hurt you.'

'We're friends.' I followed his lead, surprised to hear myself sounding almost calm when inside I was on the verge of a panic attack.

I had no idea what came next. Did we sit around and try to talk her into coming with us? Or drag her screaming and yelling down the corridor and into the jeep? Oh my God, was that why Gerry had the gun? As a last resort? To be used if she refused to come with us? She was already carrying on as if we were the Celtic Bonnie and Clyde. Here to shoot her down, in cold blood, for our own sadistic pleasure.

'We just want to talk to you, Caroline,' my voice quivered.

Her eyes hardened. 'My name isn't Caroline. And if you're not out of here in two seconds, I'm calling security.'

'We *are* security.' Gerry flashed his long outdated warrant card. 'State security! We have information that an illegal immigrant is staying in this room.'

God, he was good. I'd never have thought of that. I'd probably have flashed the gun first.

'Oh, that's nonsense.' She visibly relaxed. 'I'm not an illegal immigrant.'

'Could we see some identification, please?' Gerry would have made a perfect government agent. If he put on a decent suit and fixed his hair. 'Evidence of nationality?' he asked.

'Don't be silly. Isn't it obvious that I'm Irish?' She smiled.

'Sorry. I need hard evidence. I need to check your passport. Or your birth certificate?'

She was uneasy again. 'I don't have . . .'

'How old are you?'

'Seventeen. I'll be eighteen in three weeks.'

Gerry produced his prop notebook.

'Name and address please. Names of both parents.'

'No . . . I . . . my parents are dead.'

He didn't even blink. 'A guardian?'

'I don't have a guardian.'

'Search the room, sergeant,' he said briskly.

Sergeant? He couldn't have made it detective inspector? Why was I always . . . ?

'Now, Miss . . . ?'

'O'Reilly. Claire O'Reilly.'

I was opening the wardrobe when he called me back. 'I'll do that. You stay with her, sergeant.'

He moved at warp speed, pulling open drawers, flicking a pen through a pile of underwear, disappearing into the bathroom to appear again waving a contact lens case. 'These yours, Claire?'

'Yes.'

'Your eyes are blue. Any special reason why these contacts are brown?' His eyes drilled into her.

'You don't know much about fashion, do you?' she said after a momentary pause.

'Pretty expensive fashion.' He checked the label on the box. 'You a student?'

'Yes.'

'I'll need details.' His smile was totally disarming.

'No problem.' She returned the smile.

'You have an Irish passport?' His voice soft, almost paternal.

She nodded. He made a careful note.

'And what height are you, Caroline?' he continued writing.

'Five-five,' she answered, without hesitation.

Oh, he was good. She saw my expression and realised her mistake. 'Why do you keep calling me Caroline? My name is Claire.'

'Fine. Now get dressed, Claire. You're coming with us. We need to check out your nationality.' He nudged her towards the bathroom. 'Leave the door unlocked. Do you want the sergeant to pack your things?'

'No! As soon as I speak to your superior, you'll be driving me straight back here. With a full apology!' She grabbed an armful of clothes and slammed into the bathroom.

'Now who does that remind you of?' Gerry asked.

'Boucher in drag?'

He laughed and slapped my behind. 'God, I love this job.'

'It is her, isn't it, Gerry?'

'It's her. Throw her things in a bag. She won't be coming back here. We found her, Annie!' He high-fived me gleefully. 'Doubles all round in The Randy Goat tonight?'

'You betcha!' I laughed. 'Sir.'

30

Caroline sat in the jeep like a zombie, her stillness almost scary. Especially as she didn't say a single word. She only moved once, and that was to tug her black knitted hat lower about her ears and clutch her bulky jumper closer to her chest, as if she were feeling cold. What cold? I wondered, as even though it was now evening the temperature remained stifling. At least I thought so. But she didn't complain. Didn't make a sound. Until we pulled up outside our house and Barney came running to open the door.

That's when she started screeching.

'Get away from me!' she screamed, fighting him off.

'Be quiet!' Gerry glanced nervously along the neighbouring row of houses.

'You're not immigration officers!' she bellowed.

'And you're not Claire O'Reilly.' He pulled her unceremoniously out of the jeep, wincing when she scratched his eye with her flaying fingernails.

Barney grabbed her other arm, and between them they half carried, half dragged her into the house.

'Aggghhh!' Barney gave a bloodcurdling yell.

'What the hell?' Gerry gasped.

'Little bitch just bit my hand. See? It's pumping.' Barney held up his hand for viewing. A pinprick of red blood stained his middle finger.

'You'll survive.' Gerry concentrated on getting Caroline into the house.

I had to run to keep up with them. 'She barely marked you,' I said to Barney.

'Barely? She nearly took my finger off.' He was in high dudgeon, still simmering because he had missed out on what he considered the best part of any case – the climax.

Somewhere in the distance there was the loud bee-baa of a Garda siren.

'Get her in. And shut that door,' Gerry ordered.

'Where are you taking me?' Caroline yelled.

'Calm down, Caroline. We're your friends,' Gerry said politely.

She rewarded him by aiming a vicious kick at him, missing his damaged leg by a millimetre. If she hadn't, I might have been forced to overcome my horror of guns and do something really drastic. Even my patience has its limits.

They sat her on the living-room sofa. Pinioned her on both sides with their bodies. Gerry pointed a threatening finger at her. 'Are you going to behave, or do I have to tie you up?' he growled, his fading scars and newly bleeding eyebrow making him appear terrifying.

I went to find the first-aid box.

When I got back, she was so quiet it worried me. Still, I carefully avoided making eye contact with her – she would only be here for a short time. Best not to start feeling sorry for her, not when she could kick and maim men twice her size. Plus there was that story about the dead cat. I wasn't totally convinced of its authenticity, but still.

In her favour, she was wearing the ugliest hat I

had ever seen. Rib-knitted in coal-black wool, it looked like it had fallen off a North Sea oil rig after being used to mop up an overspill, but it showed a refreshing lack of vanity that I found very appealing. Possibly a throwback to my convent school days, when the nuns repeatedly told us that vanity was the Devil's favourite weapon, guaranteed to drag all, or any who indulged in it, straight down to hell, where we would burn for all eternity.

I put the first-aid box on the table. 'Let me check that eye, Gerry. You might need stitches.'

'What about my finger?'

'Enough about your stupid finger, Barney,' I dismissed.

Gerry's wound wasn't serious. Just a deep scratch.

'But you might have a shiner in the morning,' I warned.

Caroline watched curiously as I cleaned away the blood and gently stretched a flesh-coloured plaster across the cut.

'OK, Caroline?' Forgetting my resolution, I gave her a smile.

She looked at me as if I were vermin.

'I could murder a drink.' Barney flicked his floppy blond hair out of his eyes.

Caroline inched away from him, unsure. She didn't know who we were, of course. We could be serial killers, for all she knew. Bloodthirsty psychopaths who prowled plush hotels in search of nubile young women to maim and torture. She definitely knew by now that we weren't immigration officials. Any idiot knew that they didn't drag people *into* neat, semi-detached houses in tree-lined suburbs.

'I think we could *all* do with a drink.' I closed the first-aid box.

'Great! We'll all adjourn to The Randy Goat, will we?' Barney said waspishly.

'There'll be plenty of other nights for that.' Gerry gave him a look.

I opened a bottle of Scotch, giving Caroline a conspiratorial wink as I took down the glasses. Someone had to gain her trust. How else could we hold on to her until Boucher got here? Switzerland wasn't exactly around the corner.

I poured three generous whiskeys. Then a small one, for Caroline. What did seventeen-year-old heiresses drink anyway? Apart from champagne? I splashed soda into the glasses. Gave her a little extra.

'What is this?' she frowned.

'Whiskey and soda. Best relaxer I know.' I tried a smile again.

'I meant, who are you people? You're obviously not *professional* kidnappers.' Her voice was a sneer.

'Now listen here, you!' Barney swivelled to face her. 'You've caused us a lot of grief. So don't try that snotty act with us! Gerry has a gun!' He threatened.

'Barney!'

'OK, OK.' He backed off. 'We're private detectives! Is that good enough for you?'

When she didn't reply, he checked his finger again. The pinprick of blood had dried into a solid lump, making it appear fractionally larger. Almost like a real wound. And Barney could hold a grudge longer than an elephant. 'We were hired to find you. Fools that we are.' He tossed his floppy hair out of his eyes again.

'I'm not going home.' She folded her arms. 'I'd kill myself first.'

Barney looked as if this wouldn't spoil his day.

Gerry had been busy with his notebook, the one he insisted was a prop.

He slammed it shut. 'Have your drink, Caroline.' He pushed the glass towards her.

'No way.' She looked at me as if I were Vlad the Impaler. '*She* could have put anything in that glass!'

Before I could reply she had smacked the tumbler, sending it rocketing into the one next to it, which in a perfect domino effect sent the next one reeling. I watched in horror as Scotch and soda flooded across the low French-polished table.

This table had a history. Frequently embarrassed by my lack of domestic skills, every now and then I made an effort to rectify this defect. Usually when I wanted to show Gerry that I was as good a house-keeper as his perfect ex-wife. Wanted him to see that there was a lot more to me than just being House-slut of the Year. Three months ago I had spotted this little table in an antique shop, bought it and had it repolished at considerable cost.

It was now awash with Scotch.

'Jesus Christ!' Barney was on his feet. 'Look what you've done! You spoiled little bitch.'

I found his defence of my table quite moving until I realized he was pointing at his whiskey-splattered jeans.

'So sorry,' Caroline mocked in her high, posh voice. 'Armani casuals, are they?'

An hour later, things hadn't improved much. Despite leaving him two urgent phone messages, we still hadn't heard from Boucher, and Caroline was flatly refusing to answer a single question or give us any information regarding her disappearance. We had no idea what she had been up to for the past months. All we knew for sure was that she had spent the last ten days in the International. And even that little snippet came courtesy of the hotel porter. Gerry had contacted him, and had to promise him *another* fifty euros before we got that information.

We were now relying on Declan. He had gone to thank Flynn, the born-again drug dealer, for the tip-off. Well, actually to pump him for information so we could give Boucher a more comprehensive report.

'And in the meantime we're stuck with little Miss Superbitch?' I whispered to Gerry, as I handed him coffee.

I had already given Barney his, and put one beside Caroline, on a simple wooden chair.

I sat across the room from them, watching. Barney was fiddling with the remote control, playing with it like a child, channel surfing, his face still sulky, until he came to a heated debate on vegetarianism, which he seemed to find fascinating. One of the panelists had remarkably large breasts, which shook perilously against her paper-thin blouse whenever she drummed home her point that a world dedicated to vegetarianism could totally eradicate bowel cancer in a single generation.

Caroline watched Barney watching the vegetarian.

'I never met a private detective before.'

'No reason to assault me,' he said, his eyes never leaving the screen.

'I was being abducted! You people could have been . . . al-Qaeda.'

'Al-Qaeda?' he said dismissively. 'Do we look like terrorists?'

Her eyes widened. 'I was driven across town at terrifying speeds!'

He gave a low chuckle. 'That's Annie for you. Hard to believe she's never got a speeding ticket. She must be sleeping with the right people,' he said slyly, his eyes still following the giant breasts.

'I . . . I'm sorry for biting you. It was . . . unforgivable.' Caroline tugged at his sleeve.

'Is she coming on to him?' I whispered to Gerry.

'Leave them to it.' He was reading a text message on his mobile.

The vegetarian discussion over, another panelist was now hogging the camera, bemoaning the general lack of interest in party politics.

Barney hit the off button, and turned to Caroline. 'I suppose anyone could overreact if a gang of strangers suddenly abducted them.'

'We didn't abduct anyone.' Gerry put his phone away. 'We picked up Caroline at the request of her legal guardian. Her father.'

'Is he here?' Her eyes flashed.

'He's in Switzerland. I thought you might want to talk to us first. Tell us why you . . .'

'I need the bathroom. Quickly!'

I went with her. Waited until I heard the lock click before hurrying back downstairs. If Gerry had a plan, I wanted to be in on it.

'I don't have a plan.' He looked me straight in the eye.

'Course you do. You always have a plan,' I insisted.

'I don't have—'

'I think she's starting to trust us,' Barney said. 'And she's not the little viper I took her to be. She's tiny, isn't she? And it's bound to be frightening,

331

having people suddenly break into your hotel room and . . .'

A loud crash from upstairs interrupted this flow of sympathy.

'Sounds like she's breaking up our bathroom,' I said.

'The window!' Gerry yelled. 'She's trying to get out the feckin' window!'

Barney got there first. 'Open up, Caroline!' He pounded on the door.

'Stand back!' Gerry threw himself against it. It gave way instantly.

We stumbled in, slipping and sliding on broken glass and what appeared to be the contents of every bottle of shampoo, hair conditioner, and anti-frizz serum I possessed, plus clouds of Gerry's shaving foam.

Caroline was standing on the toilet seat, trying to climb on to the high window ledge.

'Get down from there!' Gerry yelled.

'Piss off!' she said, grabbing his shaving mirror and throwing it at him.

Barney tried to drag her off the toilet, and she threw a surprisingly hard punch at him. Gerry grabbed her arms and had to twist to one side to avoid being headbutted. Her head skimmed along his chest instead, making her scream when her hat became entangled with his shirt buttons. I reached into the melee to free it, but she was already straightening up, leaving her hat swinging on the buttons.

'Jaysus!' Barney gasped, and the three of us stood back in horror.

'Oh my God,' I breathed.

Caroline gritted her pearly little teeth. 'What are

you gawking at? Have you bastards never seen a shaved head before?'

Caroline was on the sofa, hugging her knees to her chest, her bare head shining nakedly under the light. We sat opposite, all three of us doing our utmost *not* to stare at her head. But it was impossible. My eyes simply refused to look anywhere else. After all, we'd been surrounded by so many images of her for such a long time, and in every one of them she had this long, beautiful, baby blonde hair. How were we supposed to react to this shockingly bald head? And above such an exquisite little face? It drew our eyes like a magnet.

'Two more minutes and I'd have made it!' she spat. 'I'd have been out that window, and you wouldn't have seen my arse for dust.'

'Seven years' bad luck.' Barney tried not to stare at her head.

'What?' she snarled.

'You smashed Gerry's shaving mirror.'

'Well, there's a loss!' She glared at Gerry, who was definitely in shock.

Maybe he was thinking that she didn't look much like the girl we'd seen driving the silver BMW. The one we had chased along the dual carriageway a few nights ago. That girl had looked exactly like the Caroline in our photos. Blonde hair skimming her shoulders. Big pale blue eyes. In our eagerness to find Caroline had we terrified some poor innocent driver? Almost run her off the road? Or was it possible that . . . ?

'*When* did you shave your head?' Gerry took the words right out of my mouth.

She hissed like a snake.

'I just wondered,' he said, turning away as if he had lost all interest in the subject.

Caroline clearly didn't like being ignored. 'I've had it like this for months,' she pouted.

'Then how come you've no stubble?' I snapped.

She looked at me as if I were witless. 'Doh! I shave it every day.'

I had a feeling this was going to be a long night. One of those times when I'd be bound to wonder if investigative work was all it was cracked up to be. So far, our bathroom was like a war zone, my little coffee table was ruined, Gerry was sporting yet another wound over his eye, and Caroline, who looked like a Botticelli angel in all her photos, was sitting there with a head like Uncle Fester. Was this building up to become a bigger embarrassment than the Murtha case?

Still, I continued: 'Did you ever wear a nose ring?'

She found this hilarious. 'Look at your face! You're disgusted, aren't you? At the idea of Caroline *Boucher* with a shaved head and a couple of nose rings?'

A couple? Mags had only mentioned the one.

Caroline was determined to shock me. 'You should have seen where I was sleeping! Fungus on the walls. No power. Rats the size of bull terriers!'

'Where was that? The International?' Barney asked dryly.

'In a squat in St Martin's Lane!' she boasted proudly.

'Nice.' Barney feigned disinterest.

'Have you ever squatted?' she challenged him.

'Na. I like a proper toilet.'

'We didn't even have running water. Had to go to a pub to wash.'

'So was there any *special* reason why you moved to the International?' he asked, without even a hint of a smile.

'I didn't go there from the squat!' Incensed by his refusal to be shocked, she missed the effect she was having on me. I was crushed. Listening to her talk, I realised that practically every word she uttered was underlining the fact that I owed Mags a massive apology.

'I went to a friend's cousin's place,' Caroline boasted loudly. 'A flat in a *tower* block.' She made it sound like the third circle of hell.

'Good views of the city?'

'Are you trying to be funny?'

He shook his head. 'Just making conversation.'

'Then Spike and his cousin went to England and . . .'

'Spike?'

'My friend. An artist. He had his own place in Temple Bar.'

'A gallery?'

'No,' she frowned. 'You know that slab-stoned corner by Mulligan's bar where—?'

'Oh, he's a pavement artist!' Barney's lips twitched. 'Chalks on the slab stones?'

I tried to signal Gerry. I knew he was deliberately giving Barney free reign, probably convinced that Caroline would open up more to someone nearer her own age. And she certainly was. But Barney was going to blow it, he was getting far too cocky, beginning to laugh openly at her. Caroline was young, but she was nobody's fool.

'Does he get much for his chalk drawings?' Barney pushed it.

'Well, he doesn't exactly sell the . . .'

'I just wondered, because it must be hard digging up those big slabs when he gets a cash sale. And posting them to America, now that must cost a mint.'

Caroline threw her coffee over him. Well, she tried. Most of it landed on the French-polished table.

31

Declan finally reported in, and Gerry put him on speakerphone in the hall.

'. . . some guy in Temple Bar . . . sketches tourists . . . calls himself an artist . . . she moved into his squat . . . then across to his cousin's place in the flats . . . Flynn became unhappy with them for some reason . . . he won't say, but I'm guessing this Spike and his cousin were doing smack and owed him some money maybe? . . . Caroline was possibly funding them for a while till the game got serious . . . she's nobody's fool . . . not with money, anyway . . . Flynn wants to know just how grateful we are for the tip-off . . . I said we'll let him know . . . that's when he told me Spike and his cousin did a moonlight . . . claims he doesn't know why . . . that's about it . . . oh, and he says Caroline's clean.'

'Clean?' Gerry muttered. 'I wonder if Boucher will think so? Hanging out with smack-heads isn't quite what he wanted for his daughter, I'll bet. Thanks, Declan.'

In the living room, Caroline was looking for a cigarette.

'I don't smoke,' Barney kept repeating.

'A PI who doesn't smoke?' she sneered. 'What kind of sissy are you? Everyone in our squat smoked. You're a smoker, I can tell.' She turned to Gerry. 'Give me a cigarette.'

'I was told you didn't smoke!' he said.

'Who told you that? My father? I suppose he also told you I'm a virgin?' She tried a coarse laugh, but couldn't quite pull it off.

'Your father's worried sick about you,' Gerry said grimly.

'He went to Switzerland to worry, did he? That makes sense. Has nobody here got a fucking cigarette?'

'Are you cold, Caroline?'

'No.' She flushed bright pink.

'Why do you keep tugging that big sweater around you?'

She didn't answer.

'Let me see your arms,' he ordered.

'I don't do drugs,' she recoiled. 'Look at me. Check my skin. Do I look like a junkie?'

He examined her arms anyway. Made her take off her shoes. Even checked the backs of her legs for needle marks.

'Satisfied?' She was indignant.

He hunked down in front of her. 'Caroline, if there's anything you want to tell me. Anything worrying you . . . if you have a problem . . .'

'You're my problem! Keeping me here in this fucking dump!'

He stood up. 'Stay with her, Barney.' He was gone.

She became worried. Maybe even frightened. 'Where's he going?'

'Gone to get the whip. And the electrodes,' Barney said.

'Don't be stupid. Is he ringing my father?' She ran a hand across her shaved head.

'Christ, I hope so.' Barney tugged at his still damp jeans. 'Then we can all get back to some proper detective work.'

She raised an eyebrow. 'Like what? Spying on innocent clubbers? Following shoplifters?'

He switched on the TV. 'Wonder if there's a late movie on?'

Caroline moved closer to him. 'If you let me go, I'll give you three thousand.'

'If you jump off the roof, I'll give you four,' he said.

'Go screw yourself,' she muttered.

'Aw, give over your auld flattery, Caroline. I may be fit, but I'm not a contortionist.'

'You know what you are? You're a stupid asshole.'

'Well we can't all be clever ones like you.'

She thought about this for a second, then, her head reddening with anger, she looked around for something to throw. I rescued a little glass figurine from the table. A gift from Pino and Fiona. They brought it back from their Venetian honeymoon to thank us for bringing them together. I put it out of Caroline's reach and went to find Gerry.

'Can't get him.' Gerry put the phone down. 'Even his PA is on voice mail.'

We were huddled in the kitchen. Whispering like thieves in our own home. It was getting late and we still hadn't managed to contact Boucher. All his numbers seemed to be on voicemail.

'Boucher is missing his daughter so much he hasn't left us a single open line? He can't still be in negations with the American bank. I bet he's bloody skiing.'

'Hardly skiing in mid-summer. Maybe he's mountaineering?' he whispered.

'Burying his money?' I whispered back.

At least that made Gerry smile.

'We can't keep her here all night,' I worried.

'Not without shackles.' He touched the scratch above his eye.

I nodded. 'She throws things, smokes and swears like a trooper. I wonder what other secrets she kept from Daddy? A man said to monitor her every movement?'

'Wait till he sees that bald head. The man will have a coronary,' he groaned under his breath. 'He was so proud when he showed me her photos. Said she was the image of her mother.'

'But you have to admit, it was a *brilliant* move, on her part, shaving her head. Who would have recognised her with that bald bonce. And those brown contact lenses? Masterly.'

He gave me a long look. 'So is it fair to assume that the pretty, blue-eyed, blonde girl with the string of pearls, the one we nearly ran off the road, wasn't her?'

'You said it was!' I bristled.

'Only after you said it. By then we were moving at the speed of light.'

'You told me to put the boot down!'

'Yes. *After* you told me it was Caroline driving the car.'

'Anyone can make a mistake! Especially given the night that was in it. All that rain – it was like a monsoon. And I didn't tell you to confront that poor sod in his own driveway, did I?'

'OK,' he gave in. 'That's all water under the bridge,

anyway. Our immediate problem is how to hold on to her until Boucher gets here.'

'God help us.'

'Yeah, but in case he's busy, have you any suggestions?'

'Yes! Boucher is loaded. Why can't he employ a couple of professional minders to take her to Switzerland? Like . . . tonight?'

He actually laughed. 'On Swissair? With her screeching blue murder? Biting the cabin crew? Boucher is already paranoid about his public image. Can you picture the tabloid feeding frenzy if she was busted for air rage?'

'So what's the alternative?'

We made up the twin beds in the spare room, the atmosphere between us becoming less cordial by the second as we shook out matching duvets, one of them maybe fractionally less matching, as it had several intractable coffee stains on it. Souvenirs of all the nights I used it to keep me warm in the living room while I waited for Gerry to get home from the late-night surveillances he hated. Tonight it would be keeping Caroline Boucher cosy. Her and her shiny bald head.

We spread it across the bed.

'This is stupid. Could you not come up with a better plan than this?' I threw another pillow on what was to be my lonely bed for the duration.

He was now checking the window locks.

'Gerry?'

'What do you suggest?' he asked. 'Sending her to Switzerland in leg irons?'

'I'd chance it,' I said belligerently.

'Well, it's not up to you. And remember, if we don't hand her over safely, we don't get paid.'

'What do you mean hand her over? We're only contracted to find her!'

'Read the small print, Annie. Our contract specifies that we hand her over, to a Mister Simon Boucher.' He gave a mock salute.

'Who signed that crap?'

'I did.'

'Oh.' I readjusted the pillow. Angled it downwards to cover the biggest coffee stain. I don't know why. Caroline had boasted of sleeping in a filthy squat, for God's sake. And here I was, afraid she might be offended by a coffee stain in the shape of a penis.

'Gerry?'

'Yeah?'

'You . . . you don't think he . . . abused her?'

He swung around to face me. 'What do you mean abused?'

'Well, what reason would she have for running away? She has everything.'

'Kids are always running away,' he insisted. 'Even rich ones. For all sorts of dumb reasons. They're like a different species. Primed by nature to tune in to their own needs and no one else's.'

'But that's my point. All her needs *were* met. She had everything. So why go to such drastic lengths not to be found. Something stinks here, Gerry.'

'Not our problem. We were contracted to find her.'

'And hand her over?'

'Exactly. End of story.'

'That's just it! We still don't know the real story. I don't like her, but suppose . . . ?'

'Drop it, Annie. He wasn't abusing her! And we're

not paid to suppose. We just do our job. Christ, I'd kill for a cigarette.'

'Shame Tomo isn't around, then. You could buy one from him. Contribute to the delinquency of a minor *again*!' I walked out.

'I couldn't do that, Annie,' he called after me. 'He's probably on voicemail.'

I didn't laugh. He might be satisfied with the situation here, but I wasn't. To him, finding Caroline was an end in itself. McHugh Dunning could now close the case. Job sorted. All that remained to be done was to hand her over to her father.

But as long as she was here, I couldn't relax. I kept wondering what she was running away from. Damn Boucher, anyway. If he were here to pick her up, I could put her out of my mind. Stop worrying. Hopefully move on to another case.

I had just about convinced myself to ask Gerry about that possibility when he followed me down to the kitchen and went straight for the whiskey. Breaking it open, he affected a nonchalant stance which didn't fool me for a second. Even from his back view I could tell that he was uneasy. Most definitely worried.

With the kitchen door open, every sound carried clearly from the nearby living room, so there was no mistaking Caroline's growing frustration. She was banging things around, messing with the stereo. Being generally obnoxious. Alternating the volume, flicking it up and down until my nerves were raw.

Gerry was now drinking straight Scotch.

'Want one?' He held up his glass.

'No. Not until we get madam sorted.'

'She's as sorted as she's going to be. For tonight anyway.' He poured himself another.

'She's not staying here.' I made up my mind as another loud burst of music had us both practically leaping out of our skins.

'Be reasonable, Annie. Where else can she go?'

'To hell, for all I care. Boucher asked us to find a sweet, pleasant-natured girl and . . .'

'We found his daughter instead.' He chuckled into his whiskey.

'It's not funny. We found a monster. A self-absorbed, selfish, nasty house wrecker. A girl incapable of relating to another human being on any level.'

'Don't beat about the bush, Annie.' He grinned. 'Spit it out. What do you really think of her.'

'You won't make me laugh. There's nothing funny about her. She's wrecking our house. I want her out. I have a bad feeling about her. I think she's possessed.'

'Twenty minutes ago you were afraid she was being abused.'

'Well, you can scratch that. I'd say Boucher is terrified of her. No wonder he's hiding in the Alps. I know I'd be, if I had to live with *that*.' I jumped as another loud bang came from the living room.

'She'll calm down.'

'The only thing that might calm her down is an exorcism! Her head is probably spinning as we speak. I want her out.'

'We can't just throw her out. As soon as I contact Boucher I'll be able to . . .'

'Then ring Switzerland again. It must be morning there by now. Don't the Swiss all get up early anyway? To practise their yodelling or something?'

Beaten, he went to the hall phone.

He was picking up the receiver when I heard Barney yell, 'Leave that alone! It's not yours.'

I grabbed two aspirin. Washed them down with a mouthful of whiskey.

Gerry mumbled into the phone for what seemed like an age, then listened for even longer before speaking in halting, schoolboy French. '*Parlez . . . plus . . . lentement . . . s'il . . . vous . . . plait.*'

I went to stand beside him.

He frowned. '*Je . . . ne comprends pas. Ah. Ah. Oui . . . Je compre . . . d'accord!*'

'What didn't you understand?' I asked as he hung up. 'Don't tell me they still can't reach him?'

'That's not the problem . . .' He hesitated. 'The air traffic controllers have called a lightning strike. There'll be no flights out until . . . she'll have to stay . . .'

'Absolutely not!'

'What can I do?'

'You have a gun. Shoot her. It's her or me.' I rubbed my aching temples.

'Be serious.' He tried to pull me towards him.

I shrugged him off. 'I am being serious. Where's your gun? The one you told me you *never* take out of that drawer?'

He laughed. 'Come on, Annie. Calm down. Another day and it will all be over, she'll be out of our lives. I promise you'll never hear the name Boucher mentioned again.'

'I'm warning you, Gerry, I've had it . . .'

Barney came out of the living room. 'You got a cigarette, Gerry? She's pulling the place apart—' He saw my expression and stopped mid-sentence. 'What's happening?'

Caroline appeared behind him. 'I know you smoke,' she accused Gerry. 'I found a cigarette butt in your CD player. Tried to light it and burned my fingers. Damn match nearly set fire to the music centre.'

Before I could reach her, Gerry pushed me into the kitchen.

'Just one small punch? Please, Gerry. OK, a slap? Just one! Please.'

'You can't hit a defenceless girl.' He kicked the door shut. 'You need some sleep. Go to bed. Things always look better in the morning.'

'It *is* the morning!'

'Go to bed, baby.' He caught me to him. Held me close in a comforting hug, rocking me until I began to melt against him. I was reaching up to be kissed when I realised he wasn't rocking me. He was shaking with laughter.

'What's so funny?' I pulled away angrily.

'You! When you're premenstrual you'd take on Lennox Lewis,' he laughed.

And my awful, awful edginess suddenly made sense. Everything about the day did. My anger at the weather. The jeweller. My continual overreaction to what was, after all, just childish behaviour on Caroline's part. Not evil. Had I actually threatened to kill her for damaging my furniture?

Happily, this behaviour was normal. Well, normal for three days every month. Any serious row Gerry and I had ever had I could trace back to my wicked PMT. It didn't mean he was never in the wrong, simply that my tolerance levels plummeted when I was premenstrual.

'You're so clever.' I kissed him gratefully and went looking for my diary.

I found it. Thrown in a bedside drawer. And there they were, all carefully mapped out. My monthly cycle dates. Confirmed in black and white. My period *was* due. Five days ago.

32

I plucked at the sun-baked grass and watched Fiona setting out our picnic lunch on the immaculate linen tablecloth.

I'd come to the park expecting cling-wrapped sandwiches and a flask of coffee. Instead, I was greeted by a banquet. Gleaming silverware and wine glasses so fragile I'd be scared to take them out of the press, let alone use them for a picnic lunch in a public park. But Fiona liked the good things in life. Which was probably why she'd insisted on bringing the food, terrified that I'd bring Big Macs and chips.

She wasn't to know that anything I ate today would taste like sawdust.

She reached into the picnic basket and produced a splendidly boned duck *à l'orange*, already carved. She began arranging it on fine bone china plates.

'I only have an hour, Fiona,' I fidgeted.

'Relax,' she smiled. 'Look at Calum. That's the way to enjoy this weather.'

Calum was in his pram. Sleeping on his back. Feet in the air, legs spread wide, exposing his Pampers to the glorious sun. Hardly a pose I could adopt if I didn't want to get arrested.

'So you eventually got some sleep?' Fiona adjusted his parasol to block out the sun.

I nodded. 'But I was so worried, I kept one eye

open. Then woke to find her bed empty and ran downstairs like a madwoman.'

I plucked a frosted grape from the mountain of food in front of me.

She slapped my hand. 'They're for dessert. Have your starter first.'

I spread pâté on wafer-thin toast and tried to taste it.

'So where was she, then?' Fiona munched hers happily.

'In the kitchen. Making mushroom omelettes!'

'Omelettes?' she laughed.

'Yeah. Feeding Gerry and Barney. I must have looked a right fool, bursting in like that, screaming that she had gone missing. And there she was, stuffing her face with a massive mushroom omelette. For a little slip of a girl, she can't half eat.'

I picked at a slice of roast duck. 'I warned Gerry. Told him that if she can sneak out of a room while someone is sleeping less than three feet away, how in God's name are we supposed to hold on to her until Boucher gets here?'

'What did he say?' Fiona dipped her asparagus into a butter-rich sauce.

'Oh, you know Gerry!' I couldn't hide my irritation. 'Even when you're working with him he doesn't always let you know what he's thinking. He just said that we would take turns watching her. Then looks at me and says, "You need a break." He suggested a long walk in the park. Some fresh air, maybe. That's when I rang you . . . and you mentioned lunch and . . . here we are.'

I knew I was babbling. It's what I do when I'm nervous. Right now I was terrified. Nothing to do

with Caroline – Barney could handle her. I was terrified because no matter how carefully I had checked
and rechecked my diary, I couldn't get the dates to
do my bidding. They refused to cooperate or
rearrange themselves into a less frightening order.
The one salient fact had remained . . . salient. My
period was five days late. Counting today it would
be six.

Fiona watched me, a little frown rucking her forehead, her eyes so concerned I began to wonder if the
horror was emblazoned on my forehead.

Six days late! Six days late!

She leaned towards me. 'Are you . . . ?'

I felt my lip quiver.

'. . . driving?'

I collapsed on the grass, giggling like a madwoman.
'Why do you ask that?'

Her frown deepened. 'Because I want to know if
I should pour you wine or Ballygowan?'

I sat up. 'Wine, please! And er . . . don't put the
bottle away.'

Now she was worried. 'What's wrong, Annie?'

'You know what's wrong.' I grabbed the glass of
cool Frascati. 'Bloody Caroline Boucher is what's
wrong,' I lied.

'Well, right now she's not your problem. It's
Barney's turn to watch her, so let him worry about
her. You just relax. Enjoy your lunch.' She raised her
drink in salute.

I drank thirstily, almost emptying the glass. 'But
one drink always leads to another, doesn't it?'

She refilled my glass till it overflowed, topping up
hers just as enthusiastically.

'So what?' she laughed. 'It's a beautiful day. God's

in her heaven, and . . . we can sleep this off in the sun. Calum isn't due to waken for another hour.' She lay back against his pram. 'And Barney is guarding the *prisoner*. So there's no need for you to rush back. We have all the time in the world, to do nothing,' she said lazily, and raised her face to the sun.

I stretched out on the warm grass and closed my eyes. 'Thanks, Fiona.'

'What for?' she asked sleepily.

'Everything.'

'Welcome.' She began to snore softly.

I was just about nodding off when Calum started to wail.

Calum was topped and tailed and swallowing roughly half of every spoonful of the beige goo Fiona was feeding him, the other half dribbling down his chin and on to his cute little boy's bib.

Fiona wasn't at all perturbed by this spoon-in-dribble-out procedure. In fact she seemed to be enjoying it – a woman who used to be so fastidious, she once broke up with a divine man because whenever he ate he got tiny crumbs stuck in the corner of his lip.

'So when *does* Boucher get back?' The suddenness of the question startled me.

'Tonight, I hope.' I plucked idly at a stalk of grass. 'If he doesn't come up with another delaying tactic. I haven't said this to Gerry, but I think we're being taken for saps.'

'How so?' She spooned another helping of beige goo into Calum's mouth.

I waited, and out it came again. Right on cue. Exactly half of it, wending its way down his little fat chin until it was scooped back by the pink plastic spoon and redeposited in his chubby mouth.

'He's obviously using us as babysitters until this major banking deal is sorted. He's not going to risk having Miss Beelzebub marching into his corporate office in Switzerland when he has dopes like us to mind her! Image is so-o-o important in his world. Or maybe he's afraid the American bank won't trust him with their trillions if they think he can't even control a seventeen-year-old.'

'She can't be that bad?' Fiona caught an exceptionally large beige dribble and spooned it back into Calum's waiting mouth.

Watching him swallow it, I experienced a curious mix of emotions. Mainly revulsion, of course. But somewhere underneath there was a growing interest in the whole baby feeding procedure. A weird fascination with the mother and child interplay as they . . .

'*Is* she that bad, Annie?'

'What?'

'Caroline? She can't be *that* difficult?'

'She's a nightmare.' I reached out to pat a tubby Labrador who had abandoned her elderly owner to check us out. Or, more likely, the remains of our picnic.

'Gretchen?' her owner called, and Gretchen waddled off.

'I bet Boucher is dying to see her,' Fiona said. 'I bet he's moving heaven and earth to get back here as soon as he can.'

Calum was now having his bottle, drinking his milk so tidily I wondered why Fiona bothered with the spoon.

He was finally tucked up in his pram, and we were packing up the picnic basket, when Fiona brought up the subject of Caroline again.

'She's Boucher's flesh and blood, Annie.' She glanced adoringly at Calum. 'And there's no stronger bond than that between parent and child. It's almost . . . spiritual? You'll find out for yourself, when you have a baby.'

'That'll never happen!' I snapped.

'Course it will.' She went all smug. 'Some day you'll become pregnant, and your hormones will take over and you'll . . .'

'My period is late, Fiona!' The words burst out of their own accord.

Then, to the consternation of a passing jogger and the curious Gretchen, I burst into tears, big harsh sobs that I couldn't control.

Gretchen's owner was beside us in a flash. Dragging the dog away. Apologising for the intrusion. 'So sorry. Bad girl, Gretchen! Bad girl!'

Gretchen looked back at me with big, puzzled eyes, but Fiona reacted as only a true friend would. She bit back her own delight to gently commiserate with me.

Then, 'But . . . would it really be so terrible? To be pregnant?' She helped dry my eyes.

'Of course it bloody would! I have ambitions to fulfil, Fiona. And none of them include overpopulating the world!'

'But one little . . . teeny . . . tiny . . . baby?' she dared. 'That's hardly . . . OK, OK. I completely understand. It's your body. Your choice.' She backed off.

'Damn right it is.'

'How late are you?'

'Six days.'

'Oh, for God's sake. I've often gone longer than that. Loads of times.'

'Not me. I'm regular as clockwork. Remember?'

Our eyes met. Held.

'That was different, Annie. This time you're in a loving, stable relationship. I bet Gerry would be only too thrilled to . . .'

'No! If you tell him I'll never speak to you again.'

She looked hurt. 'Annie?'

'No!'

'OK.' She put her arm around me. 'Then let's get this in perspective. Six days late is nothing! It doesn't mean a thing. You've been seriously stressed. Overworked. Under enormous pressure these last few months. It's at times like these that loads of women find their cycle goes haywire.'

'You think?' I was full of hope.

'Well, you look like shite.'

'So I might be?' I stiffened in terror.

'Not necessarily. How much sleep did you get last night?'

'Practically none.'

'Well, there you are! That's why you look rotten. Like an old hag. That's all it is.'

'Thanks, Fiona. You always cheer me up,' I tried to smile. 'Oh my God, look who's behind you. No, don't turn!'

'Who is it?'

'Handsome optometrist. Kissing a girl!'

'Not just a peck?' She tried to peek.

'Definitely not. Don't turn!'

'Tongues?'

'Like lizards.'

'Oh.' Her curiosity got the better of her and she turned to look. 'God, she's young. I thought he was gay?'

'Jury's still out.' I chewed my lip. 'Six days late, Fiona. What am I going to do?'

'I think you should tell Gerry.'

'Out of the question. I bet you're right, anyway.'

'I am?' She brightened.

'Yeah. Six days is nothing. Not even a week. Oh my God, he's got his hand up her skirt.'

'I don't care if he's got his hand up her arse! Here's what you'll do. Wait another couple of days, just to be sure. Then you get a home-testing kit. I use a new German one. I'll give you the name. It's infallible. Dead easy to use. You just pee on the stick. Wait three minutes and you'll have your result.'

'Negative?' I attempted a smile again, determined to blot out memories of the last time I had found myself in this predicament. That had led to a dark night of the soul, months of guilt, bordering on self-flagellation, as I accused myself over and over for taking a certain decision which . . .

'OK?' She waited.

'Three minutes?' My voice sounded hollow.

'Yes. You don't have to wait for weeks to do the test. You could even do it tomorrow, if you want. Three short minutes and you'll know one way or the other. Then you can decide where to go from there. Your decision.' She reached out to hug me.

I was hugging her back in gratitude, or maybe just for the sheer physical comfort of it when a deep voice called, 'Hello!'

Handsome optometrist was standing by Calum's pram, his kissing companion nowhere in sight.

'Enjoying the good weather?' He flashed his movie-star teeth, which were nearly as dazzling as his all-white outfit. He looked like he was next up to bat.

'I've seen you in the café with Annie.' He offered his hand to Fiona. 'I'm Michel. The optometrist?'

'Fiona.' She shook his hand. 'You know Annie, of course.'

'Yes. Always busy. Always in a hurry.' He seemed completely unaware of my raw, red eyes. Or maybe they were everyday fare to optometrists.

'Your baby?' he asked Fiona, and leaned into the pram.

Never one to miss an opportunity to be adored, Calum opened his eyes and gave a big, toothless grin at the world in general, and Michel in particular.

'Oh, he's adorable.' Michel fell under his spell, and for the next few seconds he and Calum drooled happily at each other.

Fiona mouthed to me to tell Michel that we were having a private conversation, which he was interrupting.

No, you, I mouthed back.

You, she pointed.

Michel interrupted this soundless conversation. 'I've been considering . . . starting a family.' He looked from me to her.

Brain overload. Too much. Way too much information for the day that was in it.

'You'd recommend it, no doubt?' He watched Calum, who was now trying to swallow his right fist.

'Er . . .' Fiona floundered. It was the first time I had ever seen her at a loss for words.

'What about you, Annie? Doesn't he make you feel broody?'

Dead silence. Then my mobile shrilled.

Sandra. 'She's gone, Annie! Caroline's gone! Her *and* Barney. All I'm getting is the answering machine. I tried and tried his mobile, but it's out of range.'

'What's happening?' Fiona asked as I grabbed my bag.

'Caroline's gone!'

'Oh my God!' she cried as if it was her problem. 'Can I do anything?'

'No. I have to run.'

As I legged it, I heard Michel say, 'I'll walk with you, Fiona.'

I could just make out Fiona's reply.

'Oh, bugger off!'

33

Sandra met me at the agency door, her eyes bulging with alarm. 'I did my best, Annie. Barney rang earlier and I could hear them laughing. She was telling him to hurry. I knew there was something going on. I said they weren't to leave the house. That Gerry would kill them. Barney said he'd take full responsibility. There was nothing I could do. Gerry is over at the dog track, and I'm not allowed to ring him when he's working undercover. I'm sorry, Annie.'

'It's OK. I'll sort it.' I tried Barney's mobile. Engaged.

I rang the airport to check incoming flights. There was a flight due in from Zurich, but not until late evening. A clipped voice declined to confirm whether a Mr Simon Boucher was on the passenger list.

I tried Barney again. Engaged. I sent him a text message. COM BAC R DIE.

I rang my home number. A too familiar voice asked me to leave a message after the tone, but I drew the line at leaving a phone message for myself.

A lightning trip to the loo confirmed my ongoing lack of menstruation. I sent Barney another text message. U R DEAD. I nearly send a duplicate to Gerry, but decided that might be rash. Sometimes periods *were* just late. Maybe not mine. But still. Every late period didn't necessarily indicate a pregnancy. I made the universe a solemn promise that if I were lucky enough not to be caught this time, I would never have sex again. Ever. Then tried to convince myself that this was almost a duplicate of the time my Honda refused to start, and I had flown into a desperate panic, ringing Gerry to tell him the car was fucked. A complete write-off. And it turned out to be nothing more than an air bubble in the tank. Please God, let this be an air bubble. Please.

I drove to the house at top speed. There were dirty coffee cups everywhere and a trail of cake crumbs leading to the kitchen. And not a single low-fat yoghurt left in the fridge. There *was* a burn on the CD player.

I was about to do another loo check, when Sandra rang. 'Better get back here quickly, Annie! They're just coming in. Wait till you see the get-up of her.'

'You knew she was safe with me.' Barney refused to back down.

'Gerry said she wasn't to leave the house. What if her father had arrived and found her missing again?'

'She wasn't missing. She was with me.'

'Have you completely lost it, Barney? What the hell were you thinking of?'

'Don't blame Barney!' Caroline stepped forward. 'I needed clothes. I didn't have a thing to wear.'

She was now draped in dazzling white cheesecloth, from head to toe. A pint-sized flower child. Pure sixties retro. The little blue-trimmed kerchief tied around her head only added to the time-warp image. She looked as if she had taken a wrong turning on her way to Woodstock, and managed to look a lot more feminine without hair than most women can with a full head of it.

Barney clearly thought so.

'She looks wicked, huh?' he grinned.

Wicked. Now there was the word I'd been searching for.

'You look like a model!' Sandra gushed at her. 'That kerchief really suits you. Most people look dog-rough in them. Like tinkers. You look gorgeous. It's probably because you have cheekbones!' she enthused, as if the rest of us had to make do with boneless pads of flesh.

'See, Sandra approves.' Barney was chuffed.

'I don't have a problem with the way she looks!' I said. 'It's the sneaking out that worried me. And your utter lack of professionalism. She makes you a mushroom omelette, and you forget all your training? And as for you, little miss. You try that again and you'll be sorry,' I threatened the vision in white.

To my horror she burst into tears. 'I told you she doesn't like me, Barney. I said she'd try to turn you against me,' she sniffled into his chest.

He enveloped her fragile little whiteness in his long arms. 'See what you've done, Annie. Do you have to be so cruel? What's got into you, anyway? You're such an old grump these days. All we did was go out and buy a few clothes. What's wrong with that?'

Three pairs of eyes glared accusingly at me.

I cleared my throat. 'Just don't leave again. That's all.'

'I need the bathroom.' Caroline crossed her legs dramatically.

'No way!'

'You can't stop her going to the bathroom!' Barney was horrified.

'Go with her, Sandra.' I gave her a push. 'And

360

don't leave her alone for a second. Stand guard outside the door, maybe even inside if you have to. Barney, I want a word with you.'

'OK.' He watched them go, a soppy look on his face.

'What if she had done a runner in the shopping mall?'

'I'm not stupid. I stuck so close to her people thought we were conjoined. She never once—'

'Got the chance to leg it?'

'I swear to you.'

'I believe you. Because if she got a chance, she'd be gone. We can't afford to relax around her. I want you to follow them upstairs and wait outside the toilets. Do it, Barney!' I ordered when he hesitated. 'Have you forgotten who she is? If we lose her, we don't get paid.'

'Yeah, I know.' He was unhappy. 'I'm to think of her like a COD parcel. It's a bit sick, isn't it? She's nearly eighteen. Old enough to make her own choices, surely?'

'I agree. And she can do exactly that! *After* we hand her back. She can bungee jump off the Bank of Ireland for all I care. But first we finish the job we're contracted to do.'

'Christ, you've changed. You used to be so . . .'

'Naive?'

'Nice. Now it's all about money.'

'Grow up, Barney. If the bank calls in our loan, we're dead. And you'll be out of a job. Besides which, you know all those mini-listening gadgets you keep asking me to order? If we botch this case, you can forget them. You'll be lucky to have a mobile phone at your disposal. Maybe you're the one who's

361

changed. Turning all dewy-eyed because little Miss Loaded put her hand on your knee?'

He looked shocked. 'She's just a kid.'

'Yeah? Well keep that in mind.' I held his gaze.

'Christ, you're turning into Gerry.' He tried to laugh.

'Well I doubt you ever will!' I delivered a nasty blow.

His face soured. 'She needs someone on her side, Annie.'

'She's had too many people on her side, and a fat lot of good it did her. She meets some wannabe artist in Temple Bar and he drags her into a hole like *The Dimmer*? She tells him she's having problems at home, and he offers her a bed in that filthy squat. Convinces her it's cool. *Like . . . it's radical, man!* I wouldn't let a dog sleep in that place.'

'That's why she moved to the flats! And . . .'

'Listen! With her lack of judgement I'd rather see her at home with her prig of a father than being conned by drug addicts. I don't like Boucher, but compared with her chosen alternative, he's a prince. Her boyfriend was doing heroin, for Christ's sake!'

The lift doors sprang open and Sandra came running out. 'Annie? I can't find her.'

'What . . . ?'

'I had to go myself. I was bursting. I'd have wet myself if I didn't . . .'

'Lock the front door, Barney.'

He slammed it shut. Clicked the lock. One of Naomi's regular customers was outside. She tapped delicately on the glass, waving politely to attract our attention.

'I'll take Dreamland Interiors.' I ignored her. 'You

go through our offices, Barney. Come on, Sandra,' I yelled.

There were dozens of possible hiding places in Dreamland Interiors. Sandra and I trawled through the lot, searching mock bedrooms at top speed, dropping to our knees to check under fancy canopied beds and behind what felt like miles of draped gauze. Nothing.

We tried the bathrooms next. All those fancy closets. Power showers. Nothing. Mock living rooms. Dining rooms. Wood-panelled studies.

The only place left was Naomi's office, but, given their history, I thought it unlikely that Caroline would hide in a place with black and white blow-ups of Naomi on every wall. We were checking behind a row of Chinese lacquered screens when we heard a ruckus coming from the office. It sounded like hand-to-hand combat.

Naomi and Caroline were pushing each other backwards and forwards in the big office. Not exactly punching, but not exactly pussyfooting around each other either. A bubble-headed glass Buddha toppled over as Naomi stumbled back against it, her hand rescuing it just in time. In retaliation, she pushed Caroline. Hard. Caroline fell against the desk, sending a Chinese lantern crashing to the floor.

'Oh my God! Look what you've done! That's irreplaceable,' Naomi screamed, and lashed out with a kick to the ankle.

Caroline reacted by grabbing Naomi's silk neck scarf and tugging it so hard, Naomi's face turned blue.

'Get Barney,' I ordered Sandra. I had seen what

Caroline could do when she was riled. But Naomi wasn't beaten yet. Her eyes bulging out of her head, she still managed to slap Caroline hard, making her drop her choke-hold on the scarf.

'Ow!' Caroline nursed her cheek in shock. 'You slapped me!'

'If you weren't pregnant, I'd have punched you.'

My gasp made them both turn. Caroline crumpled like a distressed child.

'She's . . . she's not pre . . . pre . . . ?' I couldn't say the p-word.

'Are you blind?' Naomi shrilled. 'Look at her. That kaftan can't hide her bump. And look at that inflated chest. You could sit on it.'

Caroline clutched her reddening cheek, her head lowered in despair.

'Caroline?' I reached out to her.

Naomi laughed cruelly. 'My God, Simon doesn't know, does he? Oh, I'd give ten years of my life to see his face when he gets this news. His precious little angel. His little princess. How far gone are you? Three? Four months? This is priceless.'

Fiona's pâté and duck *à l'orange* began churning in my stomach, threatening to make me hurl on Naomi's priceless Persian rug. I put a hand over my mouth.

Naomi laughed and laughed.

I left my office door open to keep the air circulating. Unlike Naomi's, my office got the sun all day, which meant that right now it was unbearably hot.

Caroline sat in front of my desk, head bowed like an errant sixth former, eyes on the floor as she waited for the head's wrath to be unleashed.

'I take it your father *doesn't* know?' I asked.

'He'd kill me.' She sounded about ten.

'I doubt that.'

'He'd never let me have it. He'd make me have an abortion.'

My stomach still playing up, I steeled myself to ask the pertinent question.

'How far gone are you?'

'Five and a half months.'

I hid my shock. Jesus Christ, this was a nightmare. Five and a half months? So all along we had been chasing a pregnant girl? I had even tried to ply her with whiskey. Would have given her cigarettes, if I'd had them. Barney and Gerry had manhandled her like barrow boys. And all the time she was . . . ? In our defence, we had had absolutely no idea of her condition. Even looking at her now it was hard to tell – her stomach had only a minor curve to it. When Fiona was five months she was the width of a two-seater sofa. It was only by looking for it that you spotted Caroline's neat little bump.

'Caroline?'

She put her head in her hands.

'Does Spike—?'

'It's not his!' she spat. 'He was only someone to hide out with.'

Despite the heat, I felt a chill creep along my spine. 'So . . . who is the father?'

'None of your business.' A flicker of the old Boucher arrogance.

'OK.' I reached for the phone. 'I'll just ring your . . .'

'No. Please. He'll make me have an abortion.'

'If you're five and a half months, nobody can make you have a . . . a termination.'

'He can. You don't know him. He can do anything. Anything he wants. My father is a very powerful man.' Her voice cracked.

I needed Gerry. I picked up the receiver.

'Who are you calling?' She scrambled to her feet.

'Gerry. He—'

'No! He'll tell him!'

I put the phone down. 'He won't. Gerry is . . .'

'I have an aunt in New Zealand. She says I can stay with her. In three weeks I'll be eighteen. I can get a passport without his signature. Please let me go. Three weeks, that's all I need. I want to keep my baby. My aunt wants to help. I have my own money. I can take good care of a baby. I've already proved that, haven't I? I didn't touch drugs! Everyone around me was doing something, but . . . but I never. I had to stay with Spike . . . anyone else would have given me up to my father. All I ever did was smoke a . . .'

'What?' I squeaked.

'A couple of tipped cigarettes. And I didn't even finish them!' She put her head down on my desk and sobbed. I reached out to touch her, then pulled back.

The first rule of any good private investigator: put your personal feelings aside.

Where the hell was Sandra? I'd told her we'd need tea and plenty of chocolate biscuits. Maybe even a couple of cream cakes.

34

'Jesus, what a mess!' Gerry was practically eating his third cigarette. 'How come nobody noticed she was pregnant?'

'You mean me?'

'Well, you hardly expected me to . . .'

'Oh, I see. I'm a woman, so I'm supposed to have a built-in pregnancy detector? On your bike, Gerry! Nobody could have guessed that she was pregnant.'

'Naomi did!'

'She knew what she looked like before. I didn't. Plus they were pushing each other around Naomi's office. Practically wrestling. It's pretty difficult *not* to notice a pregnant stomach when you're wrestling its owner.'

'Did Naomi hurt her?' He became concerned.

'No. She's fine. Tough as they come. Well, maybe not exactly . . .'

I thought of her heart-wrenching sobs. Her tear-stained face. The way she had curled into an almost foetal position as she clutched her stomach protectively, pleading with me to let her go.

'She's not as tough as she pretends. In fact she's quite vulnerable now her secret is out. Now that she's no longer hiding it under her clothes!' I knew I was making her pregnancy sound like a small mammal, but my head was wrecked. Right now I could barely think straight. In some strange, perverse way my own problem made me almost overly sympathetic to hers. Even though we both wanted different outcomes.

'Boucher just rang. She won't speak to him.'

'You didn't tell him?' I was horrified.

He took a long, slow drag on his cigarette.

'You didn't?' I slumped.

'No.'

Relief washed over me. 'Has she told you who the father is?'

'Told me? She won't even talk to *me*.'

'So what now?'

'He's the client.' He inhaled again, this time avoiding my eyes.

'And of course he *is* offering us that lucrative long-term security contract. We mustn't forget that.' Even to my own ears my tone sounded nasty.

He left his desk and went to the window, trailing a cloud of smoke, and disapproval, in his wake. 'How is she?'

'Distraught.'

'Look, even if we wanted to help her, there's nothing we can do.'

I took a deep breath, bringing passive smoking to new heights.

'We could let her go.'

He didn't act surprised, just turned to look at me, his eyes wary. 'Suppose we did.' He paused. 'She still has three weeks to go to her eighteenth birthday. By the time she gets a passport sorted, she could be seven months gone. No airline will take her then. So what happens? I'll give you the most likely scenario. She'll hide out in Dublin backstreets again. End up back with the only people she trusts not to blow her secret. A gang of junkies.'

'Th . . . they're not actual junkies,' I said, a little flame of hope beginning to ignite.

'Splitting hairs, Annie.' He looked cross.

'We could always . . . Help her get her old passport?'

'What?'

'Boucher said it's in his safe. In the house. Caroline is bound to know the combination. Maybe we could go there and . . .'

'I'm going to forget you even said that! We're supposed to uphold the law. Apart from which, what I think you're suggesting could get us five years.' He drew hard on his fast-shrinking cigarette.

'That wouldn't happen.' I hurried over to him. 'Boucher wouldn't dare set the law on us! He'd be frightened that we know too much about him.'

'And what the hell do we know about him?'

'Well . . . he must have something to hide. A man like him always has. Come on, Gerry, he abhors publicity. He'd never turn us in.'

'Jesus, Annie! Do you know what you're asking me to do? Have you any idea of the seriousness . . . ?'

'Have you any idea what that girl is going through? You're the one always saying people should be given a second chance. What chance will she have once he sees her condition? He'll have her bundled into a clinic before you can say Jack Robinson. She's terrified of him, of what he'll do. And what about afterwards? Are you prepared to take responsibility for what she might do to herself after he forces her to have a termination?'

369

He closed his eyes. 'Go away, Annie. I need to think.' He stubbed out the remains of his cigarette.

Of course it was a totally insane idea, one that no law-abiding private investigator should even contemplate. Still.

Gerry drove. I slipped a Van Morrison CD into the stereo as a mood enhancer. He didn't comment.

Ms Lynch greeted us like old friends, welcoming us into the big house.

'But why the delay?' She was curious. 'Why isn't she coming home? Mr Boucher's assistant said she's safe and well.'

'She is, but er . . .' I flustered.

Gerry took over. He explained things, taking extreme care to use only detective speak, which was guaranteed to leave poor Ms Lynch utterly baffled.

'Oh. Very good so.' She thanked him, her expression one of total bewilderment. 'Now, the clothes you mentioned? They're all packed.'

She pointed to a Louis Vuitton suitcase by the door.

Shit.

In the agency my plan had seemed foolproof. When I had sat Caroline down and explained it carefully, she had cried. Weeping with joy, she had practically kissed my hand in gratitude before calming down and giving Gerry the combination to the safe and describing its exact location in her father's study.

The plan was for Gerry to slip into the study and open the safe while Ms Lynch and I were busy selecting clothes for Caroline.

But superefficient Ms Lynch had anticipated us. The clothes were all packed and ready to go.

Right there in the fancy Louis Vuitton suitcase.

Gerry and I exchanged panic-stricken looks.

Then Ms Lynch asked the most wonderful question. One which would require a very long and intricate answer. 'How on earth *did* you find her? After all this time?'

'You'd better explain, Gerry. You tell Ms Lynch the full story while I use the bathroom. I *remember* where it is.' I gave him a look. And before he could stop me, I was hurrying upstairs.

The study door was unlocked. I tiptoed across the gleaming oak floorboards, stomach tightening in fear. Hands shaking like jelly, I pulled aside the oil painting of Caroline's beautiful mother.

Don't look at me like that, you. I'm doing this for your daughter! And your grandchild.

Caroline had only give the combination of the safe to one person. Gerry. But that wasn't a problem. I was in the room at the time, wasn't I, and I never forget a number. Caroline had been so nervous, warning Gerry that getting a single digit wrong would trigger the alarm in the Garda station. But figures were my speciality. I flexed my fingers and set to work.

The heavy door swung open soundlessly to reveal a slim pile of papers in the middle of the safe. I flipped through them until I came to a brown envelope with Caroline's name on it. And there it was. The wine-coloured passport. I opened it to double-check. Caroline smiled up angelically at me from the photo, her blonde hair shining like spun gold. I put the papers back carefully and locked the safe, dusting it lightly with a paper tissue, then glanced up at Caroline's mother again.

She's going to stay with your sister, so stop looking so worried.

The passport tucked in my bag, I went to the first-floor bathroom. Flushed the loo, splashed water a bit carelessly around the immaculate sink and messed up a neatly folded towel. A housekeeper would notice things like that.

Adrenalin still pumping like mad, I went back to the living room. Hell, if we were forced to close the agency, I could always take up safe cracking.

'Now, are you sure you have everything Caroline needs?' Ms Lynch got to her feet as I rejoined them.

'Everything.' I smiled at Gerry.

He looked like he was on the brink of collapse. 'Let's go.'

'A friend of ours has a plane to catch.' I explained his nervousness to Ms Lynch. 'A long flight ahead of them. And you know these long-haul flights. All that talk of deep vein thrombosis! Everyone gets jittery . . .'

Gerry pushed me out the door.

'Were you trying to get us caught?' His voice was raw with tension.

'Just making polite conversation,' I smiled. 'My father always said politeness will get you anywhere.'

'Did you get it?'

'Of course.'

'No problems with the combination?'

'Do you notice any Garda cars rushing up the drive?'

'I'll take the wheel,' he snapped, but a little grin of relief was trying to break out at the corners of his mouth.

* * *

372

Barney and Caroline were waiting at the agency. They slid in beside the Vuitton suitcase.

'How did it go?' Barney asked as we drove off.

'Ask Annie. She's the safe cracker.' Gerry tore through an amber light.

'I did have the combination,' I said modestly.

'*You* opened the safe?' Barney looked at me, his voice rising in shock.

I waved the passport before passing it over my shoulder to Caroline.

She kissed the back of my head. 'Thank you, Annie. I hope some day you'll have a baby. Then you'll know how much this means to me.'

Jaysus.

As we watched her plane take off for London, Barney handed me an envelope.

'She said to give this to you after she left.' He looked curious.

'I hope it's money,' Gerry said as we headed back to the jeep. 'Because we've just waved goodbye to the biggest fee we would have earned this whole year. Not to mention that security contract.'

We walked to the jeep in silence. I waited until we were well on the road before tearing open the envelope.

No money. Just a note.

Annie, I owe you this. The baby's father is Daddy's head groom. I know you met him. Not exactly Brad Pitt, huh? We only did it once. After he'd spent the day teaching me how to use a short rein.

It was over so fast I can barely remember it. Anyway, he's happily married. With four kids. But

I know Daddy. He'd ruin him. I'm trusting you
with my secret.

A million thanks.

P.S. Aunt Belinda says you're not to worry about
any fallout. She can handle Daddy.

'What does it say?' Barney asked. 'Does she mention
me?'

'Yeah. She said you were fantastic. Almost as
memorable as a head groom she once knew.'

'Cool.' He was chuffed.

I tore the note into tiny little pieces and threw
them out into the rising wind. My second act of
lawlessness in one day.

Gerry didn't ask about the note. Just chain-smoked
and drove. Barney was soon lost in thought as well.
Me too. Caroline's problems might be sorted, but we
still had to face Boucher. He was due in tomorrow,
on the very day of Calum's christening. And along
with all that, I still had an unopened box of tampons
sitting in my bedside drawer.

I hurried about the airless bedroom, setting out my
christening suit for the morning. The promising little
wind had come to nothing, died down after a brave
attempt at relieving the humidity. It hadn't rained for
weeks, yet the clouds were touching the rooftops.
Even if I'd been worry-free, this weather would have
guaranteed me a headache.

I set the alarm for six.

Simon Boucher was catching the early flight.

Gerry came out of the bathroom, his hair dripping
wet from the shower.

Most nights the sight of him clad only in a white

towel was enough to have me panting. Not tonight. Sex was the last thing on my mind right now. All I wanted was to go to sleep and wake up to find my period had arrived and that Simon Boucher wasn't about to set the law on me.

'You all right, Annie?' Gerry asked.

'I'll be fine.' Even to my own ears my voice sounded strained.

He reached out to me, wet arms glistening.

'Don't!' I pulled away. 'You're all wet.'

He frowned. 'Never bothered you before.' He dried himself quickly, dabbing carelessly with the big towel.

'I'm tired.' I turned away. 'And . . .'

'Premenstrual?' He was disappointed.

'Oh, forgive me if my female hormones get in the way of your sex life.'

He stopped towelling. Gave me a searching look, then pulled on a pair of pyjama bottoms.

I sat back, watching him dry his hair, his strong arms reaching up to show the fine black hair underneath. I usually found this after-shower ritual a total turn-on. It was practically guaranteed to have me telling him to hurry up, forget about drying off and get into bed. Tonight was different. Tonight I had other concerns.

If Gerry was still thinking about Boucher, you couldn't tell. He clearly had sex on his mind, and that overrode all else, of course. He was a man, wasn't he? He could have sex while having his teeth drilled.

'Are you still worried about Boucher?' He threw down the towel.

'No,' I said quickly.

'Don't be. I'll handle him.' He came up behind me and began massaging my shoulders, his strong fingers working against my taut muscles, dissolving my tension beautifully.

That's the trouble with Gerry. Whenever I get all riled up and start finding reasons to resent him, he manages to do exactly the right thing. I leaned back against him and he lifted my hair to kiss my neck, his tongue moving, feather-light, against my skin.

My mobile rang.

'Leave it,' he said hoarsely.

'It might be Caroline.' I picked it up.

Fiona's number came on screen. 'Any news?'

'No show!'

'I'll call you in the morning.'

Gerry was sitting on the bed, looking at me with his heart in his eyes. Sod that. He was mostly to blame for the mess I was in. Not that I could recall the specific occasion when we had taken a chance. There had been too many of them lately to keep account. But he was the one who had talked me into giving up the pill. He'd been working a private case taken against a pharmaceutical giant, and been so horrified by the long-term effects of several of the drugs he'd had to research that he became paranoid about me taking the pill. Not that any of the suspect drugs were even associated with the pill. Still, after that experience he got his knickers in a twist whenever he saw me taking it.

'Durex don't put your health at risk,' he had insisted.

Well, not when you actually remembered to use them.

I felt a hand slip under my nightie.

'Don't! I'm . . .' I squirmed.

'Premenstrual. I forgot.' He got off the bed, picked

up the towel and went to the bathroom to drop it in the linen basket.

I slid between the sheets, taking care to keep to my side of the bed. If I even brushed against him the floodgates might open. I might break down and end up telling him that I had been premenstrual for nearly a week and was going out of my mind with worry. And where would that get us? Wrapped in each other's arms as he tried to convince me that having a child would enhance our relationship . . .

I closed my eyes.

'Annie?' He touched my back.

I feigned sleep, lying so close to the edge of the bed that a single deep breath would have sent me crashing to the floor.

35

I opened one eye to check the clock. It was eight-thirty-five. We had slept through the alarm.

I shook Gerry awake, skilfully avoiding his reaching arm, and raced around getting ready, tearing the plastic cover off my cream christening suit and pulling on my matching shoes at the same time. The ceremony wasn't until two, but we had a full morning's work to get through first, and hadn't a hope of getting home to change.

Gerry was all fingers and thumbs as he dressed in his dark, formal suit. He even needed help with his tie. And cufflinks.

Then we were off. No time for breakfast. Not even a quick coffee as we drove away in separate directions.

I envied him his morning. He was enjoying his work with the syndicate who had called him in to investigate the greyhound scam. Two of them were show business people, one of them a comedian, a real character. The job didn't pay hugely, but it would keep his mind off Simon Boucher. My morning would be taken up with working the accounts and trying to avoid the bank manager. For me, Simon Boucher might prove to be light relief.

Waiting at a long red traffic light, my seat belt began to feel tight. I loosened it with trembling hands.

Told myself to get a grip. *Even if you were pregnant, you dimwit, it would only be the size of a pinhead.*

Sandra greeted me with a pile of post and a cheery, 'Guess who died? That man we were hoping to get piles of sexual harassment evidence on. Massive heart attack. Dirty old git. A lucky escape for him! So I'll mark that case off the book, will I? And Mrs Behan cancelled. She made up with her husband. Doesn't want pictures of him and his fancy woman after all. So after today, Barney has nothing to do. Declan left a message last night, says he wants to wind up the lap dancing case alone. He already has nearly all the evidence Mr Frawley needs on his manager. So that's sorted. You look great, Annie. Love that suit. You'll make a smashing godmother.'

'Thanks, Sandra.' I checked the post. 'No inquiries? No . . . new cases on offer?'

'Ha, ha, ha.'

She was right. The postbag was heavy, but with bills. The only exception a nerve-racking bank statement. Reading it gave me severe stomach cramps.

I beat Sandra to the phone. 'Good morning, McHugh Dunning Investigative Agency. May I help you?'

'Any word from Boucher?' Gerry.

'Nothing. What's happening about the dogs? Get any good tips, did you?' I tried to be jocular.

'Yeah. Never wear a dark suit around dogs. Listen, I'll be finished here in an hour. My two suspects have admitted to switching the dogs. They had no choice when we caught them on camera. But this thing is much bigger than anyone suspected, so I'm handing my evidence over to the gardai. We don't have the resources to track stolen dogs across two continents.

The Gardai say they'll owe me one when it finally comes to court. They'll use me as a witness. But I'll have to wave goodbye to my closure fee here. Can't be helped, Annie.'

Of course not. But it would leave another noticeable hole in this month's accounts. If Declan didn't tie up the lap-dancing case, this was about as bad as it got.

I put the phone down. It rang instantly. Simon Boucher.

'I'll be with you in an hour. To collect my daughter.'

'Er . . .'

'No! Don't put her on. I'll talk to her when I get there.' He hung up.

I went down to reception to check on incoming inquiries just as Barney arrived, looking like something off the cover of *Vogue*.

Sandra wolf-whistled loudly. 'Look at you! You look like a tailor's dummy,' she chortled.

I hadn't known Barney possessed a real suit. Well, not a pinstriped job that looked like a genuine Armani.

He paraded up and down for our approval. 'I'm going to try again for that model agency job.'

'You're going to be a model?' Sandra's mouth dropped open.

He chortled. 'I'm going to see if they'll hire me to investigate that spate of insider thieving the girl I met in Emerald Waters told me about. If Jim Nolan and his cohorts are chasing that gig, it must pay well. I'm hoping to charm the owner into hiring me. I've heard she likes her men young and well groomed. I even got my nails buffed. See?' He held out his hands.

I hugged him so hard I nearly ruined his suit. 'Thank you, Barney.'

He caught my face in his manicured hands and kissed me. 'No sweat, hon. I'd dig ditches to keep this agency going. Not that it's ever going to close!' He answered my worried look. 'Do you think I'd shell out three grand for a suit like this if I thought we were in danger of closing?'

'We're closing?' Sandra became distressed.

'Course not! Barney's just messing. You think he'd buy an Armani suit if we were closing?'

'He *hired* that suit! I rang the shop for him.'

I turned to see him frantically signalling to her to shut up.

Gerry was back. Waiting for Boucher. It was now two and a half hours past the time he'd said he'd be along to collect his daughter. I was weary from checking the clock, trying to ignore my nervous stomach cramps and answering calls from everyone but Boucher.

Barney was on every fifteen minutes from the modelling agency. Anxious to know the state of play. Declan rang from a belly-dancer's flat. She was packing, going home to eastern Europe, reneging on her promise to give evidence of money-laundering in the club. And our bank manager kept demanding to speak to me, no matter how many times Sandra told him I was out. Then Fiona rang, in the middle of her christening preparations, the background noise sounding like the Tower of Babel because four of Pino's Italian relatives had flown over for the celebration and somehow managed to pick up a French cousin en route.

Everyone was on. Except Boucher.

'Maybe his plane crashed?' Barney said hopefully.

'Don't be wicked. I bet he's stuck in traffic,' I said.

'Without a mobile?'

I began working on the accounts, trying not to despair. But the more numbers I tapped in, the handier the safe-cracking option appeared as a career choice.

It was almost one-thirty when the big Bentley purred to a stop outside. I ran to Gerry's office. 'He's here.'

'Go back to your own office, Annie.'

'No, I'll stay. You don't want to face him on your own.'

'That's my job,' he said grimly, fastening the beautiful dark suit I had forced him to wear, and which made him look impossibly handsome as well as businesslike. More than a match for any pompous millionaire.

I was slipping into my office when I heard the lift doors clanging. I waited a full minute before tiptoeing back along the corridor to listen at Gerry's door.

The voices were muted at first. Even polite.

Then a loud bellow. 'What?'

Gerry's voice: '. . . nothing . . . could . . . difficult . . . as best we could . . . nobody to . . .'

Another bellow. Then loud arguing. Two alpha males, neither one prepared to give an inch. Shouting each other down. I could almost smell the testosterone wafting under the door.

Footsteps approaching. I legged it back to my office, leaving my door open a crack.

'And you expect me to pay you? You *lost* her? Three

professional detectives couldn't keep control of a seventeen-year-old girl?'

'Could you?'

A pause.

'I should have known better than to entrust the safety of my daughter to a man who couldn't make it up the ranks of the *Irish* police force. Not only will you not see another cent of my money, I'll see to it that you're blacklisted by every business in the city!'

I pressed a hand to my mouth to keep it shut.

The lift door slammed.

I took the stairs two at a time, praying the lift wouldn't choose today of all days to work properly. It didn't let me down. I was racing into reception before the doors chugged open.

Boucher stepped out, his face brick red with temper.

I handed him a bill. 'Our expenses, Mr Boucher.'

'Expenses?' He crumpled it into a ball and threw it on the floor. 'I'm not paying you people a red cent.'

I blocked his path. 'I'm afraid you'll have to pay our expenses, Mr Boucher. You might get away with refusing to pay us for finding your daughter. I'm aware of the loophole in that contract. But if you don't pay the expenses incurred in the long search for her, we'll see you in court.'

He looked at me as if I were an annoying insect, something he could swat aside at will. 'Me? You may see my *lawyers* in court! You certainly won't see me.'

'Your choice. I'm sure your lawyers will be as fascinated to hear what your daughter has to say about you as we were.'

'Are you threatening me?'

'Absolutely not! I'm just explaining that we'll be

forced to use every piece of evidence at our disposal in order to win the case for our expenses. Of course, if we were unscrupulous, which we're not,' I added quickly, 'we'd . . . em . . . probably leak stories to the press?'

He didn't move.

'Did you know that your daughter shared a rat-infested squat with a group of drug addicts? You didn't? Did you know that she . . . ? Well, never mind about that! It will all come out in court anyway. What I'd like to know is why, when we found her, and repeatedly tried to contact you, you gave us the run-around? Were you just too busy to come and collect her? You thought it was better to leave her in a detective agency with total strangers? For two whole days? People collect their dogs quicker than that.'

The silence seemed to last for ever. Even Sandra appeared to stop breathing.

Boucher held out his hand, his face like stone.

I picked up the expenses sheet from the floor. Smoothed it as best I could. I'm not proud. He scanned it quickly and went to the desk.

'Sandra? Give Mr Boucher a pen.'

He scribbled the cheque carelessly.

'Thank you, Mr Boucher.' I took it. 'Will you be wanting a receipt?'

He looked as if he might drop his frozen act long enough to smack me.

'Bye-bye, Mr Boucher,' Sandra called after him pleasantly. 'Do come again.'

Gerry was standing at his office window looking into the street as Boucher's car pulled away.

'He gave us this.' I handed him the cheque. 'For our expenses.'

'Jesus,' he said in disbelief. 'He actually gave you a cheque?'

'You obviously said something right,' I laughed.

'But he was livid!' he puzzled.

'What do we care. We got a cheque. OK, we won't be bathing in champagne, but this should keep the wolf from the door for a few months.' I took charge of the cheque again.

'Did we do the right thing, Annie? Letting her go?' He frowned.

'You know we did. Christ.' I grabbed my stomach.

'What?'

'Stomach cramps. But don't worry. An old neighbour of my mum's used to call them "happy news cramps", and I used to look at her and her eight kids and wonder why. I think I know now.' I grimaced and smiled at the same time.

He didn't get it. 'But you look pale. Are you sure you're OK? I think you need a break, Annie. Why don't you take a few days off? You've been working non-stop.'

'What about you? When did you last take a break?'

'That's different. I'm used to investigative work.'

Was that where this was going? We were short of cases, so guess who was about to be given a break, then quietly pushed behind a desk again?

'A few stomach cramps won't stop me working!' I snapped.

'We'll see.'

We bloody will, I thought. I'm not going back behind a desk. Next he'd be asking me to stay home and bake bread.

'Excuse me.' I dashed out to the toilet.

The stomach cramps proved to be exactly what I suspected. I had never been so happy to rip open a box of tampons. I came out of the bathroom walking on air.

Gerry caught my hand. 'What is it?' he smiled.

'Delight?' I kissed him. 'Let's go to this christening.'

'How can you have such huge moods swings, Annie?' he puzzled.

'Dunno. Just lucky, I guess.'

We were getting into the jeep when Sandra came running out, calling Gerry. 'Ansan Insurance are on the phone for you, Gerry. Sounds important.'

I sat behind the wheel and tried not to sulk. Important? All Gerry's calls were important. Mine were just phone calls. I checked my watch. There would be hell to pay if we were late for this christening. The competition to be godparents had been fierce – all the Italian cousins wanted in on the act. One of them had even brought a special Padre Pio medal as a bribe for Pino. I couldn't wait to hear Fiona's version of that tale.

My mobile rang. 'Fiona? Oh, Barney . . . What are you . . . ? You didn't? No, of course you don't look gay. Gay hair? That's nonsense. How can you have gay hair? Well that's her problem. No, you don't have bisexual hair either . . . well she's obviously an idiot . . . come to the party after the christening . . . yes . . . lots of single girls . . . beautiful Italians I hear . . . no-o-o they won't think you have gay hair . . . OK . . . see you at the party.'

Gerry came rushing out, his carefully knotted tie

all askew again. He pulled open the door. 'Scoot over.'

'Why?'

'I'm driving.'

'Who says?'

'Oh, Annie, not today.'

'Why not?'

'Oh, for fuck's sake.'

'All right, you can drive.' I slid over. 'But we're going to have to discuss certain things, you and I.'

'Jesus, if we have any more discussions there'll be no time left for anything else.' He started the jeep with a roar. 'Guess what? Ansan Insurance want us to take over their investigative department.'

'Oh my God! That's like winning the lotto!' I screamed.

'Not quite. But insurance fraud *is* huge!'

'When did you put in for that?'

'I didn't. But don't forget we saved them a fortune when we recovered that stolen jewellery. Apparently they've been investigating *us*. No offence to Calum's christening, but they've just given us a mega reason to celebrate today! You realise that if we had that security contract with Boucher, we wouldn't be free to accept Ansan's offer,' he laughed. 'Someone up there likes us, Annie.'

'Padre Pio maybe?'

'What?'

'Nothing,' I laughed.

He gave me a look. 'Open that glove compartment. I put something in there for you. I wanted to . . .' He paused. 'I planned on giving them to you later, but to be honest . . . ah, hell, you may as well have them now.'

I tore open the glove compartment. Pulled out a little blue box.

'What is it?' I asked.

'Open it and see,' he laughed.

I rattled it. Examined its funny shape. Roughly three inches by two?

'What is it?'

'Open it!' He took one hand off the wheel to muss my hair.

I lifted the lid slowly, peeped inside, and a lump the size of the Sugarloaf Mountain blocked my throat. I threw myself across Gerry. Kissed him anywhere I could reach.

'Stop! You'll get us both killed!' He pulled over on to the hard shoulder.

Choking with emotion, I spilled the contents of the little box across my lap.

'Well?' He smiled.

I could barely speak. 'This . . . this is the best present anyone has ever given me,' I sniffled, trying not to cry on to the neat little cards. They were all so beautiful. So beautifully identical. All of them saying exactly the same thing, in the neatest, most perfect print I had ever seen.

Annie McHugh
Private Investigator

Three minutes later we finally broke from another weepy clinch.

I picked up one of my cards, examining it again.

'So perfect.' I ran a finger along it.

'So are you,' Gerry lied, but it *was* an emotional moment.

'How many cards altogether?' I was in love.

'Couple of hundred.' He touched my cheek.

'Is that all? Well, you'd better get on that phone right now and start reordering—'

I would have finished the sentence, but it's hard to talk when someone's mouth is on yours.

I drew back. 'Gerry?'

'Emmmm?'

'Is that a gun in your belt, or are we . . . going to a christening?'

We pulled ourselves together. Tidied ourselves up. Gerry started the jeep, his eyes crinkling up in the way that I had loved from the very first time I'd seen him. I clutched a bundle of the little cards so tightly they were practically cutting into my hand. We drove to the christening in the bright sunlight, my head bursting with plans.

Also available in Arrow

ANNIE'S NEW LIFE

Maureen Martella

*Annie's discovered a case of
mistaken identity . . . her own*

After thirty years of being Annie McHugh, Annie
discovers that she is, in fact, someone else. Her
beloved and hugely respectable parents forged her
birth certificate.

She hires Gerry, a private detective with a strong look
of George Clooney, to track down her real mother.
But how is it that when Annie goes to confront her
mother in her large mansion in the smart end of
Dublin, she ends up working for her instead?

Will Annie reveal the truth to her frosty new employer?
Is this the beginning of Annie's new life? And has
Annie completely finished with Gerry's services?

Annie has decisions to make . . .

MADDY GOES TO HOLLYWOOD

Maureen Martella

A gloriously escapist romantic comedy starring an unforgettable heroine

At thirty-three years of age Maddy O'Toole is stranded on Cold Comfort Farm, deep in rural Ireland, with a monosyllabic husband, two children, and her mother. The only bright spot in her week is the American television soap she's addicted to.

Then she discovers that her long-lost sister Gloria is living in Hollywood. No sooner has Gloria invited Maddy – and sent the ticket – than Maddy's on the plane. But what she envisages as a short break ends up changing her life.

For when she arrives at Gloria's hopelessly luxurious Bel Air home she falls helplessly in lust with her sister's gorgeous and gentle actor boyfriend, Carlos, none other than the star of her favourite soap.

It's not going to endear her to her sister, but Maddy can't bring herself to contemplate going home . . .

Order further *Maureen Martella*
titles from your local bookshop, or
have them delivered direct to your door
by Bookpost

☐ Annie's New Life   0099280574   £5.99
☐ Maddy Goes to   0099280582   £5.99
   Hollywood

FREE POST AND PACKING
Overseas customers allow £2
per paperback

PHONE: 01624 677237

POST: Random House Books
c/o Bookpost, PO Box 29, Douglas,
Isle of Man, IM99 1BQ

FAX: 01624 670923

EMAIL: bookshop@enterprise.net

Cheques (payable to Bookpost)
and credit cards accepted

Prices and availability subject to change without notice
Allow 28 days for delivery
When placing your order, please state if you do not wish to
receive any additional information

www.randomhouse.co.uk